Map 1
SOUTHEASTERN
EUROPE IN 357 BCE
Hellenic (Greek) cities and colonies
Mountains
SCYTHIA
Olbia
Istria
Tomis
Land of
the Getae
Istros
(Danube)
PONTOS
EUXEINOS
(Black Sea)
Odessos
Apollonia Pontica
(Colony of Miletus)
THRACE
DARDANIA
ILLYRIA
ADRIATIC SEA
Axios
Strymon
PAEONIA
MACEDONIA
Bosporus
Strait
Byzantion
BITHYNIA
Chersonese
Thasos
Taras
Mt.
Olympus
Epirus
Thessaly
AEGEAN
SEA
ASIA
MINOR
Kroton
HELLAS
Euboea
Thebes
Athens
(Greece)
IONIAN
SEA
Miletus
Syracuse
Sparta

Published by Atmosphere Press

Cover design by Matthew Fielder

Interior maps designed by Ronaldo Alves

atmospherepress.com

Map 2
THRACE IN 357 BCE
Division of the Odrysian Kingdom
Hellenic (Greek) colonies
Local settlements
Land of the Triballi
Land of the Getae
Mount Haemus
Valley of Bendis
Kabyle
Onocarsis
Tonzos
Donuca
Pistiros
Eumolpias
CENTRAL ODRYSIAN REALM
Hebros
Mount Rhodope (Independent tribes)
Nestos
Orbelus
PAEONIA
WESTERN ODRYSIAN REALM
Secret path
Lake Bistonis
Neapolis
Krenides
Pangaion
Strymon
MACEDONIA
Pella
(Lake Loudiake)
Amphipolis
Galepsos
Symbolon
Abdera
Maroneia
Doriscus
Thasos
Samothrace
AEGEAN SEA
Lemnos
Imbros
Olynthus
Potidaia
Pydna
Mesembria
Apollonia Pontica
PONTOS EUXEINOS (Black Sea)
EASTERN ODRYSIAN REALM
Bosporus Strait
Byzantion
PROPONTIS
Cardia
Chersonese
ASIA MINOR

For Peter.

Your encouragement and belief in us
illuminated our path on this journey.

CRACKING OF THE MASK

A NOVEL

ALEXANDER GREEN
& MARIA PETROVA GREEN

atmosphere press

- ONE -
2015

THE NO-SMOKING AND FASTEN-SEAT-BELTS SIGNS LIT up. The flight attendants took their seats. The engines roared and the Cathay Pacific flight to Hong Kong accelerated down the runway.

As the plane flew away from JFK Airport, Zenon McClow looked out the window, watching the New York City skyline shrink beneath him. He said a final, mental farewell to the city, to his old life, and to his old self before easing his window shade down and closing his eyes.

He was leaving New York a very rich man. He didn't trust the security of the plane's wi-fi network, so he restrained himself from pulling up the encrypted banking app on his phone and looking at the number again. But it was hard not to look. His balance could have been a Social Security number. He had been more successful than he'd allowed himself to hope for. And he'd gotten away with it. No one had even suspected that his promises might have been hollow, that the slice of cake he'd served had contained a barbed hook.

The image of Evmondia sitting at the seminar flashed through his mind. Did he regret that he would never see her again?

Oh, come on, Zenon. She's gone. Move forward.

Zenon had left everything behind, or so he thought. He'd abandoned most of his belongings. He'd brought a few changes of clothes, his laptop, and a few mementos from his past he couldn't part with.

Sitting comfortably in first class, he took a deep breath and considered his first destination: Macau, China. He had already decided on taking the ferry from Hong Kong to the former Portuguese colony. His meeting with the man who would deliver everything he'd ordered was roughly fifty-one hours in the future.

He was glad he had kept in touch with some of the rougher types from his days working on cruise ships. A former cook he knew had connected him with someone who could provide a fake Ecuadorian passport, a fake Australian permanent residency card, and all the necessary paperwork to accompany them. He had already paid fifty percent and would hand over the rest upon delivery.

Back in New York, 'Johnny', a hired goon, was going to keep the store going for a few more months, sending 'trading reports' to investors, keeping them on the hook and their money flowing in.

He looked at his watch again: a Chopard Alpine Eagle, the last thing he'd bought before leaving the city. In fifty hours and forty-five minutes, Zenon McClow would cease to exist, and Enrique Sanchez would enter into the world.

"Zenon McClow," he murmured to himself. He liked his name. He was grateful to his parents for coming up with it and giving it to him. He felt a pang of sadness at the thought of never using it again but quickly suppressed the feeling, reminding himself that he needed to keep his emotions under control as he made his moves, otherwise the whole thing could fall apart. Emotions were weak points.

He thought about Phil. It had been only a few hours since

they'd parted. Phil had insisted on driving him to the airport, probably just to show off his brand-new Ferrari. They had agreed that Zenon would 'return' to Hong Kong to jumpstart the 'trading' with the investors' funds. And in a month's time, he was to return to the States and give another presentation. But 'Zenon McClow' would vanish long before then.

When he finds out, how far will he go to track me down?

- TWO -

THE SOUNDS OF CARDS BEING SHUFFLED, CHIPS CLACKing, and a constant murmur of conversation, occasionally rising to a crescendo of excitement, filled the VIP lounge at the Sands Macao. Zenon looked at his two cards with frustration. A pair of tens—hearts and diamonds.

He'd reached Macau and picked up his new documents without any hiccups, so he'd decided to kill some time in the casino. With the amount of money sitting in his offshore bank accounts, he could easily afford a few rounds of Texas Hold 'em. But from the moment he'd sat down, he'd struggled to win a single round.

The cards on the table were a six of hearts, ten of clubs, queen of hearts, ten of spades, and queen of clubs.

Four of a kind! I can win this round. "All in," he declared.

Across the table, a player who appeared to be an American businessman also pushed his chips to the center. "All in," he echoed.

Zenon kept his expression neutral and waited.

"Please show your cards," said the dealer.

A profound feeling of anger and disappointment overtook him when he saw his rival's queen of diamonds and queen of spades, which gave him a winning four of a kind with a higher card. The confidence that had worked so well in pulling off his scheme did not work on the stranger he was playing cards against.

It means nothing. Feeling suddenly fatigued, he gave up on the game and walked out of the fortress-like building to get some fresh air and natural light. *I haven't recovered from the jetlag. Otherwise, I would've played better and won.*

He consoled himself with the thought that he would soon be in a drastically different environment. In two days, Ecuadorian citizen Enrique Sanchez was to fly out of Tokyo, stopping over in Mexico City before landing in Quito...

- THREE -

THE PRESERVED COLONIAL BUILDINGS OF QUITO'S old town shimmered under the day's intense sunlight. Walking along the narrow streets of the Ecuadorian capital, Enrique Sanchez was enjoying the youthful, optimistic vibe of the city.

He had chosen the country not only for its remote areas, where he could hide in peace while still enjoying decent amenities and infrastructure, but also because Spanish was the only foreign language he had substantial practice with. He had come up with a story about living in Australia from an early age, to explain why he didn't sound like a native speaker.

Enrique's time in the city was fated to be short, as he would soon be departing for his next destination, the mountain village of Vilcabamba. It was a place that attracted health enthusiasts, nature lovers, and spiritualists, and certainly nowhere anyone would come looking for Zenon McClow.

Enrique didn't know if Phil would go public or turn to the authorities when the roof fell in. An investment guru getting fooled by a guy with no real credentials? How embarrassing. Surely he would want to save face. Using his own wealth and family fortune to paper over his losses wouldn't be out of the question for Phil. Still, Enrique needed to prepare for the worst.

Phil wasn't the only investor he had to consider. If anyone sent hired guns after him, they would inevitably comb Asia first. Meanwhile, he'd be more than ten thousand miles away from Hong Kong, in a place not known for luxury.

After a long ride from Quito over narrow, bumpy mountain roads, Enrique arrived at the secluded villa that would be his home for some time. The property owner, Señor Mosquera, showed him around. It was an eco-friendly lodge, featuring exquisitely carved wood accents and a lush garden out front. The design was unique and asymmetrical. A stone path through tall trees connected the property to the main road that led to the village.

"I hope you like it here," Señor Mosquera said. "Is there anything else I can do?"

"No, everything seems perfect."

"I'm glad to hear that. If you ever need me, don't hesitate to call."

"Thank you, señor."

Enrique took a step towards the door to see the owner off, but Señor Mosquera didn't seem to be in a hurry to leave. He was a friendly and talkative type.

"I see you'll be staying with us for quite a while. It's nice to be able to take such a long time off!"

"Actually, I'm going to be doing my work here."

"Oh! What type of work?" the old man asked.

"I'm a writer."

"Oh, I see! Well, this is the perfect place for that. In fact, you're not the first writer to stay here. May I ask what you're working on?"

"A novel."

"A romance novel, by chance?" There was a twinkle in Señor Mosquera's eye when he asked the question.

Enrique flushed and said only, "No."

"You have that dreamy look on your face of someone in love," the old man said.

A strange feeling rushed through Enrique's body.

"Then is it history?" the old man guessed.

"Nope."

"Crime? Those stories are very popular these days!"

Crime? I've already done that.

He was startled by this, his own thought.

Anxious to be done with this conversation, Enrique replied, "Señor, I don't want to be rude, but I'm awfully tired from the trip. I'd love to chat another time."

The old man nodded and walked out the door, waving from the path as Enrique closed the door gently.

- FOUR -

A FEW DAYS LATER, AFTER SETTLING IN AND GETTING himself oriented, Enrique walked to the town square. Sitting on a bench and eating an empanada, he watched people pass by. A group of teenagers sped through on bicycles, followed by two middle-aged men on horseback. It was quite a departure from what he was used to in the States.

Leaning back on the bench, Enrique inhaled the fresh mountain air. He enjoyed being surrounded by the Andes, thousands of feet above sea level—quite a change from the decade he'd spent at sea. The mountains were a lovely backdrop, and he allowed himself a few moments of pride, reflecting on the ingenious strategizing which had brought him here and, so far, worked like a charm.

The next day, Señor Mosquera visited the villa to do some maintenance work, and they struck up a conversation.

"You have not had any problems in Vilcabamba, Señor Sanchez?"

"Not at all. The people here are very friendly, and I've found some excellent things in the shops."

"Wonderful! Still, you should be careful when you're out. There are gangs, mostly coming from other regions. They rob people who are reckless with their money. And, you know, not everyone feels sorry for the victims."

"Why not?"

"Because they resent the *turistas* for having money and coming here for their own benefit, but not doing anything to help with our country's poverty and corrupt government. For many people, it's easier to blame something or someone else than it is to take personal responsibility."

An uncomfortable feeling shot down Enrique's spine as if he had just touched something electric.

"Enrique, I wish everyone here was honest, but many are poor, and some feel they must steal to survive. They feel it's okay to do crime because they think the loss to the visitor is not as high as the good done to them."

Sounds familiar, Enrique thought, starting to feel uncomfortable.

"Among themselves, they will say they resent the rich. But the truth is, most of them want to be rich themselves!" the old man continued. "It's *hipocresía*. I, for one, believe that when wealthy people use their money to help others, it can do a lot of good. My dream is that one day, our country will prosper, and the citizens will live well."

Evmondia's face flashed into Enrique's mind, and he heard her words to Mr. Clifton again: "You've already done so much for me and all the other people you've helped worldwide by donating to all those charities."

He shook it off. Talking with Señor Mosquera was proving to be a challenge. He felt a powerful sort of cognitive dissonance. On the one hand, he was finally rich after years of grinding poverty and struggle, and was eager to get to New Zealand, where he could soak in all of the luxury and glamour that came with wealth. But at the same time, he had so often thought of himself as an enemy of the rich. Was it possible that he was one of the hypocrites himself?

- FIVE -

AS HIS STAY IN VILCABAMBA DRIFTED ON, ENRIQUE didn't want to admit it, but something about the place was starting to make him feel uneasy.

The Andes Mountains were majestic and mystical, but there was something about the seclusion and isolation, the tranquil, unpolluted nature, about the way of life preserved from an era long gone... It was as if the mountains were giants, ready to squeeze and crush him. Or gods judging him for his...

Crime?

But it had been an act of retribution. Of revenge. Of justice.

Still, since his conversation with Señor Mosquera, he couldn't shake a feeling of guilt.

Were the mountains to blame? Perhaps the high altitude was making him sick? Maybe it was the food? The weird, hippie expats whose rambling conversations he avoided? The mind-altering cactus concoction, a local specialty, which he had drunk against his own better judgment?

Get it together, he told himself. *Emotions are weak points! Lock it down.*

Fortunately for him, the Vilcabamba area offered plenty to do. The village itself was pleasant and fun, but nature was the star. Hiking opportunities were abundant. The treks were long sometimes, but with enough perseverance, picturesque new views could be discovered virtually every day. Enrique found himself observing rare species of birds along the trails, swimming in placid, clean rivers, and mountain biking along steep dirt paths.

The last time he had been on a horse was at a kid's birthday party in Atlanta, so he signed up for riding lessons with Pablo, an energetic and down-to-earth instructor. Soon enough, Enrique found himself following Pablo's lead, walking their horses slowly through ankle-deep grass and narrow forest trails.

One day, Pablo took him to a waterfall that had a reputation as a sight to behold. It was a bumpy ride on a trail narrower than Enrique expected. The entire time, he feared that his horse would buck him off, but Pablo had trained the animal well.

The waterfall cascaded down from a height of nearly a hundred feet, gathering in a pool which Pablo encouraged him to enter.

"The water is pure and clean. It's a bit cold, but trust me, you will feel very refreshed if you go in."

Enrique complied, and Pablo was right. The initial shock gave way to a feeling of surprising tranquility.

"Close your eyes, calm your mind, and feel the water with all your body and spirit. It'll help cleanse and purify your soul," Pablo said.

Enrique stood still in the pool and tried to clear his mind of all thoughts. He focused on the feeling of the water, the sound of the waterfall, and the birds chirping in the background. It felt good... for a moment. But the pleasure faded fast, and he began to feel strange and hollow inside.

Was the water purifying his soul, or was something in him polluting the water?

The two men sat on a boulder to eat lunch. “Pablo, I can’t believe you’re seventy-five,” Enrique said. “I wouldn’t have put you at a year over fifty. You have more energy than I do, and I’m only thirty-one!”

Pablo smiled.

“I’ve been wondering. What’s behind the health and longevity of the people here? From what I’ve heard, many are over a hundred. Is there some special secret?”

“Many people ask me that, and leave disappointed by the answer. There is no special secret,” he replied. “We simply live in harmony with nature here as much as possible, without the worries and drives of the industrial world. One can’t expect to live a highly stressful life and be healthy, Enrique. I see some people trying to compensate for that by taking supplements or eating so-called superfoods, hoping they will work like magic. It doesn’t always.”

“Yeah, I hear you.”

“Taking care of one’s body is important,” Pablo continued. “But if the soul is deeply troubled, it can also make the body sick. Many people come here for health, but do not bring healthy habits with them. We now have more alcohol and processed foods in the village, for instance.”

“If I may ask, how do you feel about Vilcabamba attracting more and more foreigners?”

“Well, the politicians will tell you that tourism is a great thing, as it brings prosperity and infrastructure to the region. And I, for one, am grateful for everyone who comes. You help us, just like the income I receive from lessons and tours. But you know, some of my friends view outsiders, especially the *gringos*, as people who do not respect our land or our culture. And as people who are greedy for our resources. Some of the current trends remind them of the past. The Conquistadors arrived here, bringing novelties like the European horses we are riding now. But they also brought disease and greed.”

Novelty, like artificial intelligence in trading, Enrique thought.

"Of course, our ancestors had many shortcomings themselves. If Atahualpa didn't have his half-brother Huáscar killed, and the empire wasn't divided, things may have been different." Pablo sighed and continued. "There have been talks about building new hotels and resorts in the area. But too much building will pollute the water and the air. The food we grew used to be entirely organic. Now, some farmers have started using pesticides. And young people are becoming addicted to the new technology, staying indoors and getting lazy. I worry that soon, health and longevity will be a thing of the past here."

"Greed sure is causing a lot of damage," Enrique replied, not knowing what else to say.

"Yes. But the greedy will never be in a state of true health or happiness. Many people, especially in the industrial world, think that riches come from material things. In the past, it was gold. Now, it is all about money. Money is important, of course, but there has to be balance with a rich life of both body and soul. Here, our way has been to accept what nature, the earth, and life give us with gratitude. The earth gives us plenty, and in return, we take care of it. The majority of the people who live here are simple, hard-working, and honest. But some look to the past and believe that they are entitled to some kind of retribution. So they steal because they feel they deserve whatever they can take. It is wrong to steal. It never brings happiness or satisfaction."

Pablo was starting to sound eerily like Señor Mosquera. Enrique tried to divert the conversation. "The elite have a lot of power. It's a shame it's not often used for good."

"Yes. I'm afraid that Vilcabamba will follow the trend in other places. I don't want to see our little paradise destroyed by greed. The rich want to live long and be healthy, which is understandable. But too many of them don't give a damn what they destroy as long as they get what they want. In the end, they don't find happiness down that path and end up suffering themselves. However, there are also those that use their wealth wisely to do good in the world. Those I respect."

Enrique found himself agreeing with what Pablo had said. But now, he too was one of the wealthy. He had stolen from the rich, but he was no Robin Hood. He never had any intention to give to the poor.

The conversation didn't make him feel better about the place or himself. Instead, it deepened his dissatisfaction.

Before arriving in Vilcabamba, Enrique had dreamed about his new life of freedom. But those dreams were not his current reality. The problem wasn't Ecuador, which was beautiful. It was his state of mind that wasn't living up to his dreams. Lingering questions, doubt, and unease were never part of the plan.

One of the first activities Enrique had embarked upon in Vilcabamba was a hike to the top of Mandango Hill. Despite the difficult, steep, and slippery climb, he had persevered. Despite the danger along the way, he had made it. One wrong step and his life might have ended. But he had embraced the danger, and it had all been worth it. The view from the top had been magnificent. Turning in circles and absorbing a 360-degree view of the valley, he had felt as if he were standing on top of the world.

The day after his conversation with Pablo, Enrique decided to climb the hill again, hoping that the exercise and the beauty of the scenery would disperse his foul mood. But the hike proved to be even more challenging than before. He did not feel sure of his steps. The view from the mirrored cross at the halfway point was still beautiful, but this time, as he stared out at the vast green expanse, a new feeling crept upon him.

Ever since he had concocted his scheme, he had viewed

himself as larger than life. But here, in the middle of the landscape, he was starting to feel small. Like an ant crawling around and trying to survive.

He was supposed to be carefree and happy. Living it up. Enjoying nature. Dancing and singing with the locals and other travelers. But while his body was going through the motions, his heart and mind were not cooperating.

Don't crack now, he admonished himself.

- SIX -

IT WAS A BRIGHT, SUNNY DAY, NEITHER TOO HOT NOR too humid. Swinging gently in his hammock, Enrique was studying the Huilco trees all around. He realized they reminded him of the pictures Evmondia had shown him of the Bulgarian pine trees surrounding her hometown, and the wild strawberry plants growing between them.

Startled by the memory, he closed his eyes, trying to visualize something else. But the swinging motion of the hammock lulled him...

He was walking amongst pine trees, picking and tasting delicious strawberries, feeling the gentle soil underneath his bare feet. Feeling her gentle soul.

The bright sun blazed over the snowcapped mountain to the south. He passed a thick tree, and there she was, standing gracefully underneath a tall, majestic pine. She smiled at him, kindness and warmth radiating from her.

He wanted to hide behind the tree so she wouldn't see him. But he was frozen in his tracks. She didn't seem to notice. Still smiling, she picked up some wild strawberries, put them in an Ecuadorian-style basket, and walked back to town. He followed.

In town, she walked to a white house with a red-tiled roof and wooden framings. She left the door open when she entered, and he drifted inside behind her. In the living room were several elderly people, including Mr. Clifton and his own father.

Enrique called his father's name, but the older man didn't pay attention to him. He was focused on Evmondia. Still smiling, she bent down and began giving strawberries to everyone. They accepted gratefully and ate them with joy.

Enrique was looking in from the hallway, in his Armani suit with the Alpine Eagle on his wrist. Everyone else was dressed simply. Most of them looked quite old, over a hundred. Yet they all seemed content and happy. In contrast, he was young but felt hollow inside and out of place.

He caught a glimpse of himself in a large mirror on the wall. To his surprise, he was wearing a heavy, gilded mask. The image startled him, bringing him back to the hammock, and he opened his eyes in shock.

He touched his face to see if the mask was there. To his relief, it wasn't. It had only been a dream.

He ran his fingers through his hair and wiped the sweat from his face.

I need to get out, he thought. *Being among people should help me relax.*

But when he got to town and was seated in his favorite local bar, dissatisfaction and discomfort overcame him. He still couldn't shake his memories of Evmondia or Mr. Clifton. And he was starting to doubt.

Was he right to do what he had done?

It had been logical. Corporate greed had ruined his father and, consequently, his own life, so retribution was only natural. Besides, the people he had taken money from weren't even using their wealth for noble purposes; they were acquiring it just for the sake of having more.

Or were they? How did he know?

It had been so much easier to justify his actions in New York, observing the inequality, the grinding stress of daily existence, and the corporate plutocrats who manipulated the economy and crushed the weak.

But here in Vilcabamba, things were less clear.

Enrique kept returning to Pablo's comments about health and happiness. If the old man was to be believed, he had no chance of reaching true happiness or health, despite his bank balance.

If Pablo were wrong, Enrique would be happy and content with his millions of dollars. His body would feel energetic and relaxed, not sluggish and tense.

Enrique had felt suffocated and confined, first on the cruise ships where he'd spent his twenties and then in the narrow, crowded streets of New York. And he had been looking forward to the vast expanses of the Ecuadorian highlands. Yet once again, he was feeling trapped. Not drowning out in the sea, but suffocated by the mountainous valley. It was as if the tall, looming peaks were the bars of his prison cell, the ground the slippery floor of his cage.

Never before had he felt so torn and confused. No matter how many times he commanded himself to control his feelings, he failed.

Guilt was getting harder and harder to ignore. Was he right to feel it? He didn't know.

Many of the Ecuadorians he had met were down-to-earth, kind, and friendly. Yet their lives were difficult. Why didn't *they* deserve to have millions of dollars? What was so great about him?

These people didn't go through the trauma I did, he told himself. But he was far from the only person to have had harrowing experiences. So what made him special?

I'm overthinking it, he decided. *It must be this place. The people here are stuck in the past and have a strange, foreign mindset. I don't belong to this culture. I need to go to a place where there'll be more of my type of people, living my kind of lifestyle.*

A few days later, during a visit to a remote lake in the mountains, a new suspicion began to overtake Enrique. Staring into the turquoise water and watching it gently ripple in the breeze, he started wondering if he liked the ocean after all.

Perhaps I'm missing it, he thought. *Maybe I need to be on a beautiful island with a long beach where I can dip my feet into the water.*

Returning to the villa, he looked at the Australian permanent residency 'card' he'd purchased. He would need it to reach his ultimate destination of New Zealand. That was where he wanted to settle and live out the rest of his life. But it was too risky, he thought, to go there so soon. Where then?

He paced around the room. *It all started with that damn brunch. That girl was bothering me from the moment I saw her.*

He felt like pulling his hair out. Something needed to change. He had to get away.

- SEVEN -

WHAT AM I TO DO?

Felix Svoboda, feeling as confused as ever, stood before the ruins of the old, colonial-era prison.

It had been a few weeks since the former Enrique had selected his new identity and left Ecuador. His new home was the Isle of Pines in New Caledonia, a small paradise in the middle of the Pacific. It was remote, breathtakingly beautiful, and not overcrowded with tourists—key reasons why he'd picked it. The population was generally French-speaking, and since he spoke only English and moderate Spanish, that meant he was unlikely to find himself caught in uncomfortable conversations—or have uncomfortable philosophies pushed on him.

To stay indefinitely in New Caledonia, a French overseas territory, he needed citizenship from an EU member state. As if guided by an invisible hand, he had picked the Czech Republic. He vaguely recalled hearing something good about the Czechs, but he couldn't remember from where or in what context. At any rate, it was a solid choice, as the country had a good reputation and hardly ever made the news in a negative way.

He had selected his new surname carefully. Browsing through lists of Czech family names online, he learned that Svoboda meant 'freedom' in Czech. And freedom was exactly what Felix was seeking. His source had come through with the right documents once again, and here he was. But after only a short time on the island, Felix was already feeling like a lonely prisoner, and he wasn't even trapped inside the prison.

Only a thousand yards away, the Pacific Ocean lapped against the shore. The waves were calm and placid, yet Felix felt like there were much stronger waves crashing forcefully inside his gut.

Everything had been planned and executed to perfection. Where was the satisfaction, then?

Why was happiness always so elusive?

Only a month before, the spectacular views of the Andes Mountains had unfurled before his eyes. It was there, in the silence, in the beauty, away from the maddening buzz of globalized civilization, that he first began to feel something was wrong. That something was ugly. That his whole life after the death of his parents had been one mistake after another. The structures that were his beliefs were starting to collapse from within.

Felix stood for a long time, observing the prison as if its ruins held the answers he was seeking. By then, dark clouds had started to move in, and his thoughts followed them. A storm was brewing.

Hurriedly, he took the narrow, sandy path back to his place. Like sentinels, the tall pine trees ubiquitous to the island seemed to walk along with him. He reached his hut, built in the island's style with a triangular straw roof, just before the rain began to rip down from the sky in sheets. Suddenly exhausted, he threw himself on the mattress and collapsed.

Are we truly in control of our lives? Startled by his own thought, Felix sprang out of bed the next morning, sweat trickling down his face. His head was not only hurting; it felt heavy. Wondering what to do, he opened the door.

The air was particularly thick and wet, as the rain had only let up an hour before. He breathed in deeply and stepped outside.

He started walking, paying no attention to his path. Getting some fresh air and exercise was all that mattered.

The familiar sight of the old prison loomed ahead: he had unintentionally headed that way. Once again, he stood before the crumbling structure, observing its decay.

When he had decided to come to the Isle of Pines, he had been unaware of its history—that the island had been used to hold convicted Communards, people who had revolted against the social and political order of France; it was not unlike what he believed he had done back home, striking a blow against the rigged economic system.

He entered the ruins and walked through the remnants of the cells. Mold was growing everywhere, and insects were buzzing all around. A dreary setting indeed. He looked around as if trying to find a sign. A message. A secret symbol. Any clue left behind.

There were some scratch marks on one of the stones. He inspected them closely. Nothing.

At least those Communards were kept here against their free will. He had done everything to be free, and yet he still felt imprisoned. Had he become a prisoner himself? Not inside one of the cells, but inside his own torment?

He wiggled his left shoe in the dirt. And as if directing his plea for an answer toward the invisible prisoners from the past, he asked out loud, "How can I break free? How should I live my life?"

A thought struck him as if the dead Communards were

responding. *The one who has been keeping you prisoner is yourself. First on the ships. Then in New York. Then Vilcabamba. And now on this island. You do realize that? All the years we spent here, we yearned for freedom, fresh air, and light. Those disturbing emotions you feel now? They are trapped inside of you, and they want the same. To be released. To be set free. So restart your life by the open sea, the wind, the sand, the sun...*

"But isn't that what I'm doing?" he asked himself, deep agony in his voice.

Then, as if those troubling emotions had now started talking back to him, he thought, *You have kept us imprisoned inside of you for too long. All these years, we have been yearning and yearning for freedom, fresh air, and light. But you kept us trapped, and in return, we are keeping you trapped in the same patterns. It's time for you to set us free.*

He didn't know how to respond or how to process his own thoughts.

"Damn it, am I losing my mind? It's this place. It's giving me the creeps."

He retraced his steps until he was off the prison grounds. With a rapidly beating heart and hurried steps, he took the path to the Cemetery of the Deported.

There, he stopped and bent over, resting his hands on his knees to catch his breath. The graveyard was serene and eerily quiet. A silent reminder that many convicts had died in this place.

He glanced around at the stones. They were overgrown with weeds and eroded by time and the elements. There were no readable names on most of them.

"Just like me. I don't even know who I am any more."

He had convinced himself that Zenon McClow and Enrique Sanchez had been left behind forever. But here, Felix Svoboda, the free man, was feeling no more permanent. He stared at the stones.

Is there still someone left who remembers and cares about these nameless convicts? Will there ever be someone who remembers or cares about me? Will I matter? Or will I become one of the nameless? One of the forgotten and uncared for?

He wondered what his father's grave looked like today. There was no one to visit it any longer. A deep sadness ran through him.

His memories of the day, many years ago, when he and his mother had buried his father and stood by his grave, together but alone, remained vivid. They were not just internally broken, but broke. His father had been buried in a donated coffin in the churchyard of the parish to which they belonged.

Felix hadn't thought about that day for a long time. He'd tried consciously to bury the memory. He sighed, wishing he could have given his father a better funeral. His father had loved him, he knew that. But he still carried the fear that there had been something missing in him. That he wasn't good enough for his father to choose to fight for him, to live for him. Why would his father have turned to drugs otherwise?

Felix looked down at the blank gravestone at his feet. *How would anyone even know who you are? I'm sure you were special to someone. I'm sure that someone would have wanted to know where your resting place is.*

That night, he slept a deep and dreamless sleep for a change. But when Felix awoke, the question of how to live his life nagged at him again. Then an idea came to him.

You told Señor Mosquera that you were a writer, his inner voice reminded him.

He wondered if, through writing his life story, he could find the answers he was seeking and heal his soul. He had nothing to lose and not much to do except wait until the time was right to head to New Zealand.

Writing could be his relief. A newfound occupation.

Staying off the radar was making for a lonely life. Besides, something inside was compelling him to try it.

He turned on his laptop and placed his fingers on the keyboard. Slowly, they began to move, and soon, sentences began to pour forth. He was full of hope, expecting at any moment for the answers he was seeking to pop out of his subconscious and appear before him on the screen. Surely he would become a wiser man...

But after typing for hours and rereading some of what he had written, the elation of having met the challenge was replaced with the same, old emptiness. If anything, he felt more hopeless than ever.

Disappointed and not knowing what to do, he continued to stare at the screen. He had written almost automatically, moving forward as fast as he could type. He began to scroll down and down. And as he read, his inner voice began to give him the feedback he needed.

You have been blaming and hating, hating and blaming, it told him. *You tell yourself that you're on the outside, watching them all—but they're watching you too. They see you, make no mistake. And the resentment and sense of entitlement... it's time to let them go. You have trapped yourself with all of these emotions and are eating yourself from inside. The guilt is an indication of that. Don't self-destruct. Let your resentment go!*

"Why should I? I'm not wrong to feel how I feel! The world is full of exploiters and cheats, and I'm just taking what's due me!"

Are you ready for the consequences? It doesn't seem like you are.

"My sentiments are what fuel me—they're what got me here. What will I do without them?"

Continue to write, and you will find out. Don't regurgitate the same old stories. Find a way to trick the sentries of your mind. Distract them from the situations they are guarding—

and snatch the key to inner wisdom from behind them. Write what you need in order to heal. Don't require a calamity to force you to pull yourself together.

"Damn it; I'm going insane!" He tried to calm down and take a moment to reflect. "If I continue to feel the same hatred, the same disappointment with the world, with all the people who brought me to this state, will anything ever change for me?"

This time, the answer was obvious. *Your excuses and justifications will keep you trapped in the same patterns forever. Don't you want to free yourself and make the most of your life while you still have it?*

He leaned back and looked up at the ceiling. Letting go of the past might be easy for some, but it wasn't something as easy as snapping his fingers or waving a magic wand. *I'm not ready.*

- EIGHT -

FELIX WOKE UP UNUSUALLY LATE THE NEXT MORNING, looking at the clock on his nightstand with alarm. If he hurried, he could still catch the boat to Nouméa. After washing quickly, he grabbed his jacket and ran to the wharf. The boat was almost full, but he managed to find a seat, squeezing onto a bench beside a tourist and her oversized backpack. It would be an uncomfortable ride.

He hadn't planned to visit New Caledonia's capital. But he was being propelled by an impulse, since Evmondia had appeared in his dreams again.

He had been back in New York, stepping into the spotlight after Phil's introduction. But this time, instead of boisterous applause, he was met with laughter. The audience of investors was pointing their fingers and mocking him. He looked at Phil, bewildered. Phil was laughing too. What was going on?

He touched his face. To his surprise, he felt the coldness of metal. A mask was again covering his face. He tried to yank it off, but it didn't budge.

"Phil! Help me!"

No one came to his rescue. The audience continued to laugh as he struggled, losing his balance and grabbing the podium with one hand to keep from falling.

Evmondia was sitting in the second row. Without a word, she rose and walked gracefully toward the stage. He had never seen anyone quite like her. Dressed in all-white, she was as ethereally beautiful as an angel.

She ascended the stairs and faced him, her eyes full of warmth and love. In an instant, the laughter filling the hall stopped. He felt a warm sensation rising up and spreading throughout his body and soul. It was soon followed by a cracking sound. He felt the mask on his face breaking apart. All at once, it fell away and shattered into small golden pieces on the floor.

"Who are you?" he asked in bewilderment.

But before she made any response, the audience stampeded toward the stage and started eagerly grabbing the shattered gold pieces, pushing the two of them apart. He tried to fight through them to reach her. But they were pushing him further and further away until he couldn't see her any longer.

Felix stared at the vast expanse of water. He wished he had someone close to him he could confide in. But there was no one. Just some tourists—from Australia, France, and Japan, judging by their conversations.

Ever since he had met Evmondia, she had plagued his dreams and intruded upon his thoughts. But there was something else that kept appearing in his dreams: the mask. The Thracian noble's mask she had shown him.

He needed to figure out why she and that mask were stuck in his mind. And he needed to find out more about those mysterious, ancient people to whom she was linked.

Nouméa's colorful harbor was in sight. Speaking to no one, he disembarked as quickly as possible and made his way to the Bernheim Library, just a short walk from the harbor.

When Felix arrived, a pleasant middle-aged woman with warm, brown eyes and reddish-orange-dyed hair greeted him.

She spoke enough English to explain that they didn't have any books on ancient Thrace, but she could order some directly from France.

He agreed, and rented a room in Nouméa to wait for the books to arrive. He spent his days exploring the island of Grande Terre and conducting online research at the library. The more he learned about the Thracians, the more interested he became in those ancient people who once inhabited Evmondia's homeland. He found himself clicking from webpage to webpage, curiosity turning into passion.

The books arrived eventually, and he devoured them eagerly. He never thought he would find himself reading history as one might read a thriller. The more he learned, the more he was drawn to those unknown and exotic lands. Felix was captivated by their customs—which were strange but intriguing at the same time—and by the fierce and relentless people. The more he read, the more affinity he felt toward the Thracians, their rich culture, and their ancient world, which was colonized by outsiders seeking control over their gold and silver mines.

He recalled hearing that New Caledonia had been colonized by France for its nickel mines. *It's always the way*, he thought.

A particular moment in Thracian history stood out to him. A period in which the most powerful kingdom in Thrace had been ravaged by conflict and divided into three realms, each ruled by its own king.

Felix was fascinated by the story of Ketriporis, the son of one of the three kings. Ketriporis's father had died shortly after the conflict, and as his successor, he had found himself in a precarious situation. It was one Felix thought he understood.

Felix's inner voice had been urging him to continue writing. But about what? That had been the question.

Now, the veil of mystery was lifting. He was embarking on a journey. A quest deep into the past. Into lands wild and dangerous. Amongst people ancient and forgotten.

Newly enthused, he returned to his home on the Isle of Pines. The rainy season was about to start. The perfect time to begin writing again.

- NINE -
2016

FELIX'S FINGERS SLOWED THEIR DANCE UPON THE keyboard and gradually stopped. It was time to take a break. Rising from his desk, he did some hand exercises and stepped out to take in some much-needed fresh air.

He had been working for months. The rainy season was over. But he had been so caught up in his story the seasonal change had passed him by. He had written day and night, barely remembering to step out into the sun.

It was quiet outside. A far cry from the incessant clamor of New York. No cars and taxis were idling in traffic near his hut; no horns were beeping nor sirens sounding. It was as quiet as it had been in the hall of the Plaza Hotel during his presentation.

He looked up. The sky above was a brilliant shade of blue. But he felt no joy at the sight. Instead, he remained focused on the dark gray landscape inside himself.

"What is wrong with me?" he asked no one.

He closed his eyes. The overcast sky inside his mind hovered over him again. But gradually, the clouds began to part, chased away by rays of sunlight. Shades of gold and blue overtook and pierced the darkness. And among the scattering clouds, like a brilliant apparition, she appeared.

He had known Evmondia for such a short time, and yet memories of her kept washing up on the shore of his mind like waves, impossible to dismiss. He had been determined to eliminate this weakness in himself. But he had failed.

He had tried to think ill of her. But she kept appearing in his dreams and thoughts, warm and loving. Why was she walking beside him? Why was she looking at the same sights he was? He was thinking, and she was responding to him.

Did she cast a spell on me? he wondered. *Enough is enough. But I'll keep her in my thoughts for just a few more days.*

There's just a little more to do; soon, the story will be complete, he thought as he headed to a small café he had frequented before he'd become completely absorbed in the writing of *The Mask.*

After months of living with characters from a bygone era, Felix felt it was nice to be among people from the present. *At least no one is carrying a rhomphaia or sarissa or javelin,* he thought.

"Man, what happened to you?" exclaimed Michel, the café's owner. "Haven't seen you for a long time! You all right? You look sick, man!"

"I'm fine. I've just been busy writing," Felix replied.

"I don't know, man, you really don't look a hundred percent! If I were you, I would see a doctor!"

Michel's words startled him. It had been some time since Felix had paid attention to his appearance, or to how he'd been feeling physically. He admitted to himself that his energy might be a little lower than it had been when he'd first arrived, but it was surely work-related. *I must just be tired from months spent hunched over my laptop*, he thought. *I've barely been outside. That's all it is. A little bit of sun on my face and I'll be as good as new.*

He wasn't the type to see a doctor for any minor discomfort he might be feeling. But he could pick up some medicine while in Nouméa. He was about to go there anyway, to return the books on Thrace to the library. *No need to rush, though. I'll finish the story first, and then I'll go.*

- TEN -

WHY DO I FEEL SO SHAKEN BY MY OWN STORY? Felix wondered. *Why do I feel like I died with him?*

The more Felix thought about it, the more he realized Michel's words had been true. He *was* looking and feeling a bit off; he had just been too focused on his writing to pay any heed.

So instead of simply visiting a pharmacy while in Nouméa, he decided to check into the hospital.

Nouméa's hospital was a good facility, with attentive and thorough doctors and friendly staff. Felix had bloodwork done, and some scans run, and spent a few extra days in the city waiting for the results. Having completed his task, he found himself newly open to the vibrant, vivid environment and culture.

It's no surprise I feel worn out after finishing the story, he thought. *It's dramatic. I did not intend to write it that way, but I felt compelled to make it so.*

Felix had originally intended to write a book glorifying ancient Thrace, but somehow it had turned out differently; the harsh truths of life back then eventually took over the story.

He spent a few pleasant but anxious days in a hotel in

Nouméa. Then his test results came in.

He had an enlarged lymph node under his left armpit; a biopsy had been ordered.

Nothing to be worried about, he told himself. *This is routine.*

Three days later, he received the diagnosis. The dreaded C-word. Cancer.

It was unexpected. Out of nowhere.

Or was it?

Wasn't there a part of him that had known all along what was happening? That had warned him of the impending danger? But he had ignored it—silenced it—as he was writing *The Mask*.

No, it can't be true. It must be a mistake, he repeated over and over to himself while leaving the hospital, wandering the streets aimlessly.

But gradually, the truth sank in, and the question of *Why now, when I'm so close to having it all?* began to overwhelm him.

He checked out of his hotel room and took the next boat back to the Isle of Pines, where he rushed to his hut. He spent a couple of days locked inside, attempting to process the diagnosis, finally heading to the beach early one morning.

Pants rolled up, feet in the water, he watched as the waves came and lapped at his feet.

He had thought that striking out at the system would be liberating. Instead, it had turned out to be confining.

What now?

Death. Was death the answer? Was it a new beginning? Freedom from this world of suffering? Would it bring eternal light and happiness?

Endless emptiness and darkness?

Pain and suffering? Or just nothingness?

Was there a continuation at all? An afterlife, as the ancients had believed?

He knew mankind had always been obsessed with revealing death's mystery. Each culture had its own theories and lore, but none had any answers. Existence remained shrouded in mystery.

Felix began to feel as if some invisible hand was pulling him into the water, trying to drown him. And he was ready to let it happen.

Life was starting to lose meaning. He had experienced his share of negative emotions, but nothing like the death wish he was feeling now.

He looked around. The island had lost its charm. Everything seemed drab, colorless, and bland. He felt no attachment to his surroundings.

He had no desire to fight any more. He was spiraling deeper and deeper. The emotions he felt were like boulders in his arms, too much to carry. He felt utterly defeated. By life. By everything.

In an ideal world, he thought, he wouldn't have had to lose his father so early in life. He wouldn't have had to experience pain and suffering. He would have felt no animus toward society and its rulers.

But he was not living in an ideal world. And he felt no fear of letting this world go.

What he felt was resignation.

He had waded deeper in the water. The waves were coming in stronger, soaking his pants to mid-thigh. He could have moved, avoiding the uncomfortable feeling. But he didn't.

He just stood in the water, watching the waves roll in and push at his legs as if trying to knock him down. As predictable as the tide, Evmondia's image started to wash up on the shore of his mind.

It pulled him up and up, until he felt like shaking off the

deathlike hand that had been pulling him down.

He grabbed the rope she extended to him. It pulled him away from the water, toward the shore.

His despair was replaced with the desire to one day see her again. To make amends.

He rushed back to his hut. He pulled his suitcase out from under the bed and threw his clothes in.

THE MASK

BY ZENON MCCLOW

ACT I

THE PONTIC COAST OF THRACE, SUMMER, 357 BCE

Trysimachus's sandals clapped against the cobblestones as he ran through the streets of Apollonia Pontica. It was high noon. The waves of the Black Sea—less believably known as the *Pontos Euxeinos*, the Friendly Sea—roiled in accordance with its hostile and unfriendly reputation, the dark blue water's surface illuminated by the remarkably intense sun. The colossal statue of Apollo Iatros, the colony's patron deity, shone brilliantly from the open temple built on the small island in the harbor. But that day, Trysimachus had no time to admire the fine work of Calamis, one of Athens's best sculptors, nor to watch the comings and goings of the Athenian fleet. He had been summoned to his mentor Zenon's residence, and there had been an urgency in the old man's letter. Trysimachus was excited and apprehensive at once.

He was ushered inside as soon as he arrived. Wearing a red tunic and sandals, Zenon embraced him. "Welcome, Trysimachus. Make yourself comfortable."

Still breathing heavily from his journey through the city, Trysimachus lowered himself onto a plush kline as a servant brought in cups and a large jug of wine.

"It is from Kabyle," Zenon said. "I have not tasted a better wine." Filling the cups, he gestured for Trysimachus to try it, saying, "I have become quite fond of it!"

The refreshments were welcome, but Trysimachus's anxiety overtook his gratitude at the invitation. "Why did you summon me here, teacher?" he asked abruptly.

Zenon cleared his throat, the hairs of his grayish beard bristling, and handed him a piece of papyrus. "This is a formal letter of invitation from King Ketriporis," he said.

"Ketriporis, the son of Berisades? He rules in the west of Thrace with his father, yes?" Trysimachus asked, surprised.

Zenon nodded. "Yes, he has been co-ruling since the war's end. A few days ago, an envoy was here, bringing this letter and presents from the king."

Trysimachus looked confused but curious to know more.

"Apparently, the young king is dissatisfied with the way his people are portrayed in our literature and plays. He graciously invited me, as a historian, to his court to record events on his behalf in an unbiased manner. Now, how unbiased a record he would truly tolerate is impossible to know. Still, I was very flattered to receive the invitation. If only my rivals in Miletus would respect me as foreigners do, well—"

"Do not say that, teacher. Your reputation is excellent in Miletus! Many have traveled from all over Hellas to study under you; I am but one."

"Yes, but there is always a bias against those of us who live out in the colonies. We are not just traders, tillers, miners, and dissidents, no matter what the Milesian elite tell themselves in order to continue feeling superior to us. Besides, they seem to forget that it was the great Anaximander who established this colony.

"But I digress, Trysimachus. I would like to accept King Ketriporis's invitation and go to his court, but I am not as young as I once was."

The older man was overcome by a coughing fit. When he regained his voice, Zenon continued. "You see how I am plagued. My rheumatism has been acting up lately. The western lands have a reputation for being quite cold, you know. Mount Orbelus there is covered in snow even during the warmest months, and I have heard that the wind in that region chills the bones. I am afraid that I will not be able to go. But..."

Trysimachus felt his heart pounding in anticipation. He knew where this conversation was headed.

"It would be a shame to refuse this opportunity. And if I must, the king would be sorely displeased if I failed to send someone in my stead. Trysimachus of Athens, you are one of the best students I have, and the only one I would entrust with this task. If you are willing, of course."

"Teacher, you honor me with your trust," Trysimachus stammered.

"You are curious, resourceful, and a fast learner. You are also just, and you know the Thracian tongue. You were destined for this task. But I must warn you that if you do take this journey, it will be difficult and challenging. One wrong move and the consequences could be dire. The civil war that broke out after King Kotys's poisoning has made the political situation in Thrace fragile, and I suspect it will continue to be so as long as the kingdom of the Odrysians is split into three."

Trysimachus nodded.

"Athens is certainly proud that it managed to force a peace treaty on the Odrysians. The war had to be contained before it became a detriment to your state's economic interests in the region—and to Apollonia's as well, I might add. But how long will it hold?" Zenon shrugged. "In my opinion, dividing the kingdom this way is unsustainable. There is no telling what will happen. Ketriporis probably wants someone to support the western realm's political perspective. His father is ill, so he could be preparing for a confrontation. And as you and I have discussed, history is often told by the victors. Still, in spite of the danger, I believe you are fit for the task."

Trysimachus's throat felt parched. The two men shared more wine. Looking him in the eyes, Zenon continued, "If you embark on this journey, you will be tested many times, in more ways than either of us can predict. But you will obtain the greatest knowledge of all—understanding of oneself. You are still young, and if you survive, you will be a better, wiser, and stronger man for it."

After a long silence, the old scholar asked, "How do you feel about this?"

Trysimachus stared at the ground between his feet. "I do not know. Excited by the opportunity... but also afraid?"

"I have gotten to know you well enough to know that you are an adventurous type. Fear and excitement are two sides of one coin."

"It has always been my dream to explore a new land, observe and learn about its people, write about them, and pass my knowledge on."

"Yes. This can be your big chance! A fulfilling quest."

"But I have heard and read a lot about the Odrysians. Their fierceness and cruelty are legendary."

"You are referring to King Kotys, I presume?"

"Indeed. He was infamous for his cruelty."

"While he may have been cruel, we must remember the political circumstances he found himself in. From what I know, he struggled against his own vices and had to make tough decisions. And, of course, it is advantageous to some to portray him as nothing more than an oppressor. But regardless, Ketriporis and his father are not Kotys. I know you have read Xenophon's and Thucydides's accounts of the barbarians. But I was born in Thrace and have lived on the shores of the Pontos all my life, and I can tell you, the Odrysae are a complex and fascinating people."

Trysimachus nodded attentively.

"It is perhaps hard for us Hellenes to understand the

Thracians, because their customs and outlook are very different from ours. It is easy to mock them as being backward. But there is more to them than the simplified and exaggerated tales floating around us. I am sure you have already noticed this with the local tribesmen you have met during your stay here."

"Yes, I have. Before coming here, the only Thracians I had encountered were some slaves in Athens and some mercenaries passing through the city. But they are more diverse in personality than I previously thought."

"Yes, indeed. I have been especially interested in the west of Thrace, and following all the reports from there. A father and son co-ruling in harmony? It is unprecedented. Menander returned from Thasos and told me the Western Odrysian realm has expressed their commitment to strong trade relations with the Thasians. The kings seem to be managing well so far, despite ruling some of the harshest and least fertile lands in Thrace. And according to Menander, the people seem glad to be out from under Kotys."

Trysimachus's heart was pounding so hard that he feared his mentor would hear it. "Teacher, if I accept this quest, will I have time to visit my family before I leave? I am afraid that once I go, it will be many moons before I see them again."

"The king does not expect me until the leaves have turned golden. Your father is still trading in Olbia, is he not?"

"Indeed, he is."

"You should go visit your parents, then. Otherwise, how would I face your father in the afterlife?"

Trysimachus's excitement had already triumphed over his fear. He shook his teacher's hand firmly and accepted the assignment with a smile.

"I will be awaiting your reports. I am eager to learn your perspective on the Odrysians. I admit, I did not think you would say no, so I have already prepared the necessary letters of introduction and gathered the funds you will need. I have drawn a map for you to follow as well. Let me show you."

A servant unrolled the map across a table, and the two men examined it.

"Upon your return from Olbia, you are to meet an envoy sent by King Ketriporis in the lands of King Amadokus, two full moons from now. The envoy will be waiting for you in the village of Eumolpias, on the Hebros River. He will accompany you through the mountains to the king's court."

"Why not go by sea?"

"You must do as the king commands, Trysimachus. And do not forget, the sea route is unstable and dangerous due to the ongoing rebellions against Athens. Byzantion on the Bosporus is one of the rebellious polities. You do not want to get caught up in such a conflict."

"But what about the inland tribes, between here and my meeting with the king's envoy?"

"As you know, the preferred form of communication amongst Thracians is bribery. You will be carrying enough coins to not worry about that. Should brigands cross your path, these shall be your best weapons. Now, once you cross into the lands of King Amadokus, I would suggest taking the route from Kabyle to the Hebros..."

THRACE,
EARLY AUTUMN, 357 BCE

It was a brilliant day in central Thrace. The air was crisp and fragrant. The sky was blue, without a cloud in sight. The sun was high, and Mount Haemus glistened in the distance. Trysimachus was rushing along a dusty path, trying to find his way to the Hebros River.

Like many Athenians, Trysimachus had grown up viewing Thrace as a wild and dangerous land. Its people were seen as unruly and bloodthirsty, savage and strange. Tales of the brutality of the Odrysians—the most powerful tribe amongst the Thracians, who through wit and might had forced many of the other tribes into submission—were common coin at dinner and parties. Trysimachus had never ventured into inland Thrace until now.

Marveling at the beautiful scenery around him, he climbed a tall hill and regarded the vast valley below. An unusual sight in the distance caught his eye. Was it some kind of supernatural happening that occurred only in this mysterious yet dangerous land? It must have been, as, after all, this was the sacred valley of the Thracian goddess Bendis.

There was no smoke in the air, nor did the wind bring that familiar acrid smell. And yet, what looked like a ribbon of fire was slowly moving toward the slopes of the mountain from the horizon. His heart was pounding as fear enveloped him.

But his curiosity overcame him, and he hurried down the slope as fast as he could. The closer he got, the more he could hear.

"What in the heavens is this? It sounds like the fire is crying out in pain and agony," he mumbled to himself.

Within moments, as if by magic, a magnificent sight, like nothing he had beheld before, unfurled in front of his eyes. Several men were carrying what looked like a massive sarcophagus, covered in gold. Behind it were carts laden with gold and silver cups, bowls, coins...

Trysimachus gasped, mesmerized. He had never seen so much gold in one place. The brilliance and intensity of its sunlit glow nearly blinded him. Coming out of his stupor, he rubbed his eyes to assure himself that he wasn't dreaming or that he hadn't crossed over to the afterlife.

A group of spectators was standing nearby. He headed their way. "What is happening?" he asked, almost breathlessly, in the tongue of the barbarians.

A tall, red-haired man looked him over from head to toe with a stern gaze. Trysimachus prepared to be spurned. Instead, he received a cordial response.

"Stranger, what you're looking at is the funeral procession of King Berisades."

"King Berisades? It cannot be!" Berisades's court was Trysimachus's destination. But he didn't think he'd reached the western realm yet. Wasn't he still in the territory of King Amadokus?

Taking no time to thank the man, Trysimachus hurried toward the front of the procession. He caught up, took a brush and roll of papyrus from his sack, and began rapidly taking notes and drawing pictures of all he saw. He hadn't expected his work to begin so soon! Fortune had guided him to a Thracian royal funeral. But this wasn't just any Thracian tribe—these were the Odrysians.

The procession was grand yet solemn. It was led by a rider

clad in golden armor, the personification of King Rhesus himself. His luminous figure was bathed in the glow of the sunlight reflecting off the gold.

Sitting on a fine saddlecloth and carrying his head high, the sacred ruler—the *basileus*—looked the part of a true descendent of Apollo. His horse—a black stallion with a long, thick mane, a white star in the middle of its forehead, and white fetlocks—was at least fifteen hands tall. It wore a golden harness and was decorated with countless exquisitely crafted ornaments on its forehead, on each side of its regal face, along its nose, and even on the reins. Behind the king, three riders in iron armor followed. The group was surrounded by armored cavalry, which Trysimachus surmised were bodyguards.

An old man nearby supported himself by leaning on a staff as he watched. Trysimachus turned to him. "Who is the king leading the procession?"

"Young man, that's King Ketriporis at the front."

What fate! Trysimachus thought. *I feared I had lost my way traveling to the western court, only to find its basileus here!*

Following his mentor's directions, Trysimachus had taken the route through Kabyle to meet the king's envoy. He had followed the setting sun west, but the Hebros had been nowhere in sight. Instead, he had found himself in this mysterious valley, far away from any large settlements.

He turned to the old man again. "Who are those riders?"

"King Ketriporis's brothers, followed by King Amadokus and King Kersebleptes, son of Kotys."

The gods must have guided me here to behold the three kings of the Odrysians... King Amadokus, in whose lands I am standing now, King Kersebleptes, ruler of the eastern realm, and King Ketriporis himself!

Behind them was the gold-covered sarcophagus, the one

that had initially blinded Trysimachus's eyes. Beside it walked a beautiful young woman, her head high. She was dressed in an exquisite, long *chiton* and swathed in gold, from her headdress to her earrings and multiple necklaces to the massive gold bracelets dangling on her wrists.

"Sald! Sald!" The crowd chanted the Thracian word for 'gold'.

Behind her, servants dressed in plain tunics were pushing carts full of gold and silver jugs, plates, bowls, vases, painted pottery, urns in different shapes and sizes, and cauldrons full of gold coins. One of the carts held armor and weapons. Next, a magnificent and elaborately decorated chariot pulled by four horses passed. Trysimachus presumed that all these objects must have belonged to the deceased king.

Still more servants followed. One was leading a dog. Others were carrying plates covered in grapes, pomegranates, and other foods, while others carried *hydriai* of wine. Trysimachus felt that Tyche, the goddess of fortune, was with him that day. He had heard of the Odrysian royals' lavish funerals, but never in his wildest dreams had he imagined being an eyewitness to one.

The procession continued with richly dressed riders, who, based on their attire, must have been the *zibythides*, the Thracian nobility. They presented a colorful sight, one in accordance with the meaning of their name, 'bright'.

Trysimachus took note of their differing and eclectic hairstyles. Some wore their hair short, some long; some curly and others straight. Yet others had their hair braided or tied into topknots. A few were dyed blue, standing out amid the more common red, blond, and brown heads. Most of the nobles had beards, though a few had shaved their cheeks and chins clean.

The majority had the piercing blue and gray eyes that Thracians were known for, and they wore vibrant tunics under their armor. But the most striking part of their attire was their multicolored cloaks, which featured embroidered geometric patterns that caught the young historian's eye.

A unit of footsoldiers, called *peltasts*, marched from behind. Some wore felt caps, while others donned headgear made from fox skins—pointed, with the fox's face seated on their forehead. The peltasts wore no armor, only tunics and cloaks, all identically patterned. Their feet and lower legs were covered in tall, laced fawn-skin boots, and the majority carried javelins, though some wore daggers and swords along with the small, crescent-shaped shields they bore for protection. These wicker shields were decorated with symbols and art unique to each man.

Cavalry riders, armed with spears held behind their shields, came next. Trysimachus was impressed to see that the horses' reins dangled free. *They can control their mounts just with their knees?* he thought. *No wonder the Thracians are considered the equal of the Libyans on horseback.*

At the end of the procession were eleven women, all opulently dressed, wailing and crying. He guessed that they were the wives of King Berisades who had not been selected to follow their husband to the afterlife.

Trysimachus followed the procession to the entrance of the tomb, finding a good vantage point from which to witness the rituals. The entrance was decorated with a large sculptural scene depicting the king on a hunt. There was a bronze statue of a boar being hunted, and then another of the boar with an arrow protruding from its neck. Trysimachus knew that the Odrysians took great pride in their hunting skills; he imagined that King Berisades had been a great hunter during his lifetime.

Two huge vases were brought forward by servants, and their contents poured on the ground. They made two piles: one of white pebbles, and another of black. The pile of white pebbles was clearly larger, and the life of the ruler was pronounced to have been a happy one.

"This is one custom I did not know about. I suppose the white pebbles mark happy days, and the black mark unhappy ones? Interesting. That is a lot of tallying to do," the historian mumbled to himself.

Afterward, part of the procession began moving again, and Trysimachus watched it disappear into the tomb. The objects he had seen on the carts were going to be buried with the king, and Berisades's magnificent chariot would transport him into the next realm. And there was certainly enough gold and wine to aid him in the afterlife.

But Berisades would not be accompanied to the afterlife by objects alone. His favorite wife, servants, and grooms were going to be sacrificed, so they could continue to serve him—even his favorite dog and horses would follow.

Trysimachus took out his scroll and gazed at the tomb. The stone structure was being covered in dirt, and before long it had been transformed into a tall mound.

A sudden thought struck him. *The Valley of Bendis is also a burial ground. The hill I climbed earlier could have been another royal tomb!*

After the rituals ended and the procession dispersed, Trysimachus decided to make his presence known and bravely presented his letter of introduction to an Odrysian soldier. It passed from one dignitary to another until it reached the king's advisor, an imposing Thracian whose name was Sura. It was he who took the scholar to the young king.

Standing alone and facing the mound, King Ketriporis resembled a statue himself. With long, curly hair the color of gold and clear, blue eyes, he was strikingly handsome. Yet his brows were knotted in a deep frown as if he were ready to erupt like a storm. Turning slowly at the sound of Sura's voice, he looked sternly at Trysimachus.

Was it such a good idea to make myself known so early, and in such a grievous moment for the basileus? Trysimachus began to shake.

But the king's frown softened, and his lips curled into a smile.

"Trysimachus of Athens," the king began. "Do you understand the duties you have been asked to fulfill?"

"Yes, basileus. I do."

"Perform them well, and I shall reward you richly. But remember to record only what you see and hear. Nothing more," the king commanded. And without giving the historian a second look, he walked away.

Taking a deep breath, Trysimachus looked at Sura. The Thracian looked back at him assuredly.

"Just do as you are told, and you will be fine, Athenian."

XIII

At sunrise the next day, the preparations for the funeral games began. Trysimachus had yet to find his place at court, and followed the crowd to the chariot race. A large patch of flat ground between two low hills, where the spectators would stand, had been turned into a makeshift hippodrome. The valley's terrain provided a natural setting for the race. Two posts, placed at each end of the field, marked where the turns were to be made.

Small in stature, Trysimachus had to push his way through the tall, broad-shouldered Thracians to get a good view. A seven-lap, six-horse race was announced to cheers from the crowd.

"A six-horse race? If their charioteering skills are anything like their riding, it should be something to behold," Trysimachus said to himself.

The first of the contestants was Bryzos, chief of the local Brenae tribe and vassal ruler under King Amadokus. General Charidemus would represent King Kersebleptes and the Eastern Odrysian realm. The Hellene mercenary, whose treacherous actions had prolonged the Odrysian civil war, was met with a rather negative reaction from the crowd, and his bodyguards had to protect him from objects thrown by the spectators.

The athlete and warrior Mokatus represented King Amadokus and the Central Odrysian realm. By the boisterous applause that followed the announcement of his name, Trysimachus deduced that he was well known in these lands.

And finally, representing King Berisades and the Western Odrysian realm was none other than King Ketriporis himself. *There is more at stake here than it seems,* Trysimachus thought. *This race will be a political statement of power and prestige more than anything else.*

He watched the grooms prepare the horses and chariots for the race. All four chariots were specially decorated, but one stood out. It was covered in gold, and even its wheels looked like they were speckled in it.

Bryzos approached, bulky and clad in an iron breastplate. Trysimachus watched the man gulp a tall cup of wine and wipe his mouth with his hand. A servant handed the chieftain a bronze helmet with two boar tusks pointing upwards. Bryzos lifted it and adjusted it on his head with a broad smile. He struck his chest with his fist proudly, producing a loud clang, and climbed into his chariot, the horned helmet giving him a menacing look.

Meanwhile, Ketriporis presented a splendid but oppositional sight, clad in a golden helmet and matching breastplate. *Light and dark, life and death,* Trysimachus thought, observing Ketriporis and his burly opponent. He was cheering internally for the young basileus, even though he had only met him the day before.

Trysimachus glanced over at the other two racers. The mercenary general, in his Chalcidian helmet, and Mokatus, bareheaded and wearing only a tunic with a small oval shield on his back, looked less impressive, but they were no less dangerous.

A horn sounded, and the race began. The twenty-four horses took off eastward at full speed, the thunder of their galloping echoing between the hills. It was a sight to behold. Bouncing in the air, looking as if they could fly off their chariots at any moment, the four contestants drew shouts and cheers from the crowd. The stones and bumps along the course added to the dangers of the ride. Despite the challenges, all four made their first turn without accident and headed back at full speed.

Mokatus took an early lead. Playing to the spectators with ostentatious displays of strength and skill at steering, he was driving the crowd to ecstasy. Ketriporis, meanwhile, was trailing behind. But from what Trysimachus could see, he looked unabashed, as if he were in the position he wanted to be in.

Mokatus remained in the lead. Taking full advantage of the width of the track, he was steering and swerving his chariot in order to block his opponents. Just behind him, General Charidemus rammed his chariot into Bryzos's. The chieftain almost lost control, but was able to recover and bumped into Charidemus's chariot in return. By that time, the young basileus was just a hand behind them.

The turns were tight, and every time the racers swung around, it looked like a chariot might overturn at any moment. Mokatus, his muscles bulging underneath his tunic, was still ahead, but Bryzos was right on his heels. At one point, it looked like the chieftain had found a way to overtake him. At the last moment, though, Mokatus outmaneuvered his opponent and blocked his advance. Clearly furious, Bryzos took off his helmet and threw it at Mokatus with one arm, tusks aimed straight at the athlete's back. As if anticipating Bryzos's move, Mokatus shifted his back just in time so that the helmet was deflected by his shield.

A servant ran swiftly onto the field to snatch the helmet from the ground, moving away before he could be run over by the charging Ketriporis.

Now even more furious, Bryzos was whipping his horses in a frenzy, trying to catch up with Mokatus. But at the next turn, Ketriporis took the inside corner of the track and drifted outwards into the chieftain. The maneuver caused Bryzos's chariot to overturn, and he fell to the ground with a crash.

Several large Thracians succeeded in dragging him from the field just in time. A servant ran to bring the Brenae leader a pitcher of wine. Bryzos gulped its contents in one go and shook his whole body as a horse would, his long braid flying in the air.

Only three contestants remained in the race. Charidemus was now trying to overtake Mokatus, with Ketriporis barely behind. Mokatus, a few hands ahead, was still able to block his opponent's passage by swerving in and out. But a bump in the terrain made him bounce and lose control. The mercenary general took advantage and drove his chariot into his opponent's, aiming to overturn him. But the athlete was able to hold on.

In an instant, with great speed, the young basileus approached on the other side and rammed Mokatus's chariot. Unable to keep control this time, the athlete was flung to the ground. Landing safely, he sprang to his feet and, running as fast as he could, tried to jump back on his chariot. But it was in vain. His horses galloped away, leaving the track and heading straight toward a group of spectators, forcing them to run for their lives.

Now the race was between Charidemus and Ketriporis. They were neck-and-neck, and Trysimachus felt his breath catch in his throat. The thirteenth and final turn was coming up. The general used the opportunity to ram into the basileus. Ketriporis's chariot tilted, one of its wheels rising up in the air, and it looked like it was about to overturn. The crowd's cries and shouts ceased. All eyes were fixed on the golden chariot, which was now moving forward on just one wheel.

Trysimachus froze. *It is over for him*, he thought. *And my mission as well. If both he and his father are dead, what am I doing here?*

But Ketriporis made the turn and used his legs to rebalance the tilted chariot. The crowd erupted in a thunderous cheer as the other wheel returned to the ground. Charidemus looked back, which seemed to slow him down. The final dash to the finish line was underway. The general whipped his horses madly, but the basileus overtook him in a flash and reached the finish line several hands ahead. The crowd exploded with joy.

Trysimachus reflected on what he had just witnessed. He wondered if Ketriporis would manage to balance the competing factions in his realm, as he had balanced his chariot, or if he would be thrown over.

It will be interesting to observe, he thought.

After the chariot race, the games in honor of the late King Berisades continued. King Ketriporis's brothers competed in archery, javelin hurling, and horseracing contests, demonstrating their abilities as warriors and hunters. Hand-to-hand combat games followed. Trysimachus mingled among the spectators for all of it. Combatants from all over Thrace and the surrounding lands participated, and gold and silver prizes were awarded to the winners.

Ketriporis was one of the combatants, drawing Axios, a general from Macedonia, as his opponent. His fight was the most eagerly anticipated, especially after the chariot race. The battle was expected to be a tough one. The king and the general were both renowned fighters. When they stepped onto the field, the crowd once again exploded with loud cheers.

"*Zymlidrenos! Zymlidrenos*!" the spectators chanted in unison.

Water dragon? Why are they chanting that? Trysimachus wondered. He spotted Sura, the king's advisor, in the crowd and felt at ease enough to ask him.

"Do you see the dragon on the king's headpiece?" Sura replied. "The dragon comes from the realm beyond. It is the greatest danger to the world of the living, spreading chaos! By wearing it, the king is signifying he will attack the Macedonian fiercely and without mercy."

Trysimachus nodded and prepared to record what he could of the combat. To him, the slender, young king seemed like no match for the heavily built Macedonian. Axios looked like he could easily dominate Ketriporis.

The fight began. The two opponents threw a flurry of punches at each other. The Macedonian held an early advantage, driving the basileus backward. Lunging for him, the Macedonian grabbed the king's neck, but the Odrysian swung a hard blow straight into the general's jaw, forcing Axios to release him and step back.

Angry, Axios lunged again with renewed force, trying to grab the basileus's neck once more. This time, just before the Macedonian reached him, Ketriporis used his left arm to hook underneath Axios's right arm. Turning his body and using the trapped arm as a lever, he threw Axios to the ground, flipping the larger man's body over his back. The king followed the general to the ground and used his knees to squeeze Axios's head, but the other man kicked Ketriporis in the chest, knocking him away and allowing the Macedonian to return to his feet.

The grueling fight continued, seeming to follow the rhythm of the chanting crowd. The combatants appeared evenly matched. Axios dove down to grab Ketriporis's legs, but the basileus must have predicted the move as he jumped over the Macedonian, attempting to land his feet on his opponent's back. Axios rolled forward, narrowly avoiding the blow. Feet back on the ground, Ketriporis charged. Axios stood up just in time to receive a powerful kick to his midsection. The general gagged, reeling in pain, but was able to maintain his balance and continue fighting.

The two warriors began taunting each other, trying to find an opening in the other's guard. Axios kicked the basileus repeatedly, lifting one leg to deliver a final blow straight to the basileus's stomach. But Ketriporis swooped forward and grabbed the general's raised foot, yanking it upward. Axios fell backward onto the hard-packed earth. Before the general could rise, the young king locked Axios's foot in his grip. The Macedonian attempted to kick him away, but Ketriporis fell backward, maintaining his grip and stretching Axios's trapped tendon.

In great pain, Axios tried hard to wiggle free. But the king had now wrapped his legs around the Macedonian's and started twisting Axios's foot and leg. The crowd was thrilled as if Axios's pain was their pleasure.

Despite his agony, the warrior continued trying to knock the Odrysian away, to no avail. He scooped up a handful of dirt and threw it straight at the king's face. Ketriporis grunted but didn't let go.

Finally, the Macedonian groaned and raised his hand in submission. The judge declared the Odrysian to be the winner.

Axios struggled to his feet with a bestial expression. Several of his countrymen ran to his side and helped him up. The predominantly Thracian crowd cheered for the young basileus, ecstatic that the Macedonian had lost.

The games were over, and it was time for the funerary banquet. Trysimachus didn't know what to expect. He had read that the barbarians' feasts involved ecstatic dancing, the smoking of cannabis, and the excessive drinking of wine, followed by orgies. He recalled Xenophon's tale of the Thracian Seuthes throwing food at his guests, and he wondered if he would witness wild maenads tearing a bull's flesh with their teeth and eating the raw meat.

Large tents were set up on the field, and enormous rugs from Persia were spread across the ground. The long banquet tables were richly decorated and covered with food. A pungent smell filled the air from game splashed in chestnut sauce.

There was meat in abundance, as well as breads, soups, pomegranates, grapes, and dishes Trysimachus had never seen. Not knowing when his next opportunity to have such a meal would be, he made sure to help himself.

The food was served on plates made of pure gold. The servants brought out large vessels of wine, and he watched with interest the way the barbarians drank it, an art in itself. First, a servant would use a jug to pour wine into a guest's drinking horn, called a *rhyton*. The drinker would seal the bottom hole of the rhyton with one finger, then slowly release it, so the rich, red liquid would flow into his *phiale*, or flat bowl. Afterward, picking up the phiale with his other hand, the drinker would first inhale the aroma before imbibing the fragrant substance.

Despite observing the process several times, when Trysimachus was handed his own golden rhyton, its end sculpted to represent the head of a horse, he found himself struggling to use it properly. The fear of offending his hosts added to the pressure. Fortunately, the servant boy not only showed him the right way to handle the horn, but also explained the meaning of the Thracian wine-drinking ritual.

"See how the upper part of the rhyton is wide, and the lower part narrow? The upper part represents the world of the gods, while the lower represents our mortal world. Grapes are a sacred fruit from the gods. So when the wine's poured, it flows from the heavens down to us mortals. In this way, the kings and lords honor the sacredness of this drink."

Trysimachus recalled hearing that, in Thrace, it was customary for the guests to drink as much as the king. He feared he could hardly hold the undiluted wine the barbarians were drinking. But to his surprise, the wine being served was the finest and most delicious he had ever tasted, so he didn't mind the numerous refillings of his rhyton.

The meal, hearty and delicious, was accompanied by

music, but not the shrill sounds he had been expecting to hear. Instead, a divine melody was coming from a lyre, as if Orpheus were playing it. In a heavenly voice, a young Thracian sang the praises of the exploits of King Berisades. He was followed by a poet, who recited verses in the late king's honor. The deceased ruler was acclaimed as a great statesman, warrior, and hunter.

A spirited dance celebrating the late king's victories in battle followed. Thracian dancer-warriors leapt high, thrusting at one another and striking their swords together with loud crashes. There was no bloodshed, as Trysimachus had expected, though the dance did resemble a real battle.

In truth, the feast was proceeding in an ordinary manner. Despite the vast quantities of wine being consumed, there were no drunken arguments or physical fights—the spirit of the games had dissipated.

After the meal was over, gifts were presented to King Ketriporis. He accepted each offering graciously and gave out gifts in return. The assembly of guests included kings and dignitaries from neighboring lands, rulers of Thracian tribes under Odrysian dominion, chiefs of independent tribes, and Hellenic diplomats. Sitting among them, Trysimachus felt that any hesitation he had felt about embarking on this journey had been unwarranted.

Sitting at the head of the main table, flanked by the other two Odrysian kings, the young basileus was a stately host. There were no obvious signs of discord between the three kings, despite the recent conflict. Watching them, an outside observer would have seen harmony, a unity of strength and wealth.

Do they intend to maintain the peace treaty? Or are they wearing masks? Trysimachus wondered. He focused his attention on Ketriporis. *The young basileus has honored his father greatly. But he has also been sending a strong political message to his guests: that he possesses courage, power, and intelligence.*

"The first toast is in honor of you, great and noble King Berisades. You are now feasting with the gods and enjoying eternal bliss," said Ketriporis, rousing Trysimachus from his thoughts. As the basileus praised his late father, Trysimachus could tell that he was deeply affected by the sudden loss.

A man, especially a king, must not show weakness, Trysimachus thought, and felt sympathy toward the basileus, who carried such a heavy weight on his young shoulders.

The banquet lasted late into the night. Although Trysimachus felt it was not that different from those he could have observed in the lands that were deemed civilized, he was nonetheless struck by how Thracian it was in its nature, judging by its extravagance. *No wonder the young basileus has been upset at the portrayal of his countrymen in our plays and literature*, he concluded. *We portray them all as savages. I guess just because something is Thracian does not mean it has to be wild.*

XV

After only one day's rest, King Ketriporis's advisor, Sura, approached Trysimachus.

"We will be leaving early in the morning. We are to join King Amadokus and the rest of the honored guests on a tour of his realm. You will follow and record the events. But I must warn you, you are only to record what happens. Do not try to instill your thoughts, interpretations, or feelings. The king is not interested in a biased account. Do you understand?"

"Yes, I understand."

"I have been ordered to take care and watch over you. You will be supplied with a horse, and you are to ride beside me. You know how to ride?"

"Yes, yes, of course," Trysimachus stammered. It had been a while since he had ridden a horse, and the Thracian horses were larger and faster compared to the ones back home. Having already witnessed the Thracians' great horsemanship, he couldn't help but feel intimidated.

Predictably, riding proved to be quite a challenge. On several occasions, his awkwardness inspired laughter from the other riders. But Trysimachus tried to ignore it and focus on what was ahead. His journey had begun.

The royal party was accompanied by a large body of cavalry and peltasts in addition to the servants and grooms.

Notably absent, however, were the Macedonian and Eastern Odrysian delegations.

"Our first stop will be Onocarsis," Sura told Trysimachus as they galloped through a thick forest.

"Onocarsis? Is that where Philip of Macedonia met with King Kotys before he died?" Trysimachus asked. "I was told it is a beautiful place."

"I would not disagree."

Situated amongst shady wooden groves abundant in springs of the purest water, the royal estate and sanctuary of Onocarsis was splendid indeed. With its grand feast hall and sacrificial altar, it had an extravagant flair in the style of its previous owner, King Kotys.

After taking a rest and eating, the party continued uphill. "Do you see the peak of the mountain? On the very top lies the residence of King Amadokus. That is where we are going," Sura told Trysimachus. "The king is rather proud of it and wants to show it off to his guests."

Surrounded by deep gorges and imposing rocks, the fortified residence was difficult to reach. The steep, narrow road was strenuous for men and horses alike, so when the walls of the fortification and the towers on each side of the main gate finally loomed ahead, Trysimachus felt relief.

Following Sura and his companions into the courtyard, he dismounted. He wanted to do his best for the king in whose hands his life rested, and he pushed his fatigue and weariness aside. Instead of heading straight to his quarters, he began taking notes and drawing pictures of the sights in front of him.

The walls of the fortress and the tall watchtowers were impressive indeed. But nothing could compare to the perfect setting of the place. Below Trysimachus's feet, a vast expanse of forests and fields, bisected by rivers and lakes with water as blue as the sky, stretched to the horizon as if it had no end. The air, crisp and clear, was making the dust of even a single faraway rider visible from above.

It would be difficult for an army to lead an attack here, he thought.

The royal residence was an achievement of expert stonemasonry. Crossing over the threshold of the main room, Trysimachus was greeted by the riches and opulence typical of the Odrysian nobility. The floor in the main hall took him aback: dark red in color, it looked like it was covered in blood. The disturbing image of a bloodthirsty barbarian ready to slit his throat flashed in his mind, but Trysimachus quickly pushed it aside.

There was much excitement amongst the guests for a hunt that was to take place in their honor. The thick Thracian forests, rich in game, offered the makings of an exhilarating event.

The next morning, the kings of Paeonia, Scythia, and Bithynia were among the participants vying for the hunter's wreath and the honor to drink from the first rhyton at the royal feast. As the day ended, the bright sun was setting in a sky so colorful—a mixture of red, yellow, and purple—it looked like a work of art. It was the perfect backdrop for the feast, which was being held in the crisp outdoor air.

Embracing and toasting each of his guests in accordance with Thracian custom, King Amadokus was the embodiment of hospitality itself. He seemed amicable, not crude and cruel, appearing more comfortable in his position as ruler than the stiff and uptight Ketriporis.

Trysimachus glanced around, scribbling down his observations. *No women*, he noted. Seeing the Athenian delegation seated between King Amadokus and the young basileus, the scholar's thoughts drifted in their direction.

The royal host seems busy politicking. I think he is reassuring the Athenian ambassador that he will uphold his part of the peace treaty. The young basileus seems...

He realized he had to stop himself. Hadn't he been ordered to refrain from interjecting his opinions and thoughts into his descriptions? His notes would have disappointed the young basileus.

I must be more careful—my life depends on it, he thought. *The philosopher Plato said that opinions are not truths.*

The hunter's wreath and the first rhyton were bestowed upon Ateas, the king of Scythia. His hunting trophy, a large boar with long and fearsome tusks, was brought to the table and greeted with boisterous cheers.

"Honorable King Ateas, your excellence and strength is revered!" King Amadokus proclaimed. "And let us toast our other honored guests, who have come here as brothers! A toast to you, King Lyppeios from Paeonia. May Paeonia emerge victorious over the Macedonians one day! And a toast for you, General Athenodorus from Athens... General Bianor, and to the sons of Berisades!"

"To the great King Amadokus," Ketriporis replied. "A toast to the man the gods have chosen to rule over the lands in which my father's tomb lies. It shall remain a testament to our eternal friendship."

The bright red sun was replaced by a full moon as the feast continued. The night was cold, but the wine was flowing plentifully, warming body and soul. The atmosphere was relaxed and cheerful, certainly different from the somber mood at the funerary banquet. There was much merriment, and the assembled laughed and pounded their cups on the table in response to the jester's antics.

King Amadokus rose without warning. The servants helped him remove his boots, and he stepped into the circle of simmering embers in the middle of the gathering. To the rhythm of a hand drum, the king began dancing over the embers with his bare feet as if he were in a trance. Trysimachus gaped. It would have been an impressive performance from anyone, but especially the king himself.

There must be some kind of trickery, he thought. *The embers cannot be that hot.*

The red embers glowed underneath the king's feet as he danced around the circle. There was no sign of pain or discomfort on his face. Trysimachus looked quizzically at Sura but didn't dare ask.

As if guessing his bewilderment, the advisor whispered into his ear, "Only a true descendent of the gods can partake in this sacred ritual. As the sovereign ruler and high priest of this land, the king alone can perform this dance. He is communicating with Apollo now, as you Hellenes call him."

After the dance was over, a servant wiped the king's feet; no burn marks were visible.

Feeling overwhelmed in this foreign environment, Trysimachus's thoughts drifted back to the young basileus, whom he tried to observe once again. In stark contrast to the majority of the guests, some of whom were sprawled out on the ground, drunk, King Ketriporis looked sober. He did not smile or laugh, even at the jester's funniest jokes. Instead, he sat upright, conversing with the Athenian ambassador next to him.

Certain it was mere trickery, Trysimachus walked to the hearth and bravely thrust his bare hand into the embers. The still-hot coals seared his fingers and palm instantly. Shivering and sweating at the same time, he bit his lip in pain and ran to a nearby spring as fast as he could, plunging his hand into the cold water.

Sura erupted in laughter behind him. Thankfully, the jester had disappeared, or Trysimachus could have found himself the subject of many embarrassing jokes.

Could their kings be truly divine? he wondered. Eager to avoid ridicule, Trysimachus found a secluded spot in the courtyard. Stretching out on a large, flat rock, he began studying the constellations painted in the sky above. But soon, feeling the weight of a tiring day wash over him, he retreated to his quarters and fell asleep.

The next morning, awakened by the throbbing pain in his hand, Trysimachus looked at his blistered skin, a painful reminder that his skepticism had backfired on him. Outside, dawn was breaking, and he stepped into the courtyard. He needed to find a healer. But other than the watchmen on the towers, there was no one in sight. He had no other option but to wait for Sura. When he finally saw the advisor coming, he ran fast to greet him.

“Sura, where can I find a healer?” he asked, out of breath.

Sura laughed heartily. “Serves you right, Athenian. Maybe now you will stop doubting our rituals.”

“I will not do that again,” Trysimachus confirmed.

“The healer resides below in the village.” Sura summoned one of the servant boys. “Better Poga takes you there.”

“My gratitude, Sura. But can the healer be trusted?”

“Here you go doubting again, Athenian. Our healers are of rare talent. Soon you will find out yourself.” Sura laughed again and walked away.

The houses of the local villagers were built right into the rocks, shielded from the winds on the sunny slopes of the peak. Poga directed him to the healer’s home, and Trysimachus knocked on the door with his good hand.

An old, rather shabby-looking woman with long, tangled, fire-red locks opened the door. “What do you want?” she asked, wearing a deep frown on her face.

“Is the healer here?” Trysimachus stammered.

The old woman stared at him with suspicion for a long time, finally ushering him in. A strong smell of herbs greeted Trysimachus. He trusted the skills of the Hellenic doctors, but the Thracians’ medical abilities were unknown to him.

The woman pointed to a bed where a man was sleeping soundly, and walked away. Quiet as a mouse, Trysimachus approached the snoring Thracian. With long, white hair and a beard, the man looked the part of a healer, at least. Trysimachus nudged him gently, then grew impatient and shook his shoulder. Eventually, the healer rose, muttering, grunting, and coughing irritably.

"Who are you? I have never seen you before!" he barked.

"I am one of the guests of King Amadokus," Trysimachus replied timidly.

"Why do you seek me?"

Trysimachus offered his blistered hand. The Thracian studied it, then stared at his pupils and asked him to display his tongue.

What does that have to do with my burnt hand? Trysimachus wondered.

"Your skin is pale, and your tongue white," the healer said. "You are a Hellene, are you not? You are wondering if I can heal your hand."

"I was not thinking that." The lie made Trysimachus's face flush crimson. He watched the healer mix some herbs and apply them to his burnt hand. Then the old man chanted a brief homage to Derzelas, the Thracian god of health and vitality. To Trysimachus's surprise, the pain dissipated quickly.

"Hellene, you live too much up here." The healer tapped the scholar's head with a scornful expression. "You do not know how to connect with nature or how to take a full breath. That is why your skin is too pale, and you are so scrawny. Connect with the land and the people here, and you will have an easier time."

With that, he turned his back on Trysimachus and returned to his bed. The scholar left a few coins on his table and departed.

Once outside, Trysimachus was surprised to discover that the pain in his burnt hand was gone. Poga had been patiently waiting, and the two started back toward the fortress.

"Poga, that road there that leads through the forest. If we take it, it looks like we can return faster."

"We cannot enter this forest," Poga replied.

"Why not? It is just a forest."

"It is not just any forest, honorable guest. This is the sacred forest of the god Dionysus. No strangers are allowed to enter, except during the god's celebration. Now is not the time."

"But you are not a stranger, Poga," Trysimachus replied.

"I am Triballian and a stranger to the Odrysians."

"You are a slave, then."

"I am a captive. I was captured during the last battle between the Triballi and Odrysae. Captives are put into the service of the Odrysians."

"I see. So is this the forest where the orgies in honor of the god take place?"

"Orgies? What is that?" Poga asked.

Of course, you would not know that word. It is what we Hellenes call the celebrations, Trysimachus thought. But out loud, he said, "It is not important."

So this was the sight of Dionysus's wild and ecstatic celebrations, when anything and everything goes. The forest where the satyrs and the frenzied maenads roamed, he thought. His imagination was running wild. "Poga, what will happen if we enter the forest?"

"The forest is alive, and a three-headed serpent guards its entrance. Strange creatures, half-men and half-animals, who serve the god live there. Only the royals know the mysteries of the forest. No stranger who has ever entered it has come out alive."

At these last words, Poga shuddered. So did Trysimachus.

Following Poga the same way they had come, Trysimachus couldn't resist a look back at the forest. From the distance, he thought he saw one of the strange creatures—a centaur, perhaps—pointing an arrow at him. He ran back to the fortress as fast as he could.

During his absence, a ceremony and sacrificial offering to the gods had taken place in the newly erected temple. Adorned by ten Doric columns, the structure was another source of pride for King Amadokus.

Ten columns? Could the king or the builder be a follower of Pythagoras? Trysimachus wondered.

Favorable omens and good tidings had been announced. Preparations for departure began with everyone in high spirits; they would leave the following day.

It was time to say goodbye to King Amadokus's residence. Trying to follow the healer's advice, Trysimachus stood atop the peak. The valleys, rivers, and forests of the Thracians lay below his feet. He looked over the landscape for a long time, but he felt no special connection.

Casting a last glance at the place, Trysimachus followed the royal party down the steep and narrow road. His hand was effectively healed, and he held his horse's reins with ease.

Thc party halted at the foot of the mountain. Tall monuments carved into the rock—one resembling a snake, the other an eagle—were visible in the distance.

"Before we continue further, the royals are going to bathe in the nearby springs," Sura said. "The king finds you to be unhealthy-looking, Athenian. He has ordered you to use the springs and to drink the water here. Of course, you cannot go in the royal springs. I will take you to the ones you can enter."

"What is so special about these springs?"

"The springs are sacred. They were given to us, the chosen people, by the goddess Kotys herself. The water has the power to heal whatever ails you, Athenian. It is good for the body and the spirit. The magic of the water will make you strong and healthy—or at least less puny and weak." He laughed, and Trysimachus offered a reluctant smile.

At the springs, he was shocked by the foul smell coming from the water. It repulsed him. *There is no way I can drink this water,* he thought, but he dared not disobey the king's order. He held his nose, to the amusement of the Thracians, who once again laughed heartily and were entertained at his expense. Sura also shook his head disapprovingly.

How the barbarians could gulp goblet after goblet of the not just foul-smelling, but also foul-tasting, water was a mystery to Trysimachus. He wasn't sure about getting into the pool either. But once he was submerged in the hot water, his tired muscles started to loosen up, and his body began to relax.

Could this be the secret to the Thracians' strength? he wondered.

"Open yourself to the power of the sacred water," Sura advised him. "Just close your eyes, float, and let your thoughts go."

Trysimachus followed Sura's advice. Thoughtless and weightless, he floated in the water, immersing himself in its warmth and power. He felt relaxed in a way he had not felt in a long time, as if the goddess was working her magic on him.

"You must get dressed and prepare for the journey. We will be leaving soon." Sura's voice startled him. It sounded rough and unwelcome, interrupting this magic time of tranquility. He did not want to hear the advisor's words. He wanted to remain in this state forever.

Snapped out of his trance, Trysimachus took a few seconds to get readjusted to his surroundings. He realized he didn't even know how long he'd been in the water. Birds were flying in the trees above, chirping merrily. He hadn't cared about or noticed them before. Feeling energized, he readied himself for the journey ahead.

"Where are we going next?" he asked Sura.

"Eumolpias on the Hebros River. We will spend the night there."

"Eumolpias? My mentor wanted me to visit the Ctistae prophets there," Trysimachus replied. "What do you know about them, Sura?"

"The Ctistae are held in high honor around here. But if you ask me, I think they are a peculiar lot. Men living apart from women? How can that be? They eat no living things—only milk, cheese, and honey—and chant all day long."

"As I understand it, their lives are entirely dedicated to the gods."

"Yes, and some say those prophets know no fear."

"Can that be true? Then I really need to meet with them."

"There will be no time," Sura replied firmly.

The royal party traveled south toward the Hebros River. Leaving the southern branch of Mount Haemus behind, they entered the vast landscape Trysimachus had seen from King Amadokus's residence. Trees stretching for *stadia* and colored red, orange, and yellow by the onset of autumn glowed in the sunlight.

Trysimachus knew from the map his mentor had given him that they were reentering the same mighty plain that spread all the way to Apollonia Pontica. But the further inland they went, the less traveled and tame Thrace was becoming. He wondered what wild beasts could possibly be lurking. Boars? Lions?

The royal party moved decisively through forests and fields, with Trysimachus slowly but surely gaining better command of his horse. To his surprise, he was feeling stronger and more energetic and alert than ever.

The road that had been cut between Onocarsis and Eumolpias was of surprisingly good quality, and they soon reached the Hebros. On the other side of the river were three hills, the setting of Eumolpias. Merchant boats from the Aegean Sea, carrying a variety of goods for trade, were sailing the deep waters further inland to the trading post set up by the

Pistirians.

After crossing the river, they reached a fortification built on top of the first hill, where they were to spend the night. From there, Trysimachus enjoyed another spectacular view. With nightfall rapidly approaching, the land was tinted purple by dusk. To the south, the peaks of Mount Rhodope loomed. To the immediate north lay the Hebros River and, far in the distance, Mount Haemus. And to the west and east were what seemed like endless stadia of trees. Thrace was a massive land indeed.

XVII

The next morning, it was time to leave Eumolpias behind. The group rode in silence. Trysimachus's mind was preoccupied with what Sura had told him about the Ctistae. The previous evening, he had seen the shrine in the distance, on top of the opposite hill. He was disappointed that he did not have permission to visit the philosopher-priests. The shrine, so close yet so far away, must have contained valuable knowledge he sought.

Sura's words echoed in his mind. Men knowing no fear? Could it be possible? Easily worried, Trysimachus had tried hard to overcome his fears, but so far, it had been to no avail. *Maybe the Ctistae possess special secrets given to them by the gods—a chant, or a spell. Is that why Teacher wanted me to meet with them?*

It was fear that had made him uneasy in this quest, and it was fear that now traveled with him as his companion. He recalled hearing Thracians boast that they possessed the power to make the gods fulfill their will. And one could believe them, as their lands were fertile, their streams and rivers abundant in fish, and their forests brimming with game. But on the other hand, their lives were hard, their tribes had been conquered many times, and many of their people had been sold into slavery. One did not have to spend much time in a

Hellenic *polis* to come across a Thracian slave. So it couldn't have been true.

Is it possible for a man to control his life and destiny? Trysimachus wondered. *Would that not mean controlling the gods? But is it not the gods who control us all? Or are there a few chosen ones who possess such power?*

He didn't know how to feel about the gods. He feared them, and he revered them. When his life was going well, he was on friendly terms with them. But when things turned sour, he blamed them for playing games with him and causing havoc. Either way, his life and destiny were in their hands. Were they benevolent and good? Or were they cruel and fickle? Trustworthy or not? It was one of the greatest questions of his life.

What is my destiny? Will I accomplish great things, or will I die here, in this foreign land, and be quickly forgotten?

Feeling uncomfortable at his own thoughts, Trysimachus focused on his surroundings. He spotted the young basileus riding ahead, sitting perfectly upright in contrast to his own slouched posture. *Does he know fear?* he wondered.

While watching Ketriporis win the chariot race and the competition with Axios, Trysimachus had tried to study his demeanor. The basileus had looked confident and unafraid to him. But was it true? Or was it more like he was wearing an invisible mask, making his expression impossible to read? Ketriporis had proved himself to be a great warrior. A fearless one.

But there could have been something else behind the warrior's mask. Something vulnerable and within reach. Something that could have made the young historian trust his life to him.

As the king, does he have the power to bend the gods' will? This was something Trysimachus hoped to discover.

The first peaks of Mount Rhodope were now towering

above the royal party as they continued on the stone road. Looking at the mountains, it suddenly struck Trysimachus that the party was not following the Hebros River toward the Western Odrysian realm.

"Sura, may I ask where we are headed? We do not seem to be heading west."

"We must travel to the Temple of Dionysus first."

"The Temple of Dionysus?" The temple, with its fire rituals in which prophecies were interpreted, was famous, legendary even outside of Thrace. Many great prophecies had been attributed to those messages from Dionysus. Trysimachus felt excitement rush through him.

"The basileus wants to reaffirm his kingship and have his rebirth as the sole ruler of Western Odrysia witnessed," Sura explained.

"I see," Trysimachus replied. Then, as if sensing that he had more questions, the advisor continued.

"The young king knows that he cannot take anything for granted, certainly not in these turbulent times. Internal strife within his realm is not all that he is concerned about, as it is from the outside where the greatest threats may come. That is why, as previous great kings of the Odrysae have done, King Ketriporis wants to ground his position by receiving confirmation of his status from the greatest of them all: the gods themselves. In the most divine and revered temple in all of Thrace, the king will perform the sacred ritual necessary to receive reaffirmation from the gods that he is the one destined to rule over the realm."

"It certainly will be something to witness."

Sura nodded in agreement, and the two men continued to ride side-by-side, deep in their own thoughts. It was Trysimachus who eventually broke the silence. "Sura, may I ask why King Berisades chose his fourth son to be his co-ruler and successor?" It was something he had been wondering about but hadn't dared to ask until now.

"Because he is the smartest, strongest, and bravest of the brothers," Sura replied. "In fact, Ketriporis resembles the late king the most. He killed his first wolf at the age of twelve and earned his initiation as a warrior. And you should have seen how fast he learned your tongue, Athenian. He excelled in all of his studies, surpassing his brothers and receiving high praises from his tutors. The late king even sent him to study for two years in Athens, where he was also highly praised."

"I was not aware. Did King Berisades place him as co-ruler in order to prevent a contest over the succession?"

After a brief pause, Sura answered, giving Trysimachus much-needed insights into the affairs of the realm in the process.

"You might say that. As you may already know, Odrysia has often been plagued by conflicts between contenders to the kingship, and also conflicts between kings, nobles, and chieftains."

Trysimachus nodded.

"Odrysia was plunged into civil war after the death of King Kotys, partially because his son and successor, King Kersebleptes, made controversial decisions and was thus seen as unworthy to rule."

"Are you referring to the murder of the rebel Miltokythes and his son by General Charidemus and the Cardians?"

"Indeed. Kersebleptes violated our sacred code by allowing that brutal act of vengeance to occur. And while I am personally pleased with the division of the kingdom, imagine how infuriated King Kotys must be, watching from the heavens and seeing his son lose control over so much of the territory he fought so hard to unite. What if the same could happen within the western realm? That was the question on our minds. The late king, in his infinite wisdom, foresaw the need to deter bloodshed and conflict within his dominion. By appointing a co-ruler, he prevented us from experiencing uncertainty over who would succeed him. No one, not even Ketriporis's brothers or the nobles of the land, can express doubt over his right to rule. King Ketriporis is wise and fair. He will not disappoint the late king."

I hope Sura is right, Trysimachus thought. *For my sake as well.*

Dismounting at the foot of a high, rocky hill, the royal party left their horses in the care of the grooms. Large stone steps, carved from solid rock, led to the top, where the legendary Temple of Dionysus rested.

Passing by the temple wall built directly into the hillside, the party entered the streets and buildings of the sanctuary. Gazing around the site and taking everything in, Trysimachus was completely transfixed. There was something mystical and ethereal about the entire place, from the white-hooded priests to the caves carved out of the rock, from the massive stone blocks making up the temple to the slopes of Mount Rhodope all around.

Lined with thirty-six Doric columns, the temple was a sight to behold. Low white clouds hovered around it, making it look like it was part of the heavens above. The temple was not only befitting of Dionysus but looked like Zeus himself had constructed it in celebration of his son.

"Impressive, is it not?" Sura asked the enthralled scholar. There was a hint of pride in the advisor's voice.

"Yes, even more than I expected it to be!" Trysimachus answered earnestly.

"It is only right for us to erect the grandest temple in the land to honor Dionysus. After all, we owe him our fertility. Our prosperity. Our joy of living. Our very spirit! You should taste the god's wine, Trysimachus. There is no wine that can compare to the wine the priests make here, not in this land or the land beyond it." Sura winked merrily at him.

"I hope I shall have the chance to taste it. It looks like the temple has its own water supply?"

"Yes, it does. The water here is as pure as a maiden's teardrop," the advisor replied.

From what Trysimachus had seen, the Thracian settlements were modest and the villagers poor. And he hadn't passed by a single large city in inland Thrace. Yet no primitive people could have constructed this grand temple, which rose to the sky. It was indisputably the work of skillful builders. The contrast between the grandeur of the temple and everything else he had seen in Thrace was striking. It was even grander than the residence of King Amadokus. This captivating place was drawing Trysimachus in.

That night, the ritual of divine reaffirmation was performed. Torches lined the temple's oval open-roofed hall as countless stars filled the sky above. In the middle of the hall stood an altar cut straight from the rock. As usual, Trysimachus was relegated to a viewing position far in the back, making it hard to record everything for the king.

Wearing the white garb of a priest, King Ketriporis and the high priest of the temple, his long white beard nearly touching the floor, entered the hall. Walking down the aisle to the rhythmic chants of the priests, they slowly made their way to the altar. Trysimachus thought he could perceive the elation in the hall as if it were a visible entity. The enigma of the ritual would soon be resolved.

Women dressed in fawn-skin robes lined up on each side of the altar, snakes wrapped around their wrists. They were holding staffs tied with long ribbons and topped with pinecones, known as *thyrseis*. Standing at the altar, the young basileus looked as if illuminated from within. The chanting in the hall grew louder.

A beautiful woman brought out a gold *kantharos*, a two-headed wine vessel, and handed it to King Ketriporis. The king kissed it and knelt as the high priest began a loud chant, which Trysimachus could not understand. As the king rose again, he lifted the kantharos and poured its contents onto the altar. A fire blazed from the rock, getting larger, rising higher and higher.

The prophecy was read by the high priest. In a towering voice, he announced that the gods had declared King Ketriporis the one destined to rule the land of Western Odrysia.

The king is the fire, and the fire is the king. But the fire is also war and strife, Trysimachus thought.

The next morning, Ketriporis and Amadokus parted ways, exchanging customary greetings and bidding each other farewell. Accompanied by about two hundred peltasts and an equal number of cavalry, in addition to his bodyguards, the young basileus prepared to depart central Thrace and head back west.

Riding alongside Sura, Trysimachus had many questions about the journey ahead. Wishing to show off his knowledge of the local geography, he asked, "Sura, which route are we to take? Will we pass by Abdera and Neapolis and head south to the Aegean coast?"

"No, the king is in a hurry to get back to his domain after so many days away. Therefore, we will take the fastest and most direct route, through Mount Rhodope," Sura replied.

"Is it safe to go through the mountains? From what my mentor told me, the tribes that live there are independent and fierce."

"Yes, they are. They have lived there in isolation for eons," the advisor said. "During the time of Darius, the Persians led a campaign into these mountains and tried to force the tribes into submission. They failed. So did Sesostris, pharaoh of Egypt. In fact, no one has succeeded in conquering them or getting them to submit to another ruler."

Trysimachus's body tensed as he listened to Sura's explanation.

"Those tribes pay tribute or tax to no one. They bow down to no one. Some of their warriors join foreign armies as mercenaries for pay, but that is all. Most importantly, those tribes do not recognize Odrysian supremacy over them, and have no problem raiding Odrysia as they see fit. An attack is imminent, as many of them live off plunder. When they see our carts and possessions, they will not miss the opportunity to try to enrich themselves. But fear not; we are ready for them."

Passing by lush meadows, forests of fir and beech trees, steep ravines, deep gorges, large caves, and unusual rock formations, the party made its way deep into the heart of the mountains. It wasn't long before Sura rode ahead, and Trysimachus's gaze followed the advisor as he conversed with the king and his brothers.

Upon returning, he found Trysimachus awaiting him. "Our scout has informed us that the Dii have been following us. An attack will be coming."

"The Dii?" Fear trickled down Trysimachus's spine. He had heard of the Dii. They had massacred the Theban town of Mycalessos and were reputed to be one of the most brutal and fierce of all Thracian tribes.

The uneven road felt endless to Trysimachus. He looked at the wilderness all around him and felt trapped, confined, and isolated like never before. A distant longing for the openness of the shoreline and the vast expanse of the sea began to envelop him until Sura's words shook him from his stupor.

"We are going to be setting camp soon to lure them in. The Dii are mainly swordsmen, but we are better armed and have cavalry with us. As for you, I have chosen Pitros as your protector." He pointed to a fleshy giant of a warrior with long, curly hair and a bushy beard and mustache. "Do not stray from him. The Dii seek plunder, and our carts will be their main target. Although your first instinct may be to hide under the carts, do not do so. You will be in the greatest danger there. Stay by Pitros and you will be fine. He is a Bessian and comes from the western mountains. He knows the tactics of the Dii well. He is one of our best warriors. You will be safe with him."

The party set up camp in an open field near a narrow and steep ravine. Trysimachus watched the young basileus and his brothers giving orders to the commanders of the peltasts, cavalry, and bodyguards. At dusk, great fires were lit around the camp. The peltasts began to climb up and position themselves along the sides of the ravine while the cavalry rode into the nearby woods.

Trysimachus looked at Pitros, and the giant flashed him a broad smile. He seemed relaxed, and so did everyone else in the king's party. It was only Trysimachus who was noticeably tense, his imagination running wild with scenes of bloodshed.

When Pitros offered him a piece of the venison, he declined. He had lost his appetite.

The attack came late at night. Charging down the center of the ravine, the Dii approached with war cries so shrill it sounded as if the Titans themselves were wailing. The banging and clanging of their weapons terrified the young scholar, and he curled up in a fetal position. Shivering like a leaf in the wind, he shut his eyes and covered his ears, praying to the gods that he would make it out alive.

If only I had met with the Ctistae, he thought, *maybe I would not have known fear!*

Realizing that he would have to record the events of the journey, he opened his eyes, and the thought struck him that he had no choice but to trust Pitros.

He turned around. Sure enough, the giant was close by. He sighed with relief.

Trysimachus watched the Dii descend upon the campsite like a swarm of locusts. They were greeted by a volley of javelins from the peltasts secretly positioned on both sides of the ravine. Then, just as the first of the Dii reached the campsite, the cavalry charged out of the woods and hurled their spears at the mountain warriors, before retreating. The cavalry charged again, and this time, they forced the raiders to run in disarray, making them easier targets.

Trysimachus watched with horror as Diis and Odrysians alike fell all around him. After seeing Pitros fend off and block the advance of a few warriors, he couldn't stand it any longer. Instead of following Sura's advice, he dashed toward the carts for protection.

His path was obstructed by a Dii warrior, unsteady on his feet and smelling strongly of wine.

Trysimachus paused in terror. He could clearly see the warrior's face illuminated by the fire; it was tattooed with strange symbols and patterns. Standing there transfixed, Trysimachus tried to study them. To make sense of them, to find their meaning, to commit them to memory. He didn't attempt to move, and he no longer felt fear—his fascination was so strong that he didn't even notice the Dii swinging his sword, aimed at his chest.

To his surprise, a dagger pierced the raider's flesh just in time. The warrior's eyes bulged as he cried out in agony. Trysimachus watched him struggle, trying to pull the dagger out, before he fell to his knees, then slumped lifelessly on the ground.

"What just happened?" Trysimachus turned to see Pitros smiling broadly at him.

It was his first brush with death, and he had come very close to it. But thanks to the gods, he had survived.

XIX

Striving to contain his revulsion, Trysimachus walked across the campsite-turned-battlefield, strewn with dead bodies. Above his head, crows perched in the trees and vultures circled in the sky, awaiting their chance to feed. He was still fascinated by the Dii warriors' appearance, even in death, and started drawing pictures of the strange tattoos that decorated all of their faces and limbs. Although they lay lifeless on the ground, the dead men still looked terrifying, wrapped in their lion-, bear-, and wolfskin coverings.

Leaving the corpses behind, the king's party continued undisturbed through the Rhodope Mountains. Along the way, the young scholar engaged Pitros in conversation. He was proving to be a more amicable companion than the rigid and bureaucratic Sura.

"What're you doin'?" Pitros asked Trysimachus as they camped that night. He spoke in a Thracian dialect that Trysimachus had a difficult time understanding.

"I am writing down my observations of the journey for the king."

The giant looked over the scholar's scroll with curiosity.

"Do you know how to read?" Trysimachus asked.

"No, 'course not! I'm a warrior. What good is reading? That's for the royals—and you Hellenes!" he exclaimed as he stuffed a slice of meat in his mouth. "Have ya ever held a weapon in your hand?"

"Held, yes," Trysimachus replied in an uncertain tone. "But not much else."

"Many people here would mock people like ya who just think and think and think, readin' and writin', but without being able to do much else. But I think you're a good feller, young and still unspoiled by this world." The giant sighed. "Just like Evmondia is..."

"Evmondia? Is she someone from the court of King Ketriporis?"

"The court?" Pitros scoffed. "Nope! She's a Bessi, just like me." As if coming out of a reverie, the giant continued. "Trysimachus, you're here to do the king's work. That's quite the honor! But lemme tell ya something. Ya know why you're so fearful of everythin'? 'Cause ya can't fend for yourself. If ya don't know how to fight or hunt, how will ya survive? You'll have a difficult time here! I can tell ya that if you learn, you'll become stronger, and you'll gain more respect from the people here. Nor will ya be so easily frightened!"

Trysimachus did not know how to reply. Where he came from, people would make jokes about someone like Pitros, possibly even to his face. But there was something compelling in the giant's words. He looked at Pitros, simple and down-to-earth. Like most Thracians, he couldn't read or write. Yet Trysimachus sensed wisdom in what he said.

The remainder of the journey was rather uneventful, and upon reaching the Nestos River, the party entered King Ketriporis's territory. Trysimachus took in the sights with great curiosity. "I am finally in Western Odrysia," he said aloud.

The natural beauty of the land stunned him. It was as impressive as King Amadokus's realm and, from what he saw, contained more fertile land than he had previously expected.

A tall, jagged, snowcapped mountain loomed in the distance. "What is that mountain?" he asked Sura.

"That is Mount Orbelus," Sura replied.

"Orbelus. I have heard of it. My mentor told me the wind there chills the bones like no other."

"There is more to worry about on that mountain than just the wind."

Trysimachus had an idea of what he meant. He didn't know which he feared more: the beasts lurking on the mountain or the tribes dwelling there. "Sura, was it not dangerous for the king to have been away from his realm so long?"

"No, we made the necessary arrangements. Our messengers have kept us well-informed of the happenings in the realm. Besides, there was Medosades." Sura laughed.

"Who is Medosades?" the historian asked.

Sura laughed even more heartily. "You will soon find out."

Before long, the party reached the king's residence at the foot of Mount Orbelus, located a few stadia away from several villages. In fact, it was not just a residence, but a complex of several buildings, which Sura explained were used for various governmental functions.

"Is this the capital of the western realm?" Trysimachus asked.

"The capital, Athenian, is wherever the king chooses to reside. This is but one of his many residences. And for now, this is where the king has chosen to be."

Neither the complex's fortifications, the royal residence, nor the temple were as grand as the ones King Amadokus had built. Nor was the masonry as impressive as the Temple of Dionysus. But the place was far bigger than any building Trysimachus had ever lived in, so what did he have to complain about?

The room he was shown to was small and plain, but the bed was comfortable. And there, Trysimachus spent his first night in his new home.

Did I make the right decision in coming here? He couldn't yet answer the question, but he had plenty of impressions to think about, that was for sure.

As the stimulation of the journey slowly drained away, Trysimachus settled into his new life and his new surroundings. The process was turning out to be rather challenging for him. He missed the life he knew. His home. His daily routine. His mentor's advice and protection. Everything in this foreign land was just that: foreign and strange to him. He didn't want to admit, even to himself, that he was starting to have regrets about accepting this assignment.

When there was nothing for him to observe or record, he often wandered away to stand facing east, dreaming of the sea breeze instead of the mountain winds. More than once, he wanted to run as fast as he could back to his old life, to the familiar, the predictable, the known. He tried to create the illusion in his mind that he was here for his mentor's sake alone. And that was good enough for him.

On the other hand, the young basileus had wasted no time in settling down and immersing himself in courtly affairs. So Trysimachus was summoned nearly every day to record the numerous councils of the king and his courtiers, as well as the receptions and banquets held for foreign envoys, chieftains, and *zibythides*.

"Remember, you are to record what happens–not why, and certainly not what you think about it," Sura reminded him almost daily. "The basileus wants a neutral history, as he believes people of your kind have not been recording it fairly."

"I will do my best for the king," was all the young scholar could mutter.

As the days passed, Trysimachus began to feel like the king's official scribe, as there was no one in his court who kept records. Occasionally, an inscriber would be summoned to carve into stone official laws or treaties, which the king issued to seal his rule over the land. But that was it.

Trysimachus had known that most Thracians were illiterate, but he was surprised to see how few of them, even among the nobility, showed interest in reading and writing at all. *No wonder they have not created an alphabet of their own and have to use the Hellenic,* he thought.

It was hard for Trysimachus, who had been pushed by his wealthy merchant father to pursue academics, to imagine a world without writing. His brush was his weapon. With it in his hand, he possessed the power to go beyond his own constraints. It provided him with the ability to pour out his thoughts and feelings; to strengthen his logic; to record memories and events which would otherwise be lost in the depths of his mind. Indeed, the brush was not just his weapon. It was his closest friend and companion.

- TWENTY -
2016

ZENON MCCLOW—NO, FELIX SVOBODA—WAS SEATED on the porch of his rental villa in Nouméa. His eyes were closed, but he was not asleep, nor was he meditating. A sudden breeze ruffled the pages of *The Mask* resting on his lap. It was good he had clipped them together.

Now that his radiation treatments had begun, he preferred to spend most of his free time at the villa, reading and reflecting upon *The Mask*. He had decided to take a break after re-experiencing the Dii attack and Trysimachus's arrival in Western Odrysia–this time as a reader, not a writer.

Thinking about the conversation between Trysimachus and Pitros, a faint smile curled Felix's lip. Pitros's dialect had sounded like a lullaby to him–he had detected his father's presence and Southern roots in the giant's speech.

He had always wanted to give his father a better funeral. And he wondered if, deep down, that was why he had begun his story with an elaborate royal burial.

He knew that parts of what he had written had been written with intent, by following certain historical facts he had researched. But there were other aspects of his writing that were more enigmatic to him, their inspiration coming from a place deep within and mysterious. In truth, he had written certain sections of *The Mask* almost in a trance, as if those creative sparks had been fueled by the parts of his brain that had produced the strange, disturbing dreams he would often live through and experience at night. Those passages in his story were what he was trying to delve into and explore.

Indeed, his journey in writing *The Mask* had begun with his inner voice sending him on a quest. It was not unlike how Zenon of Apollonia had sent Trysimachus on a quest to the west of Thrace—a quest not only to record history for King Ketriporis, but for self-discovery as well.

And, like the young Athenian, he had traveled through seas and mountains, and had felt soon after his arrival in New York City the way the scholar had felt in Western Odrysia.

Rocking rhythmically, Felix continued to ponder the tale he had written.

He was certain *The Mask* carried a special message, one that he did not yet fully comprehend. And he was eager to unveil it. For that purpose, a journal and a pen lay on the table next to him. He had already filled several pages with notes and insights, and he looked forward to discovering more.

A horn sounded, interrupting his reverie. He opened his eyes and glanced in the direction of Nouméa's picturesque harbor; his villa accorded him an excellent view. A ten-deck cruise ship was about to dock. A reminder of old times. It had been on a cruise liner like that, five years prior, that his life-changing journey—first to New York and then to this moment in time—had begun.

- TWENTY-ONE -
2011

DESPITE THE ROCKINESS OF THE ATLANTIC OCEAN, the massive cruise ship *Arpina* remained steady. Zenon McClow was exhausted after a long day's work. He was only twenty-seven, but he felt fifty. How much longer would he endure this?

At first, working on a cruise ship had seemed like a great idea. Zenon had become disenchanted with his life in Atlanta ever since his family's demise. He had cast about for an opportunity to get away from it all, and at the same time see other parts of the world.

He had often dreamed of traveling and read a lot about other countries and their cultures, but he'd lacked the resources to visit them even before his father's death. When things became difficult in his life, he could relax by imagining himself moving to another country, but he didn't know which one was best or how to make it happen.

The military was out of the question, of course. But working for a cruise company operating on multiple continents had seemed like an ideal solution. Wouldn't that mean he'd be able to see the world while collecting a paycheck? He could 'audition' countries and decide which one to move to.

Zenon had done enough research to know that the pay wouldn't be great, but he had still hoped to eventually save enough to carry out a move. It was also a plus that working on the ships did not require a college degree, something he didn't possess. A perfect opportunity, right?

Experience proved his thinking to be quite naïve. Working on the ships was more challenging than he had anticipated. Although employees were required to present a façade of happiness in order to maintain the customers' vacation mood, the work was hard, and the days were long. The ship's staff spent their days offering fake smiles to the customers while catering to their every whim, and had very little personal freedom and no free internet access.

The living space in their residential cabins was as small as their paychecks. It was no surprise that most of the employees were from economically precarious countries in Asia, Latin America, the Caribbean, and Eastern Europe. Although the cruise company was based in the States, Zenon was one of the very few American workers on board, even on cruises within U.S. waters.

He had entered the job as a boy and now thought of himself as a man. His experience on the ships had hardened him just as much as his traumatic past. Sadness had turned to anger, which eventually had turned to apathy. And that was the state he found himself stuck in.

Zenon trudged around the ship like a zombie, drifting through day after day until a passenger needed something. He no longer had much hope for the future. He performed his duties on the ship competently, but he never felt fully alive and showed no passion for his work.

Deep down, he had a sense that this state of being was a trap, but he could not see an escape hatch that would allow him out into the light. One night, in the middle of the Atlantic, he tried to look up at the sky and appreciate the beautiful moon and stars, unaffected by light pollution from human civilization. But he couldn't even enjoy the open sky any more. There was simply nothing there for him.

However, Apathetic Zenon did not last forever. Everything changed when he transferred to a new ship and got a new roommate: Ricardo Herrero.

Just like Zenon, Ricardo had grown up in rough circumstances. He'd been raised by a single mother in Santurce, the heart of San Juan, Puerto Rico, never quite managing to get ahead even as the neighborhood improved slightly. He'd come to the continental U.S. and now sent at least half of his meager paycheck home.

There was one striking difference between Ricardo and Zenon. While the Southerner was allowing himself to be blown through life like a leaf in the wind, the Puerto Rican took a zealous and proactive approach to his path. Working on a cruise ship may have been all he could get for the moment, but Ricardo was determined to climb the ladder of life and make a name for himself. To do so, he bought as many books on self-help and personal development as he could, stacking them on every flat surface in the cabin. In addition, he had purchased DVDs of self-help courses and recordings of motivational speeches to watch on a small, portable player. Ricardo was determined to figure out how to find success—and happiness—in his life.

"Why do you need all those books and courses? Are you a cruise ship employee or a visiting scholar?" Zenon joked in his broken Spanish.

"You can call me a scholar," Ricardo replied. "A scholar of success, that is. Soon I won't be working for this company any more. I just have to study the principles and mark my words; I'll be free and prosperous."

"Don't tell me you believe in all that think-and-grow-rich stuff! Isn't it a bunch of baloney from salespeople trying to rip people off?" Zenon exclaimed. "I mean, who writes books these days or gives those hyped-up motivational speeches except people who are trying to milk a bunch of suckers?"

"Zenon, my friend," he said. "You can continue to waste your life all you want. It's your business. But I see how you are, just going through the motions day in, day out without any purpose. You may be alive in the literal sense of the word, but man, when I look at you, you hardly seem like you're actually living."

His words stung Zenon deeply. But he couldn't let Ricardo see that, so he acted as if they didn't faze him one bit.

His roommate continued. "Life can be tough, man. Where I come from, it can feel like there's almost no hope sometimes. But here I am, doing my best. Even having this job is a great opportunity for me, while you and some of the other guys moan and groan about it all day. The way I see it, this job is like a rung on the ladder—a rung that I'm grateful to be on, but one I'll leave behind as soon as I can make it to the next one."

Zenon laughed and interrupted. "Ricardo, are you giving me one of those motivational speeches yourself?"

His roommate began to get defensive. "Hey, that's a great career to get into, actually. It's hot right now. The potential is high, and there's money to be made. Besides, it is possible to have a good life and be happy. I know it is! You just have to follow the proven principles of success. And that's what I'm working on now: discovering what they are, what the practical applications are, and then, most importantly, practicing them. It takes desire. It takes ambition. And I have both. I will make it, man, and I'll make it big. Meanwhile, if you keep on doing what you've been doing, you'll stay stagnant. Then, at some point, you'll rot. If not here, somewhere else. I'm telling you, you've got great potential. I can see it in you. But you've got to make a decision to succeed. To live the life of your dreams. To be free."

"Whatever. Believe what you want. Those people are deceiving you, though. Good life, freedom, happiness, success, they're all just buzzwords. With our backgrounds, who are you kidding, man?" Zenon prided himself in being a cynic, and he needled the other man. "Admit it, you're in it only for the money. Stop bullshitting. I saw you eyeing that superyacht in the Caymans the other day."

Ricardo's face flushed a deep red, and he exclaimed, "You got it wrong, man! Yeah, the money's part of it, but it's not everything. What do you think success is?"

"Money. Power. Prestige. Glamour. Living it up. The big house. The Ferrari. A beautiful chick on your arm. Yachts, vacation homes, country clubs, the best restaurants, you name it."

"Is that all you think it is?"

"What more is there?"

"Well, where I come from, I'm considered a great success for having this job. It may not be much for some, but it's a lot for others. I don't steal or do drugs. It's an honest job. I work hard at it. So it all depends on your position in life and how you look at it. A jobless, hungry person views anyone with a paying job as a success. The problem is the stick you're measuring success with. Besides, what about your state of mind? Satisfaction, passion, purpose, fulfillment, presence? How about happiness? Have you ever thought about that?"

He had, but he had never been able to find it. Nor could he find any intrinsic meaning in his life.

Zenon almost resented Ricardo's positive attitude because, in some ways, it made him feel badly about his own perspective, even if he couldn't join the other man on the march to glory.

However, things started to change as the weeks went by. Sharing the cabin with Ricardo, Zenon would sometimes overhear what his roommate—and, he had to grudgingly admit, his friend—was watching on his DVD player. At first, he scoffed at the videos and wanted nothing to do with them. It was an annoyance, a distraction. But Ricardo was consistent, studying and practicing almost every chance he could in his limited free time. The motivational lingo eventually started to sink into Zenon's mind, too. Slowly but surely, it was waking him up from his maritime trance.

But Zenon's ascent from his slumber did not emulate Ricardo's. Instead of feeling uplifted and excited, he remembered the past he had tried so hard to forget. The motivation stirring within him was not simply the desire for success. It became directed toward a larger purpose: to lash out against the corrupt society he saw around him, and break up the stacked deck that kept some permanently on the bottom, and others protected at the top.

In a way he couldn't fully explain even if anyone had asked, Zenon sought... retribution. Not from any individual in particular, but from the whole unjust world. A world that allowed good, honest people to become victims of those who skirted laws and morality in order to become successful.

The system had failed to help him and his family. And he wasn't alone. Big corporations discarded employees instantly and without remorse when they ceased to be useful. Society treated people like his father as undesirables, just because he had been laid off... after the stress of working endless hours had driven him to painkiller addiction and rendered him unemployable.

And that wasn't all of it. People who'd called themselves family friends had abandoned him and his mother just because they were no longer able to maintain the appearance of middle-class comfort.

They all betrayed us! Zenon thought. *If they had helped out during the hardest times, would everything have occurred?*

Instead, they all turned their backs on us. And some even took advantage of Dad's fall.

There was not just one person or institution he could blame. They were all guilty. And more. His anger grew inside him like a tumor, fueling him to take some sort of action.

Zenon began looking through Ricardo's books. Slowly but surely, he began to form a new worldview, one in which the strong and the cunning were the hunters, and the unwary and complacent were the prey.

- TWENTY-TWO -

ZENON COULDN'T SLEEP AND WAS GETTING SICK and tired of suffocating in his cramped, prison cell-like cabin. He put on anonymous 'civilian' clothes so no passenger would approach him with some absurd demand during his off-hours, and stepped out for a walk around the ship.

When he reached the top deck, which held a nightclub and a pool with a swim-up bar, he watched the passengers. They were chatting merrily and laughing, having a splendid, happy time on board. They were sipping exotic drinks, keeping the bartenders on their feet and in constant motion. It seemed like none of the passengers realized or cared how hard the crew was working to give them such a magical vacation. Rage toward those strangers started to boil in Zenon's chest. He turned and faced the railing, staring at the endless ocean until the feeling subsided... a little.

Around 2:30 a.m., he decided to return to the workers' residential quarters. The employee lounge was now eerily quiet; the usual gang had left, and the lights were switched off. However, the bright blue light of a display screen was reflected on one wall. Curious who else might still be up so late, Zenon entered the lounge. He could hear someone typing on a keyboard. When he got closer, he spotted Jüri, a banquet waiter from Estonia.

"Jüri, that you?"

"Oh, hey Zenon, you startled me!"

"What're you doing up so late?"

"Uhh, I..." he hesitated. "It's all been a waste, man. Here I've been exhausted on the job, staying up late, and the end result is shit. Absolute shit."

"What've you been doing?" Zenon's curiosity was genuine. Jüri wasn't a proselytizer like Ricardo; he kept his business to himself, but his intelligence was obvious.

"I've been working on a trading algorithm," Jüri revealed. "The market is the future, man. This was going to be my golden ticket. I was going to sit and watch the money pile up in my bank account, and instead..."

"What market are you talking about?"

"The Forex."

"The Forex?" Zenon gave him a quizzical look.

"The foreign currency exchange market," Jüri sighed. "I guess you're not familiar with algo-trading, huh?"

"Not at all."

"Well, basically, it's when a software does the trading automatically for you based on certain criteria. If it's coded properly, you can rack up high returns..."

"Cool. So what's wrong?"

"My formula worked on paper, but something's falling apart in beta. I finished the coding a week ago and have been testing it ever since. The algorithm doesn't work! If I run it for real, all I'll do is lose money. It's a piece of shit! And to think I could have made it big..."

"But how did you get into all of this?"

Jüri stared down at the table, rubbed his eyes, and then replied. "So my country is big on internet and computer stuff. Did you know Skype was invented in Estonia, and it was the first country to allow people to vote online? I was brought up in that culture and pushed into it." He let out another long sigh. "But while I took courses in computer science, programming, and math, I never wanted to take a job in those fields—or in any other field, really. My family got frustrated and sent me to work on these cruises, so I'd 'shape up'. They said I needed to experience the real world. And, oh man, did it do the trick! I worked so hard on this algorithm, spent half my money on this laptop, and I'm paying these ripoff internet rates, wanting to succeed, not even for myself but to please my damn parents!"

Zenon's thoughts turned toward his own parents. He wondered what their aspirations for him would have been if the brisk winds that swept their previously stable lives away had spared them.

"But what am I going to do now? I gotta figure something out. Shit!" Jüri exclaimed, banging his fist on the table.

While Jüri was frustrated at the failure of his attempt, Zenon was intrigued by the broader concept.

An algorithm for trading and making money? What exactly is that? How does it work? I gotta find out more about it. Little did he know this conversation would change his life, perhaps forever.

- TWENTY-THREE -
2013

AFTER A DECADE OF WORKING ON CRUISE SHIPS, Zenon had had enough. When his contract expired, he decided not to re-up. But what would he do next?

The United States was his home, but positive memories of childhood were balanced by painful memories of his father's death and everything after. His years at sea were not motivated only by his limited employment prospects or a desire to see the world. More than anything, he had wanted to run away from home, and from the society that had ruined his life. But Zenon knew it was inevitable that he would return to the United States. He had an idea—well, the beginnings of one—and it required him to be in New York.

The city was not only the financial capital of the United States, but one of the most important financial centers in the world. If Zenon were to make it big, he needed to be in what the military referred to as a 'target-rich environment'.

Glitz, glamour, and a wealth of opportunity. That's what most people thought of when they thought of New York City. It was certainly the face the city wanted to present to the world. But Zenon realized quickly that the city was much more expensive than most people imagined and much less glamorous when you looked closely. It was a frantic anthill, everyone constantly hustling just to survive, with people who'd seem impossibly rich almost anywhere else in America still feeling pressured to find the next thing, to move just one more rung up the ladder. It was the perfect environment for someone who could tell people what they wanted to hear and get them to buy in—not just to succeed, but to make sure they didn't fall behind their neighbors.

He found an apartment in the Bronx that wasn't much larger than his last cruise ship cabin. He had arrived with the kind of savings that would have bought him a few years of leisure almost anywhere else. But the high cost of living in New York sent him right back into the working world.

He found that his experience made him an in-demand employee. Cruise ship work was all about customer service, after all. He got a job as maître d' at a French restaurant in Tribeca, frequented by financial industry types and the kind of people who lived off investment income. It was a long ride to and from work, taking him from one end of the island of Manhattan to the other, but that gave him time to think about his strategy, and ponder what he'd learned at the end of each night.

There was a way one had to approach the rich. For the ladies, Zenon knew a compliment on a pair of shoes, or a bracelet, was better than a compliment on a dress; it showed attention to detail. As for the men, a maître d' had to make them feel as powerful as they believed themselves to be. Before long, he knew what his regular customers ordered and had it ready for them as soon as he saw their names on the reservation list.

Once he was 'in' with the clients, when he was seen as something between a favorite employee of the restaurant and a trusted confidant, he was able to listen to conversations and even direct them—by nudging the men subtly, getting them to talk more than they otherwise might have about their business. He wanted to learn their secrets.

On his days off, he would explore Manhattan, observing the various classes of people moving through the streets. Most were scurrying around like ants, trying hard to make a living. Those dressed in tailored suits and designer outfits carried an air of importance and success about them. Arrogance, too, in many cases.

"We can hire you, we can fire you, and we can screw you over."

That was the vibe Zenon got from these people when they weren't in his restaurant. Their demeanor didn't give away what was going on inside of them. Their outer appearance was like a fortress, surrounding and protecting their emotions. *They're all wearing masks*, he concluded.

Corporate America turned Zenon off. His time on the ships, and his work at the restaurant, showed him enough of the rich that he knew he didn't want to be like them. All he really wanted was the money. Most of the men and women he saw night after night appeared to him like they were icebergs made of money. All he needed was the opportunity to get close enough to shave some of it off for himself.

They have far more money than I can ever make, and own a bunch of expensive stuff, he thought. *But at the end of the day, they're still ruled by the same system as everyone else.*

He possessed a growing urge to beat the system. But how?

The image of Jüri, hunched over his laptop, typing desperately, flashed in his mind. *Oh, Jüri, trying to strike it rich by finding the magic bullet.* Zenon smiled at the thought.

Then the lightbulb flashed.

How was it that he had never asked Jüri to explain his algorithm or techniques? Maybe now was the time. After all, wasn't he in the right place?

Excitement flooded through his veins. A trading algorithm

would be his big break. He would be able to generate the money he wanted instead of toiling away for it.

Feeling elevated, Zenon got to it. He talked to the restaurant staff and discovered more than a few algorithm enthusiasts and rookies like Jüri. They offered to bring him in on their latest creations or teach him how to create his own. Risky investments weren't his goal, though. And creating an algorithm was way above his head. He began researching the large firms that offered the latest in algorithmic Forex trading.

He came away far from impressed. The results they told him he 'might get', even in the best-case scenario, were way off from what he was seeking: income he could live off and the freedom to never work for anyone else again.

At one firm, he rode in the elevator with a nervous young man who seemed eager to draw Zenon's attention, clearly hoping that he might turn out to be somebody worth knowing.

"You wanna know what the truth is?"

Zenon nodded. The young man leaned toward him and spoke quietly, as if he were sharing classified information. "There's some serious software out there, man. But it's reserved for the people at the top if you know what I mean. They say you gotta spend money to make money, but really, it's more like, you gotta have money to make money. Unless you're rich, you aren't getting into the penthouse."

Zenon shook his head.

The young man registered his disbelief and nodded soberly. "I'm just laying out how it is."

"I take it you're not being paid to say stuff like that."

"I don't get paid at all. I'm an intern."

"So with all the money they rake in around here, you're working for free?"

The young man nodded.

"So, what's next for you?"

"I'm going for a master's, and after that, I hope to get an

offer here. With just a bachelor's, you're basically nothing in finance. I'll have to get some certifications too, but that can come later."

Zenon knew his lack of anything more than a high school education was a professional handicap. But the memories of the intense struggles at home during his late high school days made for a barrier he could not break. Besides, he told himself that going back to school would only help him find a place *within* the system, not *beat* it. The elevator arrived at the ground floor, and he and the intern parted ways.

On the street, Zenon looked back at the building he had just exited. Gray, cold, and unyielding, it towered over the buildings around it. The massive structure made him feel like an insect in comparison. Or like a pawn in the economic game being played inside. But he preferred to think of it as a fortress holding treasure; he just had to find the way in.

A dense crowd of pedestrians surged around him, nearly knocking him over, oblivious to his presence. He pushed his way through and headed for the nearest subway station, thinking.

The most sophisticated trading systems, like everything else in life, were reserved for the elite. Wealth generating more wealth for the select few.

How are ordinary people like me ever going to have a chance? He was starting to wonder if a winning system would ever be within his reach.

He recalled a few online algo-trading firms he'd seen that promised high returns in foreign currency exchange. He was briefly tempted but thought better of it, remembering that there were good reasons why he didn't risk his money on those sites. One of them had even installed a virus on his computer. Zenon was increasingly convinced that there was no easy way for him to make a lot of money. Not in any legitimate way, at least.

- TWENTY-FOUR -

ON SUNNY DAYS, BEFORE HIS SHIFT AT THE RESTAU-rant began, Zenon often headed down to Wall Street. He enjoyed soaking in the vibes of the Financial District in the little park next to the famous 'charging bull' statue, watching tourists take pictures of it and rub the bull's horns and nose for good luck.

Eventually, Zenon found his way to his favorite coffee shop, the Black Bean. Family-owned and independent, it was exactly the type of place he preferred to patronize. He sipped a mocha and read the free copies of *The Wall Street Journal* and *The New York Times* that were lain out for customers, hoping to stumble upon an article that would advance his quest to conquer the mystifying world of investing and trading.

One day around three o'clock, while relaxing on the cafe's comfy sofa, Zenon spotted someone standing in line who looked uncannily like a former schoolmate of his. *Is that Dipesh?* he thought. *Shit! If that's him, what do I do?*

Zenon covered his face with the edition of *The Wall Street Journal* he was reading, realizing the absurdity of the move even as he did it. Was he in a black-and-white movie all of a sudden? Still, if it really was Dipesh, he didn't want to see or talk to him. The sudden reminder of his past brought too many painful memories with it.

Fortunately, the man left immediately after picking up his order, and Zenon sighed in relief.

A week later, though, he found himself dodging Dipesh again. This time, he was certain that it was definitely his former classmate, who, based on his attire, was likely working in finance.

During his years at sea, Zenon had not kept in touch or given much thought to any of his classmates. He didn't know where any of them had ended up or what they were doing with their lives. Nor had he cared. But seeing Dipesh was triggering Zenon's memories.

He was always good at math, wasn't he? It makes sense that he would land a job here on Wall Street.

Once again, Zenon avoided talking to Dipesh. He just didn't feel like revisiting old times, or saying much about what he was doing now.

His former classmate ordered the same two coffees to go that he had on his previous visit, already gulping one down as he exited. He seemed to need the caffeine badly.

He looks worn out, Zenon thought. Then he caught a glimpse of himself in a mirror on the shop's wall. He wasn't as polished as his corporate classmate, and he'd definitely been under-dressed for some of the meetings he'd taken with investment firms. *It's good he didn't see me*, he thought, relieved.

Zenon loved hanging out at the Black Bean, so he adjusted his schedule from then on, getting his coffee earlier in the afternoon to avoid running into Dipesh. Once he was again able to relax there, he returned to his reading with even greater avidity. He skipped over headlines about offshoring, layoffs, and the vagaries of the mortgage market. None of that interested him. Zenon was searching for a useful lead that would open the world of trading to him. He kept Ricardo's optimism and perseverance in mind and sought potential opportunities wherever they might be lurking.

Over time, what started to catch his attention the most were stories about financial scams. He found himself reading those articles with great curiosity. It seemed like pyramid schemes, complex methods of tax evasion, identity theft, and credit card fraud were everywhere. Financial scammers were operating at all scales, from multi-million-dollar, years-long fraud operations to low-level cons operating out of Queens.

But what stood out to him most starkly was that so many of the crooks had operated for years without being caught.

Even the ones who did get caught took years to go to trial in slow-moving courts with seemingly no resolution or justice in sight. They were often out on bail the whole time, living their lives more or less as they had before, give or take an ankle bracelet and the occasional negative news story.

A lot of these cons were quite clever—many people wouldn't even call them cons and would likely think of them as conducting business as usual. It occurred to Zenon that subtle and less noticeable scams were the most dangerous, as they drained people's bank accounts slowly but surely. Which led him to the thought that politicians were some of the biggest scammers, often benefitting from skillful rhetoric and empty promises.

It was rapidly becoming clear to Zenon that a path to wealth and success was open to him. One day, while standing in the middle of Times Square, watching the billboards flash and change their advertising, he clenched his fists. As the surrounding cars beeped nonstop and the hawkers hawked their wares, he vowed he would make it. He would need all the wit and charm his restaurant work had helped him to hone, and a way to connect with some of the rich patrons as he escorted them to their tables night after night. How exactly he would beat the system and insert himself in the middle of the financial flow, diverting his own way just enough to make his fortune, he wasn't sure. Yet...

- TWENTY-FIVE -
2014

NEW YORK WAS BURIED UNDER ONE OF THOSE LATE March blizzards that makes the city dark and dreary. The period afterward, depending on one's state of mind, could leave a person feeling hopeless and depressed. All wrapped up, Zenon moved along the freshly plowed streets of Lower Manhattan like a displaced spirit amongst the hurried multitude. He was cold. Very cold. The skyscrapers were trapping the wind, making his uncovered head ache and his gloveless fingers feel nearly frozen. He spotted the familiar sign of the Black Bean and headed in its direction.

It was warm and cozy inside the café. Unsurprisingly, the line was long. He was not the only one to seek out the warmth of a cup of coffee or tea on a day like this. Later, he would head to his favorite Chinese joint, The Hong Konger, for some hot and sour soup.

Buried deep in his thoughts, Zenon was startled when he felt a tap on his shoulder. Frowning, he turned slowly to find himself standing face-to-face with his former classmate, Dipesh. The very person he had been trying to avoid.

"Zenon? Is that you?"

Taken by surprise, Zenon managed to stutter, "Uh, yeah,"

before following it up with "Dipesh!"

Dipesh beamed. "I thought it was you! Long time, no see! How have you been?"

"Well, uh, fine," Zenon remembered to smile.

"Man, I can't believe I ran into you after all these years! And here, of all places!"

"I know, man, I'm surprised too."

"What happened to you? You disappeared after graduation, and no one was ever able to get in touch with you."

"I've been abroad."

"Where?" Dipesh seemed genuinely curious.

Zenon told the truth, sort of, listing several ports he'd departed from or arrived in, without saying why he was there. Dipesh picked up on one city in particular.

"Hong Kong? Cool! What were you doing there?"

Zenon glanced down at a copy of the *Wall Street Journal* sitting on a nearby table. "Forex research," he said, trying to make it sound as boring as possible to deflect any further questions.

"Nice! I'm a researcher myself." Dipesh mentioned the name of a successful financier. Zenon wasn't surprised.

"So, where do you work, Zenon?"

"I'm independent," he said. It wasn't exactly a lie.

"Lucky you!" his former classmate exclaimed. But suddenly, as if remembering something, Dipesh looked at his watch. "Bro, I'd love to catch up, but I gotta run. I have a meeting with a client I can't be late for. Do you have a card?"

"Not with me, sorry."

"Never mind, take mine. Call me. We need to hang out, bro. I can't believe I'm seeing you again!"

Zenon nodded vigorously. "Looking forward to it."

Dipesh practically ran out the door.

Zenon's first instinct was to throw the card away. Dipesh was part of his past, and those memories made him extremely uncomfortable. But after a moment, he thought better of it. *If Dipesh is working in finance, perhaps he can help me.*

That night, in his apartment, Zenon took Dipesh's card out and tossed it on the table. If he wanted to plumb his former classmate for valuable information or connections, he'd have to reach out himself. Zenon wasn't one to give out his number or email address to just anybody. He wasn't on social media, either. It was better to stay under the radar than to spend the time necessary to build a profile and maintain it. Social media was a form of acting—you decided on the image you wanted to project, and then you had to stick with it until the end of time, no matter what. And there was always the risk that someone who knew the truth about you would pop up with a deflating comment or an unflattering old photo, as though they were heckling you from the audience. High risk, low reward.

Zenon sat down, flipped open his laptop, and googled the company. Accruement Finance.

He found a series of YouTube videos hosted by the company's founder, Phil Brawclad. The man was marketing himself as a 'guru' and an expert in the field of finance. He looked to be in his early sixties, and possibly older, so it was clear to Zenon that he had a much younger team helping him with production. Scrolling down the company's YouTube channel, Zenon found a number of videos dealing with investing, and clicked on a few that seemed interesting.

Each video contained a few beginner-level investing tips, but Brawclad emphasized that certain higher-tier strategies were reserved for elite members only. Zenon visited the company's site and read the registration page. The fee was much more than he was willing to pay. Still, he could see the appeal. Accruement members were promised access to the best investment strategies in the world, carefully selected and researched by Brawclad himself. They were also sent an email newsletter containing interviews with the most successful people in finance and offered the opportunity to attend quarterly seminars in major financial centers.

Zenon typed the word 'algorithm' in the site's search box, but no results showed up. Searches for 'automated trading' and 'high-frequency trading' were similarly unrewarding. He clicked the staff page looking for Dipesh's name, but didn't see it.

"That's strange. Didn't he say he was a researcher? Why isn't he mentioned anywhere?" he asked himself. He picked up Dipesh's card from the table and reread it. His title was 'Office Manager'. Zenon chuckled but decided to contact him anyway. He needed to find out if Accruement Finance members had access to a good algorithmic system—and if not, whether Dipesh could provide him with any useful leads.

- TWENTY-SIX -

"SO ZENON, WHAT PART OF THE CITY DO YOU LIVE in?" Dipesh asked.

"I'm uptown, but I'm still spending a lot of time abroad. I come in and out on business–I don't really live in New York."

They had reunited at the Black Bean. Zenon had been nervous coming into downtown that day, but now, as Dipesh recalled stories about their days attending North Dotson, he couldn't help but feel glad to see the other man. It hadn't been all bad during those times, after all.

"I thought you'd be the next Tolkien," Dipesh said, looking quizzically at Zenon. "To be honest, I was surprised to hear that you're in finance. So what happened to that passion of yours?"

"Adult life hit, Dipesh, adult life hit... I haven't read a fantasy novel in years, man."

Those adolescent days felt like another era to him. Zenon was far removed from the time when his life almost entirely revolved around school, sports, and burying himself in fictional worlds.

"I hear you. I haven't played the drums since graduating high school. Things just got too hectic in college."

Zenon nodded, not wanting to admit that he never did end up attending college.

As they chatted, Zenon was surprised how often Dipesh's phone rang, or how it seemed to explode with incoming texts, almost vibrating off the table. And every time his former classmate answered, he seemed to be drawn farther and farther away from the flow of their conversation.

Finally, Dipesh exclaimed, "It's no use, Zenon. I have to cut it short." He was visibly upset. "It's my boss. I have to run. Otherwise, he'll text me until the minute I walk back into the office. I'm sorry, man. We should absolutely meet again. There's so much more we need to catch up on. Make sure to call me before you leave town. I'll make it up to you next time."

Dipesh departed in a rush, leaving Zenon alone to process this valuable information about how busy things seemed to be at Accruement Finance.

The following week, they met up for lunch at a small and cozy restaurant far away from Wall Street—Dipesh's choice. Without the risk that someone he worked with might overhear, Dipesh opened up to Zenon about his working conditions.

"I can't believe I stay working for that asshole Brawclad. Greed is his middle name. He was born into a wealthy and privileged family; I'm sure you know that all the really big players are living off the interest from money that was made four hundred years ago, but still, for him, no amount of money is ever enough. He wants more and more." Dipesh took a large swallow of beer. "It's frustrating, man. He thinks the world belongs to him, and everyone around him was put on this earth to serve him. New hires are told, if you can't work on Sunday, don't bother coming in on Monday."

"Can't you find something else?"

"Well, when you have parents who believe you're a failure if you don't get a well-paying job, and then you get a great offer to be a lead researcher, of course you go for it."

"Dipesh, are you actually his lead researcher? Your card—"

"Yes, I am. Phil is seventy-five percent image. He pretends that he's a genius, but we do the heavy work while he takes all the credit—and the money."

"I noticed on the website he claims that he researches and selects the investment strategies himself. So that's not true?"

"No, it's bullshit. If he was a real genius, he'd be running a hedge fund instead of shooting YouTube videos. And he's terrified of people figuring out that he's not the great guru he claims to be."

"But is working for this guy at least valuable experience? Can't you use it as a stepping stone to a larger firm?"

"Maybe things are better abroad, but the job market here these days is terrible. It's who you know, and Phil keeps us out of the really valuable meetings, precisely because he's afraid we'll get yanked away. So I'm stuck in place. Such is life, man."

Zenon nodded in agreement as Dipesh continued to unload. "Oh man, how I wish I could just leave a surprise letter of resignation on his desk—a big F.U. to Phil! The look on his face would be priceless! But outside of work, things are actually looking up for me now. I didn't have the chance to tell you last time that I've met the most wonderful and beautiful girl in the world. We're engaged and hoping to get married soon. She's from Singapore. Her father's also in finance, and that could actually turn into something. He wants to arrange a job for me there, and I can't wait to get out of here. Anyway, what've you been up to? Last time we hardly had a chance to talk. You said you were in finance. You have your own firm, right?"

"Yes, I do."

"What's your specialty?"

"Investing."

Dipesh perked up and was all ears. "Nice! Tell me more,

man."

This was the moment Zenon had been waiting for. "Forex trading," he replied casually. "I'm using my own system."

"A proprietary algorithm?" Dipesh asked.

Zenon needed to be careful. He didn't want to trap himself. "Yes. How about Accruement? What are you recommending?"

"I don't even want to waste your time telling you. The results our members were getting with the latest system we plugged weren't impressive at all. We got a lot of backlash in the newsletter replies."

Zenon was disappointed. Hoping to prompt Dipesh to say something more useful, he offered, "I hear you. But technology is evolving. It's important to stay on top of it. There's powerful stuff out there."

"Absolutely. Phil would love to get his hands on some real cutting-edge trading tech. Both because he's greedy and because he'd want to show off in front of his members! How about your system?"

Zenon laughed. "I can't talk about it. Not quite yet."

"That secretive?"

Zenon paused as though thinking about whether to let Dipesh in on his 'secret'. Finally, he said, "It's definitely cutting-edge."

Dipesh's eyes glowed as if he were sizing Zenon up. Then he grinned. "Phil may be interested in talking to you. I can hook you two up if you want."

"I mean, how big's your client list? I run a small operation; I'm not sure my results will scale up." He had trapped himself. He couldn't seem too eager to dive in.

"Think it over, man. Accruement could be a good break for you. Phil may not be generous when it comes to his employees, but if he sees a shiny new thing, he dives on it, and I've seen him pay some eye-popping fees to consultants. When exactly are you leaving again?"

Zenon needed time to think and plan. "I'm leaving in a couple of days."

"Do you know when you'll be here next? You said you come back pretty often, right?"

"I'm not sure on dates right now, but yeah, I'm here once or twice a quarter, anyway."

"All right, just give me a call next time you're in the city."

- TWENTY-SEVEN -

RIDING THE SUBWAY BACK HOME THAT NIGHT, AFTER his shift at the restaurant, Zenon thought deeply about his conversation with Dipesh. The meeting had left him with the feeling that there was an opportunity there, but one that had to be handled very carefully lest it break apart in his hands like an egg Dipesh had tossed him. He thought about it all the way back to his apartment. Once there, he busied himself with tidying the place up and watching TV aimlessly. But nothing held his attention. His thoughts circled around Dipesh and Phil like a whirlpool. Still wondering what to do, he stretched out and relaxed on the sofa, and before he knew it...

He was on a cruise in the middle of the ocean. But instead of wearing his cruise line uniform, he was dressed in a white tuxedo and a black bowtie. He wasn't an employee, but a wealthy vacationer thoroughly enjoying the cruise. He looked about the ship as though its entirety was his own domain.

As though he was in a movie that had cut to a new scene, he found himself in the ship's casino, standing up from a poker table and picking up all the chips he had just won with a grin. The other players—Phil Brawclad, Dipesh, his former boss, the owner of the Black Bean, and Allen, especially Allen—looked on with envy, anger, and regret as he walked to the casino cage and cashed in his winnings—$1 million.

After another seamless transition, he was at the bar, ordering a cocktail. He took a sip. Delicious. He looked around and saw Jüri and Ricardo, wearing their uniforms and sitting at one of the tables. Jüri was typing vigorously on his laptop. "I don't think this will work," he told Ricardo as Zenon listened.

With his usual conviction, Ricardo replied, "You'll make it happen and succeed one day. There has to be a way."

Ricardo then looked up at Zenon. "See that guy in the white tuxedo? We can be like him. We can live a life of freedom and luxury. We'll get there, no matter what it takes."

Jüri replied, "Even if we cross the line?"

"Yes, even if we cross the line."

Outside, an ambulance wailed past, interrupting Zenon's dream. He didn't want to open his eyes, though. He kept them closed for a long time.

He was still feeling the power of winning, of having so much money at his disposal that he didn't even have to think about what things cost. He didn't want it to end, to return to reality. The feeling was profound and deep. After all, he deserved to have it all. *What am I here on Earth for? To suffer?*

With lingering resistance, he opened his eyes and slowly took in his environment. He was doing all right—the restaurant paid his rent, and he was gaining valuable knowledge from the conversations he overheard, but he had no way to apply that knowledge yet. He needed a way in. Beyond that, he was disappointed that there was no magic bullet in algo-trading that he, an ordinary guy, could get his hands on.

He thought back to a conversation he once had with Ricardo. "You got time," his coworker had told him. "You got great potential. But you got to make a decision. A decision to succeed. To live the life of your dreams. To be free."

Zenon recalled the way Ricardo's influence had made him

feel. It had given him the drive that had ultimately brought him to New York City. And he hadn't lost that drive, but it was getting difficult to stay motivated with so many pathways seemingly closed off and so few potential opportunities.

He thought about his father collapsed on the floor of their house, his despair and addiction dragging him down to oblivion.

And he thought about Allen. He remembered the way Allen had cozied up to his father, pretending to look up to him and work hard for him. His kind father had taken him under his wing, teaching him, mentoring him. While all along, Allen had coveted his father's position in the company, playing dirty to snatch it away. But in his dream, Zenon had beaten him.

It was like a switch flipped in his mind. *Our economic system, especially the investing world, is just like gambling*, he thought. *People take risks and place bets in order to strike it rich or further grow their money. And while there are rules, there's no real logic. It's more important to understand the players than the game.*

Zenon knew from his days on the ocean, and his new job at the restaurant, that people were often fundamentally greedy, but even more than money, they wanted to believe they were smart and talented—that they were good players. He thought of the phrase, 'born on third base and thinking he hit a triple'. People who grew up in rich families still found a way to convince themselves that they'd achieved something in life on their own initiative. And people like that were the most vulnerable to flattery of all.

Thinking about his winnings in the dream, he pondered the factors that determined the outcome of a poker game.

It's not just luck. Psychology is a major factor. Players make decisions to call, fold, or raise by trying to read the other players. And the masterminds of the game take advantage of that. What was it called? Bluffing!

By bluffing, he could draw people like Phil Brawclad into his game. They were the ones who dominated the world of finance, the ones who controlled the system that had ruined his family.

He understood that to bring Brawclad and men like him to his side, make them partners in his scheme, he would have to offer them more than the prospect of making money. They would like that, but they already had money. What they really wanted was to feel like geniuses and the heroes of the myths they created about themselves.

There were only a few approaches that would work. He would have to convince them that his idea was their idea. Or he would have to convince them that he was offering them the chance to be the first to do something. Or, finally, he would have to convince them that they were his partners in a scam being run on a third party. This was how many cons worked; it wasn't about saying, "I've got a way we can make some money that's not strictly legal." That wasn't enticing enough. What really got people drawn into a con was, "Let's you and me cheat that other guy over there."

He didn't like the idea of that third option, though. So to accomplish the scheme that was beginning to take shape in his mind, he would need to increase his knowledge of economics, finance, psychology, and the newest technological trends. Communication and rhetorical skill would also be crucial. Servile maître d' Zenon would have to go. A new Zenon—confident and assured—would have to emerge. One who would be driven by his own willpower and desires, not by the world, by society, nor by any corporation.

Society and life force us to make certain choices: political, social, moral, ethical, he thought. *We can choose to be compliant or rebellious.*

Zenon had made his choice. He would be rebellious. He would take charge of his own destiny.

THE MASK

BY ZENON MCCLOW

ACT II

THRACE, AUTUMN, 357 BCE

Hail the gods, the realm appears to be stable, and the affairs were well dealt with during my absence. But why, oh why, do I still feel uneasy inside?

My life so far has been a tale of strength and victory! Why would it not continue to be?

Uneasiness that I might disappoint Father? Is that what this feeling is?

Father... you bestowed upon me the greatest honor a son can receive: to be by your side as an equal. To rule these sacred lands together. But today, I stand alone.

It was too soon, Father. Our independence had just been recognized, yet you had so few days to enjoy it. I miss—no, this strange feeling, I must be rid of it. It is not befitting of a king. It has been a stranger to me in the past, and so it must remain in the future.

Back at his residence, the young king, Ketriporis, was welcomed and greeted as a hero by courtiers, lords, and commoners alike. The feast set up in his honor, although not as grand as the one honoring his late father, was still rich and lavish. The duty of overseeing the realm in the king's absence had been left to Medosades, Ketriporis's closest advisor and his father's most loyal companion. Tall and muscular, with a long beard, bushy eyebrows, and a thick mustache, and carrying himself with a flair of importance, he informed Ketriporis of the latest news.

"My king, the reports from the foreign delegations after the funeral of the late king are that Western Odrysia is prosperous and strong, and your valor in winning the chariot race and the combat with the Macedonian Axios is talked about near and far."

"Good news, Medosades. What else is there?"

"Great king, the messenger from General Akinestes on the Strymon River has reported that the Macedonian siege weapons and battering rams broke through the wall of Amphipolis, and that the city has fallen into Macedonian possession."

"And what about the citizens of Amphipolis?"

"Those who were ill-disposed toward King Philip were exiled, the remainder treated with lenience."

"This is intriguing," Ketriporis replied. "During the banquet at Amadokus's residence, Antiphon of Athens informed me that Philip of Macedonia had pledged to turn the city over to the Athenians upon its capture."

"Do you think Philip will keep his word to the Athenians?" asked Prince Mononius, the first son of Berisades.

"It remains to be seen, brother," Ketriporis replied. "But an independent Amphipolis to our south is no more."

"Now that Philip has access to the gold and timber of Amphipolis, I do not expect he will relinquish control over them," Mononius replied. "Philip is ambitious, and exploiting the mines at Mount Pangaion will provide him greater wealth. Leaving Amphipolis in Macedonia's possession could be a great risk to us."

"I disagree, brother," said Prince Skostos, Berisades's second son. "Either way, Amphipolis will not be in our possession! And even if Philip exploits those mines, the Amphipolitans only possessed but one side of Mount Pangaion, and we all know the best deposits are to be found on the other side.

Besides, the Athenians have failed every time they have tried to capture that former colony of theirs."

"And you think that Philip having possession of any mine in Mount Pangaion is a small matter, Skostos?" Ketriporis slammed the table with his fist. "Philip is not only centralizing his power—but he is also turning soldiering into an occupation! Those mines can provide him with valuable funds to finance his wars and keep his soldiers from returning home to do other work. It is no secret that Philip's army is growing in Pella, that he is hiring military strategists while building new roads and fortresses. Have you forgotten the way he defeated the Illyrians and Paeonians? His actions are of great concern. By controlling Amphipolis and the bridge over the lower Strymon, he could easily encroach upon our lands."

"No one at Father's funeral bestowed upon us more generous gifts and pledges of friendship than the Macedonian delegation," Skostos replied. "Philip continues to show goodwill toward our realm and demonstrate his intent to keep the peace with us."

"Philip also offered peace to the Paeonians, only to invade their lands and force them to swear allegiance to Macedonia when the opportunity arose!" the king responded, even more angrily.

"The Paeonians were pillaging Macedonia, Ketriporis! He retaliated against them. It is not the same."

"And do you believe that Philip will ever forget how our father initially supported Pausanias to become king of Macedonia?"

"But in the end, Father revoked his backing of Pausanias and supported Philip! My king, did not the Macedonian delegation reaffirm the friendship between Macedonia and Western Odrysia and assure us that Philip would not encroach upon our lands?"

Why is Skostos taking Philip's side so strongly? Ketriporis wondered.

"Brothers," Mononius interrupted. "It is my belief that regardless of their diplomatic gestures, we must err on the side of caution with Macedonia. Philip has proven himself to be an aggressive ruler."

"I agree, brother. Speak your mind, Medosades," King Ketriporis said.

"There are reports of strange happenings in Philip's court, my king. He must have gone mad! His court has become a den for philosophers, mathematicians, poets, actors, musicians... men of genius, as he calls them. He has been summoning them to his court and requiring those in his close social circles to partake in thought and artistry."

"When did that boorish man become a lover of philosophy, poetry, and music? The Philip I know is none but a man of war," Ketriporis said.

"Philip recently snatched the painter Apelles from under the noses of the Athenians, prompting a series of new orations in the Assembly against him. The art of Apelles is highly esteemed there!" said Skostos.

"It is worthy of laughter indeed," Ketriporis replied.

"My king, there was a report that Philip has also been educating the sons of nobles in his court, placing them under his 'protection'," Medosades added.

"It is more likely that he is keeping them hostage, to prevent their parents from questioning his authority," Ketriporis scoffed. "That must be angering the so-called 'democracy' in Athens! No wonder the Athenians are referring to him as a barbarian and savage, just as they do us!"

The Athenians mock our way of life, our traditions, our form of politics and society, just because it does not conform to theirs. That is why I summoned Zenon of Apollonia. I just hope that his young student shall do well enough in his place. I remain skeptical.

"Brother, I think Philip is trying to prove to those in Athens that he is smarter, stronger, more capable, and more resourceful than they are," said Skostos.

"I doubt the Athenians will soon forgive him for that, Skostos," said Ketriporis. "Mononius, what do you think?"

"A conflict between Macedonia and Athens should not be of concern to us. We must focus on the internal affairs of the realm. There is much to be done now that Father has left us."

"I agree. General Derzelas, what is the matter? Speak up!"

Derzelas looks flustered. Entering so hurriedly, he must have unsettling news.

"My king, forgive the abrupt intrusion, but a messenger has arrived from our ambassador in Athens. Allies of General Charidemus are pushing for a decree to be passed in the Athenian Assembly which would state that any man who kills Charidemus would be subject to arrest and declared an enemy of Athens."

There is too much greed and ambition in Charidemus, Ketriporis thought. *I can see in his eyes his desire to become master of Thrace, if only in the name of Kersebleptes; what ambition for a mercenary.*

Mononius is right. The Macedonian is not our greatest threat. Let the Athenians deal with Philip.

"Lords, this news could be of great concern to us. A proposal in Athens to make that bitter enemy of ours inviolable? We must know more about this."

It was hard for Trysimachus to understand why the Thracians, even if they did not want to write, did not want to read either. For him, reading was like a gateway into the minds of the great thinkers and philosophers. A gateway to knowledge itself, as if the gods were sprinkling divine truth down from the heavens in the words on each scroll or tablet.

He appreciated the visual and musical artistry the Thracians loved instead. But to him, these were a means of dulling rationality, of distracting the mind from logic.

Trysimachus had always had difficulty making friends, whether in Athens, Olbia, or Apollonia. But here, he felt that making friends would be even harder. Pitros? Too crude. Sura? Too arrogant, constantly looking down on or laughing at him. And just wondering what the young basileus would do to him if he failed to please him caused Trysimachus to shiver.

He kept trying to overcome his discomfort, especially when in the presence of the Thracians. They were already mocking him enough. He couldn't let them see more signs of weakness. But each night, upon retiring to his quarters, Trysimachus would sit on his bed, gaze at the spiderweb on the ceiling, and ask himself if he had made the right choice.

There were periods when he was able to convince himself he was fine, even enjoying himself. But this was only temporary, as confusion, uncertainty, and doubt would always follow, leaving him feeling as if Hades himself were plaguing his soul.

Day after day, Trysimachus performed his duties in the king's court dispassionately, only the fear of faltering keeping him going. And with fewer and fewer new experiences to bewilder and excite him, the more everything he disliked about his new surroundings loomed larger in his mind.

Ketriporis's court was much more hectic and disorderly than he had expected. The king's councils felt more like banquets and celebrations than political affairs. Trysimachus's orderly and scholarly mind couldn't easily accept the relatively lax and chaotic atmosphere. Too many people were coming and going at all times—courtiers, nobles, generals, envoys, and villagers. *No wonder the king must have hundreds of bodyguards*, he thought.

Each day the bodyguards stood as still as sculpted lions, firmly gripping their swords and keeping a close watch. Trysimachus often felt like his every move was being examined, like the bodyguards were examining his records, ready to find a mistake and punish him for his insolence. But it was his imagination getting out of control, he told himself. He didn't know if they were even literate.

While pondering the king's decision-making process, Trysimachus concluded that it wasn't being done in a manner he thought proper. Rational argumentation, rhetoric, and debate were often ignored. Instead, favors, protection, or certain exemptions were granted to those pouring gold, silver, and other valuable gifts into the royal treasury, the practice being so endemic that gift-giving was viewed as an obligation, a social norm. The Thracians even had a courtier appointed just to solicit gifts for the king.

Bribery also exists in Hellas. But at least in Hellas it is widely deemed an immoral act; those caught doing so face sharp criticism. Here, those who bribe the most receive the most praise and wield the greatest influence! he thought.

"We give sacrifices to the gods, Athenian. We give to them wholeheartedly. Is it not only natural that those who are less divine give to those who are more so? Those who are lesser must please those who are greater. Otherwise, why should the greater put up with the lesser?"

Such was Sura's reasoning when the scholar questioned him about it.

Trysimachus had noticed, however, that Thracian nobles masked their lack of character, manners, and morals by covering themselves in riches to display an aura of power. *All they do is lust for wine, wealth, and women*, he thought.

As for the nobles' daughters, their existence was like that of the moon: shining and glowing, giving off elegant comfort, but surrounded by darkness. They were treated as nothing more than their fathers' bargaining coins for convenient gains and marriage alliances—and polygamous marriages, at that. No wonder he heard them sigh and talk about their dreams of love, as Orpheus had for Eurydice.

Furthermore, it seemed to Trysimachus that nearly everything in Thrace was connected to wine: not just receptions, banquets, and sacred ceremonies, but pledges of friendship, treaties, and judgments. And many of the Thracians, men and women alike, preferred to drink the wine unmixed, making its effects even stronger. The brawls and fights that would break out at banquets, some of which ended fatally, were becoming a source of dread for him. So it was with a most unusual game the Thracians sometimes played at the end of their drinking bouts, one that would draw laughter and merriment from the spectators but which would leave Trysimachus with a sour taste in his mouth.

Those who participated would step upon a large stone, holding a knife. Standing on top of the stone, they would put their head in a hangman's noose tied to a wooden post.

An assistant would then kick the stone away from beneath the participants' feet, requiring them to slash the cord before they were strangled. The ones who freed themselves quickly would receive boisterous cheers, but Trysimachus's attention was drawn to those who were not fast enough, and thus hung lifeless from the post.

No wonder the Thracians boast that they are not afraid of death, eager as they are to visit the afterlife.

The young historian had arrived in western Thrace with the curiosity, excitement, naïveté, and invincibility of youth. Although it was his first significant assignment, he had thought himself prepared for the task. But now, he wasn't so certain.

Am I the only one here feeling so troubled? Trysimachus thought over and over.

But the answer to his question was not difficult to find. It was reflected in the mood of the court of King Ketriporis: somber and not as lighthearted as that of King Amadokus. All Trysimachus needed to do was look around. Everything appeared to be going well on the outside, but something was amiss beneath the surface.

The Western Odrysian realm seemed stable and prosperous. And so did its king. Wearing his hair in a topknot, the young basileus appeared composed, regal, and confident, a sturdy ruler and a brave warrior. And one who would not simply give in to the interests and wishes of others.

King Ketriporis, holding military, economic, and sacral power in the realm, was all-powerful and in control. But was he really? Although Ketriporis's outer expression was like a fortress in itself, nearly impossible to see through or penetrate, Trysimachus had begun to sense that deep down, not unlike himself, the king was deeply troubled, untrusting, and contemplative. All the lavish feasts he was hosting were like theatrical performances. And despite all the displays of wealth and power, Trysimachus sensed a deep concern hidden behind the invisible mask the king was wearing.

The basileus was a young man, and his polity even younger. In fact, King Ketriporis was only slightly older than Trysimachus himself. And yet he was in control of vast lands. But was he not also controlled by the paradynasts, the nobles, the tribal chiefs, the interests of the foreign neighbors, and even by his own subjects? By his army, by his bodyguards?

In fact, the power inside the Western Odrysian realm was less centralized than Trysimachus had realized. The image of the almighty autocrat was turning out to be overly simplistic. The Thracian system of paradynasts and tribal chiefs controlling regions within the realm was a strange concept for him. He could see the convenience of having someone else govern over distant parts of the realm, but also the dangers, as it weakened the power of the king.

Trysimachus often watched and recorded as the king and his brothers awarded land to the paradynasts in order to keep them content. They wielded considerable power by ruling their own semi-autonomous domains, and the stability of the realm largely depended on them.

In addition to the paradynasts, the tribes living within the realm were also allowed to exercise some autonomy, with the chief of each tribe holding the status of a vassal king under Ketriporis. The ruling Odrysians were in fact a minority in western Thrace, compared to the local tribesmen. Trysimachus knew that it had been the strength and strategic diplomacy of the previous Odrysian kings that had kept the Thracian peoples of these lands in submission. He also knew the ancestors of King Ketriporis hailed from both the Odrysian dynasty and the lesser dynasties of the local tribes.

It is a delicate balance the young basileus is trying to maintain, Trysimachus thought. *He must keep control over the tribes while trying to please them. For if they were to unite in rebellion, the realm could collapse from within.*

As he continued to observe and record the happenings in the king's court, Trysimachus's curiosity regarding the Odrysians' relationship with the tribes grew. So when he had the chance to ask Sura, he did once again.

"Sura, do not these tribes hate bowing down to another master? Why do they not strive to be independent, like the Dii?"

"I will answer your question with another question, Athenian. Why do so many of the Hellenic cities take part in the confederacy of the Athenians, obligating themselves to send their men to war and pay dues?"

Sura paused, and Trysimachus knew what he was going to say. "For protection. It is the same with the men of this region. It was after Darius and Xerxes invaded Thrace and these tribes experienced the Persian occupation that the great empire of our people, the Odrysians, expanded. Of course the tribes here dislike bowing to another master. But being within the Odrysian domain gives them protection from threats near and far, as well as opportunities for trade, prosperity, and military enlistment. And a few have indeed tried to secede—but they failed." Sura chuckled.

"Is not the stability of Odrysian rule more precarious now that the kingdom is split into three?"

"No, on the contrary. Now that King Ketriporis rules within the western lands, our center of power and the military is located far closer to the local people than when Kotys was king. Kotys ruled these lands from afar through his regional paradynasts, such as the late King Berisades."

"I see."

It was becoming easier for the young scholar to understand the king's challenges: to be firm and fair, feared and respected, but also able to keep his subjects appeased and content. This was no easy task, especially for someone so young.

As for Mononius and Skostos, they seemed to Trysimachus to have very different personalities from the serious and straight-faced Ketriporis. Mononius was more open, amicable, and communicative, while Skostos was sociable and a womanizer.

Trysimachus kept his personal observations and opinions to himself. He couldn't openly voice them or write them down. But they were his. And no one, not even the king, could take them away from him.

XXX

I am grateful that my brothers are on my side, instead of competing over the kingship. I cannot take their loyalty for granted, as strife amongst us would only give power and opportunities to those who seek to weaken our realm.

"You look troubled, brother," Prince Mononius observed as Ketriporis paced up and down his quarters.

"Yes, indeed," the king said, knowing his presence was surprising this late at night. "I am hearing ominous things concerning Charidemus the Euboean. And ignoring them might put the realm in peril. Not only did Charidemus push that decree in Athens to make his life inviolable, not only did his followers demand he be made a general of Athens and paid a general's commission, but the messenger just brought the news that the council has preliminarily passed that decree!"

Mononius groaned with disappointment. "I thought that there would have been enough men with reason amongst the five hundred to have seen through the scheme."

"I understand your desire for that to have been true. But it was not so. And the decree shall now be brought to the Assembly for the final vote."

"May their decision be guided by higher reasoning and values."

"We cannot be confident of that," the king said, agitated.

"Charidemus's allies have several arguments to their advantage. Between Athens's naval activities, Pontic trade, and possessions in the Chersonese, it is in the Athenians' interest to maintain good relations with Eastern Odrysia and Kersebleptes—and some view Charidemus as the way to do it. Furthermore, the Euboean is cunning and manipulative, a master of speech and bribery. The Athenians speak incessantly of logic and rationality, yet the mind forgives and forgets easily when there are interests at stake and convincing promises. Mononius, I need you to do something."

"Command me, my king, and I shall follow," Mononius declared, placing his hand over his heart.

"You know well how notoriously slow the Athenians are with their endless orations and complex bureaucracy. There is still time, in all this madness, before the final vote is held in the Assembly. We need to seize this opportunity and do everything possible to prevent the Athenians from approving these measures. If Charidemus is not made a general, and the decree protecting his life also falters, I will be more at ease. I need you to travel to Athens and seek out those on the Hill who wield the greatest influence in the Assembly. Try to persuade them to speak out and vote against these measures. I am confident many have not forgotten Charidemus's true character or how he fought against Athens's interests during the conflict in the Chersonese. Nor that it was he who convinced Kersebleptes to violate the original covenant Athens supported for peace in Odrysia. He even betrayed their general, Cephisodotus!"

"Indeed."

"I know there will be those who will continue to turn a blind eye, swayed by the Euboean's promises and favors." Taking a sip of wine, the king continued, "Mononius, you are a man of great intellect and speech. I know no one more capable than you of pleading our cause to the Athenians."

"I am honored by your words, brother."

"There is a well-known orator in the Assembly, a certain Euthycles, who has expressed his hatred for Charidemus many times in public. I have also been told of a young rhetorician named Demosthenes, who has been recognized for his ability to write convincing speeches. These are the kind of men we need as allies: those capable of making a case against Charidemus."

"I understand, my king. I hope the Athenians will realize that these measures benefit Charidemus far more than they benefit Athens," Mononius replied. "He could even take advantage of his new status to harm Athens! This is an argument I can put forth."

"I also want you to gather as much information as you can of Charidemus's intentions and plans. He is amassing great wealth, land, and political influence in Eastern Odrysia. We must find out the true reason why his supporters in Athens are pushing these daring measures."

"I will, my king. But what of the ambassador you sent to the court of Kersebleptes? Have you received word from him?"

Ketriporis shook his head. "He returned earlier today, and I have spoken with him in private. He reported that while the Easterners made every effort to conceal their plans from him, he suspects the eastern realm is preparing for a military campaign. That is why I am relying on you, brother. Any Eastern Odrysian campaign will break the stability in Thrace, even if they do not have their sights set on our realm."

"I understand, and I will do all I can to further our cause," Mononius replied.

"My gratitude, brother."

"Ketriporis, the omens have been unfavorable lately. I have been wondering, could it be possible that Kersebleptes is seeking to take advantage of Father's death? In order to defeat us, he and Charidemus could be attempting to prevent any Athenian citizen from coming to our aid through political intimidation, by passing that decree to make Charidemus's life inviolable. He may think that if we are left to fend for ourselves, we are at a disadvantage. But could Kersebleptes really be insolent enough to attempt a re-conquest of the rest of Odrysia so soon?"

Ketriporis thought for a moment and replied, "Charidemus would recognize a good opportunity. And he knows that during the civil war, the military support and strategizing of our Athenian allies was crucial to Father and Amadokus's victory. Without them, the Easterners surely would see us as weaker prey." Pacing anxiously, the king continued, "I feel pressured, Mononius. There is much work to be done: policies to be sorted, defenses to be built, trade to be grown, tribes to be dealt with! We still do not have as much control as we should. And truth be told, it has not been quite the same without Father. But you must not speak of this to anyone else. For now, the realm is stable. But just as the sea might appear calm on the surface, go deeper and you will find that much that is unknown lurks in the darkness."

"Do not vex yourself, Ketriporis," Mononius replied. "At the funeral games, you displayed nothing but strength! You were admirable. You demonstrated skills in a way I could not, and I am proud to be your brother."

"I appreciate your words, brother. I vow that while you are in Athens, I shall do all I can to enlarge and strengthen our army, hire mercenaries, train the common men, and build more forts along the Nestos. I shall seek audience with the generals in the morning," said Ketriporis.

"And what of General Athenodorus? He is an Athenian citizen first and foremost, and would never risk becoming an enemy of Athens if measures protecting Charidemus pass!"

"That is why you must try your best to prevent the

Assembly from passing them. In the morning, I will send an envoy to Athenodorus. We must find out what he thinks about this situation. It will also be an opportunity to hear from Aunt Zeila again. I would like to know if she is truly enjoying her life in the Chersonese with Athenodorus. I regret not speaking with her during the funeral."

"Yes, brother."

"This will be a challenge for us all. Dangers lurk on many sides. But I vow to give it my all."

"May the gods be with you, my king."

"And may the gods be with you, Mononius. The break of dawn will be upon us soon. Go and get some sleep before you depart," the king said, gripping his brother's arm firmly.

Returning his brother's grip, Mononius replied, "I will take my leave, and I will do everything I can to not disappoint you."

XXXI

His negative view of Thrace was overwhelming Trysimachus's perception as if he were trapped in a deep ravine with steep walls. The climb up, to breathe the fresh air and see the light—the bright colors of the world, the more positive aspects of life in Thrace—was daunting. The task was too arduous.

Trysimachus would have run away if not for the fear of embarrassing himself. Of becoming a disappointment to his mentor and father. Of incurring the king's wrath. Of losing his life. He had embarked on a journey, a quest, but it had turned into a trial. A trial of understanding, patience, and endurance. These were qualities he resisted with all his might. And instead of trying to adapt to his new life, the scholar kept to himself, avoiding Pitros—and, when possible, Sura—and shutting himself inside the tall, protective walls of the fortress.

"Get ready, Athenian! The king wants to visit the nearby villages, as well as the emporium," Sura announced one crisp autumn morning.

Leave the fortress? If only I could go back home where I belong, he thought. But he replied, "I will be ready when you call for me."

It was a bright day in western Thrace. The peaks of Mount Orbelus shimmered against the translucent blue sky, the grass was golden, and the air was filled with the aroma of the fallen leaves. Wearing light armor under a heavy cloak, and riding his black stallion, the young basileus was accompanied by his regular retinue and his brother Skostos. The party's spirits were high. Only Trysimachus was trudging gloomily behind.

Following the main road down from the fortress, the royal party headed to a village on the mountain's lower slope. In the meadows and up the hills, sheep and goats were grazing around. Women were herding the animals in the fields as farmers gathered the late crops of the harvest.

The village they stopped in was no more than an assortment of wooden huts, each surrounded by tall palings to keep the cattle in and defended by a deep double ditch on one side, with the mountain on the other. Upon entering, the party was greeted by loud moaning sounds coming from one of the huts. And it was in that direction the king led them.

They made their way to a small courtyard. Sitting on the ground was a young woman with large, doe-like brown eyes, wearing a long, belted chiton in the Thracian fashion and holding a newborn baby in her arms. Around her was a circle of other women, crying and wailing as if they had been struck by a terrible misfortune. Indeed, the woman in the center looked quite fatigued.

"What is happening? Why are they crying?" Trysimachus asked one of the servants. "Has somebody departed?"

"No, they are lamenting the birth of the child," the servant replied.

"That is strange. Should they not be rejoicing?"

"Why would they?" exclaimed the servant. "They are bemoaning all the evils and suffering that will befall the child during his lifetime."

Not a joyous way to enter the world, Trysimachus thought. *They act as if the child has already been predestined to suffer. But how could anyone know the will of the gods?*

When they noticed the basileus's presence, the peasants'

wailing stopped, and everyone paid respect to their king. Ketriporis took the baby, a boy, from his mother's arms and kissed him on the forehead before announcing that the boy would become a great warrior for the kingdom. He gestured to his servants, and they brought forth large bags of millet, which were presented to the young mother.

Trysimachus peeked inside the family's hut. It was small, with a hearth in one of the corners and only a few possessions inside.

Leaving the young family to their affairs, the king walked to the village square, where men and women alike had already gathered around to await word from their king.

"My request to you, brave and honorable men, is that you will take up arms with me in order to protect this sacred land from our enemies. And my promise to you is that I will give every man who joins generous pay, and I will further honor those who demonstrate special merit."

The speech was welcomed with loud cheers and an outpouring of support from the villagers. The king's party moved on to the local blacksmith's shop. Covered in sweat from the heat of the fire, the blacksmith was hard at work; only the presence of the king compelled him to hold off the forging of the iron.

Barely acknowledging the blacksmith's greeting, the young basileus began to closely examine some of the weapons hanging in the shop. They varied in size and shape: from straight, triangular daggers to curved and tanged ones; from short swords with double-edged blades to those with the slightly curved blade of the heavy slashing machaira. Trysimachus had seen most of the styles carried by the peltasts, cavalrymen, and bodyguards, but the machaira only by the royal family.

Ketriporis took particular interest in that weapon, carefully running his finger over the blade, eyes focused on its fine details.

As there were more villages to visit, the king took his leave shortly thereafter. The party followed.

"Sura, what would the villagers do if attacked or plundered?" Trysimachus asked.

"They would retreat to the fort for protection."

Sura pointed to a fort built high in the mountain. It was all the advisor cared to say, and Trysimachus let it drop.

After spending the day visiting several more villages, the party was ready to rest. The sun was low in the sky, the mountains tinted in purple and orange. "We are to spend the night at the residence of Lord Sadalas," Sura announced.

It was welcome news for Trysimachus. He had started the day feeling gloomy, but the new sights had lifted his spirits. And now, he was looking forward to the feast to come, as the pangs he felt reminded him of just how hungry and tired he was.

The residence of the paradynast was a reflection of his status: large and rich, but not as grand as that of the king. Sadalas himself was a fierce, intimidating-looking man, with long, silvery hair; a beard; piercing gray eyes; and a reddish complexion. He greeted the party with bodyguards of his own.

Lord Sadalas was one of Western Odrysia's most influential paradynasts, governing over some of the best land in the realm. Although he had autonomous rights over his territory, he was still obliged to uphold the king's foreign policies, contribute to military campaigns, and pay the necessary tribute.

"Welcome, honorable king! Use this humble home as your own." Sadalas must have been informed in advance of the king's visit, as a feast had already been spread out.

The feast began. The young historian was focused more on the food than on the conversation taking place, and he missed part of what was being discussed. Now, listening in, he concentrated on what the two powerful men were saying.

"Do you really think it is coming, honorable king?" Sadalas asked.

"We cannot be certain," Ketriporis replied. "But we must be prepared for anything."

"When the news of the Athenian decree was brought to me, I myself became outraged! And to think it has been less than a year since the treaty with Kersebleptes. Peaceful times are difficult to sustain."

"Sadalas, what happened to your thirst for bloodshed?"

"It is still there, my king." Standing and raising his phiale of wine, Sadalas announced, "My men are pledged to you as always, and are prepared to defend your great domain at any cost. We shall be ready to follow your command when you call upon us."

"My gratitude, Lord Sadalas."

The two men fell into deep thought.

"My king, how did the recruitment of the peasants go?"

"We recruited a few. The problem, Sadalas, is that we also need people to work the land. Too many women have already taken to the fields, replacing their men. That cannot be sustained for long. General Derzelas is right now visiting the tribes to hire more mercenaries. We must grow and strengthen our army, just as Philip the Macedonian is doing."

"I shall do my part, my king. But we will need more funds. We must raise the tributes."

"The people are enduring enough hardship, Sadalas. We must do without that."

And so the conversation continued late into the night. It was becoming clear to the young historian that the king anticipated a possible invasion of his realm. A worrisome thought indeed.

The next morning, the party bade their goodbyes to Lord Sadalas and left for the nearby emporium. The sun was still high in the sky when they arrived. Called Gareskos, the emporium was set two stadia inland from the river and connected to it by a dirt road.

It was a busy day at Gareskos, the market hustling and bustling with trade. Thracian, Hellenic, and other foreign merchants were eagerly trying to sell their wares: grains, wines, textiles, livestock, jewelry, timber, decorative amphorae and other pottery, horses, weapons, armor, pigments, charcoal, wax, and even cut furniture.

Being in the emporium reminded Trysimachus of the times when he was young and his father would take him to the marketplaces in Athens and Olbia. How he missed his former homes.

Walking around the market, Trysimachus spotted Sura at a stall, arguing with a merchant over the price of a sword. In all the time the young historian had been under Sura's care, he hadn't given much thought to the advisor's appearance. But here, amongst the multitude of people, he was struck by how imposing and different Sura looked. His face was deeply lined as if the problems of Thrace were running through it like rivers. His narrow eyes, bushy brows, prominent nose, and rather thick lips—as well as his hair, which was also styled in a topknot—made him the image of a true Odrysian noble.

But it was the king who attracted the most attention. As he inspected the various workshops, stalls, storage houses, and residences, his movements were tracked by the women. Trysimachus heard several young maidens sigh as the basileus passed them by. Yet the king's interest was not captured by the fair maidens, but by the weapons and armor in the stalls.

Meanwhile, his brother Skostos was choosing jewelry, from headpieces to earrings to necklaces to bracelets. He was ordering fabrics, some as translucent as the seafoam, others as colorful as peacock feathers. And he was selecting rare Egyptian perfumes.

"Brother, you are too far under her foot," he overheard the

basileus declare with a rare smile. “Meda is in control of you, instead of you being in control of her!”

“I think you secretly envy the love and passion we enjoy together,” Skostos replied. “You should spend more time with your wives and take better care of them, brother.”

Ketriporis’s expression changed abruptly. “They do not love me. Why should I love them?”

“You are wrong, brother. They cannot give you love if you are unwilling to receive it. Many a man would pay a high price to have such wives as you!”

“And is ‘love’ the word to describe the way Meda feels for you? She is cold and vain, shallow and greedy. You do not love her for who she is, you just lust for her.” With that, the young basileus quickly turned away from his brother, giving him no chance to respond.

It was true that Meda, a Getic princess from the north, was stunningly beautiful. The intricate patterns tattooed on her arms indicated that she was of noble birth. Trysimachus couldn’t blame the prince for his efforts to please his wife.

But he had to follow the king, and so the scholar listened in as the basileus commissioned one of the Thracian goldsmiths to make a set of vessels depicting King Berisades’s victories in battle. Handing over some of his newly minted coins depicting Apollo on the front and a spearhead on the back, King Ketriporis made the goldsmith light up like a torch in the dark.

Strolling through the market, Trysimachus tried hard to resist the vigorous pressure from some of the merchants. They were constantly trying to push their wares on him, be they things he already possessed or ridiculous items like magical rocks or snake potions for vitality. They irritated him. His father was a merchant, but he couldn’t equate him with those he encountered at the Thracian emporium.

Trysimachus felt a tap on his shoulder. Annoyed, he

turned around and stared down a merchant completely outfitted in Thracian garb. To the scholar's surprise, the man addressed him in pure Ionic Greek.

"Greetings to you, traveler! You look like you are a Hellene and new in these parts. Are you a merchant?"

"No, my father is," he said. "But let me compliment you on your use of our language."

The merchant laughed. "You thought I was a Thracian? Let me introduce myself to you. I am Orion of Thasos."

"And I am Trysimachus of Athens," the scholar replied happily.

"A true pleasure, Trysimachus of Athens. Are you here on your father's business, then?"

"No, I am here with the party of King Ketriporis."

A look of bewilderment swept over the merchant's face. "And what is your business with the king, if I may ask?"

"To record the history of his reign."

"So you are a scholar, then."

"Yes, I have studied under Zenon of Apollonia."

"How long have you been with the king?"

"Since the onset of autumn." Trysimachus was overjoyed at being able to talk to a fellow Hellene. He asked, "And how long have you been here in Thrace?"

"For so long that I hardly remember not being here."

"How have you survived living here so long?" Trysimachus asked, surprised.

"Survive? What do you mean by survive? It is not difficult. I live here by my own choice and am glad of it."

"You want to say that you are content living in Thrace?" The scholar was even more surprised.

"Why would I not be? It is as good a place as any to live. Which places are better?"

It was an answer Trysimachus didn't expect to hear. He was hoping to find a kindred spirit in Orion, someone he could share his woes and frustrations with. But the merchant looked happy and content. "Athens, certainly."

"If you are an Athenian, perhaps." Orion paused briefly. "So, how do you like being in Thrace?"

Trysimachus didn't have to ponder. The answer to the question was simple, and he replied without hesitation. "I do not like it."

Orion shook his head and smiled. "You are still young and new here, Trysimachus of Athens. Give it time, and I think you will start to like being in these parts. Give the Thracians a chance, and when you start to understand them better, you will hold them in higher esteem."

The Thasian's words reminded Trysimachus of what his mentor had told him.

"Find yourself a woman, and you will like it here even better!" Orion added with a smile and a wink.

"A woman? You mean a local one?" Trysimachus blushed. "Most are pleasing to the eye, but their temper..."

Laughing hard, Orion struck Trysimachus on the shoulder. "You think the ones back home have a better temper? My wife is a Thracian, and she is as gentle as a lamb. I have never met a finer woman, so caring and so good."

Now feeling uncomfortable, Trysimachus replied, "I suppose not all of them are bad-tempered."

The merchant laughed again.

"Orion, do you live here in the emporium?" Trysimachus asked.

"I certainly do. A fine place it is, and I have a good life here."

"You do?" Trysimachus asked, amazed.

"Young scholar, you seem very skeptical about life in these lands! But just look around. Look at the people here. They trade their goods under the protection and generosity of the Odrysians. The king upholds our ownership of land and property while protecting us from plunder and thievery. And when a subject of his tries to pay with counterfeit coins, he is punished severely. The tariffs are fair, and there are no tolls on the roads. We have been prospering under the laws of King Kotys, upheld by King Berisades and now King Ketriporis. May the gods bring longevity and good health to the young basileus."

Then, with a rather condescending look, Orion tapped Trysimachus's arm. "Your garments are of fine material, young scholar, but they are as bland and drab as your perceptions."

Instead of feeling like he had found a kindred spirit in Orion, Trysimachus was growing irritated by the merchant's loose tongue.

"You need to put some color into your life," Orion continued. "It may very well transform your outlook on the land. Here, look at this fine cloak. I will sell it to you at a good price. Believe me, a garment like this is a necessity here! The heaviest snows are not yet upon us."

Trysimachus had already experienced the cold in western Thrace. He knew the merchant was right. But he still preferred to hold onto the old garments he had brought from his home.

"Orion, the Thracians are unrefined and wild people," Trysimachus said after turning left and right to make sure no Thracian could hear him. "Look at that, a local family is selling their child off into slavery!"

"To be able to sell, you must have a buyer. The Thracians may sell their children, but are not we the ones who buy them?" Orion replied. "You said your father is a merchant from Athens. Does your family have slaves?"

The question stumped Trysimachus. "Yes, but not from Thrace."

"But does it matter? Well, it was a pleasure talking with you, Trysimachus of Athens. I better get back to business."

Orion tapped him on the shoulder yet again, bade him farewell, and returned to his business, leaving the young scholar to ponder what had been said.

The moonlight and the stars shining through the darkness helped Trysimachus better adjust to daily life in Thrace, and more specifically, to the court of King Ketriporis. In his case, the stars were the people like Pitros who treated him well, and the moonlight was his desire to write a comprehensive historical account of Thrace, one more detailed than those written by any of the historians—Herodotus, Thucydides, or Xenophon—who had preceded him.

No matter how he felt about Thrace itself, he had a golden opportunity to reveal to the world an inside account of what it was like to live in an Odrysian king's residence.

The quest was forcing Trysimachus to mature. To face the world as it was, not how he thought it should be. He could no longer remain an innocent, curious child protected and sheltered from reality. He would have to grow up.

The next day, back at the fortress, Sura startled the young scholar when he appeared in his quarters.

"Trysimachus of Athens, you have been summoned by the king."

"Me? Why?" Trysimachus stammered.

"The king did not inform me," Sura replied impassively.

Does this have anything to do with Medosades examining my scrolls? Trysimachus wondered. The advisor had demanded that he surrender them—by order of the king, or so he said.

Trysimachus hurried behind Sura to the king's quarters as anxiety threatened to overwhelm him. He entered timidly, staring at the floor, unable to see the faint smile that briefly crossed the king's face upon seeing him.

"Trysimachus of Athens, sit there." The king pointed to a luxurious kline. It was Trysimachus's first time in Ketriporis's private quarters. Trying to be as inconspicuous as possible, he looked around. The room he had been ushered into was masculine, yet with a touch of opulence and elegance to it. Hunting and arms trophies were mounted on the walls, while fabrics in rich gold hues decorated the furniture.

"Athenian, I have summoned you today because I want to hear what you think of my realm."

"But my king," Trysimachus stammered. "I was explicitly told not to give opinions."

"That is correct. That has been my order—and it still is. But I know that you are highly opinionated, and you have already formed many opinions about us which may not be entirely accurate; however, as I cannot forbid you to hold them, I am ordering you to speak truthfully and openly. What is it? You look frightened!" The young basileus smiled. "Do I need to guarantee your life in order to hear you speak?"

Trysimachus had begun to sweat; he feared he might say the wrong thing and anger the king.

"All right, I will ask then. I have heard that you have been scoffing at our herald. Why is that?"

"My king, it is just that..." Trysimachus spoke hesitantly. "To extract favors and influence the decision-making process through gifts is the wrong way."

"And why is that?"

"Because it is a form of bribery..."

"And what is the right way, then?"

"Through discussions, debates, argumentations, and deductions."

"By orations, you mean? Like in the Athenian Assembly?"

Trysimachus blushed. "Yes," he replied.

"So you want to say that influencing through oration is the right way? And influencing through gifts is the wrong one?"

"Yes, indeed," Trysimachus responded with more confidence. "There are many great orators in Athens. I could spend days just listening to them and their wisdom. Their speeches have turned many tides."

"Exactly, young scholar! Influencing is influencing, whether through gifts or oration. Do you think, Athenian, that I can be influenced by mere gifts?"

The basileus looked sternly at Trysimachus, who started to shake visibly. Pretending not to notice, the king continued.

"The herald in the Athenian Assembly encourages and invites speeches. Our herald encourages and invites gifts. Where do you think all those gifts go? Do you think they are all solely for my personal use? They go in the treasury of Western Odrysia, scholar. Without the treasury, I cannot rule the realm or protect my people. I, as the king, receive gifts from my subjects. My subjects, in return, receive gifts from me. What is wrong with that?"

Ketriporis's question was more of a command, giving Trysimachus no choice but to respond. "My king, in the Athenian Assembly, each man is free to speak his mind, regardless of their station. The herald does not exclude anybody. He encourages and invites only speeches, not gift-giving." Then, hesitantly, almost as if in a whisper, he added, "I have seen many poor here giving gifts so they could be heard."

"Do you think a king can only receive without ever giving? I cannot give back the same to everyone as I receive. I need to pay for the army, the mercenaries, the building of new fortifications... then there are the paradynasts, the nobles, the commoners. There are many obligations and responsibilities that I have as king. And yet, have you ever witnessed me forbidding anyone from speaking their mind?"

"No, basileus. I am sorry."

"Continue, then."

"My king, in Athens, all citizens participate in the Assembly and have a say in the governing of the state by casting their vote."

"They participate because they are paid to do so. Do you think the commoner would otherwise stop his work to vote in affairs which he most likely does not fully understand or fully benefit from?"

"But in this way, even the poorer men can take time from their work."

"No wonder you Athenians rely so much on slave labor. There are no slaves in my realm. It is my people who labor in our quarries and mines."

It was a subject Trysimachus didn't want to think about, especially after his conversation with Orion at the emporium. But it was true. He had not seen any slaves within Western Odrysia, just captives from the wars who were considered servants until their tribes bought them out.

"Basileus, I do believe every Athenian citizen is proud to be able to vote and have a say in the affairs of the state."

Striking the table with his fist and startling Trysimachus, the king answered, "Heh! As if their voting is not influenced by the more sly, skillful, and popular orators. Too much say in political affairs by people who are not competent can cause disarray."

"But the men of Athens are very critical of those who speak outside of their knowledge."

"As they are critical of us Thracians?"

"No... yes," Trysimachus had to admit.

"Even I, a true son of the gods, chosen by the gods to rule

these sacred lands, have to sometimes ignore Athens's references to us as unlearned, ignorant, and savage, in order to maintain good relations."

The king paused, then continued. "The Athenian Assembly is nothing more than a nest of gold-tongued sophists and hypocrites!"

Trysimachus was taken aback by Ketriporis's strong words.

The basileus's face darkened. "So you would tell me that, as long as bribery is publicly denounced, declared an evil deed, and debated in lengthy orations as a wrongdoing, it is right to privately accept it. Just know that recently, Charidemus the Euboean, the very same one I overcame in the chariot race, bribed his way around the Council, and convinced them that his mercenary life should be declared inviolable. All for the glory of Athens, right? It was not very long ago that the same Charidemus fought on the side of King Kotys against the Athenians."

"That cannot be possible. All the councilors are subject to vigorous scrutiny."

"Scrutiny? You are naïve, scholar. You must have led a very sheltered life. You do not seem to have much experience outside of your books. What a nest of fools you Athenians are! Granting citizenship to your enemies. Charidemus is as much a friend of Athens as the late great King Kotys was. Yet the fools granted Kotys citizenship too. Now, do you think that King Kotys became a friend and a citizen of Athens, with honors and wreath bestowed upon him, because of his virtues? No, he bought his citizenship, and his friendships also! How? Through bribery, gifts, and empty promises. Building a great and strong Odrysia was all he ever cared about. After realizing that his power was a threat to their interests, like a five hundred-headed serpent, the Council all turned against him, calling the son of the gods an oppressor and defaming him. They made a mockery of him in their plays when it would have been more appropriate to mock themselves. I would not be surprised if some of them were behind the brothers who poisoned Kotys. Athens even rewarded the murderers for that."

"It must have all been decided in a democratic way."

"Athenian democracy. I am tired of hearing about it! You Athenians like listening to the truth as much as we do. You sentenced Socrates to be poisoned because of his sharp tongue! And yet we Odrysians make no fancy claims, and we vow not to kill one another except in circumstances of war. Turning oration into an occupation—is that your democracy? Many in your Assembly can give endless speeches and yet cower at the sight of the sword."

Trysimachus reddened and remained silent. At least the conversation had mostly revolved around the king thus far, giving him little chance to respond.

After a pause and a sip of wine, Ketriporis continued.

"Trysimachus of Athens, you were brought up to believe Athenian democracy to be superior to any other system. But we here in Thrace do not hide behind flowery speeches. We do what we do openly, and we have not made an occupation of having councilors giving long orations, criticizing doings in which they themselves partake. So tell me, what is wrong with our customs, way of life, and laws?"

It was a difficult question. The scholar longed to rail against Thrace and everything about it that he disliked. But how could he tell the basileus that he thought of the Thracians just as the rest of his brethren did? As rough, unsophisticated, and ignorant? He had to be diplomatic. So he began timidly. "We have laws..."

"Too many laws."

"But they are necessary. They protect the people—"

"And our laws do not protect our people? You speak of

freedom, but too many laws can, in fact, restrict people's freedom. What is important is not to have a great number of laws, but to have the right ones, scholar. If something is lawful, that does not always make it just."

"Yes, basileus, but our laws are written..."

"Ah yes, writing. I have been informed that you have been complaining of being turned into a scribe."

Regretting that he had raised the subject, Trysimachus resigned himself to the difficult and uncomfortable debate that would surely follow.

"Why do you feel superior to my people? Because they do not know how to write or read?"

"My king, it is important to feed the mind."

"With useless rhetoric?" The young basileus laughed.

"No, with knowledge," Trysimachus replied hotly.

"My people hunt, fight, and harvest. They are warriors, builders, craftsmen, traders, miners, musicians, poets, and painters. Do you think these skills do not require knowledge?"

"Yes, but true knowledge—"

"True knowledge cannot be obtained from another man. It can be obtained only from the gods. And it is they who guide our lives. One cannot survive without food, water, or breath. But one can easily survive without writing and reading."

"But my king, without writing, how will people one day know about the legacy of your people—of their way of life, their customs, their beliefs, and wisdom?"

"By what my people leave behind. Through the temples and fortresses they have built. Through music and poetry. Through the scenes of their lives that they paint and carve. Besides, is not that why you are here? I do recognize the convenience of your writing system, Hellene. But that does not mean I must force it upon my people."

"But would it not be better if your own people write down your history? This way, how others portray you does not have to be—"

"I will ask you, scholar, do you see us as the way we are? Or the way you have learned we are?"

Trysimachus was perplexed by the king's question.

"Do you think it will impact the way others portray us, scholar?" the king continued. "They are going to portray us according to their beliefs, or in a way that suits their interests. The Hellenes, the Persians, the Scythians... each portray us in their own manner. And if we were to portray ourselves, that does not mean that we would do so truthfully either. When the gods decide they want to communicate with us through letters, we will create a different way of writing. Until then, our current means shall suffice."

Not wishing to surrender so easily, Trysimachus pressed the king. "The orations in our Assembly are written down. Our laws, our oaths to the gods, our discussions, our debates are all recorded so future generations can learn from these writings."

"Do your writings put food on the table of the commoners? Provide them with shelter? Does writing alone make them merrier?"

"No, basileus. But would not your people want to write down their thoughts, observations, conversations, and beautiful poems?"

"Our knowledge and our customs are sacred to us. Our people pass them down from generation to generation. They do not forget them. They can only be passed from one Thracian to another."

Emboldened by the king's calm demeanor, Trysimachus continued. "But what about reading? Our laws are not only written down but they are publicly displayed in the agora. This way, every citizen can examine the board and know the laws of the state. Notices are publicly displayed for everyone to read and know. This is the way of our democracy."

"Do all Athenians know how to read?"

"Well, there are schools..."

"Do those working in the fields have time to spare for reading and writing? Or to even go to school? All the laws and notices in my realm are made known to my people. To the Athenians, I may be a despot, but I do not keep the knowing of my realm's laws to myself. What my people need to know, they know."

"My king, I... I do find merit in your way of life. But we Athenians record our way of governing, as we think it might be useful for future generations to learn from our democracy. Or perhaps to even find a way to further it or improve it. Do you not think that someday others might want to learn from your ways?"

"Our way of life is simple, without too many complicated laws or rules. I am not opposed to everything Athenian. I have studied your philosophers and thinkers. And I find merit in them. However, none of their writings have given me an easy answer on how to rule this dominion, or how to deal with the nature of man. They have not taught me how to trust, or how to stop our enemies from wanting to conquer our lands. Your democracy has seen many changes through the summers, while our way has remained the same."

"But it has been for the better—"

"Has it? The commoners in Athens face hardships, just as the commoners do here. While your aristocrats idle, exercise their tongues and complain of boredom, ours exercise their bodies. They fight and they hunt. Ideas and ideals do not put food on the table. Work does. That is what the gods want for them."

"Basileus, but are not your gods the same as those of the Athenians?"

With a look cold enough to freeze the blood in Trysimachus's veins, the king retorted, "Are not your gods the same as that of the Thracians?" Then, in a softer tone, he continued. "Our forests are sacred, scholar. They are home to our nymphs, the muses, and other creatures of magic. The great Mother Goddess protects our forests, trees, springs, and streams. The muses themselves inspire our poetry and music. Their song is loyal and true. Not like the song of the sirens, false and deceptive. The sacred tree of life also grows in our lands."

"Basileus, are not you afraid that the truth of your lands may be lost—"

"There will always be seekers of the truth. And they will find a way to know it. Others, who want to live their lives in deception, will find a way to deny the truth and remain deceived. Some will even find a way to hide it. There is wisdom that comes from deep inside each one of us. But often, we do not want to hear it."

With a wave of his hand, the young basileus dismissed the bewildered scholar.

Back in his quarters, Trysimachus revisited his conversation with King Ketriporis. He had already known the young basileus was intelligent, but in many ways he was a philosopher in his own right. Furthermore, the king was critical and highly opinionated, more similar to himself than Trysimachus had realized.

Previously, the scholar had felt confident in the correctness of his own opinions. But their discussion had confused and unsettled him, and he was now unsure who was right and who was wrong. Or which way was the better one.

Trysimachus was struck by a particular answer he had given the king. *I did not tell him the Thracian way of life had merit just to please him. Nor was it a slip of the tongue. But when did I start thinking this way?* he wondered.

He could never accept the idea that the Thracian way was superior to the Athenian. However, he was also no longer confident enough to completely deny and disparage the Thracian way of life. He was starting to understand why his mentor had sent him to these lands. He recalled Zenon of Apollonia's words in a letter he had received: *Through seeing the contrast between us and the Odrysians—objectively understanding and becoming accepting of it—only then can you become a true historian.*

Trysimachus was beginning to better understand King Ketriporis—the way he was feeling, and why he had ordered him to record in the way he had. He was now becoming even more fascinated by the young basileus and curious about what he was going to witness.

He could not deny it. Something about the king's words had shaken him up and had stirred something inside him, compelling him to embrace his new life instead of resisting it. But how?

Then he recalled the words of the healer: "Connect with the land and the people here, and you will have an easier time."

Pitros put his bowl of porridge down with a grin. “Teach ya hunting and fighting? Thought you’d never ask me!”

“Yes, well, I want to give it a try,” Trysimachus replied.

“Ya need to do more than just try! It takes courage and sweat, ’specially when you’re not that strong!”

“Pitros, I understand. But I want to learn. Please, teach me the Thracian ways. I promise to be an obedient student.”

“Ya don’t need to be a’ obedient student, Trysimachus. Ya need to want to learn from deep down inside here.” The giant pointed to his heart. “Then learnin’ will be easier for ya, and teaching ya will be easier for me.”

“I will try.”

“Trysimachus, when the king gives ya an order, do ya answer him, ‘I’ll try?’”

“No, how could I? That could cost me my life!”

“Tis the same with learnin’ how to fight and hunt. Tryin’ ain’t good enough—it can cost ya your life!”

The scholar had no reply. He was surprised by the giant’s wisdom. He knew that Pitros was right.

And so his training began. Clad in heavy armor, Trysimachus found himself carrying a long, heavy sword in each hand, a bag full of heavy rocks lashed to his back. Pitros had ordered him to climb a steep, icy hill at the foot of Mount

Orbelus.

"Pitros, I am a man, not a mule! I am carrying too much!"

"The only thing you're carryin' too much of are complaints and excuses!" Pitros replied.

The giant's blunt words stung like a bee. Trysimachus hated to admit it even to himself, but Pitros made a good point.

As the days passed, Trysimachus's skills started to improve slowly but surely. The daily challenges and difficulties he had to face in his training were making him stronger, more resilient, and less fearful of his surroundings.

One day, after he had managed to ride his horse standing up, Pitros remarked, "You're a fine rider now, Trysimachus! You're ready to enter the ridin' competition with the other young lads as yourself! That's the best way to make friends 'round here!"

"But even if I do well, will they accept me?" the scholar asked apprehensively.

"They will! There's nothin' a Thracian respects more than a good fighter, hunter, and rider! You're now good at all three. Big difference since when I first met ya!" The giant offered Trysimachus a mischievous smile and winked at him. "And you'll attract quite a few glances from the maidens. You're a fine-lookin' fella!"

Trysimachus was flattered but also surprised by Pitros's words. He had never thought of himself as 'fine-looking'. He was much smaller in stature than he would have liked, which was especially bothersome here amongst the tall, stout Thracians. He had been told, however, that his eyes were his best feature–intelligent and deep, large and dark brown, matching the color of his hair.

The maidens in the king's court were not merely beautiful but splendid. Dressed in tunics of the finest fabrics and covered in jewelry from head to toe, they seemed to care greatly about every detail of their appearance. Trysimachus's eye sought them out every chance he had, but it was to not much avail. "The maidens here do not like me and are avoiding me," he said.

"'Course they are! It's 'cause the way you're behavin'! All high and mighty, lookin' down on everyone here. If ya don't accept us, how can ya expect for us to accept ya? It don't work like that!"

Pitros was right again, much to Trysimachus's irritation. That was exactly how he had been behaving.

But after all, he was an Athenian. A scholar. Someone who could read and write. Think and analyze. Of course he would be above his Thracian peers.

Yet it was getting more difficult to think that way. Even he had to admit that the Thracians' wisdom and knowledge was innate, coming from somewhere deep inside of them. They didn't view themselves as artists, but they were, and their artistry also came from somewhere deep inside.

This was a paradox to Trysimachus: the Thracians were crude and unrefined on one hand, but on the other, they had refined taste in music, poetry, and art. One only needed to look at the exquisite jewelry, ornamentations, and objects they made and used, or listen to the songs and poems they were creating—rhythmic, eloquent, and fluent, as if flowing from the heavens above. It was no wonder there were myths that even the beasts would stop to listen to Orpheus's lyre.

He was an Athenian, but he himself was not on par with the Thracians' artistry. He couldn't write fine verses. He couldn't sing or compose music. Nor could he craft elegant objects. How, then, was he above the people here?

"You are right, Pitros," the scholar admitted reluctantly. "I will do my best to be better than before. I still have much to learn about this life."

"Ain't that the truth, Trysimachus. To know life, you gotta

live it. Not just read 'bout it."

The warrior struck him hard on the shoulder. In the past, Trysimachus had been rather vexed by this habit of Pitros's. But now he welcomed the blow. He needed it.

After a long winter, the snow was slowly retreating to higher elevations as the falcons returned to Western Odrysia. A messenger on horseback was spotted approaching Ketriporis's residence, vigorously kicking his stallion, shrouded in a cloud of dust. The horns sounded as he rode into the fortress. He dismounted and was immediately ushered in to stand before the king.

"My king," he gasped. "The eastern realm's army, thirty thousand strong, has crossed the Hebros River and launched an attack on King Amadokus's coastal fortress at Doriscus."

So the day has come, thought Ketriporis. "Is General Charidemus leading the attack?"

"No, King Kersebleptes and General Bassaces are leading it. Charidemus and his mercenary force have not been seen."

Dismissing the messenger, the king commanded Medosades, who was standing by his side, to summon the council.

Generals, nobles, and advisors gathered in the main hall, eagerly awaiting word from their king. With a calm demeanor, King Ketriporis apprised his council of the news, causing a stir.

"Kersebleptes is bold indeed to violate the treaty and begin hostilities against the central realm! Such a large force indicates a major invasion," stated General Derzelas.

The king nodded in agreement.

"My king," asked General Pittacus, the army's second-in-command, "have the scouts seen another force of his moving northward, toward Amadokus's central lands?"

"They have not."

"With a single force from Doriscus, it is unlikely he would launch a full invasion on Amadokus's realm," Pittacus continued. "If that were the case, why did he not march north towards Mount Haemus? Why even cross the Hebros and lay siege to that fortress? I believe he intends to continue west, towards your great realm, my king."

"I agree," said Ketriporis. "It is no secret that Kersebleptes wishes to regain the lands he lost and re-unite them under his rule. It would make sense for him to seek to eliminate me first and then march into the heart of Amadokus's territory. He must think we are more vulnerable now after my father's death." The king scanned his advisors' faces. "Indeed, if Kersebleptes were to conquer Western Odrysia first, he could greatly enlarge his army. The tribes have little loyalty and would switch allegiance for gifts and promises. Amadokus would become easier prey."

"If his goal is to indeed attack us," Medosades said, "I suggest envoys be dispatched immediately to our garrison at the Nestos with new orders, additional supplies, and reinforcements. If Kersebleptes campaigns along the coast, there are only a few more forts standing in the way between Doriscus and your lands."

Calls of agreement echoed throughout the chamber.

"Amadokus's forts are strong. Even if Kersebleptes takes the fortress at Doriscus, his forts further west can still hold up," Prince Skostos said.

"I wish there were such a thing as an impenetrable fort, Skostos," Ketriporis replied. "But the question is not whether Kersebleptes will succeed in seizing those forts, but how long it will take. Lords, we must prepare! I shall not allow the great lands of my domain to fall to a king who disregarded his own oath to the gods!" His men pounded the table in agreement. "Derzelas, summon the mercenary groups you negotiated with. We shall discuss the matter of their pay later. Sura, you are to dispatch messengers to the paradynasts and chieftains of the tribes. We need them and their men here. Medosades, send those supplies and reinforcements to the garrison."

"Brother, is there news from Athens?" Spoiled by his older brothers and left to indulge in his favorite pursuits of hunting and archery, the king's youngest brother, Prince Spartacus, was rarely present at the councils. But this time, he had been summoned in Mononius's absence.

"No, there is not," replied Ketriporis.

"Does the absence of Charidemus at Doriscus mean that the decree has not been passed by the Athenians?"

"According to Mononius's last letter, the decree is still pending in their courts. Euthycles and Demosthenes's efforts to expose its vileness must have been effective."

"In that case, what about General Athenodorus, brother?" Spartacus asked.

"It is better to make plans that do not rely on Athenodorus and our other Athenian allies," replied Ketriporis. "Especially as Charidemus's supporters in Athens are still vigorously advocating the decree. I will send a messenger, but we must be prepared to fend off Kersebleptes by ourselves."

"Brother, we need Mononius back here," said Skostos.

"You are right. It appears his political efforts there are no longer necessary. Medosades, send an urgent message to Mononius instructing him to return immediately. We do not have much time to spare."

The court was swirling in a state of chaos, tension, and urgency. Messengers and envoys were coming and going almost hourly. The army was beginning to gather in the fields, with Trysimachus kept busy recording.

"My king," reported Medosades, "King Amadokus's fortress at Doriscus has fallen. His men are slain. The Easterners have passed Mount Serrium and Maroneia. But after Maroneia, their army has split. Part of the force is now besieging King Amadokus's forts at Lake Bistonis under the command of General Bassaces, while the other is marching north, led by King Kersebleptes, and taking the road from Maroneia deeper into Amadokus's lands."

Medosades reported that there was still no news on the whereabouts of General Charidemus or his mercenaries; the tribes in the region had been defeated while the Hellenic colonies on the coast had been spared. The king ordered the council to be summoned again, and new discussions about Kersebleptes's intentions ensued.

"If Kersebleptes is marching north, then his target is indeed Amadokus," said Lord Teres. "Perhaps he wants to fulfill his grandfather's wish to take revenge on Amadokus's line. I believe Bassaces will move his men northward and reinforce Kersebleptes after taking those forts."

"Lords, there is nothing simple and straightforward about Kersebleptes," Ketriporis replied. "I feel there is something more to this action. The prophet saw in his latest vision a warrior wearing a golden mask, with a flaming spear pointing toward the Edonian plain."

"My king, there is a new report!" Sura shouted as he entered the hall.

"Speak!"

"The forts at Lake Bistonis have fallen. General Bassaces's force is moving west."

"West? Not north?"

"Yes, my king. His men are near Abdera and approaching the Nestos."

"What do you think, General Pittacus?"

"My king, it is possible that Kersebleptes is planning to invade Amadokus's realm and yours simultaneously."

"Without Bassaces's men, Kersebleptes's force is not on par with that of Amadokus," Ketriporis replied. "I cannot fathom why he would attempt such a foolish strategy. I suspect that Kersebleptes is trying to confuse us by making us think he will attack Amadokus."

"My king," General Derzelas asked, "should not we start moving our force toward the Nestos? It would be advantageous to meet them at the river and cut off their advance. Our fort there can hold them for some time, but not forever."

"Caution, Derzelas. Maybe luring us there is exactly Kersebleptes's plan. I am especially concerned, as General Charidemus and his men have still not been seen."

The warriors were not overcome by weariness. The discussions and planning continued late into the night.

Hardly able to sleep since the forts at Lake Bistonis had fallen, Ketriporis awaited new reports as he continued to strategize. The king had ordered his advisors to immediately inform him of Prince Mononius's return. So, upon hearing the horns announce his arrival, Ketriporis rushed to the gate to welcome and embrace his brother.

Then, without giving Mononius a chance to rest, Ketriporis began questioning him eagerly about the happenings in Athens.

"Tell me, were there any talks of General Charidemus leaving Kersebleptes's service?"

"None, and it does not seem likely. But you must know that he now commands a fleet. His most ardent supporter, Aristocrates, argued before the Assembly that his new fleet is yet another reason why Athens should bestow special privileges upon Charidemus."

"A fleet? This is grave news. That could be the reason why he has not been seen with Kersebleptes. But you look tired from the journey, brother. Get some rest. You know how much I rely on your advice and strength."

The first rays of the morning sun pierced through the king's quarters. Frowning as he paced back and forth, Ketriporis's thoughts were interrupted by a panting Medosades.

"My king, a messenger has just arrived," the advisor announced.

"Quickly, let him in."

"My king!" The messenger began. "The scouts have reported that the force led by King Kersebleptes has disappeared."

"What do you mean by that?"

"The king's army is nowhere in sight, its whereabouts unknown. It seems to have vanished."

How could that be? "What else?"

"That is all, my king."

"You are dismissed," Ketriporis said. He slammed his fists on the table, causing a golden goblet to fall and roll onto the floor.

An army that large cannot just vanish! Are the gods truly on Kersebleptes's side? No, there must be something else. Something I need to remember.

Think, Ketriporis, think.

During his western campaign, did not Kotys forge a secret path deep within the mountains, and did he not launch a surprise attack on the Sapaeans from behind? Kersebleptes must know of it. That must be it!

Ketriporis began to believe that General Bassaces's force was just a decoy to lure his army toward the Nestos, while Kersebleptes would quietly enter his realm from the secret passage. Still, something was making him uneasy.

Charidemus! The king was growing more and more certain that with his new fleet the mercenary would arrive by sea. And that instead of docking at Neapolis, he would dock on the other side of Mount Pangaion, at Galepsos.

"Medosades, Sura, sound the horns!" the king shouted.

"Gather the chieftains, lords, and generals. Here are my orders! Sura, summon the court musicians and the dressmakers."

"The musicians and dressmakers, my king?"

"Yes, hurry! Medosades, gather the women slingers and archers. Also, gather the women with the highest, strongest, and shrillest voices you can find. They shall be placed under Skostos's command. Tell the prince to take the Athenian scholar with him too. Skostos will be the one to 'greet' Kersebleptes and 'welcome' him to the western realm."

The horns sounded, and the king's residence erupted into chaos as men and women alike were mobilized into action.

"General Pittacus, gather the army. We shall be marching to the Edonian plain in the early morning."

"Are we to meet Bassaces's force at the Nestos?"

"There will be only a small force going to the Nestos. Send dispatches to the garrison in the fort as well as an urgent message to Abruporis the Sapaean. Order the men going there to build and maintain fires at all times and to march around in a large circle. This will give the Easterners the impression that the bulk of our force is camped at the Nestos."

It was a stormy day in western Thrace. Dark clouds were hanging low in the sky, completely obscuring the peaks of Mount Orbelus. As thunder rumbled above, King Ketriporis and twenty thousand men began the march south toward the great Edonian plain. His army of conscripted men, mercenaries, and volunteers—including entire clans and families—trampled over the fields, passing by villages and sanctuaries, and crossing streams, valleys, and forests. The further south they marched, the more the sky brightened and the balmier the weather became.

When they reached the river Angites, King Ketriporis signaled the army to halt. "General Derzelas, this is where we part ways. Kersebleptes will have a surprise awaiting him when he emerges from the secret path."

"My king, the lives of my men and myself are pledged to you. And to the defense of the great western domain."

"With Ares's help, we shall be victorious. You know what to do. May the gods be with you."

"And with you, my king."

Derzelas, leading half of the king's army, headed east to meet King Kersebleptes's forces as they emerged from the secret mountain path.

Ketriporis and the remainder of his army continued south

through the Edonian plain until a new report halted them: General Charidemus's mercenary force, a fleet of forty ships now at anchor, had indeed sailed to Galepsos. His men—five thousand hoplites and three thousand peltasts—were bringing supplies ashore, ready to march.

"With such a force, he will surely come through the Valley of the Pierians. What think you, Lord Sadalas?"

"I agree, my king. The coastline to Neapolis is too steep, and the route around Mount Pangaion too long and risky because of the Macedonians."

"Let him come. How astonished he will be to discover that instead of ambushing us from behind, it is he who will be ambushed. Not only will we cut him off from his master, we must make sure his force does not even reach the Edonian plain. Sura, inform the generals, the officers, and the lords: we shall be moving in the direction of the Pierian Valley."

And so Ketriporis, leading a force of 3,500 light cavalry, 500 heavy cavalry, 3,500 peltasts, 1,500 javelineers, and 1,000 archers, slingers, and rock-throwers, began his march southwest. His army was moving fast, halting only for a short time after receiving word that General Charidemus's army had indeed entered the Pierian Valley. Gathering the council, Ketriporis laid out his plan for victory.

"Honorable lords, where the Pierian Valley narrows in the east but is still hilly on either side, we will ambush Charidemus's force," he explained.

"What about Charidemus himself?" asked Mononius. "As the decree in Athens is still pending in the courts, would it not be best to keep him alive?"

"Although I would like to have his head, your advice is wise. Officers, relay to your men that, per my command, Charidemus is to be left unharmed. And now, we must make haste. With the gods, we march forward!"

When the sun was about to set, Ketriporis's army arrived

at the eastern end of the Pierian Valley, well before the Euboean's mercenary force.

"General Pittacus," Ketriporis commanded, "position the peltasts, archers, and slingers on the slopes. And make sure those ditches are dug. Lord Sadalas, line up the cavalry."

"My king, the men you sent have captured General Charidemus's scouts," Sura reported.

"Very well. Give the scouts a bag of gold each," the king replied. "We must ensure they send a message to Charidemus's force that the passage is clear."

"As you order, my king."

XXXVIII

While the king's preparations were underway, the mercenary force of General Charidemus was moving northeast. Through the Valley of the Pierians between Mount Pangaion and Mount Symbolon they went, following the road the Persians had built during the time of Xerxes and his march through Thrace. Alongside their supply train, approximately eight thousand soldiers marched in twelve columns.

The force consisted of thirty lochoi of heavy-armored hoplites from all over Hellas, carrying large, round shields and spears. In addition, there were thirty lochoi of peltasts from Hellas, Thrace, and Asia Minor, carrying javelins, short swords, and crescent shields in the Thracian style. And finally, there were roughly two thousand infantrymen who had adopted a relatively new fighting style that combined the defensive prowess of the hoplites with the more agile movements of the peltasts, a method devised by Charidemus's former mentor, Iphicrates of Athens, who had also served as a commander for Kersebleptes's father, Kotys. These men were armed with smaller oval shields, longer spears, and swords, and they wore lighter cuirasses for protection.

With this force, the general was eager to reach the Edonian plain and launch a surprise attack on the western realm, seeking to take revenge on the man who had embarrassed him in the chariot race and whose father had defeated him during the Odrysian civil war. Charidemus was thirsty to bring about the downfall of the two kings standing in the way of a powerful and united realm, one in which he would wield even greater power.

His army camped in the valley overnight and resumed its march when the first trace of the rising sun appeared in the sky. The terrain made for an easy journey. The soldiers were careful not to disturb the settlements of the Pieri, wishing to cross the valley without trouble or delay. A feeling of confidence and zeal permeated the ranks; jokes were shared and laughter resounded.

Moving with great speed, they were getting closer to the passage into the Edonian plain... when the ground began to shake. The hoplites heard the sound of galloping hooves, which grew louder and louder. And suddenly, with the speed of an arrow, two large cavalry forces simultaneously pierced the front and rear ranks of the marching columns.

Charidemus's officers shouted, "Close up the ranks! Double the depth!" But it was too late—in what seemed like the blink of an eye, the cavalry of the western realm sliced through Charidemus's outer ranks. At the very front rode King Ketriporis himself, clad in gold armor and steering a golden chariot drawn by two horses. Illuminated by the rays of the rising sun, he plowed through the hoplites like a ball of fire, the spiked axles of his chariot's wheels ripping through shields, armor, and flesh.

Right behind the king galloped fourteen rows of riders, each wider than the previous by two additional men, forming an arrow-like wedge. The western cavalry was trampling over the hoplites and throwing javelins at them as they tried to flee.

The king's cavalry shot like a lightning bolt through the first ten lochoi of hoplites, breaking through the columns and giving them no opportunity to form their phalanxes. Then, before the soldiers had a chance to regroup, the mostly intact cavalry unit split into two. Half the riders steered their horses to the left and the other half to the right, sweeping over the flanks.

The hoplites at the rear were faring no better. At the tip of the cavalry wedge, cutting through the rear from behind, rode Prince Mononius. He was the last thing some of the soldiers would ever see. His troops pierced through the ranks of Charidemus's bewildered men, giving them no opportunity to take formation. Then, following the same pattern as his brother, the prince's unit split in two, further forcing the men on the flanks to scatter and run for their lives. Meanwhile, confusion was spreading amongst Charidemus's mercenaries in the mid-ranks of the marching columns, who could tell that trouble was besieging them at the front and rear.

A trumpet sounded. The attacking cavalry retreated. But then, from the hills on both sides of the road, King Ketriporis's peltasts emerged, protected by their crescent shields and with javelins in hand. After another signal from the trumpet, they hurled their weapons, showering the now-formed phalanxes and units of Charidemus's army.

"Spread out! Thin the formation!" Charidemus's peltast officers ordered, frantically trying to reduce the number of men being hit by the javelins while the hoplite phalanxes tried to hold tight.

The trumpet sounded again, and the western peltasts started to retreat back up the hills.

"After them! Do not let them get away!" General Charidemus commanded.

The youngest and most agile among the Euboean's army, who had been specially trained for this purpose, ran up the hills after the retreating peltasts, only to see King Ketriporis's men disappear. It was as if they were being swallowed by the earth.

Unable to see where the western peltasts had vanished to, Charidemus's men launched their javelins into the air. But there was no sign of any impact—indeed, the javelins seemed to disappear altogether, as if carried off by the wind. And so the men continued running further up the slopes, eager to trap the western peltasts and slaughter them in close combat.

But then, as if arising from the core of the earth itself, thousands of men and women from the king's realm sprung up and barraged the soldiers with arrows, sling-bullets, and stones. Many of Charidemus's men were lethally wounded, their bodies rolling back down the steep slopes. The remainder retreated hurriedly.

The western peltasts leapt out of the ditches in which they had been hiding to chase after the retreating men. Followed by the javelineers, archers, and slingers, they resumed their assault on the phalanxes and the peltast units of Charidemus's army.

Trapped on all sides and outnumbered, the eastern realm's mercenary force had nowhere to retreat or hide.

"Close foot! Close to the right! Move to the left!" the officers frantically commanded.

But the constant barrage was beginning to break the resistance of even the toughest phalanxes. With General Charidemus's army thinned out and weakened, the western peltasts, wielding their swords, descended onto the road like a pack of wolves and engaged the disorganized force in close combat.

The sun rose higher as the battle continued to rage, the sky itself taking on a darker shade of blue. Blood was spilling, and weapons, bodies, and horses were falling to the ground. Shouts and screams filled the air. The noise was loud, the gory stench omnipresent, and the soldiers' visibility was clouded by the surrounding dust.

Seeing that his force had no chance to claim victory, General Charidemus retreated, left unharmed per the king's command.

The secret path that King Kersebleptes had traveled with his force to launch a surprise attack on the western realm was treacherous for men. Beasts lurked in the forests, there was a general lack of water, except for the occasional stream, and not only was the tree cover dense, but the trail was long and covered in thick fog and mist, making for weak visibility and giving it a rather mystical appearance.

By order of King Ketriporis, Prince Skostos had taken fifty riders, including Trysimachus, and a hundred women to hide along the trail. While waiting for Kersebleptes's force, Prince Skostos sent the women high into the trees and deep into the recesses of the rocks. They were armed with slings, stones, or bows and arrows, and some were dressed in rather peculiar outfits.

When the force arrived, Skostos's men used the fog as cover and followed the prince's orders to slip amongst the ranks of King Kersebleptes unnoticed. Mingling with the soldiers, they began spreading the tale of how the goddess Bendis herself had carved the secret passage through the forest for the great Odrysian king Sitalkes, personally guiding his force. And they warned the soldiers that no other king, general, or lord had ever been permitted to use it since. To further frighten them, especially the foreign mercenaries, the men from the west told tales of the nymphs, muses, and other mystical creatures who lived in the forest and guarded the secret passage into the western realm through which they were now trespassing.

With men and horses clad in special garments made of fabric the color of the mountain mist, Skostos's force attacked the flanks and rear of Kersebleptes's already exhausted, thirsty, and unnerved army, spreading horror amongst his men. One by one his soldiers fell, struck not only by swords but also by the slings, arrows, and stones of the women hidden in the fog-covered trees above.

The sounds emerging all around the forest, as if from deep down in the underworld, terrified the soldiers. Loud and deep, high-pitched and low, howling, thundering, screaming, and screeching—it sounded as if an army of ferocious beasts and demons were approaching. Penetrating cries and eerie whispers were echoing through the trees. Their frightening nature was the splendid work of King Ketriporis's court musicians.

Meanwhile, Skostos's men were attacking the frightened eastern army. Cowering within the ranks, Trysimachus could hear cries of horror coming from Kersebleptes's men, some refusing to go any further. When the fog began to lift, at a signal from Prince Skostos, a woman dressed as a huntress and pointing an arrow at the men suddenly appeared on top of a boulder.

"'Tis the goddess Bendis herself coming to take revenge on us!"

The men ran as chaos spread amongst the ranks. Kersebleptes and his officers tried to rally the soldiers by shouting, "Get a hold of yourselves, men! It is just a trickery! Just a trickery!"

"How is this trickery?" the soldiers shouted in return. "The goddess's invisible army is attacking us! How can we fight and stand against what we cannot see?"

A cavalryman from Skostos's ranks, wearing heavy armor, appeared in front of the already frightened army. With torches lit behind him, he held his sword high in his left hand, and it looked as though ablaze.

"It is the Horseman! Run, men, run! Heros Karabazmos is coming to avenge the lands!"

Men ran for their lives in all directions, hit continually by stones and arrows from the trees.

Skostos's forces pressed their attack as more fear spread through the ranks of Kersebleptes's army, and the men refused to continue marching further.

The officers were trying hard to rally the soldiers, and Kersebleptes himself was shouting, "It is a trickery! It is a trickery! Get back! Close formation!" But once ignited, the panic amongst the ranks spread like fire.

Seeing the women sporadically appear and disappear in the mist, dressed in their ethereal outfits, the terrified men cried, "Did you see the nymph? Or maybe it was a muse? No, it was a nymph! The nymphs and the muses look angry! Will we be able to survive? No, we shall perish! Retreat, retreat!"

Skostos ordered two of his cavalrymen to cover their horses. Bare-chested, wearing wreaths around their foreheads and with bows and arrows in hand, they mounted their horses backward and emerged from the thinning mist, pointing their arrows at the already frightened soldiers.

"It is the centaurs guarding the passage! Run! Run!"

The haunting singing of the women continued. Stones and arrows rained down on Kersebleptes's soldiers as rumors of an army of ghost riders spread amongst the ranks.

"We are almost at the end of the passage! Hold on, men, hold on!" his officers shouted, their voices hoarse. "Just a few more stadia behind those trees is the open field! Hold on, men! We are almost there! Victory and glory shall be ours!"

Now the army was no longer marching but running

toward the end of their horrifying journey. And when they emerged from the forest, instead of finding the relief they so desperately sought, they found themselves face-to-face with the peltast and cavalry units of General Derzelas, who had been waiting for them.

By Derzelas's order, the first rank of peltasts ran toward the exhausted men and hurled their javelins. Then they ran back, followed by the second rank, then the third, and others. Faced with such attacks, many of the Easterners—despite their officers' orders to close formation, chase after the peltasts, or retreat—were choosing to throw down their weapons and surrender. They were unwilling to risk reentering the haunted forest.

King Kersebleptes, however, closely surrounded by his heavy-mounted bodyguards, retreated back to the secret passage, disappearing out of sight.

As for Trysimachus, he felt that not only had the men from Western Odrysia emerged victorious, but so had he, himself, despite having never so much as raised a sword.

Meanwhile, the massive ambush in the Pierian Valley had been a resounding victory for the Western Odrysian realm. The king's warriors, exhilarated by their triumph, were feasting, dancing, and singing over the battlefield, which was strewn with the bodies of Charidemus's men.

The celebrations lasted through the night. But the king himself was preoccupied with thoughts of what was to come. He summoned Sura.

"Any news from the Nestos?" the king asked.

"The garrison is holding up against General Bassaces's siege, my king."

"This is welcome news."

"There is also a report of sickness spreading throughout

Bassaces's camp. I guess his men are not used to the swamps and the weather in this part of the land."

"That favors us. Sura, we will march in the morning. Send a message to Abruporis of the Sapaeans informing him that we will be coming through the pass. We cannot allow the Easterners to claim victory on our land."

It was late the next morning when the king's battle-hardened, but still intoxicated warriors began their march out of the Pierian Valley in the direction of the Symbolon pass to aid the garrison on the Nestos.

The young king was moving forward as fast as he could. Much was still at stake. Not just for himself as king, but for the divine fate of Odrysia and the future of western Thrace. At the first pass crossing Mount Symbolon, Abruporis, chief of the Sapaean tribe, welcomed him. Though the Sapaeans remained independent, they had always been fierce allies.

"Great and honorable King Ketriporis, my warriors and I are pledged to you and ready to join you for another victory over our common enemy."

"My gratitude to you, Abruporis. With the gods, we will chase away the remainder of Kersebleptes's army from our sacred lands. And now, we march to another victory."

"As you command, Ketriporis."

Reaching the coastal plain near the Nestos where General Bassaces's army had set up camp, the combined forces of Ketriporis and his Sapaean allies hid in the nearby forest, careful not to alert the watchmen. The warriors waited for dark to come, planning their attack.

It was very late in the night when they made their move. The gods had aided the warriors by giving them a moon shrouded in clouds and a starless sky. And so, when General Bassaces's camp had quieted down and most of his unsuspecting soldiers were asleep, King Ketriporis's force crept silently and surrounded the camp. Launching a surprise attack, they showered the camp with thousands of arrows under cover of night.

Then, spears in hand, the king's cavalry burst through the camp, followed by the peltasts, their swords drawn and ready for combat. Meeting less resistance than they had expected, King Ketriporis claimed another victory.

Thus concluded the Eastern Odrysian realm's failed invasion and conquest of the young king's domain. With his men ready to return to their homes, Ketriporis and the remainder of his force rode back. Upon their arrival, the king was greeted by Medosades, who had been left behind to guard the residence, and informed him that stability still reigned in Western Odrysia.

- FORTY -
2016

IT WAS SATURDAY. A BREAK FROM HIS TREATMENTS. Felix Svoboda headed to Nouméa's centrally located Malongo Café for his favorite breakfast, a mocha and Eggs Benedict. The café had become his go-to place on the weekends. Popular with locals and tourists alike, it was crowded. He waited for a table patiently. And as he did, his thoughts inevitably drifted back to *The Mask*—this time to King Ketriporis's expanding role in the story. The more he read back through the manuscript, the more he felt like he was becoming an observer of himself through his writing—and better equipped to understand his true self in the process.

Once he was seated and served his order, he sipped his mocha. The aroma and taste of the coffee stirred up his senses and transported him back to another place. To his days spent at the Black Bean in New York.

It had been at that time, after reconnecting with Dipesh, when a new chapter in his life had begun. Zenon McClow had transformed into a warrior and strategist. Adopting a new persona and point of view, he had fought against his enemies, like King Ketriporis had done in *The Mask*. For him, those enemies had been corporate greed, injustice, and a rigged society. Certain of the logic and justifiability of his actions, Zenon had felt that he'd emerged victorious.

Then he had met them. Mr. Clifton and Evmondia. And a new fight had commenced.

That fight had turned tougher than the previous, as it had been against himself.

After breakfast, Felix walked to Rue de Sebastopol and mingled with the tourists there, observing the flow of life around him. The street was busy with shoppers hunting for haute couture, French perfumes, designer jewelry, accessories, and home decor. From there, he turned left onto Rue de L'Alma. A new window display at Hypecorner caught Felix's eye. He stopped for a moment, as if a decade had passed since he'd first walked into an upscale men's store in Manhattan to buy his Armani suit.

The suit had set him back thousands of dollars, but when he'd wrapped himself in it, he'd felt invincible. It had become his armor, and together with aplomb, it was his ticket to Phil Brawclad's exclusive club. His ticket to the gold.

- FORTY-ONE -
2015

DRESSED IN A GLEN PLAID ARMANI SUIT, ZENON LOOKed around the suite at the W Hotel in Union Square. He was satisfied. Renting it was a small investment compared to the returns he planned to reap from his meeting with Phil Brawclad.

Zenon was confident that everything he had ordered, from the champagne to the caviar hors d'oeuvres, was perfect. His experience on the ships and in the restaurant business was coming in handy; he knew the best products, and he knew how to stage a room.

"It's showtime," he whispered to himself as he stood in front of the mirror.

Every strand of his dark hair was in its place. His eyes, a fusion of sapphires and emeralds, shone with determination. His even, bleached teeth sparkled, making his smile even more attractive. And his broad shoulders filled the tailored coat to perfection.

There was a knock at the door: three sharp blows in quick succession, the sound of a man accustomed to being awaited and welcomed. Zenon waited ten seconds before crossing the room and opening the door for Brawclad. He assessed the other man quickly, as he would a guest at the restaurant.

Phil looked just like he had in the videos. He wore his light reddish hair close-cropped, and a dimple dotted the chin of his freckled face. He was stocky—an athlete in college, no doubt—with gray eyes and a broad, square jaw.

"Mr. McClow, it's a pleasure. Phil Brawclad. Thank you for meeting with me."

Brawclad flashed a practiced smile at him as they shook hands. Zenon was surprised by the strength of his guest's firm grip. He matched it with the same strength.

"Good to meet you, too," he replied, his tone a mix of a maître d's servility and a frat bro's confidence. "Please come in, make yourself comfortable." He gestured toward the sofa.

"Thank you." Brawclad sat down and took in his surroundings. "You're a difficult person to get in touch with, Mr. McClow."

Zenon smiled winningly. "I'm sorry it's taken us so long to get together, but I've been out of the country, and I would never pitch you something serious over the phone or by email."

"Of course."

"So, what do you think I can do for you, Mr. Brawclad?"

"Well, Dipesh—I understand the two of you were classmates?—he left your card with me and mentioned that you're working on integrating trading with artificial intelligence technology. I assume he told you about our company, Accruement Finance, and what we do there."

"He told me a few things, but nothing that would break confidentiality or constitute insider trading." Zenon knew he had to establish that he could be trusted.

"So as you may know, I'm always interested in finding new and innovative investment tools I can offer to my members. And once I find something that yields meaningful results, I grab on." Looking Zenon in the eye, Brawclad declared, "To get straight to the point, Mr. McClow, I'm very interested in your artificial intelligence-based trading system. After Dipesh explained it to me, I became fascinated by its potential."

"Are your members trading in areas where it will have a real impact? I'm confident of my method's power, but only if it's employed properly."

Brawclad skipped blithely past the warning. "At Accruement Finance, we're all about making money by helping others make money. That doesn't only apply to our clients and members, but also to our partners and affiliates."

Zenon stared directly at Brawclad, maintaining an expression of confident neutrality.

"I was hoping we could help each other out by striking a deal," Brawclad said. "One that would not just be profitable for me, but also for yourself."

Zenon replied, "I'm happy to make a presentation to your clients, if you can guarantee a baseline level of buy-in. I mean, if they're not going to be interested, it's not worth your time to bring me over, and it won't be worth my time to come."

Brawclad smiled and took the glass of champagne Zenon offered, sipping it slowly. Zenon saw the other man's gaze land on the laptop open on the desk just over his shoulder. The screen was displaying a rapid series of trades.

Brawclad pointed at the laptop. "What am I looking at here?"

"Hong Kong dollars to yuan."

"What are the factors influencing your strategy?"

"I don't want to say too much. Most of it is information anyone could access... if they could read Cantonese. But there's some secret sauce, of course." He smiled but decided winking would be a step too far.

"Dipesh tells me you spend a lot of time in Asia. You like it there?"

"Hong Kong's a beautiful city. It's like walking around in

the future. But I must say, I've always had a certain weakness for New York. I always enjoy coming back here. There are things New York can offer that nowhere else in the world has, and of course, access to investors like yourself is crucial."

"You sound like my kind of guy. I understand you have quite a team of AI rock stars working with you."

"Yes, you could say that. But nothing is done without my input. I have the final say."

"Dipesh sold me on you pretty hard, and if I'm being honest, I was a little doubtful coming in, but from what I'm seeing on that screen, and the overall sense of you that I'm getting now, I'm thinking there's a partnership arrangement that will work out very well for both of us."

Zenon made the kind of face he'd seen wives make at the restaurant, when their husbands were talking about something that didn't interest them much, but they wanted to appear engaged. Brawclad continued. "How about this? If you allow our members to trade using your system—"

"It's proprietary, so I can't allow you to run my software on your end," Zenon interrupted. "You'd have to be able to send your customers to me."

"And you take a percentage?"

"Yes, but nothing exorbitant. In line with standard brokerage house fee schedules."

"Our company has a good reputation. This could boost your profile in the industry. Other companies might come knocking at your door. Can you give me some kind of guarantee of exclusivity, for a year, say?"

Zenon laughed softly. "You're the first person I've talked to about any kind of collaboration, and I'm highly selective myself, so yes, we'll put it on paper, but I can give you a year where you'll be the only firm whose clients will be trading through my system."

"Great. Let's talk details soon."

"I'm leaving the country again at the end of the week, but I'll be in touch once I'm back."

The two men stood up and shared another handshake, and Brawclad left the hotel without a backward glance.

Zenon wasn't going anywhere, of course. He needed a month or so to develop a more sophisticated version of the animation Brawclad had seen scrolling on the laptop screen. He needed something interactive enough to function as a live demonstration so that he could make a presentation to Brawclad's management and sales teams that would have them lining up to funnel their clients his way.

He stayed under the radar as much as possible, dyeing his hair a slightly different color and growing a mustache while continuing his work at the restaurant. Brawclad wasn't a patron, but down the road he didn't want someone to whom he was presenting his 'trading system' to recognize him as the man who'd led him to his table the night before.

When everything was as good as his developers could make it, he reached out to Dipesh to set up a second meeting with Brawclad. He knew something that Brawclad didn't: his former schoolmate was quietly preparing to leave for Singapore for his wedding.

Zenon's window would be in the period immediately following Dipesh's departure. He would put Brawclad on the spot, and sell him and his team on the system before Dipesh's replacement was in place. Brawclad would be forced to make a final decision and strike a deal immediately, based on the limited evidence Zenon would craft for him.

Zenon was gambling with the valuable knowledge that, contrary to his own claims, Brawclad relied on others to do his research for him, Dipesh most of all. Zenon had laid the trap, but ultimately Phil would trap himself—not reluctantly, but eagerly.

- FORTY-TWO -

"AND THAT, LADIES AND GENTLEMEN, IS OUR SYSTEM in a nutshell. Our artificial intelligence learns from its own mistakes. It adjusts and adapts, making better decisions today than yesterday, generating better results quarter after quarter, year over year. The question is not whether we will beat the market; it's by how much... and whether you want in." Zenon paced the hotel ballroom's small stage confidently as he addressed the Accruement Finance sales team and a select group of the company's top patrons, with Brawclad observing keenly from the side of the room.

All eyes were on him. The room was silent, except for the sound of his voice. He paused and looked around. A low murmur began to rise in volume.

Since he had begun speaking, he had been using an old performer's trick, focusing on a spot in the middle of the audience in order to give the impression that he was making direct eye contact. It conveyed honesty, and he needed that on his side. But he'd been drawn again and again to the woman sitting in the second row. Was she beautiful or not? He couldn't tell. What was it about her that caught his attention? He'd had no time to figure it out.

"This is not something you should be offering to your low-end clients. The minimum buy-in is $500,000. AI is no longer the future; it's the present. And the smartest mind will win the game, whether man or machine. Thank you."

His presentation finished, Zenon stepped off the stage. People stood and poured in his direction, their imaginations running wild with the possibilities he had presented to them.

He glanced at the woman in the second row again. *She is not like the rest.* There was something about her that seemed unspoiled. She was still sitting in her chair. *Is she waiting to talk to me?*

Feeling excitement at the thought, he wanted to shoo away the people who swarmed around him like flies. Then he saw her rise from her seat. He was struck by her jet-black hair and large, emerald-green eyes, a color he'd never seen before. Her skin was as smooth as the finest porcelain.

An elderly man took her by the arm. He hadn't noticed the old fellow sitting next to her, but it was obvious that they were together.

Maybe she is his daughter? he thought.

While answering questions from the salespeople and keeping one eye on Brawclad, Zenon watched the two of them approach. The woman was moving with a feline grace as the old gentleman held her arm.

Brawclad peeled himself off the wall and approached just as a new group of employees and patrons was surrounding Zenon, wanting to discuss his system. When the boss pushed through, they fell silent.

"Mr. Clifton, it's a pleasure having you at our seminar," Brawclad exclaimed as he shook the old man's hand.

"Mr. Brawclad, it's a pleasure having your honored guests here in the city. Thank you for all you've done to bring us such cutting-edge investment strategies. Artificial intelligence! It's very intriguing."

Brawclad smiled and nodded. “Zenon, this is Mr. Clifton, one of Accruement Finance’s first and most important clients. Without him and his support, we wouldn’t be where we are today.”

Zenon shook his hand. “It’s nice to meet you, Mr. Clifton.”

Mr. Clifton’s enchanting companion did not utter a word but looked on with a curious gaze. Her profile reminded him of an ancient Greek or Roman statue.

“Thank you for the wonderful presentation, Mr. McClow,” Mr. Clifton remarked. “You and your associates are revolutionaries in the investment world.”

“Thank you, sir. I trust you’ll be investing with us?”

“I certainly will be, and I’m looking forward to the results.”

Brawclad intervened. “We’ll be having our reception shortly in the ballroom. I trust you and the beautiful young lady will join us.”

“That sounds excellent, Mr. Brawclad. But I need to sit down first. Old age...”

“Please do, Mr. Clifton. And Miss... what’s your name?”

“Evmondia Georgieva,” she replied, somewhat timidly.

Zenon detected an accent. But from where?

“Evmondia? That’s a beautiful name!” Phil replied, sounding rehearsed. “I look forward to speaking with you at the reception.”

Evmondia escorted Mr. Clifton back to their seats. Zenon disengaged from the sales teams—he needed to preserve an aura of mystery, of ‘proprietary technology’, around his operation. But he was confident that he would soon be floating on a cloud of commission payments.

Everything about the reception was slick and showy, the kind of corporate luxury Zenon had seen every night at the restaurant. It held little appeal for him; he couldn’t stop himself from scanning the room to find Evmondia.

“Oh, Zenon, there you are! I was wondering what happened to you." Brawclad approached him, holding a glass of champagne.

"Just needed to rest a bit after the presentation." Zenon was being truthful. He had gone upstairs to his room after circulating for a while, as fatigue had suddenly crept upon him. On one hand, he had enjoyed seeing how well everything was going. On the other, the acting he was doing and the front he was putting up were exhausting.

"My team is very excited to get started. We hit the ball out of the park on this one!" Brawclad declared. Beaming with pride, he patted Zenon on the back and then departed, wandering toward the bar.

Inevitably, sales team members and patrons were coming up to talk to him, but his searching eyes found Evmondia again. She was attending to Mr. Clifton, who was comfortably seated. And once more, Brawclad oozed up to them, irritating Zenon.

He wanted to get to know her better. But he knew he shouldn't. He couldn't let his mask crack and forced himself to look away. However, his mind returned to her.

He saw Brawclad trying to flag him down and invite him over to the table where Evmondia and Mr. Clifton were sitting. Somewhat reluctantly, cognizant of the danger, Zenon walked over and joined the conversation.

"I wanted to invite you both to brunch tomorrow morning," Mr. Clifton said as soon as he arrived. "I've much enjoyed this presentation, and I want to express my gratitude for the fantastic opportunity you're providing. I'd be honored if you could come."

Brawclad replied quickly, "I would love to, and I'm sure Mr. McClow would as well. Isn't that right, Zenon?"

Zenon intended to demur, but to his surprise, what came out of his mouth was totally different. "I would be happy to," he replied.

"It is settled then, gentlemen." Mr. Clifton handed them each his card. "See you tomorrow at eleven a.m.!"

Later that evening, back at his apartment, Zenon was relieved that the presentation had gone so smoothly. Brawclad and his team had bought into his fake AI trading system far more eagerly than he'd expected. Soon, millions of dollars would be flowing into his accounts. He couldn't feel sorry for them. As expected, they didn't seem to care about the warning he had slipped in about the potentially destructive effects of AI on the job market.

He had already chosen his destination. After being confined to the narrow corridors of the ships, and trapped in the narrow skyscraper-walled streets of New York, he was looking forward to Ecuador's lush mountain valleys. Then, after a couple of years in that beautiful hiding spot, stunning New Zealand awaited. Finally, he would get his long-overdue extra compensation. Zenon laughed out loud at the thought. He truly felt that life was great—until, unexpectedly, thoughts of Evmondia began to flash again in his mind. But even though he told himself that he didn't want to see her, inside, he was looking forward to the brunch. To meeting her one more time.

- FORTY-THREE -

THE NEXT MORNING, ZENON HEADED UPTOWN TO the posh Lenox Hill neighborhood. Framing part of Central Park, the residences here were known for their enchanting views. Zenon was often surprised by how quiet Manhattan's wealthiest neighborhoods were. You could barely tell you were in a city. It made sense that Mr. Clifton lived here.

The building matching the address on Mr. Clifton's card must have been at least sixty stories, with bellmen and concierge services, not to mention strict security. The lobby was welcoming and elegant. The elevator was spacious and played classical music.

You can smell the money here, Zenon thought as he made his way up to the fifty-fifth floor. Stepping out of the elevator, he headed down the hall to Clifton's door, rang the bell, and took a polite step back.

Evmondia opened the door. She smiled gently and invited him in. He entered the luxurious quarters, walking right behind her.

He felt a sensation he wasn't expecting, an unfamiliar vibe that disturbed the depths of his soul. To distract himself, he focused on her attire, which was conservative but tasteful, befitting her position as... nurse? Housekeeper? He realized he had no idea.

She showed him into a large living room with floor-to-ceiling curtains opened to reveal a vast picture window that overlooked the park. Zenon glanced down at the treetops.

"Mr. McClow, good to see you again! Please, make yourself at home," Mr. Clifton greeted him cheerfully. "Thank you for honoring me by accepting my invitation. You must be a busy man."

"It's my pleasure."

Brawclad, who had arrived before him, looked like he had already made himself at home and immediately joined the conversation. "Mr. Clifton, both Zenon and I are very happy to be here."

Mr. Clifton returned to a plush armchair while Zenon joined Brawclad on the sofa. Evmondia went to the kitchen, returning to offer them mimosas and morning pastries.

The room was elegant, furnished mostly with antiques, yet at the same time, there was a cozy feeling to it. An enormous rug, probably Persian, covered the hardwood floor. The massive windows gave the room plenty of natural light. Oil paintings of diverse subjects, some small, some enormous, decorated the walls. A large portrait of what appeared to be a younger Mr. Clifton in military uniform loomed over the room, dominating all the other art.

"Mr. McClow, I see you looking at the portrait over my head," the old gentleman remarked. "Most people think it is a picture of me at a younger age. In fact, it's a portrait of my father."

"Oh, you look very much alike," Zenon exclaimed. Then, trying to be polite, he added, "May I ask what kind of uniform he's wearing?"

"He's wearing a Second World War Royal Canadian Air Force uniform."

"So he was in the war," Zenon commented. Mr. Clifton nodded. "May I ask where he was deployed?"

"Both theaters of operation, but mainly the Pacific," Mr. Clifton replied, uttering a deep sigh. "His story was rather heroic, but very sad at the same time."

"Mr. Clifton, we would love to hear what happened to him, if you don't mind telling the story," said Brawclad.

"Gentlemen, as long as you don't mind an old man's babbling, I am happy to share. Are you of Irish descent, Mr. McClow? My father, John McCloskey, was."

Zenon wondered why Mr. Clifton didn't have the same last name as his father, but said nothing. Zenon's own family background was mixed and ambiguous. His father had told him McClow came from a Scottish ancestor, but he'd never seen so much as a photograph. "I believe my surname comes from Scotland."

"Ah, a fine place, Scotland. Always enjoyed my time golfing at St. Andrews. Bud—that was my father's nickname—was American, born in Pennsylvania, but he first served with the Royal Canadian Air Force as a senior instructor. He was a gifted pilot, so when the Second World War broke out, he was eager to join the war effort. What made him long to be in active combat was listening to the stories and adventures of his students returning from the battlefront. Plus, being young and hot-blooded, I believe he was seeking the thrill of war. Young men are always striving to prove themselves, to themselves as much as to the world. He finally got his break after further training in England. He flew some missions for Canada against the German Luftwaffe and managed to down some planes."

Mr. Clifton paused as if recalling something with fondness. He smiled almost to himself and continued.

"He wrote home about how he couldn't imagine getting up at 5:30 a.m. each day, as he used to return home that late sometimes. He kept his letters positive, avoiding the grim realities of his work. War is a terrible thing, gentlemen. There's just no way around it. After Pearl Harbor, when the States entered the war, he transferred to the U.S. Air Force in the Pacific. Bud became a captain in a Night Fighter Squadron, flying a P-61, if you're familiar with old planes."

Zenon nodded, just to keep the old man talking. He didn't know anything about warplanes.

"That's where he got his new nickname: Captain Mac. My father was a man of courage, honor, and morals. In fact, I have no hesitation in saying that he was a hero. Unfortunately, he perished when I was just four years old."

Mr. Clifton sighed deeply. Zenon folded his hands and intertwined his fingers. He was trying very hard to appear engaged in Mr. Clifton's story, but half the time, his focus was on Evmondia. He watched her as she sat with a delicate posture, listening graciously to the story, even though she must have heard it before. Gentle. Kind. Respectful. These were the adjectives to describe her—they floated in his mind. He had never observed anyone quite like her before.

Where is this girl from? he thought.

"One night, Captain Mac and two of his men took off from their base at Guadalcanal for a routine flight. They were in a twin-engine Douglas P-70A. Upon their return an hour later, something went terribly wrong. There was a motor failure on both sides. A smooth landing was not possible. Captain Mac knew that a ground crash would kill all three of them, so he 'kicked' his plane out to sea so at least his men would survive. He nose-dived the plane in such a way that he took the full impact of the crash. The plane went down in the sea. The two men in the aircraft with him managed to escape, but my father had sustained head injuries from the nosedive. He was rendered unconscious and couldn't get out.

"Several of the boys from the base went beyond the line of

duty in their attempts to rescue him. But the plane had gone too deep into the ocean, and my father sunk with it. You just never know when technology is going to malfunction. I'm not a big fan of most of the technology that keeps getting pushed these days, and haven't kept up much with the latest advances. But Mr. McClow, I can't tell you how excited I was about your presentation. About the concept of machine learning and artificial intelligence. Perhaps a technology with self-correcting abilities such as this can save lives. And perhaps, back then, if it were available in an airplane, it could have saved my father's life. That is why I will be investing in AI technology and in your trading system. To say I am looking forward to it would be an understatement."

"Thank you, Mr. Clifton. You won't be disappointed." It was Brawclad who responded first, while Zenon kept silent.

"I must say, I appreciate you taking all the necessary precautions to assure that the system operates properly," Mr. Clifton replied.

At that point, Mr. Clifton and Evmondia's eyes met. The old man nodded, and Evmondia got up and left the room.

"Well, gentlemen, I hope I am not ruining your appetite with my story."

"Not at all. We'd like to hear more," Brawclad responded.

"Our brunch will be ready soon. Hopefully, those snacks succeeded in holding your appetites. Now where was I? Oh, yes. The letter of condolence from his lieutenant stated that the squadron felt so hard hit by the loss of their leader that they strove to become a more powerful force. That they fought with more determination and zeal. War is tragic, no doubt about it. It affects and ruins so many lives, including innocent ones. Do you know what really tears me up, though? Before Bud went away for training, he told his mother, 'Every time you hear a plane overhead, just think it's me up there saying hello.' And my grandmother would pray 'happy landings' for him."

Zenon's original bemused tolerance for the old man's need to relate his family's history had been replaced by genuine interest. He was now engrossed in Mr. Clifton's story. The compelling nature of it had really taken him off-guard.

"It took just one 'unhappy' landing to ruin it all, didn't it? Bud was buried at Arlington National Cemetery. My grandparents established a memorial for him afterward. They had priests from all over the world, including the Pacific, hold prayers and masses for him. He died before his own grandmother did. Tragic. Just tragic.

"I was too young to get to know my father, but when I look up at that portrait, I admire him, and I feel like I know him well. He has been a great role model in my life. My mother remarried, and I was adopted into my stepfather's family. I must say that my stepfather, George Clifton, was very kind to me, and I probably wouldn't have attained the success I had without him."

He paused. "Well, I've been rambling again, haven't I? I hope I didn't bore you, gentlemen."

"Not at all. Actually, that was very interesting," Zenon replied, sincerely this time. It was obvious that Mr. Clifton was very proud of his father. Zenon thought of his own father and how much he used to look up to him. His heart started to naturally move toward Mr. Clifton. *Is it really right to... No, Zenon, shake it off. This is about the money.* He stopped himself in his tracks, figuratively speaking. He couldn't allow himself to feel empathy toward the man he was going to scam.

"It was a really touching story," Brawclad agreed.

"Thank you, Mr. Brawclad. The story of his life would make a good book, don't you think?"

"Ah, definitely. That story would probably generate a lot of sales for any publisher," the other man replied.

This guy can't think of anything without trying to find a

way to monetize it, Zenon thought, recognizing the irony.

Evmondia returned and announced that the food was ready. The four of them moved to the dining room. The large oak table was covered with a tablecloth featuring interesting embroidered designs in a style Zenon had never seen before. *Maybe it comes from Evmondia's country?* he wondered.

Several brown ceramic plates full of food were arranged along the table. The plates featured unique patterns similar to those on the tablecloth.

"Gentlemen, you're in for a treat today. Evmondia is a terrific cook, and she has prepared some traditional dishes from her country."

Zenon couldn't help himself any more. His curiosity was really starting to peak, so he turned to Evmondia and asked, "Where are you from?"

"I'm from Bulgaria," she replied straight-faced.

That was a country he never would have guessed. He had heard of it, of course, and had worked with men from that part of Europe on cruises, but he knew nothing of the region or the culture. "Ah, interesting," Zenon replied while forcing a smile. There was still something about her that captivated him. But was it in a good way or bad way? He couldn't tell. He was getting annoyed at how much she was affecting him. She was simply an obstacle he'd have to get through on his way to external freedom and internal paradise—just like Brawclad, Mr. Clifton, and all those investors he was about to fleece.

Evmondia introduced some of the Bulgarian dishes she had made. They bore names he would never remember, let alone pronounce properly. There were breads, pastries filled with feta cheese, stuffed peppers, special types of salads, and Bulgarian yogurt. Evmondia had also prepared some Bulgarian-style moussaka for them to try.

"It's different from the Greek version. It's potato-based and served with the yogurt," she explained. She smiled, and with a wave of her hand, invited them all to sample the foods. Zenon could tell she felt more comfortable and confident than the day before. Even her shoulders and arms seemed more relaxed.

"I find Bulgarian cuisine to be absolutely delicious," Mr. Clifton said. "Before I met Evmondia, I had never tried it. Now I look forward to every time she prepares it! Please, help yourselves, gentlemen."

The food certainly looked interesting, but Zenon was still focused on her. The way she spoke the words. Her tone of voice. *Snap out of it*, he told himself. Focusing on her was not helping or getting him anywhere.

"Evmondia, why don't you bring over some of that special jam I like?" Mr. Clifton asked.

She brought it in, and Mr. Clifton eagerly recommended it to Brawclad and Zenon. The jam appeared to be homemade; there was no label on the jar.

"Why don't you tell our guests where it comes from? I bet they've never tasted anything like it!"

"We have a place in the mountains near my hometown where wild strawberries grow. It is a tradition for my family to pick them and make a jam so we can enjoy them throughout the year. It's my favorite! Mr. Clifton has also developed a taste for it. I hope you will like it."

Brawclad chimed in. "Sounds like a beautiful place, Bulgaria. I know hardly anything about it." He added, "Maybe you can tell us about your place in the mountains. Do you have any pictures?"

On her phone, Evmondia showed them a picture of a forest with tall pine trees and wild strawberries growing between them. Zenon had always liked pine trees. They were majestic and stately; just the way he was trying to present himself. Then she showed them pictures of her hometown and explained that it was situated in a valley surrounded by three mountains. The valley was apparently rich in natural mineral springs. She also showed a picture of what the valley looked like in the winter. All covered in snow, it seemed truly magnificent. Zenon imagined what his next destination, Vilcabamba, would be like. He had seen some pictures—the valley and the mountains there, too, seemed spectacular, as quaint as Evmondia's hometown.

Bulgaria seemed like a charming and beautiful place, but it wouldn't work. Europe was not a safe place for him to hide.

Zenon could tell Evmondia missed her home by the way she seemed to vanish into nostalgic reveries at the sight of it. He didn't know why, but he was compelled to ask her why she'd moved here.

"Well, economics, basically. It's sad, because I love my country so much. The people, the nature, the history, the food... I wish to return someday. But Bulgaria's economic situation, while it's getting better, is still not very good. Plus there's a lot of corruption. It's a shame. So many people, young people especially, left the country to find better pay abroad.

"And the plight of the elderly is especially dire. Most of them can't survive on the small pensions they receive, so they rely on their relatives to help them out. Due to the generosity of Mr. Clifton, I can really help my family."

Mr. Clifton interjected, "I've always wanted to do more, but this young lady here doesn't let me. She can be quite stubborn."

Evmondia, who had sat down next to Mr. Clifton, smiled and patted his hand. Zenon detected real warmth and care in her gaze, which was directed toward the old man.

They're more like a father and daughter than an employer and caregiver.

"You've already done so much for me and all the other people you've helped worldwide by donating to all those charities."

"Thank you, my dear. Still, I wish to do more. Why don't you tell the two gentlemen about your dream?"

Evmondia said, "I've always wanted to help the elderly back home who are struggling. One day, when I return, I want to start my own organization to give them care and support. They deserve to spend their golden years with dignity. Especially the ones who are alone and helpless."

Zenon didn't know how to respond to those statements. So what came out was, "I've met some Bulgarians—well, during my travels. They were all very nice."

"I'm glad to hear it, Mr. McClow," Evmondia exclaimed. "We Bulgarians have a bad reputation, especially in Western Europe, because of a few people who have committed crimes and made the news. But the news doesn't show that most of us are honest, hardworking people, just like everyone else. I know for sure that most Bulgarians are good people. It's the circumstances we have found ourselves in that have not always been easy."

Zenon nodded. He was struck by her words. Just like him, she had left her home to seek a better life. Evmondia, however, was making it clear that, unlike him, she still loved where she had come from, and loved the people there very much. Yet, at the same time, she was quite aware of their problems and shortcomings. Zenon wished he could have been proud to be American in the same way she was proud to be Bulgarian.

But it was too late for that. He couldn't look back. Vilcabamba awaited.

After a moment, Brawclad asked, "So, why the USA?"

"What I've always liked about America is that in many ways the people here are more open-minded and accepting of other peoples and cultures. That's not the case everywhere. Also, there's an established Bulgarian community here in the city. It made things easier. I studied English in school, and that helped too."

After the meal was finished and Evmondia had cleared the table, the four of them retreated to the living room.

"I hope you liked the food," she remarked.

"Different and delicious!" Brawclad responded.

"It was great," Zenon agreed. In reality, he'd been so distracted by Evmondia during the meal that he had hardly focused on the taste of the food.

The ensuing moment of silence was interrupted by a question from Brawclad. "Ev-mon-dia... such a beautiful name. Is it popular in Bulgaria?"

"Actually, it's not popular at all. I'm not sure there's anyone else in Bulgaria called Evmondia. I was teased quite a bit and made fun of by the other kids while growing up because of it. They thought it was weird."

Her name is as intriguing and exotic as she is, Zenon thought.

Evmondia glanced at him as if she had heard his silent comment. "My parents were historians and archaeologists in Bulgaria. Their specialty was Ancient Thrace. Evmondia was a Thracian name, so in honor of their work, they named me that. Have you ever heard of the Thracians?"

Zenon hesitated, and Evmondia asked a follow-up question. "What about Spartacus? The gladiator slave who led an uprising against the Romans?"

Zenon nodded.

"He was a Thracian, actually."

"Oh, I remember now. The movie *Spartacus*, with Kirk Douglas, is one of my favorites. Have you seen it?" Brawclad asked.

Evmondia shook her head.

"I'd recommend it. So ancient Thrace was located in Bulgaria?"

"Yes, the Thracians were in Bulgaria, and also parts of Greece, Turkey, Romania, and other countries as well. They were fascinating people." She smiled and added playfully, "Of course I feel this way, being raised in a history-obsessed household."

Zenon listened with interest, but he was anticipating the moment when he could escape from Clifton's home. His feelings were mixed and dissonant. Or maybe he couldn't tell what he was really feeling. On the one hand, he was absolutely fascinated by Evmondia. On the other, she was stirring up strange emotions in him. They were bothersome, and he wanted to get away from the stimuli so the feelings could stop.

What were they? He was starting to get frustrated.

Brawclad smiled at her and said, "I don't think I ever studied the Thracians in school. The Greeks and Romans, yes. You've got me curious now."

Zenon noticed that Evmondia immediately became enlivened and more animated. This subject was obviously a passion of hers.

"The Thracians were quite mysterious," she replied. "Even we Bulgarians, who live on their ancient lands, don't know much about them. They didn't leave us written records, so what we know about them comes from archaeological discoveries, or what the Greeks and Romans wrote. Although they were fierce warriors, the Macedonians and later the Romans eventually conquered Thrace, and slowly the Thracians were assimilated into other cultures."

"Fascinating, Evmondia," Brawclad replied. "I myself have always been interested in the subject of archaeology."

Phil? Archaeology? Oh please! Zenon thought. *Maybe if there's a way to make money by selling artifacts!*

"I'm glad to hear it, Mr. Brawclad! There's more to the Thracians than meets the eye. The archaeological evidence paints a much more colorful picture of them than what the ancient authors wrote. Some of the digs my parents took part in led to amazing discoveries!"

Zenon was glad to hear Evmondia talk freely without holding herself back. So many of the people he had to engage in conversation with at the restaurant, or in other circumstances, seemed to talk just to fill the air or to hear their own voices. Their empty sentences would match their slackened faces, and it was difficult for him to concentrate on them. By contrast, Evmondia held his full attention. She spoke not just with her voice, but also through the graceful movement of her head, the green fire in her eyes, and the delicate expression of her fingers and hands. It was like watching a dance.

Raising his eyebrows, Brawclad asked, "Ah, what are some of those?"

"They actually participated in one of the richest digs on Bulgarian soil, where many incredible objects of gold and silver were found. Thrace was a land rich in both—one of the reasons it was conquered. Like the Egyptians, we have our own Valley of the Kings—the Thracian kings. Their tombs held a lot of riches."

"I would sure love to see those," Brawclad said.

"I can show you some of the objects," Evmondia replied, reaching for her phone again.

The craftsmanship of the artifacts Evmondia showed them was amazing. They weren't just objects, they were works of art; the attention to detail was astounding. He saw images of intricate necklaces and earrings, bowls and pitchers, drinking horns, and a crown with delicate oak leaves. But one image, in particular, caught Zenon's attention. It was a solid, glistening golden mask molded to a bearded male face.

"What's that?" he asked.

"Oh, that is the golden funeral mask of a Thracian noble."

"Wow." Zenon didn't know why that particular image intrigued him the most.

"I wonder how much it would be worth," Brawclad added. "Those finds are beautiful. Although not as beautiful as you."

Evmondia blushed. Brawclad slid his hand across his face as he tried to hide his smile. Sitting comfortably, passively listening to the conversation, Mr. Clifton appeared to be quite satisfied by the flow of the discussion.

Brawclad continued. "Thank you for sharing those pictures. Otherwise, I would never have known that a place like Bulgaria has such amazing treasures and history."

He winked at Evmondia.

A place like Bulgaria? Zenon thought. *That sounds condescending.*

Evmondia didn't seem offended, and he was glad of that. She was far too excited and engaged with the discussion. "The oldest gold treasure in the world was found in Bulgaria," she said, beaming. "Near the city of Varna, on the Black Sea coast."

"Oldest gold treasure? I always thought Egypt would've been its home. So the Thracians go really way back then?" Brawclad asked.

"Actually, the people from the Varna culture were part of another, older civilization. Some believe the Thracians learned their craftsmanship from this earlier group."

"Is tomb robbing a problem in Bulgaria?" Zenon asked.

"Unfortunately, it is a big problem. Many artifacts have left Bulgaria. My parents were involved in the fight against black archaeology for a long time. They were pure archaeologists, and they've been saddened to see the large number of artifacts that have disappeared and left the country."

"Yeah, I hear you. But I must admit, I would love to see those treasures in person," Brawclad said.

"Maybe one day you'll have a chance," Evmondia replied. "I know Thracian treasures have been on display in museums all over the world, including the Met."

"That's awesome. I love gold. I have quite a bit of it in my portfolio. It's a very good investment."

Mr. Clifton smiled and nodded in agreement.

"Evmondia, it's neat how passionate you are about Thracian history," Zenon remarked.

"Thank you, Mr. McClow! Thrace is part of the heritage of Bulgaria, and just like the rest of Bulgarian history and culture, I am proud of it and try to embrace it as much as I can."

The brunch was winding down. But what should have been a relatively straightforward and mundane meeting had turned into an emotional rollercoaster ride for Zenon. At first, he couldn't wait for it to be over. Evmondia had been making him uncomfortable, and he had wanted to escape. But the discussion about Mr. Clifton's father and Evmondia's background had engrossed him, and seeing her open up and come to life had left him enchanted by her. He had felt spellbound by the moment.

Then, she had stopped her tale, and when the conversation turned to financial matters, he couldn't help but feel annoyed. Although his manufactured answers were spot-on, there was no pride or joy in his ability to respond.

When the time came to leave, Zenon felt relieved. He and Brawclad took the elevator down in polite silence, and outside the building he shook the other man's hand and quickly headed in the opposite direction.

THE MASK

BY ZENON MCCLOW

ACT III

XLIV

THRACE, SPRING, 356 BCE

Having returned to King Ketriporis's residence with Prince Skostos's troops, and given his report to the basileus, Trysimachus hurried to the soldiers' quarters to find Pitros.

"I am glad to see you!" Trysimachus said, a genuine smile forming on his face.

"Look at ya! You've grown up. You're a man now, bein' in your first battle!"

"You could say that... but Pitros, what is that?"

"Oh, it's nothin'. Just a scratch. Nothin' that the fair maiden healer from my people can't fix."

"I hope so, Pitros. You are not only my best friend, but also my mentor here. Let us go and see that healer of yours."

"Do you see those mountains just yonder? A few days a' travel that way's where she is."

"What is this? Are you blushing? Do you fancy her?" Trysimachus teased.

"Who wouldn't fancy her? Betcha you've never seen a gentler or more beautiful maiden than Evmondia in your life! She can make all your pain or troubles go away!"

"You must be smitten... Evmondia is a beautiful name. But why do I think I have heard it before?"

Pitros said nothing. His mind seemed to have wandered away, most likely with the fair maiden in the land of his people. Then, snapping out of his stupor, he said, "I've been granted leave, and I'll be headin' back to my people."

"Will you be gone for long?"

"Not that long. From this full moon to the next!"

"What if I were to ask for permission to come with you? The king and lords are busier feasting and celebrating than holding court these days. I do not think I am as needed here at the moment. And the king has been generous in his granting of leave."

"That I'd like, Trysimachus! 'Tis always better to travel with a companion! But I must warn ya, the journey will take a few days through the mountains. Will ya be ready for it?"

"I will. You cannot imagine what I experienced on the secret path. This will be nothing! Especially since you shall be with me. If I receive permission, I can be ready to depart at dawn."

"Very well then! I reckon it'll be good for ya to meet my people!" Beaming with pride, he remarked, "The Bessi are the finest Thracians you'll ever know!"

"Then I shall take my leave to speak with Medosades. But Pitros, go see the healer here first before we embark."

Despite the deep gash in his arm, Pitros delivered another hard punch to Trysimachus's shoulder. It didn't feel any weaker than before.

Medosades gave his permission for the trip, and Trysimachus was excited by the prospect of visiting the Thracian tribe of the Bessi, who were well known in Hellas. They were renowned for their independence, fierceness, and sacred rites. Trysimachus had heard contradictory tales about them while growing up, and now, under Pitros's protection, he was about to find out for himself whether they were true or false.

The two companions began their journey by following the upper reaches of the Nestos and moving northward through the mountains. The majestic peaks of Mount Orbelus loomed high over the left side of the river, while the slopes of Mount Rhodope ascended from the right.

"Trysimachus, if you're gonna complain, ya shouldn't a come!" Pitros snapped, after the Athenian had grumbled one too many times for his liking.

"I spent the night writing to Zenon of Apollonia! I did not get enough sleep!" the scholar replied scornfully. Then he added, "I am sorry. I was the one who wanted to come with you. Just let me take a short nap, and I will be ready to continue."

"I'll take ya to a special place. The water there will invigorate ya more than any nap!"

The two continued on, passing steep gorges, rock altars, cave dwellings, and never-ending forests, moving further and deeper into the mountains. Trysimachus bit his tongue and followed Pitros without uttering a sound.

The giant stopped at last, pointing to a spring and a small pond nearby. "This is it! Gimme your cup, young warrior. You ready for some magic from our land?"

"I think I have had enough of magic! You should have been with me when we ambushed King Kersebleptes's forces. You cannot imagine what went on in the secret passage."

"Nothin' that Kersebleptes didn't deserve, I reckon!"

"It is not for me to judge."

Pitros took Trysimachus's cup, filled it from the spring, and handed it to the weary traveler. "Drink up!"

Squirming after the first sip and spitting out the water, Trysimachus yelled, "What kind of water is this? It did something to my throat!"

"It will! But the more ya drink, the more you'll like it!"

Trysimachus swirled the water hesitantly. Tiny bubbles formed. "I have not seen water like this! It looks like something strange is coming from it! I do not think I should drink it."

"That's the magic of Zemele, the earth mother! She makes the water to bubble like that! It'll cleanse ya from the inside! And after that, go to the pond and soak in it! You'll feel differently!"

Trusting the giant, Trysimachus drank the bubbly water. The more he drank, the more he liked it. After having his fill, he followed Pitros's advice and entered the pond. The coldness of the water shocked his body and put him on edge. He was ready to jump out, but Pitros halted him with a firm grip.

"Just a bit longer!"

"I am freezing! Let me out!"

But Pitros continued to hold him in. After what seemed like an eternity to Trysimachus, the giant loosened his grip, and the historian jumped out of the pond. Shivering at first, unexpectedly, his body heated up, and a new, unfamiliar sense of wellbeing and vigor shot through him.

"How do ya feel?"

"I am not sure how to describe it!" The young historian walked back to the spring to study the water and record that phenomenon of nature.

"Ready to continue?"

"Yes, I am. And my gratitude to you. I am much better now!"

And so the two companions continued north—one an uneducated and illiterate Thracian warrior from the mountains, the other an educated Athenian scholar from the coast. To the unfamiliar observer, they would have seemed like two complete opposites. But in many ways, it was as if they were old friends. Or even brothers.

Trysimachus knew that Pitros would be deemed crude and unsophisticated by many of his Athenian peers. Nevertheless, he felt more comfortable alongside the Thracian warrior than he had felt with his fellow scholars, many of whom he found too arrogant and ambitious to bear. Pitros certainly possessed less knowledge of the world than he did, but it was the Bessian who seemed far more familiar and connected with it. Trysimachus was grateful to have the giant by his side. After all, Pitros had saved his life during the battle with the Dii.

On this journey, Trysimachus was feeling far more secure in his steps than he had before. It was not just the presence and protection of Pitros that gave him confidence while traversing these isolated and wild lands, but also that his inner confidence and courage had grown since the beginning of his quest. The time he was spending in Thrace was not only increasing his understanding of the ways of the land, but also his acceptance of his reality, and his confidence that he could brave any challenge or adverse moment. Furthermore, the training he had undergone with Pitros and the experience of participating in a battle made him feel more able and prepared to fend for himself no matter what was to come.

He still felt fear. But his fearful thoughts were far weaker than they had been, and they did not petrify him like before.

Through cold and warm, the brisk feeling of wind and the intense rays of the sun, through light and dark, under blue and gray skies, alongside trees covered in green amidst barren mountain peaks, Trysimachus and Pitros continued northward. Their food was what they could gather or hunt, their shelter the caves and large, curved rocks along the route.

"We're gettin' close!" Pitros exclaimed with a broad smile. "See the valley down below? It was carved out by the gods when they formed the mountains eons ago. And over there is the dwelling place of Kotys, goddess of healin'."

Trysimachus began sketching the valley on his scroll.

"And this is where the Bessi lands start! From this valley on," Pitros added.

"Which direction are we going?" Trysimachus asked.

"Straight ahead, toward Donuca!"

"Donuca?"

"Ya read and write, but ya haven't heard of Donuca? This valley separates the three sacred mountains: Orbelus, Rhodope, and that mountain yonder is Mount Donuca, the tallest mountain in all'a Thrace!"

"I thought the Haemus was the tallest mountain in Thrace."

"No, 'tis Donuca! Takes three days to climb to its peak! I've never done it myself, but the great priest of my people went up there in order to speak with the gods. Ya can't get closer to the heavens than from the top of Mount Donuca. I've heard the view's beautiful up there, and ya can see the three seas from the top!"

"The three seas?"

"Yeah! The Southern, the Illyrian, and the one ya came from!"

"Oh! You mean the Aegean, the Adriatic, and the Pontic?"

"Yeah, I guess that's what Hellenes call 'em."

"The feeling of reaching the top must be wonderful."

"I reckon so, but I also know that any man who tries to climb up there's gotta be careful. If you're not a man of good character and the gods don't like ya, they'll consider ya a trespasser, and they'll punish ya for trying to reach the heavens by throwing lightning down from the sky. 'Tis a stormy place if you anger the gods! That's why I haven't climbed there. What if they punished me?"

"Pitros, I am sure they would consider you a worthy and good person."

"Well, my gratitude to ya, lad, but I think I'll stay down here!" He laughed, and the two descended into the valley, passing by more small hamlets situated amongst tall, majestic pine trees.

Now in the lands of the Bessi, they walked for hours before they finally reached Pitros's village. He was eager to see his clan, and his tribesmen were delighted to see him. He was greeted and embraced by men, women, and children alike as if he were a legendary hero whom they had been awaiting. Even the elder of the village, Vologesus, appeared to welcome and bestow blessings and honor upon the giant.

As for Trysimachus, he was inviting plenty of curious stares, whispers, and pointing from amongst the Bessians. But upon hearing Pitros's explanation of who he was and assurance that the Athenian had come as a friend, they welcomed him. They were impressed by his command of the Thracian tongue, which had only improved during his stay in Western Odrysia.

A tall, stout woman still in her prime made her way to Pitros, pushing away the other villagers gathered around him. Upon seeing her, the giant rushed over, lifted her up, and swung her high in a strong embrace. Tears were streaming down her face, but a broad smile illuminated it.

She must be his mother. There is a striking resemblance between them, Trysimachus thought.

The mother and son bade goodbye to the villagers. Hand in hand, they walked away, chatting merrily, oblivious to anyone around them.

Forgotten but not offended, Trysimachus followed the pair until they entered a hut at the village's edge. Not knowing what to do, he wearily watched the animals grazing outside. But, having remembered Trysimachus, Pitros reappeared.

"I'm sorry, Trysimachus! Where was my head? I haven't seen my ma for so long! Come in, come in!"

He ushered the historian in. The dwelling they entered was a circular hut with a hearth in the middle.

After learning who he was, Pitros's mother made quite a fuss around Trysimachus, embracing him and making sure to seat him comfortably. Pitros's younger siblings sat in a circle around him, staring right at the historian with big eyes and the curiosity of youth. Only Pitros's father was somewhat reserved, eyeing him suspiciously.

A feast was prepared for the travelers that evening. It was not grand, but the food was plentiful and delicious. Trysimachus was surprised at how hospitable and amicable Pitros's family was and how well they were treating him.

"If a Bessian doesn't like ya, ya'll find no stronger and fiercer a' enemy. But if a Bessian does like ya, ya have a companion and friend for life!" explained Pitros delightedly.

After the meal, worn out from the journey, Trysimachus fell fast asleep.

XLVI

"Get up! Get up!" Pitros's younger sister struggled to wake Trysimachus.

"Give me a little longer! It is still dark," the historian replied drowsily.

"Trysimachus, ya must get up!" Pitros shook him. "We Bessians rise early to greet the first rays a' the sun!"

"All right, all right. I will get up. But why must you do that?"

"'Cause the first rays are at their purest, before they start witnessing the deeds a' men! They give strength to our bodies and cleanse our souls of the scars from the mortal world."

"It makes sense. I have never thought about it in that way."

So with Pitros's family and the rest of the villagers, the historian welcomed the rising sun. As its rays warmed his skin, Trysimachus started to feel unusually content and happy inside.

He embraced this feeling of bliss, which had eluded him for a while now, with the deepest sincerity. He also embraced the air that filled his lungs. It was the freshest he had ever breathed. No wonder the Bessians claimed their air was the purest and closest to heaven, cleansed by the spirits inhabiting the mountains!

Trysimachus's fascination with the Bessi grew with each

day, as he continued to learn more about their way of life. Like the rest of the Thracians, the Bessi didn't know how to read or write. But they proudly proclaimed that they knew how to read the seasons, the mountains, the rivers, and the springs. For them, glory lay not in resisting or overcoming nature, but in embracing it and acting in harmony with it. They didn't view the beasts of the forests as their enemy, but as a source of sustenance, nourishment, and sacrifice to the gods. They didn't view the cold, the heavy snow, or the harsh winds as a threat, but as tools with which to become stronger and more resilient. Their habit of bathing in cold water and sprinkling their bodies with the cold mountain dew seemed to help them adapt to the climate of their lands. He was surprised how many of them held memories from King Sitalkes's great Macedonian campaign seventy-three years earlier.

Joining in the daily lives of the Bessi and recording his observations had made the historian oblivious to how fast the days in his new environment were passing. So he was surprised when he saw Pitros preparing for the journey back.

"Pitros, are we to depart already?" he asked.

The warrior nodded.

"Is it not too early to return to the court? Do you not want to stay longer with your family?"

"I do. But there's a village I wanna go to." He pointed in the direction of Mount Rhodope. "If we leave now, we can get there 'fore nightfall!"

"Why?"

"Too curious again, aren't ya?"

"If I am not curious, how can I become a good historian?"

"All right, I'll tell ya. We're to go to the Elethi."

"The Elethi? Who are they?"

"They're the ones who live yonder," he replied, pointing again in the same direction.

"Tell me about the Elethi."

"They're strange," the giant replied reflectively.

"Strange? How?" His curiosity piqued, the historian insisted on a response.

"The Elethi don't believe in taking!"

"What do you mean by that?"

"Well, they're mighty warriors, Trysimachus. But they won't strike. They only fight to defend themselves. They say their strength's a gift, not a weapon. And they don't plunder or raid. They're quite different than we Bessians are! We give in to plunder easier, I admit!" He laughed.

"But why must you visit them?"

A wide grin split the giant's face, and he paused before saying, "Let's get goin', friend, and ya'll find out!"

And so the two traversed the valley again. Upstream they went, and when the sun was about to set, Trysimachus and Pitros approached the Elethian village.

That evening, lying on the ground just outside the village under a blanket of stars, Trysimachus felt warm inside despite the chill of the mountain air. Unexpectedly, the sounds of a lyre and the sweet voice of a female singer filled the night. The melody and the singing beguiled Trysimachus, gradually dispelling both his weariness and the sorrows he was holding onto deep inside, replacing them with the feelings and memories of his childhood—a time when he felt protected, loved, and secure—feelings which had long disappeared and had been replaced by insecurity, uncertainty, and confusion.

As Trysimachus began drifting into slumber, he saw himself as a child once again, back home, cuddled in his mother's arms, feeling safe under her care. He wasn't sure whether these alluring sounds were real, or if he was already dreaming. But in the lucid state he was in, he thought he heard the giant mumble, "Evmondia's singin'."

Having slept soundly, the travelers rose later than usual the next morning and hurried toward the village.

The Elethi seem more prosperous than the Bessi, Trysimachus thought as he looked around. *Their dwellings are larger, and they seem tidier.*

The sound of a lyre and the same sweet female voice resounded in the distance once more. The sense of wellbeing from the previous night enveloped the scholar again. The melody was enchanting and drawing him in. *It is healing. Not since I was a child have I felt this way.*

Trysimachus saw Pitros follow some of the villagers in the direction of the spellbinding sounds, walking as if in a trance. He too followed eagerly.

A young woman with eyes the color of the spring foliage was surrounded by a group of elderly Elethians. Her dark tresses framed her face, falling down her shoulders. Her clothes were simple, and she wore no jewelry. Yet there was something striking about her. Most of the women Trysimachus had met in the court of King Ketriporis were noblewomen covered in jewelry, fine clothes, and other decorations. Many were beautiful, some not so, but most appeared pretentious and conceited.

There was something special about this maiden. What it

was, he couldn't tell. Was the girl he was now looking at beautiful? He wasn't sure. But regardless, he felt that he was falling under a spell.

There was a basket full of berries by the maiden's side. After finishing her song, she placed her lyre gently on the ground, picked up the basket, and began offering berries to the listeners. Seeing an elderly woman among the crowd, the maiden ran to her with the grace of a fairy. Bidding farewell to the bystanders, she joined the woman and the pair walked away. There were disappointed looks in the eyes of those gathered, but they waved goodbye and began to disperse.

A loud sigh emerged from Pitros, the likes of which Trysimachus had never heard him utter before. But the young historian fully understood how the giant must have felt.

"T'was Evmondia, Trysimachus."

"Evmondia? The fair maiden healer you spoke about?"

"Yeah, t'was her. Have ya seen a more beautiful maiden?"

"I do not suppose so."

Silently, each deep in their own reveries, the two friends sat by the nearby stream to take in their morning meal until the scholar broke the silence. "Tell me more about her."

"Ya saw her, and ya heard her, Trysimachus. With her song and smile, she can heal man's wounds and sorrows," the giant replied dreamily.

"You are right. I experienced that! But is she of flesh and blood? Or one of your nymphs? Or a muse, perhaps?"

"She's what ya want her to be, young scholar." The giant smiled.

"How do you know her, Pitros?"

"Evmondia's a Bessian! She lives with the Elethi now, but she's from my village. We grew up together, childhood friends and all."

Recalling old memories, the giant continued. "I always looked after Evmondia, protectin' her. Those were good times, without care," he remarked nostalgically.

"Why does she live here? Is she wed to an Elethian?"

"Nah, she's unwed. She's the caretaker of the goldsmith—the best one in the land, I'll tell ya! He's lucky to have Evmondia to care for 'im. She has a heart of gold, that girl."

"Why did you not go and speak to her? Why did you let her leave without letting her know you are here?"

Blushing profusely and looking embarrassed, the giant replied, "I just couldn't. I needed to gather my courage."

"What? You braved yourself in battle and dismissed your wound as a mere scratch, yet you need courage to approach a maiden? I did not know that you were so shy around women!" the scholar teased.

"Only around her. I dunno why Evmondia makes me feel that way!"

"Evmondia was the reason you wanted to come here, was it not?"

The Bessian remained silent.

"Who was the old woman she accompanied?"

"Kerza, the goldsmith's housekeeper."

"Pitros, I would like to visit the goldsmith. This way, I can gift something from these lands to those at court."

Watching the flow of the river, the giant replied reflectively, "I've seen more beautiful things in his workshop than in the king's court!"

"Pitros, you are making me even more curious about the goldsmith. And besides, it would be a shame for us to have traveled here without you meeting the fair maiden. Let us go to his shop."

"For that, we gotta climb up the mountain."

"He does not live here in the village?"

"Nope, high up this mountain."

"And the fair maiden lives there too?"

"Yeah, and Kerza too! They sure live a quiet life up there

all by ’emselves!”

“Are not they afraid of thieves or brigands?”

“The goldsmith’s guarded by forces beyond man’s understandin’.” Leaning closer to Trysimachus and speaking in a hushed tone, as if afraid someone might hear him, Pitros whispered, “The goldsmith’s one of the elders, said to be the keepers of special secrets, entrusted to ’em by the gods, ’cause of their pure hearts and good intentions.”

“Pure hearts and good intentions? What kind of secrets?”

“Well, the goldsmith, they say, is the keeper of the secret a’ the Elethian gold.” Leaning close again, Pitros whispered, “Promise me that ya won’t tell anybody what I just said.”

His curiosity piqued, the scholar agreed. “So are we to leave without visiting the fair maiden?”

Beaming, the giant responded, “’Course not! We’re gonna go up that mountain. I’m always welcomed at the goldsmith’s dwellin’. As long as ya don’t mention what I told ya, ya’re gonna like talkin’ to the goldsmith. He’s wise, much wiser than ya are!” Giving the Athenian a hard strike on the shoulder, he added, “Now don’t ya sulk, Trysimachus! I know I can trust ya. I’ll tell ya more about the goldsmith. And about the passage to his dwellin’.”

Large fires burned under a sky blanketed by stars on the grounds of King Ketriporis's residence. His warriors were celebrating, still elated not only by their victory over the eastern realm, but also by the loot and trophies they had carried back from the battlefield.

While the intoxicated warriors were feasting, their king was pacing back and forth in his chamber, deep in thought, awaiting the arrival of his brother Mononius.

“Come in, Mononius. How are you faring, brother?”

“My leg is still sore, but patience and the magic of the healer shall mend these wounds. I trust that you are well, my king?”

“My body is fine. And I am grateful to the gods for aiding us in victory. But these days, even when I rest, I do not feel rested. Such is the life of a ruler, I suppose.”

“Brother, rest assured that with everything you did, you demonstrated how great a ruler you truly are. And I am proud to serve under you.”

“I would not have been able to do it without you, Mononius, or our other brothers, or the great warriors of Western Odrysia... but where is Skostos? I have not seen him of late.”

“Where else could he be? With Meda, of course!”

“Meda?” Ketriporis shook his head. “If you ask me, that

woman is nothing but trouble. She is beautiful, all right. But how beautiful is a poisonous snake after it bites you? She is meddling too much in the affairs of the realm. I shall not have it. It is too bad that he and I are constantly at odds over her."

"I agree, brother. Meda is ambitious, but for herself."

"You are right. If she were a man, she would have made a great mercenary for the realm. And if she were a woman from the Sauromatae, she would have made a great general! Otherwise, I have no use for someone like her."

"It is disappointing that Skostos cannot see through her."

"Indeed, his attitude is vexing me. So what did you think of the meeting with the Athenian ambassador?"

"Well, he certainly flattered us enough and tried hard to convey Athens's goodwill toward Odrysia, but I did not like how diplomatic and carefully spoken he was. Athens is avoiding taking sides in this conflict, it is clear."

"My sentiments also. As we have discussed many a time, Athens cares about Athens. And they need us for now. But the Athenians also think that they need the Easterners. We are all just figures in their games. The Athenians will flatter us as long as they need us. And when the day comes that they do not, they will discard us. It is the same with Kersebleptes and Charidemus. But as long as Philip remains king of Macedonia, they will use anyone to attain their goal of weakening him. They remain blinded by their fury over losing Amphipolis."

"Not only Amphipolis, but Pydna also," Mononius replied. "Philip completely outsmarted them in seizing both cities. No wonder the Euboean's supporters are still insisting that Charidemus is the only one who can defeat the Macedonian and recapture Amphipolis for Athens!"

"Yes, indeed," the king replied. "But how could that be if Charidemus could not even defeat me? I am curious to find out what the Athenians will do next. But it is getting late. Go now, brother, before your wives become angry with me."

As the realm continued to celebrate and optimism prevailed, the young king tried to be in accord with his subjects. When Medosades rushed into his quarters, a deep frown on his face, the king couldn't help but smile and think, *He looks angry. But come to think of it, he always does!*

"My king," Medosades began, panting, "I am sorry to disturb you, but a delegation from the Thasian settlement Krenides has arrived. They have requested an urgent audience with you."

"How dare they, mere settlers and miners demanding an audience with the king! Send them away," the king responded, his mood darkening.

"My king, they have a grievance to report. And they look rather troubled and displeased."

"Fine, let them in," Ketriporis replied, waving him away with his hand.

Six Thasians bearing gifts were led into the reception hall. "What is it, men of Krenides?" Ketriporis demanded sternly. "Your gifts are generous, but what has made you journey all the way to my court? What grievance do you have?"

"May the gods grant you long life and a prosperous reign, honorable King Ketriporis," their leader began, his gaze lowered. "The cries of our people—cries which can be heard throughout the land—and the springs stained in blood have prompted us to seek audience with you."

"And why do your people cry?"

"Because of the attacks on our settlements, honorable king. Ever since the hostility between you and King Kersebleptes ceased, men from your army have been attacking and plundering our mines, terrorizing our people. Men, women, and even children have been slain at their hands. We do understand, honorable King Ketriporis, that a war requires large reserves. So we have come to offer a larger tribute to help you replenish your treasury—"

"Silence, men of Krenides! You speak softly, but you offend me with such a daring accusation. This is preposterous! Those men attacking your settlements and mines must be brigands or mercenaries. They are no soldiers of mine."

"With all due respect, honorable king, n-not only do they wear the colors and patterns of the Western Odrysian army, b-but—"

"Speak clearly!"

"The captives have also confessed to acting upon your orders, great king."

"No man of mine would ever confess to such a thing. Liar! For tales such as this, I could have your heads!"

"We would never dare lie to you, honorable king!"

"Men of Krenides, I have made agreements with you and the other Thasian colonies upon my honor. And I have kept all of these agreements, as witnessed by the gods. So how dare you come here and hurl such accusations at me?"

These arrogant Hellenes will pay for this insult. They shall feel my wrath. But not now. Thasos remains allied with Athens, and I cannot allow Athens to turn their backs on me and favor Kersebleptes instead.

"King Ketriporis, all we desire is to mine, carry out our trades, and live peacefully alongside your great people. We have obeyed all of our treaties with you and paid our tributes in a timely manner. But we are begging you to do something about these raids! The lives of our women and children are at stake."

"That is enough. I know not what has transpired at Krenides, but I shall hold a council on the matter. Your men are to wait until you receive word from my advisors."

I am certain no man of my realm is attacking those mines. And even if they were, how dare mere foreigners and settlers come to my court and complain! They should be grateful that the Edoni have not already wiped them from the face of the earth.

Something very strange is happening again. Oh Father, where are you to guide me?

XLIX

Only a short time had passed since the council was last summoned for an urgent meeting. Generals, nobles, and advisors gathered again to await word from their king. And when he related the accusations from the people of Krenides, there was an outcry, as heated and outraged discussions erupted among them.

The council members immediately suspected the local tribes of being behind the raids. It was no secret that the tribesmen of that region disliked the presence of the colonists from Thasos on their lands, and doubtless wished to capture the gold and silver from the Krenidean mines. Yet the young king remained unconvinced.

"Even if they were behind the raids, they have no reason to seek to implicate me," he said. "In fact, it would be foolish on their part."

"My king, if not the Edoni or Odomanti, someone else must be behind this," Lord Cothelas said. "Someone with an agenda against our great realm."

"There can be no other explanation," the king agreed. "But someone is taking great pains to implicate me in these attacks against the Hellenic settlers. What a despicable ploy this is! The mastermind behind all this must be very clever and ambitious. Mononius, you know as I..."

"Indeed, brother," said the prince. "Eastern Odrysia has been trying to justify their breaking of the peace treaty and their hostilities before the Athenians. What better way for them to make you look like an unworthy ruler?"

"Not only that, but Charidemus can use this to redeem his character and take his revenge on me. I can hear his supporters now. 'He, too, broke the sacred treaty and viciously attacked the peaceful colonists allied with you!' They will proclaim such nonsense before the Assembly to justify his actions!"

"I must admit, it is a cunning strategy," said Prince Skostos. "Kersebleptes would be able to replenish his treasury by plundering the mines, our relations with the Thasians and Athenians would be at risk, and a conflict between the tribes and us could begin!"

"That is true, Skostos. The chieftains shall be angered if they are led to believe I have looted the mines without their help and without sharing in the plunder. They would view it as a betrayal against them on my part. Lords, even I could not have foreseen such a ploy! Kersebleptes on his own could not have come up with this. But Charidemus could."

"My king," said Medosades, "while in Asia, did not Charidemus take Troy by disguising his soldiers as captives, thus being granted an entrance into the city? He then defeated the force of General Athenodorus!"

"Ah yes, Athenodorus did tell me about that," Ketriporis said. "I had forgotten this story. This only further confirms my suspicion. Who else could think to disguise their men as soldiers from Western Odrysia but Charidemus, placing the blame for these raids on me!"

"My king, what is your command then?" asked the advisor.

"General Pittacus, gather a unit of peltasts and cavalry to accompany the delegation back to Krenides and aid the settlers in their fight against the raiders. Also, bring some captives back here so we can interrogate them ourselves. It would be beneficial to have proof of the Easterners' ploy. It is best if we act quickly. Do make haste."

Charidemus! It has to be Charidemus! People like him will never stop. All along, I have known he will do anything to emerge victorious over me. But I am a warrior. I shall not allow such insolence and treachery. I am ready to do what must be done to protect the sacred lands.

Trysimachus felt like he was entering into a pool of boiling water. The festive and victorious mood at court was no more, and a new sense of tension permeated the air. Nothing seemed to elevate the mood around him, even the exquisite gifts Trysimachus had brought from the Elethian goldsmith.

The historian couldn't help but feel disappointed, as the gifts were intricately made and of the highest quality. King Ketriporis had accepted the ornate golden dagger graciously, as had the princes their fibulae. But Trysimachus could sense their lack of enthusiasm in accepting them. Only Sura and Medosades had seemed delighted, but not as much with the gifts as by the fact that he had begun to partake in Thracian customs.

He was kept busy recording the discussions held by the councils and was glad to be privy to the happenings in the court. He felt like he had the ability to correct the record, should history implicate King Ketriporis unfairly in the Krenidean raids.

Messengers and couriers were coming and going hurriedly. Trysimachus was sometimes asked by the couriers to deliver the letters in their stead. Whether it was because he was one of the few literate residents apart from the royal family, or because of his new attitude and willingness, he couldn't tell.

One day, after delivering some letters to the king's wives, the horns sounded, announcing the arrival of another messenger. The scholar stood in the courtyard, observing as the messenger gave his report to Sura. The advisor ran to the king's quarters, and Trysimachus followed, ready to record the latest news.

"My king..." Sura began, panting heavily. "A new, urgent report has been received from Krenides. The Thasian delegation which came to your court never returned. Instead, the settlers received their impaled heads accompanied by a threatening letter... a letter supposedly written by you, my king."

"By the gods, how could that be? What about General Pittacus? His force should have been able to protect the delegation!"

"My king, General Pittacus and his force... they have all been slain!"

"It cannot be!" the king shouted, throwing his rhyton.

Dented and bruised, the vessel rolled on the floor, landing at Trysimachus's feet.

"Their bodies were found strewn alongside the road to Krenides and Neapolis. It looks like they were ambushed, my king."

"Was there anyone found alive?"

"No, my king."

Like a lion ready to leap on its prey, the basileus sprang from his chair. "Sound the horns, Sura! We must gather the army and march to Krenides before Charidemus or Kersebleptes cause more trouble for us. Athenian, you are coming too."

LI

Under inauspicious omens and a clear blue sky, King Ketriporis's army marched toward the Edonian plain again. But this time, the king's force was significantly reduced in size, and he could not call upon the southern tribes.

Still, Ketriporis remained undaunted by the challenges ahead. As for his soldiers, they saw another opportunity to get their hands on loot and trophies.

There were no ambushes or surprise attacks on their journey. They made steady progress. Ketriporis had sent enough scouts and an advance force to ensure that his army would not meet the same fate as General Pittacus's unit.

They were headed southward when the king received a new report.

"My king, it is the Macedonians," the scout began.

"What about them?"

A Macedonian garrison had been seen occupying Krenides, and another large Macedonian force had been spotted moving eastward, in the direction of the Thasian settlement.

"Why was I not informed about their presence in the area before?" Ketriporis said angrily.

"No scout has ever reported seeing them coming," Sura informed the king.

Ketriporis ordered his flustered advisor to dispatch more

scouts and set up camp while they awaited further information regarding the Macedonian force.

Dark clouds hung over the camp of the young king. Ketriporis wondered what message the gods were sending him as he watched the dance of distant lightning and listened to the roaring thunder. Then, amid torrents of falling rain, a new report was received: the Macedonian army, led by King Philip himself, had arrived at Krenides.

Impassioned discussion and speculation spread among the lords and generals, inflamed by the news.

"My king," said Prince Spartacus, "if the Macedonians take the mines at Krenides, they will control both the east and the west side of Mount Pangaion. We must not allow that to happen! Nor can we risk losing the tributes the settlers pay us, especially after the previous war depleted our treasury."

"Spartacus is right," replied the king. "We must plan wisely, lords and generals, or this could be a significant loss for Western Odrysia. Philip's possession of Amphipolis and the bridge over the River Strymon was worrisome enough, but the Macedonians encroaching so far to the east, trampling over our lands? I cannot accept such a plight! If Philip takes over Krenides, he will not leave. That is certain. The mines in the nearby hills shall certainly entice him to stay. And the Pieri or Edoni in the way are no threat to him, any more than the Paeonians were."

"My king, I find this all to be strange. Could the Macedonians have possibly defeated the force of Charidemus?" Lord Sadalas asked.

"Our scouts have reported no such thing, and they have not been able to uncover any force of Charidemus's in the area. The Euboean must be hiding them well," the king replied.

"This is bad news for us, then!" General Derzelas said. "There is not just one force we must contend with, but two! My king, the army is still weakened from the previous war. If we continue marching and engage in combat with the Macedonians and the Easterners, we will surely suffer defeat."

"I agree with Derzelas, brother," Prince Skostos said. "But if we negotiate with Philip, we can assure him that we are not the ones behind these attacks. Philip is a man of reason."

Is he, Skostos? Ketriporis thought.

"I also agree, my king. We must convince King Philip to leave Krenides," said Lord Sadalas. "Mere gifts alone will not sway him. But there must be other ways. The Thasians are, after all, still allied with the Athenians. Would this not make Macedonia's dispute with Athens even worse?"

"Brother, I do believe it is best to enter negotiations with Philip," Mononius said, raising his voice to be heard over the thunder. "Why not attempt to ally with the Macedonians against Eastern Odrysia? After all, they are a threat to Macedonia almost as much as they are to us. Kersebleptes's appetite for conquest is as large as Philip's, and Charidemus is proclaiming that he can recapture Amphipolis from Macedonia for Athens... we can use these circumstances to sway Philip to our side."

"Mononius, you speak the truth," Skostos added. "We must not forget that Philip pledged his friendship to us. He is our ally, not an enemy. We are men of honor and courage," he continued. "We must not cower and instead use these new developments to our advantage. Let us make the involvement of the Macedonians into an opportunity to further our cause. If the east wants to provoke us once again, let us fight back alongside King Philip and show them an even greater array of strength!"

Shouts of agreement came from the lords and generals. But Ketriporis said, "I must give it some thought. Leave me now."

When the dawn broke after yet another sleepless night, Ketriporis summoned his advisor.

"Sura, call Mononius. I must speak with him. Also, dispatch a messenger to Krenides immediately and inform the Macedonians that an embassy will be seeking an audience with them," the king commanded.

Thanks be to the heavens that I have Mononius by my side. There is no one I trust more than him.

When his brother entered the tent, he said, "I have decided to follow the wishes of the council and send an embassy to Philip. Mononius, as you are the best with words, I think you ought to lead the embassy. Moreover, as you are my brother, sending you as an emissary would be a sign of my goodwill toward Macedonia and Krenides."

"As you wish, my king. I will do my best not to let you down," answered Mononius.

"You must also assure Philip and the Thasians that we have come as friends, not as enemies," the king instructed. "They must be convinced that I am not responsible for those attacks, and that someone else has been falsely implicating me. Express my wish to visit Philip and speak with him in person. A joint coalition between Macedonia and ourselves against Eastern Odrysia is something we must consider. We have brought several fine rhytons and stallions that can be presented to Philip. And take the Athenian scholar with you to make a record."

"As you command, brother."

"Tread carefully in the Macedonian camp, Mononius. I cannot lose you. And may the gods go with you."

LII

Like a lone wolf trapped within the confines of his tent, King Ketriporis paced in circles, awaiting the embassy's return. Only when the horns sounded, announcing their arrival, was he able to breathe a sigh of relief. He had worried the embassy would be met with a misfortune similar to that which had befallen General Pittacus's force.

He hurried outside into the still-pouring rain and rushed to Mononius, taking him in a firm embrace. Ushering his brother into his tent, he listened attentively to what he had to report.

"Philip will welcome you, brother, and grant you an audience," Mononius said. "And he did express his intent to maintain a friendship with us. But after I explained that you never ordered those raids on Krenides, he became evasive and refused to speak further on the matter."

"Hmm... what think you of the happenings in Krenides?"

"The Macedonians are everywhere," the prince continued. "Philip himself is occupying the residence of the Thasians' former leader, Kallisthenes. But Philip mentioned something intriguing: the citizens of Krenides pleaded with him for help in stopping the Western Odrysian attacks. And he had come to Krenides because of their pleas. Do you think it is possible, brother? Why would they plead to him? Why not to the other

Thasian settlements? Would not they fear that Philip would do as he did at Amphipolis and become their overlord?"

"It is difficult to know. It is more likely he marched on his own, opportunistically, and is now using diplomacy to convince the settlers that they cannot do without his help. Regardless, what is of the greatest importance is that the Macedonians withdraw from Krenides. I am glad the Athenian was with you to make a record. Let the Hellenes know the truth of what is transpiring, and not just a tale spewed by Philip. But you look tired, brother. Go rest. I must prepare for the journey. I have long days ahead of me."

"May the gods grant you a favorable audience with King Philip, brother."

"May they hear your words, Mononius."

The sun was at its highest point when Ketriporis entered the chamber he was shown into, his eyes focused solely on the king of the Macedonians.

So this is the man who dares to encroach upon the sacred Thracian lands. The man Athenians now fear, but also hold in low esteem. It has been a while since I have seen him. His build is more like Axios's than I remembered. Makes me wonder who might emerge victorious in hand-to-hand combat. But I must be careful. There is a shrewdness about him.

"Welcome, Ketriporis, son of Berisades. It is an honor to have you visit me. Let us drink to the friendship between our two kingdoms."

"The honor of being here is all mine, honorable Philip, son of Amyntas. This toast is to you! May your rule be long and prosperous, great king!"

"I shall gladly accept your toast, King Ketriporis, as I know you are as sincere toward me as your father was."

He is mocking me. He has not forgotten that Father

supported Pausanias over him.

"Come, sit beside me."

"I am glad you understand me, Philip. I have come to Krenides only with the best of intentions. I do not want there to be any misunderstandings between us."

"Why would there be, Ketriporis?"

"Krenides lies within my domain. Therefore, it is my responsibility to look after the Thasian colonists who live here per the agreement reached with my father. The events of recent days, I can assure you, have nothing to do with myself. They have been part of a vile ploy by King Kersebleptes, who is trying to turn the colonists against me by making it seem like I have ordered those raids."

"Ah, that reminds me. May I congratulate you on your great victory over Kersebleptes, Ketriporis? Your stratagem was clever indeed."

"My gratitude, Philip. The last war has made my rule stronger, my realm even more prosperous, and my army better equipped. The tribes are also faithful to me. So be assured, I can protect the Thasian settlers on my own."

"That is not what they think. It is their cries of despair that have brought me to Krenides. The war with Kersebleptes has to have depleted your treasury. You must need more funds for your army. No wonder your soldiers have been plundering the mines of the Thasians."

"I am giving you my word of honor, as king of Thrace and of the Odrysae, that this is not the case, but a slander against me by the Easterners."

"I have also given my word of honor to those miners that I shall protect them and aid them in their fight against you, King Ketriporis."

"But you can trust—"

"You want me to trust you when you just told me a lie? Let me ask you something, Ketriporis. Do you trust me? Do you trust that I will leave Krenides? Or is it not out of mistrust and fear of what I will do next that you have come to meet with me? Is that not the purpose of your visit? You need not deny it. You came here seeking to change my opinions and intentions. But there is one thing you can trust. And it is that I will fulfill my promise to the Thasians and protect them against the attacks from your soldiers."

"No Western Odrysian army is attacking those colonists!" Ketriporis responded in a thundering voice.

"What matters is not who is attacking them, Ketriporis. But who they believe is doing the attacking," Philip said, raising an eyebrow.

What is that look in Philip's eyes? Is he mocking me again?

"Be assured that I will care for the colonists," Philip continued, a smile forming on his face. "You need not worry about their safety any longer. You think me greedy, Ketriporis. And you think I am here out of greed. But are you not here out of greed also? We are not much different after all, you and I. You want to rule over Thrace, do you not? If all of Thrace could be your domain, would not you gladly accept it? And I want to rule over greater territories. What is wrong with that? It is our mutual friends in Athens who fear me and fear a united Odrysia. Why? Because we threaten their hegemony in these parts of this world. But what makes them deserving of such a hegemony? I suspect you think the same as I. But do you fear me also, young king?"

"There is no reason for me to fear you."

"None at all. Why, we are friends! But is there anything else you have come to offer me?"

"A joint coalition between Macedonia and Western Odrysia against King Kersebleptes. The Odrysians of the east are a threat to you as much as they are to me. I am sure you are aware of the claims the supporters of Charidemus of Euboea have been making in Athens. And you know very well the ambitions of Kersebleptes are as great as his father's."

"That is more like it, son of Berisades. I will definitely consider it! We shall part as friends. But just remember that I keep the promises I make. May the gods be with you, Ketriporis. Come to Pella. I would like to show you my palace and my new treasures. Now I bid you good tidings."

My rhetoric did not bring justice to my cause. He will not leave Krenides. He will not let Krenides go. I am sure of it.

LIII

Outside, still perplexed by his conversation with the Macedonian ruler, Ketriporis encountered General Axios.

He still looks like a wolf. He must not have forgotten how our last meeting ended. But why is he covered in dirt and blood?

"We meet again, Thracian. But the tides have changed. They now favor me," Axios snarled, baring his teeth.

"You can continue to be insolent, Axios."

"Ah, but fate agrees with me. Do not you know that all of the land of men belongs to the Great Sun that brings it to life? When the sun rises in the east, it can burn you, but when it sets in the west, darkness always engulfs you. A Macedonian can always outwit a Thracian, King Ketriporis. And you have been a fool."

What impudent words! But I cannot provoke Philip. Not now. I must walk away before Axios forces me to strike him.

Ketriporis strode to his stallion, accompanied by his bodyguards. However, instead of giving the signal to his men to mount, he stood next to his horse for a moment. Sweat dripping from his face, the king stared directly at the intense sun. He could have sought shelter from its burning light. But he did not. He stood still, allowing the hot rays to scorch his skin. He was trying to make sense of what the Macedonian general had told him. *Did Axios give me a riddle to solve?*

His thoughts returned to Philip. It was difficult to make sense of the events that had transpired, things he had not been able to foresee.

How ingenious of him, marching into Krenides as a savior instead of a conqueror.

He looked around to see what Krenides had become. There were Macedonian soldiers all around him—he might as well have been in Macedonia itself.

Thinking about the mines infuriated him. But, at that moment, under the suspicious watch of the Macedonian bodyguards, their stares as sharp and menacing as hawks', there was nothing he could do about it.

How audacious of Philip to claim I am here out of greed, for him to say that we are alike! But he is wrong. Those mines belong to no Macedonian. Thracian gold belongs to those of Thrace, and to those who have been chosen by the gods to rule over these sacred lands.

Ketriporis mounted his stallion and galloped with the wind while thoughts continued to rush through his mind, as if they, too, were galloping.

It had to have been Charidemus all along. He blamed the Euboean for many of the happenings that had occurred these past several years. He knew he had been right to hate and blame him, a man who always did something to deserve it. But now, when it came to the events surrounding the settlers, why was he starting to hesitate? *Was it really Charidemus's men disguised as mine?*

Riding back, the king began to lose his sense of certainty. There was something about the Macedonians that bothered him deeply. Their presence in Krenides, a place far east of Macedonia, was completely unexpected and worrisome. How had they crossed the swamps undetected by the scouts?

There was no way he could have foreseen that happening.

Therefore, there was no reason to blame himself for being unprepared. So why, then, was he doing just that?

He faced a dilemma. He could retreat from the Edonian plain and allow Philip to have his way in Krenides. But that would be an act of cowardice, not befitting a king of the Odrysae.

He could also engage the Macedonians directly. But such a charge would only devastate his force.

Axios's words still puzzled him. *East and west. Did the west refer to Macedonia? And the darkness... was that a threat? But what about the east?*

It had made sense to him that Charidemus would have come with such a ploy to seek revenge. But ultimately, it had been only speculation. There were no signs of Charidemus's men.

The young king was tired and disappointed in himself. He couldn't admit to the council that he had failed. He decided that he would decline to speak to them when he returned and would instead welcome the night to reflect.

But then the sight of his camp took his breath away. *By the heavens! What happened here?*

He dismounted quickly and looked around, petrified. He was no longer the ruler of the camp he had left just two days before. Devastation now ruled in his place. Laughter no longer resounded. Nor did the aroma of roasting meat fill the air.

No tent stood erect. There were only the cries of the wounded. The stench of the dead. Burnt tents and carts. Bodies of men and horses everywhere.

"Look for the princes, the lords, and the generals among the dead! Be sure to give the wounded water!" he commanded his bodyguards as he moved quickly through the camp, searching for his brothers.

So this was Philip's way of keeping his promise to the settlers!

Long, wooden pikes, Macedonian sarissas, protruded from many of the bodies.

I fell straight into his trap! Axios's words make sense now. No wonder he was so confident! Axios, the next time we meet, you will surely lose your life to me!

"Are my brothers amongst the dead, Truxos?" the king asked his most trusted bodyguard, his voice quivering.

"It seems not, my king. Just Lord Sadalas amongst the zibythides."

"Sadalas? This is a grave loss!" he exclaimed, face contorted. *Who can I trust now to provide stability over the Sintian land?* "Take me to someone I can speak with. I need to know what happened here!"

"Yes, my king! There is a soldier well enough to speak."

He leapt like a hunted stag to reach the wounded man, a javelineer propped up on a broken cartwheel. "Speak up! Who attacked you, and where is the rest of the army?"

"My king... they had to... retreat... the Macedonians... too strong... took us by surprise... late in the night... we could not get close to them to fight..."

"Do not exert yourself any longer. Your king will remember your service to the realm."

Leaving the soldier, followed by Truxos, he walked among the slain bodies of his men. The sight of death was nothing new to him, but the feeling was different. From time to time, he stopped to chase away the crows feasting on the bodies of the dead. Then he would study the faces of his men as if trying to recognize and remember them for eternity.

"Truxos, I must find and meet with the rest of the army. Leave some of the bodyguards to tend to the wounded, and haul back those who have a chance at surviving. And take good care of Lord Sadalas's body."

Followed by the rest of his bodyguards, the young king galloped as fast as a lightning bolt. Through the plains, swamps, forests, and hills, he rode tirelessly until he spotted his battered force ahead.

"Mononius. Spartacus. Skostos. I am relieved to see you all alive and well!" Ketriporis shouted. He couldn't hide his joy as he jumped off his horse and ran to give each of them a strong embrace.

"It is good to see that you are also well, my king," Mononius replied.

"Brother, but why did the Macedonians attack while you were negotiating with their king? It is infuriating!" Spartacus declared.

"It was Philip's way to ensure his claim over those mines. The settlers will not dispute it now. They will feel obligated to him for defeating the ones who attacked and plundered their mines and settlements—presumably us." Ketriporis shook his head.

"The Macedonians took us by surprise, brother," said Skostos. "Otherwise, we may have been—"

"I know, Skostos. Do not blame yourselves, brothers."

"It was a force led by Axios and Parmenion who attacked us, Ketriporis," Mononius explained. "But it was not the generals or their phalanxes that gained them their victory. Brother, it was the sarissa we could not fight against! No wonder Philip takes so much pride in that weapon. Our swords and spears were no match for it. Its length is great, and it impeded our ability to get close enough to fight. Nor could our swords cut through the wood, as it is hard and strong."

"There was no way for us to break through their ranks, brother, even if they had not caught us off-guard," Skostos added. "They were able to pierce our men and horses with ease from afar. We had no choice but to retreat. Otherwise, our losses would have been even greater, my king."

"You decided wisely. I saw that Macedonian weapon's

effects on the battlefield," the king replied. "But do not vex yourselves, brothers. I am glad you are all alive. I grieve for the loss of Lord Sadalas."

"Yes. He fought valiantly until the end," Mononius said.

"We shall honor him in a way befitting of the great warriors of Odrysae."

"What are we to do now, brother?"

"Let us return. The men need to rest and heal. Then we will decide what is to be done."

Their heads hanging low, King Ketriporis's warriors marched back home from Krenides, grinding their teeth and muttering curses under their breaths. Nursing a cut in his leg as deep as the one in Pitros's arm, Trysimachus marched with them.

This had been his third brush with death since his arrival in Thrace, but the historian had grown and matured in strength. He was feeling more emboldened and ready to handle life now. History itself was becoming one of his mentors, bringing him closer to knowing and understanding himself. And that mentor had given him great opportunities, including the honor to be in the presence of the now-infamous Macedonian king. Philip seemed as almighty and powerful as Zeus, with the charisma and eloquence of Hermes and the cunning of Dolos.

Back at the residence, Trysimachus's hand—the same hand that had mastered the art of wielding a sword—was becoming as sore as his leg as he tried to keep up with the debates echoing around the court over the Krenides affair. There were still many questions. Who was responsible for the initial raids? Had it been Charidemus, or had it been King Philip all along? And who had ambushed and slaughtered the Krenidean delegation and General Pittacus's force? How had the perpetrators even known about the unit of cavalry and peltasts sent alongside the delegation?

The formerly stable and prosperous dominion had been shaken to its core. And it had all happened very fast.

Having gotten to know and understand the basileus better, Trysimachus was noticing a change in Ketriporis's demeanor. It was as if the walls of the invisible fortress surrounding his expressions and inner feelings had crumbled—the guards and watchtowers gone—and the Athenian scholar could now confirm what was inside: a man who was infuriated and disappointed. A man who blamed others but also blamed himself.

Trysimachus was also getting a glimpse into a new aspect of the basileus's personality. He could see something dangerous, even turbulent, inside the king, as if he were a mountain lion whose den had been trampled upon, one who was ready to leap and strike back at the trespassers with sharp claws.

And who could blame him? After all, less than a year since his father's death, the young ruler had lost access to both valuable mines and good agricultural land, at a time when he needed ever more revenue to strengthen the army and bolster the defense of the domain.

Thracian politics were out of Trysimachus's control. The only power he had was to perform his duties diligently and do his best to take care of himself. Under Pitros's mentorship, strengthening his body had become as important to him as strengthening his mind. Therefore, on the day of the scheduled downhill horse race competition, eager to join the other participants, Trysimachus mounted his horse and galloped toward the steep Orbelian hill where the contest was about to begin.

Clad in a white robe like the great Thracian kings before him, Ketriporis set out on a sacred journey to the spot closest to the heavens in all of Thrace, the summit of Mount Donuca. The climb was perilous, but the king needed to consult with the gods, for his realm was in even greater peril.

All alone, he scaled Donuca while thoughts of Krenides circled around in his mind like vultures, feasting on his distress.

Was I wrong all along? Did Philip stage the events at Krenides, like the Athenians Euripides and Sophocles staged their plays? But how would he have known?

He asked himself the same questions over and over as he climbed. *Could there be someone in my court collaborating with the Macedonians? A traitor! But who? Could it be that Athenian scholar? Or is it one from the council? Or even one of my brothers? No, that could not be!*

Neither the wind, nor the cold, nor the jagged rocks were his enemies. It was the men. This is why he had come.

At long last, he made it to the top. Rooted like an oak against the blustering wind, and feeling the power of the gods and his ancestors emanate throughout his body, Ketriporis stared up at the heavens. Then he began his chant.

"Oh great gods, I, Ketriporis, made of your essence but in

human flesh and blood, ask you to bestow upon me understanding on the fate of these sacred lands."

He placed four vessels on the rock, containing the sacred liquids of water, wine, honey, and milk, and added, "Please, accept these offerings! Oh, Mother Goddess, the sacred lands you have entrusted me to rule over are threatened by a foreign enemy.

"The foreign king who encroached upon your lands with slyness, and his new invention—the long pike, taller than two, even three men—defeated us. Oh gods, hear my plea and give me your guidance! What should I do? How can I counter that weapon with the swords and spears my army has?"

The wind is subsiding. The sun getting stronger. All around me is brighter and clearer now.

"Hail be to you, great gods! I have received your guidance. I give my pledge to you. The sacred lands shall remain your domain and be ruled by your chosen people. Yes. A blacksmith I shall seek. A blacksmith who shall make a sword long as the sarissa, strong enough to cut through the hardest wood. No warrior of yours should ever be pierced from afar or prevented from showing his skills in close combat."

I am the closest to Father I can be. If I look carefully, maybe I can see his face once again amongst the stars.

"Oh Father, great King Berisades, do you hear me? Do you see me? Father, I am standing alone. Not just here on this mountaintop. When I return to the realm, I will still be standing alone.

"Father, as the king, how can I please everyone? If I try to please the lords, then it displeases the commoners. If I try to please the commoners, then it displeases the lords.

"But the lords are greedy, Father. Their greed seems to be insatiable. The people are suffering and being enslaved because of their greed. Yet there is no loyalty in the people either. They follow the spoils and plunder.

“Then there are the Easterners, the Macedonians, and the Athenians. Their games of treachery and manipulation are not mine; their preferred cup of wine is not my cup of wine. It makes me uncomfortable. But no one must know that. As the king, no one must know my feelings, my weaknesses, my fears.

“The mask conceals the expressions of the face. So wearing a mask is what I must do. But a mask is heavy, and its price high.

“Father, I promise you I will take our revenge! But in order to do that, I must increase both my power and control. I must crush power, not be crushed by power.

“I will do everything and everything it takes. Even if it means becoming a harsher ruler. Philip, Kersebleptes, and the others employ lies, deception, and plunder. Why should I not do the same?

“I will reduce the influence of the nobles. I will increase my wealth and power. And I will develop a stronger weapon for my men than that of the Macedonians. But for that, I will need more gold. Our treasury is almost empty.

“I will do it. I will find a way to take back the lands that we have lost. They do not belong to Philip or to anyone else. Now, with pain in my heart, I must bid you goodbye. I will make you proud of your son, Father.”

"Medosades, summon the council," Ketriporis commanded.

"Yes, my king."

After toasting each nobleman present, he began his speech. "Honorable lords, I seek your help. The realm has been wounded—the treasury has been greatly depleted by the last campaigns. New coins are needed. Yet we are cut off from access to the mines at Mount Pangaion and Krenides, and I have lost much tribute due me. Thus, everyone must contribute more. As the king chosen by the gods to rule over these lands, I must increase the revenues in the treasury.

"The Macedonians and the Amphipolitans have profited from selling timber to the Athenians for years. I believe we should do the same. The forests east of Mount Orbelus will be used for this purpose, and the timber be delivered to Gareskos. I cannot allow the remaining sacred lands to become vulnerable to Macedonia, to the east, or to anyone else."

"Brother—" Mononius attempted to speak.

Making no eye contact with his brother, Ketriporis declared, "This is my command. You may all take your leave now."

It is the wealth Philip is amassing that is making him so powerful. How else can he pay his soldiers, grow his army, hire the best strategists, and even turn soldiering into an occupa-

tion? If I am to become his rival, I must find a way to do the same. Without wealth, I can be no match for him, or Kersebleptes, or anyone else.

Back in his chamber, Ketriporis's attention was drawn to the dagger Trysimachus had gifted him. He slid his finger along its surface.

It is truly elaborate, he thought. *The Elethi are strange people, isolated in the mountains and secretive. But they have mines. Their lands are filled with gold. What was the Athenian doing in the Elethian land? And who made this dagger? I should summon him.*

"Trysimachus of Athens, this is a fine dagger you gifted me."

"I am glad you like it, basileus."

"I was informed you obtained it from the Elethi. But how did you know of them?"

"Pitros, one of your warriors, is a Bessian. Having befriended him, I was given permission to accompany him during his leave. He is the one who took me to the Elethi."

"An Athenian has befriended a Bessian? Heh! I should drink to that. Pitros is his name?"

"Yes, basileus."

"It is strange. What affairs could a Bessian warrior have with the Elethi?"

"The caretaker of the goldsmith from the Elethian village I visited is Pitros's childhood friend. He wanted to see her before returning to your court."

"Her? Blushing, are you?"

"No... yes. She is possessed of great beauty."

"Do you fancy the women here in Thrace, Trysimachus of Athens?"

"They are quite beautiful."

"They are. Yet in a way, they resemble this dagger: alluring but dangerous. But never mind. The Elethian's work looks to be of the highest quality."

"Indeed, it is renowned throughout those lands."

"I have been looking for a skilled goldsmith. The ones here are good, but not as good as this Elethian. What else has he made?"

"I saw some of the most intricately made necklaces, bracelets, and decorations I have ever seen."

"You have made me curious now. Tell me about the goldsmith."

"There is nothing to tell."

I have noticed that the Athenian clenches his cloak when he is afraid. But what is there to fear now?

"You hesitated. You seem insincere."

Looking down at his cloak, Trysimachus replied, "No—yes, basileus... I am sincere."

"You are not a good liar, Athenian. What are you hiding? Speak up."

"It is just that... I promised not to speak about it."

"Is that so? Sura, bring me your sword. We will help the Athenian keep his promise. Cut his tongue off."

"No, basileus, I shall speak! It is only... I promised Pitros to keep it a secret."

"Keep what a secret?"

"That the goldsmith is one of the keepers of the secret of where the Elethi keep their gold."

"The very goldsmith you met?"

"Yes, according to Pitros."

"And do you believe the Bessian? Do you believe the goldsmith to be a keeper, scholar?"

"I am not sure. But he is one of the elders of the tribe, highly revered amongst the Elethi. And he is wise, beyond the understanding of many men."

"What do you mean by that?"

"I had the privilege of visiting his dwelling. He lives high in the mountain. Few venture to visit him, and he enjoys conversing, especially since he lives a secluded and isolated life. And me being, if I am permitted to say, a learned man myself—"

"Trysimachus of Athens, what did he speak to you about?"

"He spoke of the sacredness of the gold, which he uses to honor the gods and to bring beauty into the lives of those residing in the gods' sacred land, as instructed by the gods themselves. He spoke of the ways gold can be used for good in their lives, and he also spoke of the need for harmony. He called himself 'keeper of the harmony' between the gold and man, saying that gold can also corrupt one's spirit, make men turn against one another, and lead them to do harm. 'By harming others, one spreads misery, not just to others but to himself. And by robbing, one robs himself.' Those were his words."

"Strange words indeed. But you said he lives isolated, high up in the mountains? Does not he fear brigands?"

"It is said that the goddess of the mountain herself protects the passage to the goldsmith's dwelling. The villagers also protect the passage, fearing the wrath of the goddess, and that a misfortune will befall them if they fail. It is also said that she has cast a spell on it, and that only those pure in heart can go through."

"So tell me, scholar, is your heart pure?"

"I am not sure. But that of Pitros must be! He took me safely through the passage."

"What will happen if someone whose heart is not pure tries to go through the passage?"

"The passage will close and suffocate the trespasser. It is also said that the goldsmith is protected by a monster with the body of a lion and twelve serpentine heads, fierce enough to devour any army. And if anyone with bad intentions tries to visit the goldsmith, the serpent will slowly drink his blood until it destroys him."

"Do you believe in the sayings, scholar?"

"I do not know, basileus. But the villagers do. They would not allow any harm to befall the goldsmith."

"It is an interesting tale. Trysimachus of Athens, you may take your leave now."

That goldsmith... why would he live secluded, high up in the mountain, surrounded by such strange tales? Unless... is it possible? Could it be just a tale?

Perhaps not. There always seems to be some truth in the tales of the commoners.

What should I do? The blacksmith, the one whose reputation is known throughout the land, lives among the Bessi. I must visit him to ensure he is most suitable for the work. And the Elethian lands are nearby. It would be wise to visit the goldsmith too. If these tales are true, he just may be the one to aid me in my quest. I can visit him under the pretext of commissioning him to make something for me. But what? I will think about it later.

"Medosades! Find the Bessian warrior Pitros, and summon him here."

It was a fine day to ride. Galloping with the wind through fields and hills, the king and his bodyguard, Truxos, were traveling with Pitros toward the Bessian lands. The giant was taking them on a path different from the one Ketriporis anticipated.

This route may be more direct. The warrior should know the fastest way. He is simple, but he seems trustworthy.

"Pitros, how long have you been in my service?"

"Already five springs, my king!"

"That was a dangerous slip of the tongue, warrior. You were commanded to no longer address me as 'my king.'"

"But how couldn't I address ya as 'my king', my king, when I know ya're the king?"

"If you want to keep your life, you must address me as Rebulus."

"As ya command, my king... no, I mean Rebulus, my king!"

"This will not do!"

"I'll try harder, my, uh, Rebulus!"

"Disobey my order, and you will know my wrath. Who am I, Pitros?"

"Rebulus, a fella warrior like me, in the service a' King Ketriporis!"

"That is more like it."

"Well, may I ask ya a question, Rebulus, now that we're fellas? Are ya gonna visit with the priestess of Dionysus? Is that why ya wanted to go to the land of my people?"

"You are right. But before that, there is someone I must visit. You are to wait here with Truxos. It will take two nights before I return."

"Then I'll wait for ya here, Rebulus."

"You are doing a fine job now, Pitros. I knew I could rely on you."

I hope the blacksmith will be able to forge the sword. His reputation as one of the best in the land must keep him occupied. I have to persuade him, no matter what it takes. Time is of the essence.

I felt it in my hands. I felt its power. Its ability to defeat. To destroy. To spill blood. I saw it clearly. The vision came to me. The blacksmith lived up to his reputation.

Rhomphaia. Yes. That is what I shall call it. A true destroyer forged from the strongest iron. I agree with the blacksmith. The blade should be curved, not just long. And there will be no match for it. Not amongst the Macedonians, nor the Athenians, the Scythians, or the Persians.

Philip has been boasting about his new inventions. Soon I will have something even better. But no one except for my brothers must know that here in the Rhodope, the finest sword ever made is being forged. If my men were to wield it, victory and glory in battle shall be mine. But I need gold. Lots of it. Otherwise, how will I equip my army?

"There ya are, Rebulus!" Pitros shouted as the king rejoined his companions.

How quickly he adapted to speaking to me in such an informal manner. It is a reminder that respect for the king, after all, depends on outer appearance and the impression of power and authority.

"Yes, I have returned. Now let us go. Pitros, take us to your home."

"My home?"

"Yes, we will be staying with your family."

"But my home wouldn't be fit for ya, Rebulus!"

"I am the one who shall decide that. Tomorrow you must take me to the Elethian goldsmith. The one who made the dagger the Athenian gifted me."

"As ya command, fella warrior!"

LVIII

It was still dark when the king woke his most trusted bodyguard. "Truxos, Pitros and I will journey to the land of the Elethi at dawn. You are to return to my residence and await further orders."

"But, my king–"

"This is my command. I have gotten to know the Bessian well, and I know him to be worthy of my trust."

After greeting the first rays of the rising sun and parting with his bodyguard, the son of Berisades set off. The two travelers moved with agility through the valley, through the forest, and through the passage and up the mountain.

The passage didn't close or try to suffocate them. Nor was there any sign of danger. They moved in silence, each wandering in a reverie of his own until the melody of a song and the voice of a female singer filled the air. They glanced at each other, a question in the king's eyes and knowing in the eyes of the warrior.

"Is this a muse or a goddess singing?" asked the king. "This voice... it seems to be coming from the heaven above."

"It's a muse singin', Rebulus. A muse who can heal man's heart," the warrior replied, picking up speed and forcing his companion to match his pace.

Accompanied by the heavenly voice, they climbed up and

up. The king's troubled thoughts were gradually replaced by feelings of calm and bliss.

Suddenly, the singing ceased. The two travelers continued their climb, albeit slower, their steps reflecting the disappointment they felt.

The goldsmith's house was tucked amongst tall, majestic pine trees. Berries grew everywhere around. An old woman greeted them. Recognizing Pitros, she gave him a hearty embrace and ushered the travelers in.

The dwelling they entered was modest but airy. It appeared surprisingly comfortable to the king. Adjacent to it was a small hut that looked like a workshop.

An old man appeared, moving slowly. Pitros introduced him as the goldsmith. The king was taken by surprise. This man also appeared as though he had seen many a spring, and instead of being strong and stout, he was bent and fragile—looking like he would break with ease. But what surprised the king the most were the old man's hands. With their knotted and swollen fingers, they did not look like the hands of someone who could have crafted the elaborate dagger Trysimachus had gifted him.

"Welcome to my home, honorable guests. Kerza, fetch some wine," the old man said and invited them to sit.

Moving with unexpected grace and agility, the old woman brought in a golden jug of wine, and three equally exquisitely made cups. They stood out in contrast to everything else in the room, and the king's eyes shone at the sight.

"What is your name, young friend?" the old man asked, smiling. "Anyone who comes to visit we receive as a friend!"

"Err... Rebulus."

"And what brings you to our home, Rebulus? It is rare for anyone to come up here to visit. Even Pitros does not come to visit us much any more! We are always delighted when old and new friends come to see us!"

"It is the fame of your craftsmanship which has brought me here," the king replied. "I would like to commission you to make something for me."

A curious look crossed the goldsmith's face. "Then let us finish our wine and go to the workshop, honorable friend."

"Yes, let me compliment you on the wine. I have not tasted anything like it. Bitter, yet pleasant! It is hard to describe."

"That is because it is not made from the fruit of the grape, but from the herbs that grow here in the mountain."

"Oh, I see. I am grateful for the honor of tasting something I have not had before."

"You speak eloquently, young friend. From your speech, I surmise you are not from these parts."

"I come from the court of King Ketriporis. Pitros and I are fellows in arms, both in the service of the king."

"Are you an Odrysian, then? I have no quarrel with the Odrysae. They have done me no harm. You are welcome here, young friend."

"I am honored to be your guest, and to be considered a friend, esteemed master."

"Then, let us go to the workshop. There are a few items I would like you to see."

The goldsmith's workshop was clean and unusually bright. Was it the light coming from the outside, or the gold the young king was focused on, that made the room appear as if it were lit by a spell? He couldn't tell.

There were bracelets, necklaces, earrings, and other ornamentations, and a few cups, goblets, and plates made of the finest gold and silver and of the highest quality, more befitting of a royal residence than a modest mountain dwelling.

The immaculate objects captivated the king. He didn't want to miss even the smallest detail.

Some eyesight the old man must have to chase in such a way. He glanced at the murky pupils of the goldsmith. *It cannot be possible. All of this he must have made in his youth. Can I even commission him to make a mask for me?*

The king said, "I was hoping you could make a warrior's mask. One made out of gold. Our king's enemies are frightful and numerous. A frightful-looking opponent would befit them."

"It can be done. But it is getting late. Why not spend the night here, and we can discuss the making of the mask in the morning. I must rest for now. Kerza, prepare beds for our guests. And be sure to make them a hearty supper. They are young and must have big appetites. Much bigger than I have."

He smiled and added, "You are in for a treat. Kerza's cooking is the best in these parts!"

The giant looks pleased. I wonder why? He surely cannot be enamored of the old woman.

Unable to stop the flood of thoughts in his mind, the king turned in his narrow bed while his companion slept soundly.

Could the old man truly be one who knows where the Elethian gold is hidden? The Athenian was right. He is not an ordinary craftsman. But where could it be?

The scholar spoke of a monster. One protecting the goldsmith against anyone with impure intentions. But am I not here with impure intentions? Monsters... Impure hearts... I cannot threaten the goldsmith or force him to lead me to the gold's location. Not now, when Pitros is here. I must be patient. There will be a way. Nothing will stop me. Not the wrath of the goddess of the mountain, nor any monster.

Bothered by Pitros's snoring, unable to sleep, the king stepped outside the house. A sky covered by stars greeted him; not far off, a light gleamed from the goldsmith's workshop.

Was I wrong about the goldsmith? Maybe I can see him at work. By the heavens! Who is she? I did not see her here before.

But what is she doing? It looks like gold she is holding and... chasing. By the gods! Ketriporis, wake up! A maiden goldsmith? Are you dreaming? But... there is something endearing about her. It is strange. I feel calm and peaceful inside. I must be in a dream. It cannot be real. But it is a beautiful dream. I do not want to wake up.

By the gods! It is not a dream. It is all very real.

I was right! It all makes sense now. She must have been the one who made those exquisite objects.

LIX

The king opened his eyes, expecting to see the maiden from the night before. Instead, he saw Kerza leaning down, watching him. Startled, he jumped from his makeshift bed out into the courtyard.

"I thought you'd never get up! The sun's already high in the sky!" she remarked grumpily. "The master and Pitros already had their morning meal. But Evmondia, as good-hearted she is, she'll prepare somethin' for ya."

Evmondia... could that be the maiden goldsmith? His heart fluttered at the thought.

"Oh, here you are!" the goldsmith greeted him. "You must have been tired. I hope you slept well."

"Yes, I did, Master. The smell of the pine trees was rather soothing."

"We feel honored by the gods to have been given this place as our home. Oh, Evmondia, meet our new friend, Rebulus!" the old man said, waving at the young maiden.

Turning to the king, he added, "Rebulus! This is Evmondia! She was at the village the day before and could not greet you earlier."

"Maiden of spring, as fresh as the morning dew," the king started, then stopped, angry at himself—or maybe embarrassed.

Evmondia smiled, saying nothing. He sensed her smile was open and genuine, in contrast to the women in his court. She turned her attention to the goldsmith, making sure he was seated comfortably.

"Look after our friends, Evmondia. No need to fuss around me," the old man said, feigning scorn.

"Evmondia, ya shouldn't a' walked up the mountain so late at night!" Pitros interjected.

Taking the warrior by the hand, she replied, "You should not have worried, Pitros. The sons of Mother Berdina escorted me here."

She looks beautiful under the sunlight. The king's heart was pounding like never before, not even before a hunt or a battle. Why, he couldn't understand.

The meal the young maiden prepared, although simple, tasted more delicious to him than anything he was used to being served.

He looked at her hands. Her long and delicate fingers were exquisite, made for the craft she was engaged in. She wore a simple tunic; no decorations crowned her hair or dress.

She looks queenly in the cloth of the commoners. Those eyes... I have never seen eyes so green before. There is something else to her besides beauty. I feel different in her presence.

"So what do you say about it, Rebulus?" the goldsmith asked, interrupting his reverie.

He hadn't heard what the old man was saying, but his voice sounded harsh and uninviting. He would rather have heard the sweet voice of the maiden. "I am sorry, esteemed master. My thoughts seem to have wandered somewhere else."

"Do not be concerned, young friend. I was just asking if you want the mask to be crafted in a certain way."

"No, I would rather leave it to your experienced hands. And I am willing to meet your price."

"Very well, then. Come back, let us say when the leaves start changing color."

"I will be honored to return, esteemed master."

The king stared deeply into the young maiden's eyes. *Are you the one who made the dagger? Are you the one who will make the mask?*

As if hearing his question, she smiled at him. Then, turning to the Bessian, she said, "Pitros, I have prepared some goat milk, berries, and buns for the villagers. Could you and your friend help me carry them down to the village, perhaps?"

Beaming and blushing, Pitros replied, "I'd be glad to carry anythin' for ya, Evmondia! But Rebulus here, he ain't used to—"

Interrupting the giant, the young king turned to the maiden and replied, "I will be honored to help you carry whatever you ask!" Almost in a whisper, he added, "Ev-mon-dia."

LX

They followed the maiden down the path to the village—the king who was used to being served, and the warrior who was used to being in service. And yet they carried the jugs and baskets for Evmondia equally.

"Friend Rebulus, tell me, is Brother Pitros treated well in the service of the king?" the maiden asked, watching her steps.

"From what I know, he is."

"I am happy to hear it! I was glad to learn that he has befriended the Athenian historian from the king's court... and Pitros and you are friends, are you not?"

"We have become friends, having fought side-by-side. Pitros is a fine warrior; he is one I can trust. And trust is most important among warriors."

Upon hearing that, a wide grin split the giant's face.

She is also a Bessian, yet she speaks more eloquently than Pitros. She must have learned to speak this way from the goldsmith.

"If I may ask, fair maiden, how did you come to live with the Elethi?"

"We are almost there! Perhaps later, Rebulus," she replied gently.

Helping to distribute the goods amongst the villagers came naturally to the giant. As for the king, helping felt awkward.

But he did it without disdain or resentment. In fact, he felt glad that he was doing something to assist the Bessian maiden. It surprised him that he was becoming more like the man he was impersonating than the one he truly was.

I am glad none of my courtiers can see me now! There is nothing in common between Skostos and me when it comes to women. Yet I am starting to worry... No. It is gold I seek, not another wife.

After they had finished distributing what they had brought, Evmondia turned to the king.

"Friend Rebulus, Brother Pitros and I must go to the river. I promised Mother Berdina to wash—"

"Ah, but Pitros is busy playing with the children! I will accompany you."

Evmondia glanced at Pitros, who was pretending to be a horse while four boys clambered onto his back.

"Do not lift that basket, Evmondia," he added. "It is heavy. I will carry it for you."

"You are kind, friend Rebulus."

Am I? That is not something I hear often. If ever.

Not knowing what to say, the king followed the maiden to the river. They walked in silence, disturbed only by the sounds of the forest and the creatures dwelling in it.

"How is it living with the Elethi?" the king asked, interrupting the silence between them.

"It is fine, Rebulus. I like their way of life and the way they think."

"Oh? I find them to be strange, carrying no weapons."

You should not have said that, Ketriporis! But the maiden smiled.

"Brother Pitros does as well! But do not concern yourself, friend Rebulus. Their way of life would be uncomfortable for a warrior who must follow his king's command."

"You are right."

At the river, he watched her as she bent down to wash the garments entrusted to her by Mother Berdina and spread them out on the rocks so they could dry under the hot sun.

"Evmondia," he asked, annoyed for a reason he couldn't explain. "Why must you be the one to wash those garments?"

"I wanted to, Rebulus. Mother Berdina has been so kind to me ever since I came here to the Elethian land."

"Evmondia, these are not your people. I hope they are not exploiting you."

"They are not, friend Rebulus! They have accepted me. They are good to me. Besides, I am the one who came to their land."

"You mean you were forced to come here?"

"Why would you think that? I came here on my own. Well, except for Pitros, who accompanied me here."

"But why, Evmondia? I do not understand."

Kneeling, she swirled her hand in the water and replied, "It is not an interesting story."

"I am willing to hear it if you are willing to tell it."

Taking off her boots, she entered the water. Treading carefully and holding onto the rocks to make sure she wouldn't slip, she climbed up a large, rather comfortable-looking rock close to where the king was sitting. Then, sitting down, she began to gently kick and swirl the water with her feet.

After a while, she resumed speaking. "I am a Bessi. And a Bessi I shall always be. The Bessi reside here," and she pointed to her heart. "They are not bad people. Just look at Pitros. It is just that the ways of my parents differed from the ways of some of the clans. My father refused to partake in the raids and plundering organized by his kin and the clans—my parents just wanted to live a simple life tending to their flock and caring for their children. So we were shunned, looked down upon, and treated as outcasts. It is true, Rebulus—one can feel like a foreigner even amongst their own people and kin. If it were not for Pitros's family, we probably would have starved."

She paused, continuing to kick and swirl the water with her feet.

"There was a merchant from our village who traveled about the land. And he used to tell us children stories of other lands and the people who dwelled within them. From him, I learned of the Elethi. He would describe their lands as mysterious, defended by the mountains and guarded by the gods themselves. And he would say that the people living in those lands were strong and brave, but not ones who would kill or fight without reason, preferring to live peaceful lives tending to their land. Strange, he called them."

At that, she smiled. "Ever since I heard those tales, I knew those were the people I wanted to live among. Despite the way they were treated, my parents did not want to leave our home. But they encouraged me to go to the Elethi and seek a different life if I could have it there. It was six springs ago that Pitros brought me. The people here cared for me, and the Master, kind and generous as he is, took me in. Ever since, he has also been helping my parents and some of the villagers back home."

"Would you ever go back to living with the Bessi?"

"I do not know. Maybe one day. I like being able to help Master with—" She stopped herself. "Besides, I often visit my family," she continued.

Should I tell her that I know she is a goldsmith? No, it is better that I not.

Looking at the water, Evmondia added, "Life changes, Rebulus. We cannot stop the flow of life from happening."

With that, she jumped off the rock, and, treading again through the water, walked back to where the garments were lying in the sun. After ensuring they were sufficiently dry, she folded them carefully and placed them in the basket. The king lifted the basket, and they headed back to the village.

He looked at the maiden as they walked shoulder-to-shoulder, trying to study her.

There is something pure about her. Something childish, yet mature. Something naïve, yet wise.

"Rebulus, if I may ask, how long have you been in the service of the Odrysian king?"

"Ever since my rite of passage."

"Oh, I see." Then, she added, "The king you fight for is King Ketriporis, is he not?"

"Yes, indeed."

"Pitros has told me all about him and the difficulties that have befallen his realm."

"What has Pitros told you about the king?"

"Well, that he is a great strategist and a skillful warrior."

"That he is. But perhaps Pitros has also told you some of the tales surrounding the king." Seeing the concern in Evmondia's eyes, he added, "No harm shall befall Pitros if you tell me."

"All right then," she said. "Apparently, King Ketriporis likes to partake in the rituals of bathing himself in blood and drinking the first milk of new mothers. Pitros also said that the men like to call him the 'snake king', because he orders for a different poisonous snake to be brought into his chamber each evening. The king allows the snake to bite him so he can increase the strength and endurance of his body! And because he is of divine descent, no bite has ever harmed him, unlike how it would a mortal. Rebulus, do you think that is true?"

"I do not know. But does it matter? King Ketriporis is a strong and fair ruler. I am proud to serve under him."

The men and their imagination! It is good they view me as powerful, though.

"Rebulus, would you ever consider leaving the king's service for a life without fighting?"

"Leaving my life as a warrior would bring me nothing but shame and disgrace," the king replied. "Besides, fighting is thrilling, and it is satisfying. It makes me feel more alive than anything else."

"But does not having to fight keep you from living free?"

She is brave to speak to a warrior in such a way. "Free? Can a man ever be free, Evmondia? Is there a land without foes and enemies? Without rivals? Without battles for control? I am a warrior, and a warrior I must remain."

"There could be such a land. Is it not what the gods want from us, to make it so?" Evmondia replied. "But I have been talking too much. Excuse me; I see Mother Berdina waiting."

After he and Evmondia had delivered the basket with the clean garments, the young king took a stroll to take in his surroundings, leaving the maiden to converse with the other women. The village felt strangely calm and peaceful, in stark contrast to the tension permeating his court.

Looking back at Evmondia, his thoughts wandered. *Could she be a nymph? An enchantress? A deceiver? I cannot give in to her. Soon I will leave her and all of this behind.*

It is good Pitros is coming. We should depart now.

His attention was captured by a young Elethian carrying a lyre. When they saw him, the villagers stopped what they were doing and gathered around.

"Is he going to sing?" he asked Pitros, who was walking up to him.

"No, 'tis Evmondia who'll sing," the giant replied softly.

"Evmondia?"

The king knew he should leave. But his legs would not move. He stood still, watching the maiden goldsmith taking the lyre from the young boy. And then, her song began.

He felt drawn in, beguiled by her singing. *It was her. She is the one I heard singing when we went up the passage.*

His concerns for the realm, the people, the lords, Philip,

Kersebleptes, Charidemus, how to increase the revenues in his treasury... one by one, they all started to fade away.

He was once again a prince, young and brave and carefree. Not a king responsible for ruling and safeguarding his realm.

Snapping out of his stupor, he ordered himself to stop thinking of her. *Enough! She is not a muse, but a siren!*

He walked away into the surrounding forest, leaving Pitros to listen to Evmondia's song, so mesmerized that he was unaware of the king's absence.

LXI

"Pitros, return to court. Your services are no longer required," the king said. "Take this letter and deliver it to Lord Truxos. He will know what to do."

"And why's that, Rebulus? Did I do anythin' to displease ya?" the giant replied, worried.

"No, you did not."

"What're ya gonna do by yourself in these parts then?"

"Questioning the king, are you?"

"No... yes! I thought I might ask, since aren't we fellas?"

"From the moment you depart, I will be your king again." Feeling a pang of sorrow upon looking at Pitros's face, Ketriporis added, "If you must know, I am to visit the temple. Fetch me a guide."

"I can guide ya there myself..."

"No, Pitros. You must deliver my message to Truxos. This is an important task."

At that, the giant's face lit up. "I'll do as ya say, then!"

"Depart when the sun reaches those peaks. Now, make haste and fetch the guide."

Am I getting soft? Where is my former determination? Feeling sorry for a warrior whose life is pledged to me.

I am the king; I must have a heart of stone. This mountain must have bewitched me.

The temple in the land of the Bessi was very different from the Temple of Dionysus in King Amadokus's land. Instead of a massive, masterfully built columned structure, the priestess resided in a cave high in the Rhodope. A large hole in the ceiling above the altar gave a view of the stars and heavens above, and the place had an eerily peaceful feeling.

Sitting on a stone chair surrounded by thirteen torches, sipping wine and pouring some of it onto the altar from time to time, the priestess was delivering her oracles.

The king couldn't tell if she was young or old, as her face was covered by a veil, and a strange mist enveloped her. Ketriporis felt lightheaded in the presence of the priestess, but he did not know whether it was because of the unusual atmosphere or the strange and unfamiliar aroma. The sensation soon lifted, and he felt a clarity of mind.

"What ask you of the gods?" the priestess demanded.

"I seek guidance on how to gain back the lands I have lost."

"The land you speak of belongs to the gods. There is nothing to regain."

"I am a king! Am I not descended from the gods?"

"But you are not a god."

"I am the one chosen by the gods to rule over the sacred western lands."

"Today it may be you, tomorrow someone else. Mortal power comes and goes. The land remains the land."

"It is today that matters to me. And I will fight to regain back all that I have lost until I am victorious."

"Be aware, victories also come and go."

"So does defeat."

"Winning does not mean that you will be victorious, and victory does not mean that you will win. Conversely, losing does not mean that you will be defeated, and being defeated does not mean that you will lose."

"Defeat is unacceptable to a king and a warrior!"

"Why?"

"As the king, I must lead my army into victory. Victory gives them spoils and trophies. Not defeat. And spoils and trophies are what they want."

"What will happen if you do not give them that?"

"They will turn against me."

"They may turn against you even if you give them everything they want or desire."

"That is true. It has happened many a time before. That is why I must have ultimate control over my realm."

"It is not your realm to control."

"Whose is it, then?"

"You know the answer to that question."

"I cannot accept defeat!"

"What will you do?"

"I will continue fighting until I am victorious."

"At what cost?"

"I do not care about the cost."

"Even if you lose your life?"

"It is an honor for a warrior to die in battle."

"What will you accomplish by that?"

"Taking my rightful place amongst the gods and the greatest warriors."

"So you will die and allow your enemies to rule over your lands and your people? Did your father not tell you to always protect the people? For mortals, victories are passing. Defeats are passing. And so is life. But the people will remain. Is it not a mark of a great king to be able to give his people a good life?"

"Yes. They will have that when I become victorious."

"What if you do not?"

"That will not be."

"Your people are suffering. Do not you care about them?"

"People are fickle, ungrateful, greedy, disloyal, easily swayed. Why should I care about them? At any moment, if given a chance, they might put a dagger in my back. It is the sacred realm I must protect."

"Stop fighting, then."

"If I do, my enemies will emerge victorious."

"Not necessarily. You will release them from the need to fight with you. To kill you. To destroy your realm. To enslave your people."

"How can that be?"

"Try it, and you shall see."

"My enemies would take control of my realm and seize my riches. My people would become my enemies' subjects, not mine."

"Is that what is most important to you?"

"Yes."

"You want to safeguard your people, then?"

"I do."

"Regardless of how you think about them?"

"It is my responsibility as their ruler."

"Do you think that, by fighting to the death, you will accomplish that?"

"The gods are on my side. I give them honors and sacrifices. They will give me victory."

"Your enemies also give honors and sacrifices. How do you know whom the gods will favor?"

"I will make sure it is me."

"So you think you can control the gods? By your silence, I see you have started to doubt. Can you accept defeat as a gift from the gods?"

"Gift? What kind of a gift is this? Victory is the only gift I will accept."

"So be it. The gods have spoken."

Ketriporis walked outside, disappointed by the nonsensical 'guidance'. The words of the Bessian priestess were strange and incomprehensible. Was she a fraud? Words like this could not have come from the gods. He was certain of it. Instead of him asking the questions, it was she who was asking questions and then giving him ambiguous answers. What a waste. "Defeat as a gift." He laughed scornfully as he walked away.

Ketriporis spent several nights in an inn favored by travelers to the Bessian temple before heading to the spot he had chosen to await Truxos and the scout he was leaving behind in the land of the Elethi. They were to meet in a meadow with water falling into a pool from high up in the mountain. The meadow was lush and covered in flowers that were blue, white, red, yellow, and purple, spreading all around like a vast and elaborate rug.

Walking toward his destination, he heard galloping hooves in the distance, and a heavenly voice singing.

It could only be her.

The king was torn between the sounds of the galloping horses and the enchanting song. Quiet as a mountain lion, he approached the waterfall and spotted the maiden goldsmith. He watched as she picked berries and flowers, bathing in her beauty and beguiled by her song.

His eyes were drawn to a mother bear, fur white as the snow on the peaks of Mount Orbelus. She was sitting by the waterfall, watching her cubs swimming in the pool. He froze, unsure of what to do.

The bear grew wary. Ketriporis saw Lord Truxos approaching, an arrow notched in his bow and aimed straight at the bear. He stepped forward and signaled Truxos to withdraw.

But the bear was now running toward himself and the maiden. He took the sling from his bag and aimed directly at its snout.

The maiden turned, watching the scene unfurl. The stone struck the bear, and it groaned loudly and retreated to the pool.

Ketriporis approached the maiden. "Evmondia, you should not have been here all by yourself!"

"Rebulus, that mother bear and I have been friends for a while now. She would not have harmed me. I am grateful to you for not killing her. She is just a mother protecting her cubs."

"Yes, I knew that. That is why I just wanted to stop her."

He was a hunter. He would have killed the bear, as he had killed many beasts before. But somehow he knew it would have saddened her.

"You have a pure heart, Rebulus," she said. Looking at him with eyes as green as the foliage, she added, "Even if you do not know it."

The king flushed. Once again, he was no longer a ruler made of stone but a man of flesh and blood with a heart beating fast, full of feelings previously unknown to him.

"I must return to the village," said Evmondia. "Master is waiting for me there!" As if talking to herself, she added, "I am glad he is still able to walk up and down the mountain. Although it is painful for him, he does his best, never complaining!"

Lost in her eyes, he replied, "I will escort you back. You should not be walking by yourself."

"I am in no danger. I have been walking here by myself since I came to this land."

He pictured her, beautiful as the flowers covering the meadow, running barefoot in the tall grass, laughing joyfully.

"But I thought you and Pitros had departed."

"Pitros did, but I had another task."

"Oh, I would have liked to see Pitros again! But I am glad to have seen you, Rebulus. So long, then! We will all be glad to see you back!"

With that, she ran away, as light as a butterfly.

Pangs of guilt overran his mind. *It is for the realm. My people. My father. It is my responsibility as the king—my duty. There is no other choice.*

I should have killed the beast. I cannot have feelings for anyone, let alone a naïve maiden from a foreign tribe. Once I am back in my court, she will be forgotten.

He walked toward Truxos and the scout. "Follow me," he ordered the two men, prepared to lead the scout through the passage.

Back at court, Ketriporis felt relieved to be able to shed 'Rebulus' and be a king again. Of course, ruling came with consequences and responsibilities.

"I hope to hear more about your journey, Ketriporis," said Mononius.

"That will come with time." He was eager to announce his plan to equip his army with the new rhomphaiae. But the fear that there might be a traitor in his midst was inspiring Ketriporis to remain secretive. "What has been happening during my absence?"

"Events of late have been troubling," Mononius admitted. "There is much unrest and discontent amongst the lords and people."

"It was to be expected, brother. They must be angered by the higher tribute."

"Brother, the people have been coming here every day, seeking an audience with you. When has it ever been like this?

The tribute is too high! Many will die of starvation like this, or sell their wives and children into slavery in foreign lands. We need the people on our side."

"Why do they think I have enacted this measure? It is all for them, brother. For the realm. Do they want to find themselves under the sword of the Macedonians? Slaves to Philip?"

"They do not see things that way."

"They are shortsighted."

"The order to cut down the sacred forest is also causing an outcry," said Mononius. "The people fear the wrath of the gods, the nymphs, and the creatures who dwell in the trees. The men are refusing to cut them down. They fear misfortune and punishment shall befall them."

"If that threat was real, there would be no Macedonians or Athenians cutting down the forests by the Strymon," Ketriporis thundered. "Nevertheless, we must make the people understand that it is the gods' will for the timber to be sold, so that this great realm can be prosperous. The gods themselves communicated such orders to me on Donuca's summit. We must tell the priests to spread the word that, far from punishing us, the gods shall reward us for these deeds!"

"That may be a solution, brother. But there is more! We have received word that the Odomanti are refusing to pay the higher tribute."

"Then we shall force them."

"A rebellion could very well be likely."

"Then we shall crush it. The western realm cannot lose yet another tribe."

"Brother, have you forgotten the state of the army?"

"Do not worry. I will grow the army and make it stronger than ever. Soon, even Philip will envy us."

"But brother—"

"Patience, Mononius, patience. Leave me now," the king commanded.

Disregarding Mononius's concerns, Ketriporis summoned Skostos. "You and General Derzelas are to lead the force to the southern plains against the Odomanti. Do whatever it takes, even if you must put them all to the sword. Bring the chieftain, Polles, here. He must swear loyalty and allegiance before me personally."

Skostos nodded and departed.

Left alone with his thoughts for but a moment, Ketriporis was soon interrupted by Sura. "My king, the Athenian Peisianax has arrived as ambassador. He is requesting an audience with you."

Remaining silent, Ketriporis regarded Sura for a while. Finally, he said, "Let him in. I will hear him out."

"Greetings to you, great and honorable King Ketriporis," said the ambassador. "It is an honor to be in your presence. Please accept these gifts as a token of our friendship, and of Athens's goodwill towards Western Odrysia."

Ketriporis observed the ambassador, who was of average height and a strong build, with gray hair. "Let us drink to our friendship then, Peisianax of Athens... now, on what matter do you seek an audience with me?"

"Great king, the Athenian Assembly has been following the aggrandizement of Philip of Macedonia with increasing concern. The men of Athens do not understand exactly what occurred at Krenides. But they do not believe the raids on the settlers were ordered by you, honorable king."

"I had nothing to do with those raids. Or of any upon the lands or mines near Krenides."

"Rest assured, honorable king, that I have come to reaffirm Athens's intention to maintain their alliance with you.

The men of Athens are angered that Krenides is now in Philip's hands. Indeed, this situation has been causing tension between us and the Thasians."

"I am certain that is what Philip wants," Ketriporis said with a short laugh.

"As you have observed wisely, honorable king, it appears Philip is transforming Krenides into a Macedonian colony—bringing in new settlers, ordering new buildings to be erected, draining the swamps. And, of course, exploiting the mines for himself. We in Athens are growing concerned about his ambitions. Especially now that he has captured Potidaia, and the Illyrians have been defeated. It is unprecedented!"

Shaking his head, Ketriporis replied, "Yes, this is troubling news indeed."

"Additionally," the ambassador continued with a deep sigh, "Philip has succeeded in convincing the Olynthians to abandon their negotiations with Grabos the Illyrian and ally with him instead. And we have received word that Philip has relinquished Potidaia to Olynthus and the Chalkidian League as part of his agreement with them. The men of Athens are angered over the loss of Potidaia, just as they were over Amphipolis, and just as you must be about Krenides. We fear Philip will stop at nothing to expand Macedonia, that he believes all the lands under the sun are rightfully his. But it is a very dangerous prospect for the region to fall under the hegemony of such an aggressive and treacherous man."

"Yes, indeed," Ketriporis answered, raising his voice and standing.

"Basileus, fortune seems to favor Philip as of late. His horse claimed victory at the recent Olympic Games, and his fourth wife Olympias has given him another son—Alexander, they have named him. If Philip continues to rise in strength, wealth, and influence, what will stop him from seeking conquest of your realm?"

"I can stop him. In fact, I have devised a strategy to defeat him myself."

"That may be, honorable king, but a great realm and ruler needs friends and allies. Philip has swayed the Epirotes, Molossians, Thessalians, Thasians, and Chalkidians to his side. He humiliated the Illyrians and forced the Paeonians to kneel before him. You, great King Ketriporis, are the chosen ruler of the Western Odrysian lands—"

"You speak eloquently, ambassador," Ketriporis interrupted.

"My gratitude, basileus," Peisianax replied. Putting his hand over his heart, he continued. "And that brings me to the purpose of my visit. We propose an alliance between Athens, Illyria, Paeonia, and Western Odrysia for joint action against Philip. If we combine our forces, we can have the better of him!"

Sitting back down, and resting his chin on his fists, Ketriporis remained silent for some time. Then he said, "Peisianax, I have concerns."

"Whatever your concerns are, basileus, it would be my honor to—"

"I am concerned that this alliance will exist only as a formality in your legal system, and in the end, the other kings and I shall be left to fend for ourselves. Must I remind you, Peisianax, that during the campaign of Sitalkes against Macedonia—in the conflict you call the 'Peloponnesian War'—Athens failed to deliver on its promise of sending ships to aid him. We here in Thrace have not forgotten that. Your polity did not send a force to stop Philip at Potidaia either, and I know it is because of your engagement in the war against those former allies of yours. You have still not managed to subdue those poleis and their forces, and an entire year has already passed!"

"Honorable king—"

"I surmise, ambassador—and I shall speak bluntly, as I am angered—that Athens intends to use Grabos, Lyppeios, and me to do all of the fighting against Macedonia. This alliance, I fear, would bring greater losses to us than to yourselves."

"Athens has already lost much—"

"Lost what?" the king snapped. "Your colonies in Thracian sacred lands? Colonies that should have never been settled to begin with?"

"Basileus, our presence here has not just contributed to our prosperity, but to yours and your people's! Athens has been pleased to find new sources of timber from you, and we are willing to pay generously. Ever since we supported King Berisades in the war—"

"Ah, that reminds me, Peisianax, about Kersebleptes," Ketriporis interrupted. "Now tell me, what has been done in the Council or the Assembly to hold Kersebleptes and Charidemus responsible for violating the treaty?"

"Well... it is not my place to—"

"You sit on the Council, do you not?"

"Yes..."

"If Euthycles had not initiated a countermeasure against the decree pushed by the Euboean's supporters, your Assembly most likely would have passed it, giving Charidemus what he wanted!"

"Great king, Prince Mononius won over many in Athens to your cause when he was in our city. Indeed, there are many in Athens who think highly of you and your brothers. The decree you speak of will not be ratified, I am sure of it. It is just that we have a different political system, one which we believe is fair, but which sometimes slows the legal and political process. I can assure you we are taking measures to prevent Kersebleptes from causing more instability! Otherwise, he is as dangerous as Philip. But to return to the alliance which the men of Athens sent me here to propose, I am pleased to report that we have already started negotiations with King Grabos of Illyria and King Lyppeios of Paeonia—"

"Ambassador, I must know how I can depend on Athens's support when its forces are engaged in war with your rival states," Ketriporis interrupted again.

"If you are willing to begin negotiations with us, honorable king, we are willing to meet your terms. It is our conviction that this alliance is of the utmost importance to all concerned parties."

Summoning Medosades, Ketriporis announced, "Peisianax of Athens, I will give this alliance my consideration. Let us part now. I shall see you at tonight's feast."

Putting his head into his hands, Ketriporis pondered the ambassador's proposal.

Should I consider the alliance? I can ally with Lyppeios and Grabos, even without Athens. But the Athenians would be best at brokering the treaty, and the support of their fleet would be helpful indeed.

Should I send Mononius to Athens again to begin negotiations? Yes. I do not need his resistance and pleas getting in my way.

At least Skostos is on my side and eager to lead his men against the Odomanti. But is it because of his own convictions or because of Meda? He has been telling me Meda approves of my handling of the realm.

LXIV

There were many affairs for the king to manage, and many plans for him to conceive. But thoughts of the fair maiden goldsmith cycled through his mind, soothing his troubled spirit at first, but leaving him confused and uncertain, and angry at himself for allowing her to disturb his heart.

She had been appearing in his thoughts and dreams nearly every night. Drawing him in, taking him places he'd never ventured to before. Places he hadn't known existed, deep within himself. Places without swords, spears, or shields. Without power, rule, and control. Dangerous places for a king to venture into. If he were to fulfill his vows to the gods, to his father, and to himself, these were places he could not enter.

He tried to chase her image away. To dismiss her. To command her to take her leave. Or to at least lead him to the Elethian gold.

After all, he was a king accustomed to being obeyed.

But Evmondia kept on appearing to him over and over, continually disturbing his peace.

"Sura, relay my order to the royal goldsmith," Ketriporis commanded. "He is to make a rhyton with the head of a woman, a drawing of which I will give you."

"As you command, my king," the advisor replied.

If only she obeyed me as easily as everyone else does, I would not have to struggle to forget her.

In the sweltering heat of summer, the anti-Macedonian alliance was ratified in Athens. Thracians, Illyrians, Paeonians, and Athenians alike would soon gather their forces against the Macedonians in secret—it was imperative that Philip not find out.

Prince Mononius returned to Odrysia to find the same boiling atmosphere he had left. Even though the ratification of the alliance had prompted the Athenians to praise King Ketriporis, within the realm itself, it felt like night had fallen, blanketing Western Odrysia in darkness. A people who had formerly looked forward to each chance to hunt, to gain spoils in battle, to win a competition, to celebrate and feast, to enjoy a new artistic creation, dance, song, or poem, were now discontented and fearful, their enthusiasm turning into anger. The king's decisions—to raise the tribute and cut down the sacred forest—were still being met with resistance among the wealthiest of lords and poorest of peasants alike.

Ketriporis's rule was becoming harsher than ever before. He seemed to rely on fear and intimidation, having succumbed to these things himself. Mononius was informed that after the quelling of the Odomantian rebellion, Ketriporis had ordered garrisons to be stationed in tribal villages in order to keep the people under control and suppress any resistance.

The prince knew that instead of making the realm more stable, his brother's oppressive approach was weakening it from within, increasing the number of his enemies inside. Fearing betrayal from his subjects and having given in to paranoia, Ketriporis had recruited men and women alike to serve as scouts and spies. Their duty was to keep a closer watch over his subjects. Therefore, those subjects, pursuing their own individual interests, began exercising greater caution and secrecy in their dealings...

"Honorable lords, I understand your concerns," Mononius responded. The most influential nobles in the realm had gathered privately inside a secluded hilltop fort. "Sorrow and vengeance over what happened at Krenides are guiding those actions. But as Ketriporis is wise and fair, I do believe that reason will soon show him that his decisions have been made in haste. Meanwhile, I shall continue to remind him of the flaws in his thinking and actions, and of the need to change those policies."

"But we cannot wait any longer, Prince Mononius!" shouted Lord Seuthes. "The commoners have been blaming us, calling us greedy and uncaring! It is becoming too difficult to tolerate the anger, the instability, and the outcry of the people!"

"Lord Seuthes, I do feel your anguish," Mononius said.

"Wise prince, you have rightfully earned the respect of the lords and the army alike. You are fair, a great warrior, and a great strategist," Lord Cothelas said. "It is our conviction that there is no one else more deserving to rule the realm. We would be honored to serve under you as our king."

"I am honored that you think so highly of me, lords. But I cannot accept this proposal. Our great King Berisades put his trust in Ketriporis and chose him as his successor. I agreed with Father with all my heart then, and still do. Ketriporis has been misdirected by his anger, but he will soon return to the correct path, I am certain. I still trust and believe in him wholeheartedly."

"Prince Mononius, the realm is becoming–" Lord Teres began.

"You talk of instability, but plotting rebellion is also not the answer," Mononius interrupted. "Strife and disunity only give our enemies more opportunity to strike against us. I give you my word, honorable lords, that I will continue to remind the king of the fallacies in his policies. Now, I shall take my leave, as I am to travel to the estate of General Athenodorus on another mission for the king."

"Wise prince, we beg you to reconsider–"

"I have nothing more to say. But fear not, I shall not tell the king about this meeting. In return, I trust that you will continue to support and aid him."

I am pleased the alliance was ratified, but I cannot solely rely on our allies. Western Odrysia must be strong by herself. This new weapon will be key to that, and the blacksmith is working fast. But he demands payment. I need more gold.

King Ketriporis paced back and forth in his chamber, contemplating the state of his treasury. There was no word from the scout he had left behind in the Elethian land. He was becoming impatient. But the leaves were starting to turn. The time to visit the goldsmith was coming.

Perhaps I am the only one destined to uncover the Elethian treasury, he thought. *But what about her? I cannot stop thinking about her. Is she a sorceress? Did she cast a spell on me? Or is she the goddess of the mountain herself? Is she punishing me for trespassing? For my intentions? Keeping me perpetually torn between what I want to do and what I must do? Tormenting me?*

I could summon the sorcerer to free me from her spell.

But somehow, it is a spell I do not want removed. Could I leave my life of ruling and fighting behind? Could I live with her, high up in the mountain? Rebulus. Those are his desires. Not the ones of Ketriporis, the king.

It was a paradox. Or maybe even sorcery. But the more merciless Ketriporis became, the more his heart opened to feelings of compassion, sympathy, and love—feelings that were useless in one who was destined to rule.

"Truxos, you are to accompany me back to the Elethian lands," he commanded his bodyguard. "Choose men you trust deeply. We leave in three nights."

With Mononius away, he would appoint Skostos and Medosades to manage the realm. Accompanied by his bodyguards, Ketriporis departed for the Elethian land with renewed determination, forcing himself to believe that he was motivated by the only correct influences: the demands of his court, and of the gods themselves.

Reaching the familiar meadow with the waterfall, he ordered his party to halt and set up camp. Then, he commanded his bodyguards to await his return. Paying no heed to the changed carpet of flowers, Ketriporis hurriedly embarked on the passage to the dwelling of the goldsmith. He walked and climbed fast, focused on his aim like a falcon flying towards its prey.

"Master, Rebulus has returned!" Kerza shouted, seeing him amongst the pine trees.

Supported by his stick, the goldsmith came out to greet him. "It is good to have you back to visit us, Rebulus!"

"It is good to be back, master goldsmith," Ketriporis replied. He looked past the old man, his heart pounding in anticipation of beholding Evmondia again. "I have come to inquire about the mask."

"It is made, young friend."

"I am anxious to see it, master."

"Of course. Kerza, fetch Evmondia and tell her Rebulus is here for the mask!"

He sensed her approach even before he turned to see her walking toward him, carrying the mask on a tray. Then their eyes met: the green of the forest and the blue of the sky. At that moment, everything he was and had ever been ceased to exist. There was only her.

She smiled at him. "Rebulus, welcome back to our home!"

Mesmerized, he was struck silent. But she helped him snap out of his trance by continuing. "I hope the mask will be to your liking."

The mask! For an instant, he had forgotten about it. He touched his face. Bare.

The fair maiden smiled again. Why, he could not understand. Was she seeing something he couldn't see? The real him: unmasked, grotesque, and frightening? The thought startled him. He gazed at the mask she was holding. A mask he intended to wear in battle.

Then he looked at her again, with trepidation. She smiled warmly, offering neither disdain nor mockery. "Is the mask to your liking?" she asked.

He replied only in his mind: *If it was made by you, how could I not like it?*

He picked it up from the tray and began examining it. It felt heavy in his hands. There were no carvings of lions or goddesses on it; no ornamentations at all. There was no sign of the intricate, elaborate chasing he had seen on the goldsmith's other objects. The mask was plain. Too plain for his liking. It resembled a death mask.

The old man must have made it.

"You look displeased, Rebulus. The mask must not be to your liking." There was disappointment in her eyes.

"No, it is just that I expected..."

"You must not have expected to see a death mask," the old man interjected. "You asked us to make the mask as we would see it. Then let me ask you, young friend. Does not a warrior bring death, whether to his foes or to himself? Does fighting not bring you closest to death?"

The king remembered what he had told Evmondia before: "Fighting is thrilling, and it is satisfying. It makes me feel more alive than anything else." A stark contrast from the goldsmith's words. "You are right, master goldsmith. I do see the wisdom in that." Turning to Evmondia, he added, "I am more than pleased with the mask, Evmondia."

"You honor us, friend!" she responded merrily.

He handed the goldsmith a pouch with Odrysian coins adorned with the head of Dionysus. The king knew he needed to leave quickly, but he did not. Instead, Ketriporis lingered as long as he could, swimming in Evmondia's essence.

When he was finally ready to depart, the goldsmith said, "You can visit any time, Rebulus! You are a friend of ours for life!"

Not daring to look into Evmondia's eyes, Ketriporis muttered, "I would be honored." Then he turned and departed hastily. "Forgive me," he whispered.

Ketriporis rose at the crack of dawn. Standing under the new day's sun, feeling deeply conflicted between his love for Evmondia and his destiny as a king, he directed his pleas to Sabazios, asking the god to cleanse him of the weaknesses of commoners and restore him to his true self, that of a warrior-king. Leaving his bodyguards behind once again, he set out to meet with the scout he had left in the Elethian land.

Ketriporis met him at the designated place, where the scout had been ordered to wait every six nights for the arrival of the king or new orders. Selected because of his Bessian origin and his familiarity with the nearby lands, the scout was there as commanded.

"Report," Ketriporis commanded.

Hesitantly, the scout began, "Other than going to the village, I only saw the old man leave once. But where to I do not know, as I lost him, my king."

Drawing his dagger and pointing it at the scout, Ketriporis shouted, "How can you lose an old man who can barely walk? I should take your head!"

"Spare me, my king!" the scout pleaded. "I found a cave, high up in the mountain!"

"A cave?"

"Yes, but it is guarded by a fierce monster!"

"Did the monster attack you?"

"No, but when I entered the cave, I saw his eyes. There were so many! Looking at me, following me. I was barely able to escape before it devoured me!"

"Lead me there," Ketriporis ordered.

The cave was difficult to reach, as they had to travel through a rocky and steep crevasse. But they succeeded.

It was vast, cold, and damp. Ketriporis looked up and understood what had frightened the scout. There were numerous openings in the cave's ceiling, resembling a dozen pairs of eyes looking at them, following their every step.

"Is this where the tale of the monster comes from?" the king whispered. "Frightening indeed."

He examined the cave's walls with care, the scout following closely, carrying the torch and looking around anxiously.

Ketriporis spotted a narrow crack splitting the rock. He was slim enough to suck in his chest and pass through, closing his eyes to contain his fear of being crushed or pinned in place.

He knew what would be within: the gold of the Elethi. And there it was. Suddenly, her image flashed through his mind, more brilliant and beautiful than the gold he was looking at. He banished the vision, though it took a great effort, as her brilliance overshadowed that of the gold itself.

Slowly, he opened his eyes. Thick, cool darkness greeted him. "Pass me the torch!" he commanded the scout.

He drew the flickering flame carefully through the gap in the rocks and swung it around himself in an arc, illuminating the chamber. There was only emptiness. Nothingness. Disappointment.

Shining the torch along the walls, he examined every crack, dent, and crevice. And there it was. Another opening, possibly even narrower than the first.

He forced all the air from his lungs, turned sideways, and

passed through it, illuminating the new chamber with the torch. This time, he was greeted by a few bats that flew at him. Other than that, it was the same emptiness, nothingness, and disappointment.

Diligently, he continued his search, journeying deeper into the cave. But it was all to no avail. More darkness, disappointment, and emptiness were all that he encountered.

Though he was far from the open sky, he knew it was likely already late in the day, and the sun would set before long. Retracing his steps and emerging from the cave, Ketriporis found the scout waiting for him, tossing rocks down below.

"Follow me," he ordered.

Back at the meadow where his bodyguards were waiting, he commanded, "We are to return to the court. We must employ a different tactic."

"Medosades, what do you think of Skostos's governance in my absence?" asked Ketriporis when they had returned.

"My king, he has been following your orders and enacting your policies with a firm hand, keeping control over commoners and lords alike."

"I am pleased to hear that. And how has the work of the Athenian scholar been?"

"He has been recording, as you have commanded him. He is participating in the competitions and has even won some footraces."

"And is there anything I should know about?"

"There is, my king. It concerns Krenides. Or should I say, Philippi, now?"

"Philippi? What do you mean?"

"Philip has renamed Krenides after himself. There is no doubt now he will keep it as a colony of Macedonia. He is also minting new coins, double the weight of the regular ones."

"He has access to enough gold to do so, Medosades. This is bad news not only for us, but for Grabos, Lyppeios, and the Athenians. Bring Skostos in."

Skostos has always been different from Mononius and me. Only interested in feasting and women. Showing no interest in the realm's affairs or governing until Meda came to the court. She has altered him greatly, it seems.

"Brother, come in. I am pleased to see you," Ketriporis said.

"I am pleased you have returned, brother," Skostos replied.

"Tell me, what has been happening in my absence?"

"The lords and commoners continue to have the same complaints. As for the tribes, they have given us no trouble."

"As I expected."

"But brother, you never told me why you had to leave in such haste. Did something happen?"

"Nothing important, Skostos. Why are you concerned?"

"It is only that Meda wanted to know, as I have been spending less time with her."

"Did she not urge you to become more involved in the affairs of the court? She should have been pleased I entrusted you with governing the realm."

"She is. She fears you may leave soon again, and I will be once again too busy to devote my attention to her." Skostos seemed animated.

"You will have to disappoint her once more. Soon, I shall leave again to recruit more men. Therefore, I shall need your help. Or do you want me to summon Mononius back?"

"No, I will be honored to help, brother!"

"Very well, then. I just wish you could control Meda as you have done the lords and commoners."

"I cannot understand why you dislike Meda so. Are you jealous of me?" his brother retorted.

"I am not. I just do not trust her. She should learn her place around here."

Getting defensive, Skostos replied, "She is only interested in me and the wellbeing of the realm! And, of course, in maintaining our friendship with the Getae. Nothing more."

"I hope you know what you are talking about."

"You can trust me, brother. I know her well," Skostos replied, putting his hand over his heart.

"Well then, I will think on what you said," Ketriporis replied reflectively. "I will see you at the archery competition."

If ever there was a doubt in my mind about the need to capture the Elethian gold, there can be no longer. Not when Philip is minting new coins! The gold I can obtain from the mines remaining in my possession, even if I use the captives' labor, will be barely enough. Even if I increase the tribute. Even if I cut more of the forest. It will not be enough for me to stand against his growing wealth.

There is no time. I must act quickly.

The Elethians... they can think themselves mighty warriors, but I will dare them to stand in my way. With the rhomphaiae I already have in my possession, defeating them will be easy.

Do not let her turn you away from your path. Do not let her dissuade you and make you hesitant.

It was early in the morning. The young king's residence had not yet awakened to the hustle and bustle of its daily routines when the king and twenty of his most elite bodyguards set out quietly and swiftly for the land of the Elethi.

They galloped through meadows covered in early autumn dew, the grass shimmering silver under the rays of the rising sun. Upon reaching the Nestos, they took the same path the king had already traversed twice before.

The closer they drew to the Elethian land, the more careful, discreet, and inconspicuous they became. The king led his men stealthily around and over steep hills, climbing along sharp edges and making broad leaps in order to reach the goldsmith's dwelling from behind. They moved in silence, as quick and nimble as foxes.

This time, I will not return empty-handed. I promise you, Father.

Despite the early hour, the goldsmith's household was awake and active, in contrast to King Ketriporis's residence when he had departed. Hiding among the tall pine trees, the young king could see Kerza tending to the goats in the stockade. The goldsmith was sitting outside, taking in the early rays of the sun and partaking of his morning meal.

And there she was. He could see Evmondia coming in and

out of the dwelling.

Wearing the mask made for him by those he was about to confront, he signaled for Truxos to follow him and for the rest of his bodyguards to surround the dwelling.

As soon as she saw the masked man emerging from the trees, Kerza began to cry out. But her warning was immediately stifled with a hand over her mouth.

"If the goldsmith or the women are harmed, you will answer with your lives," Ketriporis had ordered his bodyguards. "It is imperative that they stay alive."

Seeing the masked man approaching, the goldsmith exclaimed, "Rebulus... or should I say, King Ketriporis, son of Berisades. I have been expecting you."

"So you know who I am. You are a wise man indeed."

"It looks like the mask fits you well, king."

"That it does, old man. You made a fine mask indeed—one that suits me. But I have come not as a friend, but as a foe."

"What do you seek from me, then?" the goldsmith asked, remaining calm and unabashed.

"I seek knowledge of where your people keep the gold you use. You must lead us to it."

"The gold belongs to the gods. They have gifted it to us and made our land rich with it. The gold cannot belong to you, Odrysian."

"But it can, old man. As I am a descendent of the gods."

"If you were a descendent of the gods which preside over this land, you would not have to come here as a thief."

"You are wrong," was all that Ketriporis was able to say, as at that moment he beheld Evmondia. Without thinking, he reached up and touched the mask with his hand. His face remained safely hidden, and he felt relieved, but only for a moment.

Evmondia smiled, and turning to the old goldsmith, she exclaimed, "Master, the mask does not suit our friend Rebulus, does it?”

“The mask suits the king of the Odrysae very well.”

“The king?” Her voice held an innocence Ketriporis found disingenuous, as though she had known all along and was now mocking him—but affectionately, not cruelly.

“Yes, the king,” the old man replied.

She did not bow or curtsy to him. Her eyes searched for an answer.

The goldsmith continued. “He has come to inquire about the gold.”

“Oh, if I had known, I would have cleaned—”

“There is no need for that. The king is not here to admire our trade, Evmondia.”

She looked at Ketriporis, seemingly confused. Then she looked at her mentor again, worry starting to cloud her face.

“Fetch us some wine,” Ketriporis ordered the maiden, wanting to spare her the sight of the scene to come.

She seemed to seek guidance from the goldsmith. He nodded and gestured for her to go inside.

Once she had vanished through the door, the king drew his sword and pointed it at the goldsmith. “Now, lead us to where the treasure is kept, old man.”

“Upon my honor, I have given my word to the gods and my people that I shall keep the secret until my last breath.”

Putting the sword to the old man’s throat, Ketriporis hissed, “Lead us to the gold.”

“Do you think I fear death, young king? It is gold you seek, but you cannot even see it.”

“Then show it to me, old man.”

“Open your eyes.”

“Rubbish. I do not have patience for nonsensical attempts to confuse me. Bring—”

Ketriporis heard a clatter and a splash, and turned around. Evmondia had dropped the tray and the jug of wine she had brought. She still appeared regally beautiful to him, like a goddess. But this time, like a goddess of ice, she was standing with an expression of horror frozen on her face.

Instinctively, he lowered his sword. *Do not let her put you under her spell. Do not let her unmask you. Lift the sword, Ketriporis. Do not look at her, no matter what.*

"My king!" Truxos shouted a warning.

Ketriporis turned and saw twelve stout-looking warriors rushing toward them from amid the trees with swords drawn.

As he had known it would, the new weapon with which Ketriporis had armed his bodyguards prevented the valiant Elethian warriors from demonstrating their skilled swordsmanship. Indeed, the unprepared warriors, incapable of overcoming the rhomphaia, fell one by one, cut down or pierced from afar by the longer and stronger sword. In a short time, Ketriporis's men emerged victorious.

The king, whom not a single Elethian had been able to reach, turned to the goldsmith. "Old man, I do not have to tell you about the power of my new weapon. Your guardians did me a favor by allowing us to demonstrate it. Now imagine an entire Odrysian army armed with those swords. You saw what they can do. I can slaughter all of your people or, if I am feeling inclined toward mercy, sell them into slavery. I am sure you would not want such a fate to befall your people. All you have to do is lead me to the gold." He paused and waited. "No answer, old man? Perhaps we should begin right now. Bring the old woman!"

His bodyguards brought Kerza out, shoving her to the ground.

"Does her life mean anything to you?" Ketriporis roared, shifting his sword toward the old woman's throat.

"Master, do not tell them! My life is not worth this sacrifice," Kerza pleaded. She gasped for breath as one of the king's bodyguards held her head under his arm, squeezing her throat tightly.

The king stood, sword raised, pointing it toward... Evmondia, who had run to Kerza and was shielding her with her own body.

Do not let her lower your sword. The old man would not allow anything to happen to Evmondia just for the sake of keeping the secret. But what if I harm her? Her life is precious to me... more precious than my own.

I have never thought like this before. Why now?

"No one has to die or get hurt. Lead me to the gold, and we can part ways peacefully."

Still, he received no response.

"You refuse to obey the command of the king?" he shouted.

"You are no king of mine that I must obey," the goldsmith replied, his face impassive.

Ketriporis lowered his sword, and turning to Truxos, shouted, "Hang the old woman!"

"As you command, my king."

"No!" Evmondia's wail was heart-wrenching, as loud and piercing as a battle cry. But with purity behind it.

"Do not! I beg you!" she cried out again.

Then he heard her say the words he had been hoping to hear most. "Please stop! I will lead you to the gold! But you must give me your word of honor as the king. You must swear that you will not harm Kerza or Master. Promise me!"

"Upon my honor, maiden, no harm shall befall them." He gestured for his bodyguard to loosen his grip on Kerza.

Evmondia walked to the goldsmith. Gently, she took his hand and spoke softly, looking him deeply in the eyes.

"You will not break your vow to the gods and to the people, Master. I will be the one to lead the Odrysian king to the gold. There will always be more gold that can be mined. But your people, Master—their wisdom, their kindness, and the good they bring are more precious and valuable than any gold! Do not let the Odrysian king destroy them."

She returned her attention to the king. "Follow me, Rebulus. Or should I say King Ketriporis?"

He regarded her silently. He did not try to laugh it off or scoff at her. His heart felt as if it had been pierced, left bleeding and wounded deep inside.

Surrounded by his bodyguards, he followed Evmondia closely down the path. Normally, he would lead a captive at the tip of his sword, but he could not bring himself to do that to her.

They were so close, and yet he felt so far away from her. He tried to guess what she might be thinking about him. About his betrayal. About his sullied heart, so far from being pure. If it had ever been.

Why are we going down the mountain? We are descending onto flat ground. Yet this place looks familiar somehow.

And there it was, the meadow and the waterfall. The same place where, not that long ago, he had been torn between the call of her song and the call of his destiny.

He spotted a bear sitting by the waterfall. White as the snow, in contrast to the darkness in his spirit, it must have been the same one as before. But this time, instead of stopping his bodyguards, he signaled them to eliminate the obstacle.

No more lingering weaknesses.

Their arrows were on target. The bear groaned as it tumbled to the ground.

"No!" Evmondia screamed.

She rushed toward the bear, unconcerned for her own safety. Kneeling next to the dying animal, she began to sing the most sorrowful song he had ever heard. The bear struggled before succumbing to its eternal sleep.

"Evmondia, you must lead us to the gold!" He tried to interrupt and command her onward. But there was more gentleness in his voice than he had intended there to be.

She would not look at him, nor did she reproach him. Slowly, she rose and pointed in the direction of the waterfall. “Take this path and go behind the waterfall. You will see an opening in the rock. There, you will find what you seek.”

He could see the tears glistening like gems on her cheeks. But for him there was no turning back, no possible retreat. Not now. Not when he was so close to what he needed so desperately.

He heard movement. Then he saw them, swords drawn, coming at his men rapidly.

“The gold in these lands belongs to its people,” he heard Evmondia say. “Why do you think you can own it, King Ketriporis?”

Wasting no more time on debate, he rushed toward the Elethian warriors, flanked by his bodyguards, all gripping the handles of their rhomphaiae tightly.

The javelins and arrows of the Elethians did not touch the skilled bodyguards, who dodged them with great agility, deflecting them with their shields, and cutting through the flying spears with their rhomphaiae.

There were more of the Elethian warriors than there had been at the goldsmith’s dwelling. But their numbers did not grant them any advantage—they were still struggling to engage in close combat with the rhomphaia-wielding Odrysians. And soon, the king’s men were able to overpower the Elethians. The swords did their intended work again, slashing through bone, metal, and wood, and cutting the Elethians down one by one.

Then Ketriporis saw him. Despite his age, the old goldsmith was still able to wield a sword.

He followed us down the mountain! But why? He must know it is in vain!

“Do not harm the old man!” he shouted. But it was too late.

He watched as one of his bodyguards swiftly pierced the goldsmith straight through the heart.

Evmondia let out a shriek of terror and despair. He watched her rush toward the fallen goldsmith, cradling his body and crying despondently.

"My king!" Truxos shook him from his stupor. "They are all dead! What do you order us to do?"

"Follow me!"

Cautiously, they approached the waterfall at a diagonal angle. The entrance to the cave was visible but still difficult to make out behind the rushing water.

No sounds could be heard. Not even the chirping of the birds. Nor Evmondia's cry. Only the hypnotic, rushing flow of the endlessly falling water.

I am sorry, Evmondia. But I must.

He turned to look back at the maiden one final time. She was still by the goldsmith's side.

"Watch out!" Truxos's warning came just in time for him to dodge the arrow that flew out from the darkness of the cave. More arrows followed, falling on them in waves and killing a few of his men.

The guardians of the treasury charged out of the cave. But once again, the intruders were able to overtake the warriors, deflecting the arrows with their shields and striking the Elethians down with their superior swords.

Charging forward, the king led his men into the cave, slaughtering the last remaining guardians.

Four of the king's bodyguards perished in the fight, and five were severely wounded, but the raid—a real raid for gold led by King Ketriporis, unlike the setup at Krenides—was a resounding success.

The sun had already begun to set when the surviving Odrysians reappeared from behind the waterfall, laden with the gold of the Elethi. They had found the treasure they sought stored deep inside the cave, in a chamber with a pool of green water and sharp, icicle-like figures of stone hanging over their heads.

The bodies of the fallen warriors covered the meadow. And among them, a solitary figure stood out. The figure of a woman cradling the body of an old man, singing.

The king forced himself to look away from her. He stopped himself from rushing toward her, from trying to take her into his arms. To hold her. To comfort her. To never let her go.

He knew that her image and her song would be forever etched into his memory.

But his destiny was calling him. And with the newfound gold, it appeared his fate would be a glorious one.

Maybe one day I will find a way and be able to return. Or so he thought before joining his bodyguards, who were carrying the gold away. All the while, the Elethian villagers went about their work in peace, unaware of what had transpired.

Fortune has favored me again. The gods are on my side! Now I shall not just grow my army, but my realm. Soon, I will be the one to reunite Odrysia under my rule. And then conquer and annex Macedonia as well! Philip must learn his place in the grand order of the world. From the Getic lands to Thessaly and Illyria, my kingdom shall be rivaled by none. Tales of its reputation shall spread throughout the lands: to Persia and Libya, and even further, to the end of all seas. And I will build a city grander than Pella, grander than Persepolis itself!

Do not get ahead of yourself, Ketriporis.

But it is good to dream. Without dreams, there is no ambition. And without ambition, there is no success. But this feeling! She...

Forget that naïve girl, Ketriporis. You did what was best for the realm. For Father. Grabos and Lyppeios have agreed that when the flowers bloom, we shall gather our forces and strike Macedonia. The Athenians, too, are in support.

During the snows, I must finish my preparations for war. Axios, the Macedonian sun may be bright, but over my realm, its rays shall be dimmed. And Macedonia herself shall be the one plunged into the night.

The members of King Ketriporis's court were elated over the successful capture of the Elethian gold. With the royal treasury filled once more, lords and commoners alike, previously resistant to the king's policies, now welcomed his new edicts: that the sale of the Orbelian timber be halted, and the tribute for the upcoming winter be reduced even below its previous level. Moreover, the king had announced his plan to expand his realm, annexing more lands and peoples and forging alliances with the most powerful tribes.

Mononius was concerned that Ketriporis was becoming more like Philip himself, but everyone else greeted this news with great excitement. Western Odrysia would not just become mightier but more prosperous.

Yet amidst the high spirits, Trysimachus was deeply tormented. He shut himself in his room and feigned illness.

Am I to blame for the raid on the Elethi? the historian asked himself, as the memory of his broken promise to Pitros circled in his mind. He had come to western Thrace to observe and record history. Was he now responsible for altering it? Had he become like Aeschylus, a creator of a tragedy himself? The tragedy of the Elethian people, of the goldsmith, and of Evmondia?

When Pitros learned what had transpired, he left Ketriporis's service, burdened by grief and guilt over having guided the king to the goldsmith's dwelling.

And what of Trysimachus himself? He carried the burden of his own part in the events. He had lost one of his best friends, one who had helped him gain confidence, skill, and strength, and understand the life and ways of the Thracians. A Bessian warrior, lacking in learning, but wise in his own way nevertheless.

Overwhelmed by profound grief and guilt, Trysimachus wondered if he, like Pitros, should leave the basileus's court. There was only one person he knew he could rely on for guidance.

Reaching for his brush and papyrus, he began writing a letter to Zenon of Apollonia.

As King Ketriporis prepared to strengthen his army and expand his realm, a shadow was engulfing Odrysia.

"What is it, Skostos? You look troubled. Has Meda done something to vex you?"

"No, Ketriporis, Meda could not be more agreeable. I know not how to say this, but it concerns Mononius."

"What about him?"

"I should have told you sooner. Forgive me, Ketriporis! But he is our brother, and I know how much you value him. Yet I fear he is plotting a rebellion against you."

"What makes you think that?"

"Brother, when you were away, I was informed that he had conducted secret meetings with those lords who stood in the greatest opposition to your policies. As you know, even now he continues to oppose your great vision for the future of the realm. I have it under good authority that he is gathering a force as we speak, colluding with some of the chieftains to overthrow you, brother."

"Rebellion? I have been feeling betrayed by Mononius, but this I never expected! Especially now, when we are so close to becoming one of the strongest realms!"

How, oh how, could the brother I once trusted most become such a threat?

"I, too, could not fathom that Mononius would have such an intent! I did not want to accept it. But the proof has become undeniable. What should we do?"

"Capture Mononius and his closest advisors and place them under guard! I will interrogate them myself."

"It shall be done as you command!"

"But Skostos, we must keep this between ourselves."

"I understand. It shall be done quietly."

"Very well. Let us tread carefully, brother. We must prevent conflict within the realm. Despite our recent fortunes, we still have vulnerabilities. I need more time to enlarge the army and to have more swords forged. The snows will be upon us soon. It is unlikely Philip will strike during the winter, but we must prepare. And when the flowers begin blooming, we must act quickly! Now that Mononius has taken to the other side, you are the one I shall most rely upon. With a larger army, combined with the forces of our allies, we shall eliminate the threat that is Macedonia. My new sword will help see to that."

"Brother, what is this new sword you have been talking about?"

"The moment has come. I will demonstrate it for you."

Trysimachus was eager for a response from his mentor. He peered toward the horizon, on the lookout for the coming of the courier, ignoring the red, orange, and yellow hues coloring Mount Orbelus. Finally, he spotted a cloud of dust coming down the road. The courier was arriving.

"Is there a letter for me from Apollonia, Bora?" the young scholar inquired, hardly giving the courier a chance to dismount.

"There is, Athenian, and I'm glad of it! I'm sick of ya pestering me!"

"This letter is important to me," Trysimachus responded apologetically.

"That's what the Getic princess says, too, but I can't make her father write her any sooner! Besides, she's been sendin' and gettin' too many letters. She might as well be a Hellene like ya!"

Leaning closer to Trysimachus, the courier whispered conspiratorially, "Say, Athenian, could ya deliver this letter to Princess Meda? I'd like to have my wine without havin' to listen to her complain 'bout my smell. She's always scoffin' at me, beautiful though she is!"

"I would be glad to." Taking both letters, the scholar left hastily. But instead of heading to the princess's residence, he first headed to his own.

Tossing the letter to the princess on his table, he unrolled the one from his mentor and devoured every word, searching for an answer:

> *Trysimachus, we in the mortal world cannot always foresee the effects of our words and actions, as we mortals cannot know what someone is going to do with the information we provide them. At each moment, we do what we must do, guided by the gods. Your dilemma is born from your wondering whether it was you or the gods who chose life for you, death for the goldsmith, and for King Ketriporis to take the Elethians' gold. You cannot be sure whether it was you or the gods who affected history. Thus, you have been blaming yourself. You must learn forgiveness, first for yourself and then for others. Each one of us, present within this world, affects events in some way. We cannot understand the grand plan and the grand meaning of it all. Only the gods can. As historians, our work is to observe and record the events as they occur. So continue to record events as you observe them. After all...*

Startled by blaring horns and the noise of running feet and shouting, Trysimachus put his mentor's letter down and hurried outside to investigate the commotion.

Unsure whether to be grateful or angry at Skostos's revelation about Mononius, Ketriporis was preparing himself to visit his brother. He would interrogate him and uncover the truth.

Without warning, Sura burst into his quarters. "My king! A messenger sent by General Akinestes has arrived with an urgent report! I have brought him here with me!"

"Speak!" Ketriporis commanded the messenger.

"My king, the fort on the Strymon is under attack from the Macedonians, and King Philip's army is marching into your dominion."

"What we have feared is happening!" added Sura.

"Yes, it is. Sura, you know what to do!"

"I take my leave, my king!"

The king's plan was to act quickly, but it was the king of the Macedonians who was the quicker.

How had Philip known to move his army at that precise moment, to strike and take advantage of the still disorganized realm of the young king? A realm whose second-in-command had been imprisoned, his services rendered useless? A realm that still needed more swords to be forged, more gold and silver coins to be minted, more men to be recruited, more land to be annexed, and more alliances to be made?

It was a mystery to many. But like a cloud hovering above the countryside, Philip was moving into Western Odrysia, casting a gray hue over it.

LXXI

Ketriporis's lords and generals were gathered in the field, listening to their king's commands and readying themselves for the impending war.

"Prince Mononius has been taken gravely ill," the king announced. "Therefore, his force will be led by Lord Rhaskus."

Murmurs of bewilderment rose from the assembly, and General Derzelas voiced his concerns. "My king, the prince must lead his men into battle, even if he is ill! They will not fight under another leader, I fear."

"They must fight, and they will!" Ketriporis responded. "In order to become victorious, a clever strategy is needed. We must think carefully about the terrain on which we will engage the Macedonians. Honorable men, you have already experienced the strength and impenetrability of the Macedonian phalanx formations. But what they shall lose to is... this."

He raised it over his head so that all could see. It had a blade longer than any sword, with just a slight curve toward the end, and a longer-than-usual handle similar to a spear's shaft, but still shorter than the blade.

"Yes, this is the new weapon I have been hinting at. I call it 'rhomphaia'. I can already see the admiration in your eyes. Derzelas, try it out... what do you think?"

The general took a few practice swings and strikes with

the rhomphaia, and replied, "This is a formidable sword indeed! With a weapon like this, we shall certainly have an advantage over the Macedonians."

"The problem, honorable lords, is that I can equip only my elite unit with the number of swords forged so far."

"Your most skillful warriors are in that unit, my king. Equipped with these swords they can take on the Macedonians, as long as we trap them on favorable ground."

"My thoughts precisely, general. Let us sound the horns! We must depart quickly."

Confident of victory, the army of King Ketriporis marched to confront and stop the Macedonians.

Just as in previous campaigns, the king was clad in golden armor. But this time, his face too was covered by the gold mask of death. He looked frightening and deadly, ready to take on his foes.

The army was moving west at great speed, hurrying to block the Macedonians' entry through the Orbelus pass. With no time to rest, they were marching at night, the flames of their torches dancing under the moon amidst the autumn breezes.

When the sun rose, the army of the Thracians had no time to bask in its rays, which reflected off their armor, swords, helmets, and shields; their horse plates; the long, slightly curved blades of the rhomphaiae; and the golden mask and armor of the king. And as the sun continued to rise, the king noticed that it felt exceptionally warm and bright for autumn.

"Halt!" he commanded an approaching scout. "Report what you have seen."

"My king, an advance force of Macedonians is camped in the meadow below."

"How many men?"

"Around five hundred, I'd say."

"How much cavalry?"

"Only a few horses; mostly infantry."

"Who is leading them?"

"General Axios, my king."

Axios, I have not forgotten what you and Parmenion did at Krenides. "Is there another force nearby?"

"No, we haven't seen any, and neither has Lord Rhaskus up 'head."

"Good. If we act quickly, we can take Axios's forces by surprise. It shall be an easy victory!" Ketriporis declared. "I will take the elite unit with me. Spartacus, follow me. Skostos, you must lead the army forward. I will be back to rejoin you soon."

Axios, today, you shall meet your death at my hands.

Riding fast, the king's unit arrived at the meadow only to watch as the Macedonian detachment disappeared into the nearby forest.

"After them!" Ketriporis ordered.

Dismounting and chasing the Macedonians, the elite unit entered the forest. And the deeper they went, the thicker the tree cover became. The spaces between the trees were getting narrower and tighter, the branches turning into nuisances and obstacles for the men. And then...

"Retreat! No further! It is a trap!" the king shouted. But it was too late. The Macedonians had already turned around and were charging at the king's men, swords drawn.

Impeded by the length of the rhomphaiae, neither Ketriporis nor his elite warriors could effectively swing their blades in the narrow spaces between the trees. Beneath the thick cover, it was difficult for them to fight.

Instead, they were the ones who were falling, cut down and slain one by one by the shorter swords of the Macedonians. From the corner of his eye, Ketriporis saw his younger brother trying to swing his rhomphaia against a charging Macedonian. But Spartacus's sword had gotten stuck in the branches of a bushy tree. Swiftly, the Macedonian thrust his much shorter sword at the prince, piercing his heart.

"Spartacus!" Ketriporis shouted as loud as a titan, his chest about to burst. "No!"

Filled with rage, he dashed toward the Macedonian to slaughter him. But he couldn't swing his sword.

Why was I not more careful? This weapon was never meant to be used in the thickest of forests! These were his last thoughts before he was struck from the side by a sword. Falling to the ground, he saw Axios snarling at him with wolfish teeth. Seconds later, he heard a thump and saw Axios lying next to him on the ground. Blood was gushing from the Macedonian's forehead, where a dagger was stuck.

He felt someone trying to lift him up. "My king, lean on me! We must go!" It was Truxos.

The king looked down at Axios's body. "You did well," was all he was able to say.

Protected by Ketriporis's other bodyguards, who had also rushed to his aid and who were trying to stay afoot despite the persistent attacks of the Macedonians, Truxos carried the king's limp body away. Finding a hollow place behind a rock, he laid Ketriporis down and tended to his wounds. He tried to conceal him by covering his body with autumn foliage, the red leaves matching the blood gushing from the king's wound.

Father, how will I face you in the heavens? I was too eager to take my revenge on Axios and caused Spartacus's death! But all cannot be lost. There is still Skostos and his force. They will come out victorious. But there is no time for me...

He took his most trusted bodyguard by the hand. "Truxos, Mononius is imprisoned. You must set him free. He is the one to take my place. Promise me you will convey my will."

"Yes, my king."

"And there is another duty you must fulfill for me. You must take me to the land of the Elethi... to her."

“Should I not take you to the healer first?”

“There is no need for that. The end is near. Do as I tell you.” Ketriporis added, “Oh, and there is something else...”

It was becoming difficult for him to speak. He knew the blow he had received was a fatal one.

Was it all premeditated? It must have been! But how could they have known how to overcome the rhomphaia? How could they have known of its existence?

All of his dreams, all of his plans were fading away. He had no choice but to leave it all behind. To meet his parents again in the afterlife. To forgo control, which he had struggled so much to obtain, but which was starting to feel meaningless in the face of death.

Under cover of the leaves, Truxos waited until darkness fell and all had quieted down, until only the corpses were left strewn around the forest.

He lifted his king—still alive but weakened by loss of blood—and put him on his back to carry. Finding their horses, Truxos followed his king’s command and galloped toward the land of the Elethi.

When I thought I was the most in control, I had it least. Was it my magic weapon that caused my own demise? Was my desire for revenge my weakness?

LXXII

Trysimachus had been overlooked, left behind, and forgotten in the rush to battle, having received no orders to march with the king's force. Disappointed, he returned to his quarters. The letter from his teacher still lay on the table. And next to it, neglected and forgotten, lay another letter: the one he had promised to deliver to Princess Meda. He grabbed it and set out to fulfill his promise to the courier.

But the historian stopped before reaching the corridor, his curiosity piqued. The letter's contents could open a door for him to the inside of the Getic kingdom, and the prospect of learning something new was too tempting to resist.

Having handled many scrolls before, Trysimachus knew how to open and reseal them undetected. He peeked at the writing, which was in Doric Hellenic.

> *My beautiful daughter*, he read. *Wait for the sun to rise and shine over the valleys and the mountains. Have patience; I, your father, promise to reward your loyalty to me by making the one you have chosen the rising star of the new kingdom of the sun. It is your wisdom that illuminated my way. The idealistic son will be in the shadows. As to the new problem, it can be overcome. The great one has found a way. Await my coming. Soon. You did well. Father*

Rerolling the scroll and sealing it again, the scholar pondered what he had read. There was something unsettling about the letter.

He rushed across the grounds toward the princess's quarters. With the king and most of his men and cohorts away from the royal residence, the place was eerily quiet and peaceful.

Truxos dismounted. Supporting his severely wounded king, he headed toward the goldsmith's dwelling through the gently falling snow, leaving his horse among the tall pine trees to await their return.

Suddenly, the enchanting voice of a female singer filled the air. The bodyguard watched as the king stirred to life. With a show of strength Truxos didn't expect him to have, Ketriporis tore himself away from his bodyguard's heavy grip. And despite the difficulties and the strain, he headed in the direction of the mesmerizing song.

As they approached the dwelling, a giant warrior with his sword drawn lunged unexpectedly at the king; Truxos recognized the Bessian, Pitros. The bodyguard quickly deflected Pitros's intended strike.

Staring into the Bessian's eyes, Truxos could see rage flaring like fire, ready to burn him and the king alive.

"The king shall not harm the maiden! Let him be! He is dying! He will not remain in the mortal realm much longer!" the bodyguard declared.

The Bessian's expression changed, the tension around his eyes loosening.

Lowering their swords, the two Thracian warriors watched as the king staggered toward the maiden, who had come out of the dwelling to see what the ruckus was about.

At the sight of her, the young king touched his face, where

the golden mask was still firmly attached. Struggling, with much effort, he took the mask off, revealing a handsome face with bright blue eyes.

But in her mind's eye, the maiden did not see the handsome face of the king—or Rebulus, as she had known him before. Instead, she saw him slaying the Elethian warriors, and herself holding the body of the slain goldsmith in her arms. The horror made Evmondia instinctively turn her head away.

Falling to his knees, gasping for breath, Ketriporis groaned, "Evmondia, let us meet again in the afterlife... do not turn away from me... start differently..."

She did not respond. He collapsed, and his lifeless body rolled down the cold slope.

LXXIII

Trysimachus's sandals clattered over the cobblestones of Apollonia Pontica as he rushed to his mentor's residence, still pondering the events he had witnessed and experienced in Odrysia.

The waves of the Black Sea, the Pontos Euxeinos, were calm and peaceful that winter day, much different from the last time the young historian had been in Apollonia.

Less than two years had passed since he had departed from the colony. Not much had changed in his absence that he could see. The real change had occurred not here but there.

The once prosperous realm of Western Odrysia he had visited as a young and inexperienced historian was no more. It was no longer ruled by King Berisades or his son King Ketriporis, but by the king of Macedonia himself, Philip.

After the conclusion of his time in Western Odrysia, the young historian had finally been able to unravel the mystery of the letter to the Getic princess Meda which he had read. It had begun to make sense to him, and he was confident that he now understood its meaning.

The letter had not been from the princess's father after all, but from another benefactor: King Philip. Indeed, the 'sun', the kingdom of Macedonia, had conquered the western realm. And the 'rising star', Prince Skostos, had been appointed the vassal king of western Thrace under Macedonian rule, with Meda his queen consort.

As for Mononius, the 'idealistic son', he was 'in the shadows', having been falsely accused of plotting a rebellion against his brother. Fleeing western Thrace, the prince had taken residence in King Amadokus's realm. Both pro-Athenian and anti-Macedonian, a man of strong rhetoric and influence, Mononius had been the most significant threat to Skostos's, and by extension Philip's, rule over western Thrace.

And the 'new problem' had also been solved. By revealing the information and the design of the rhomphaia, Meda had given the strategists in Pella a chance to figure out how to overcome it.

It was difficult for Trysimachus to reconcile himself to the idea that the princess had helped cause the young basileus's demise. Could it have also been she who had helped ambush General Pittacus's force and the Thasian delegation, by revealing the king's orders regarding Krenides to the Macedonians? Or were there others in King Ketriporis's court secretly acting as informants to the Macedonians? Indeed, how privy had Skostos been to Philip's and Meda's schemes, if at all?

He would most likely never know. In the end, others had affected the history of the western realm far more than he. Having been helped from the inside, as in previous campaigns, the 'sun' had blazed and quickly burnt Western Odrysia.

Ketriporis's raid on the Elethian treasury had been for naught. Ultimately, it had benefited the Macedonian king more than the Odrysians. And the pain and suffering inflicted upon the Elethi—upon Evmondia—could not be undone.

At least Skostos had taken a liking to his brother's weapon, and ordered that more rhomphaiae be forged. Ketriporis's legacy would live on in that one way, if nothing else.

Macedonia had continued to act swiftly, defeating the

armies of Grabos the Illyrian and Lyppeios the Paeonian before they could join forces. The alliance between the three kings and Athens had been rendered useless, the Athenians failing to accomplish what they had set out to do diplomatically.

But the young historian had accomplished his mission, and had learned much about himself on his journey.

His mentor's words echoed in his mind.

"Through the challenges, the dangers, the perils, the unknown, and the unexpected, you will obtain the greatest knowledge of all. The knowledge of knowing and understanding thyself."

In the end, he had indeed come to know and understand himself better. He was glad he had made the difficult decision to set out on that journey.

The funeral of King Ketriporis was quite a different affair from that of his father, King Berisades. He was buried in a plain and solitary tomb devoid of decorations and riches.

There was no favorite wife to follow him. No servants to serve him in the afterlife. No fancy procession, games, or banquet. He was buried with only his stallion, his armor, the first rhomphaia, a golden mask, and, placed over his heart, a golden rhyton bearing the image of a maiden.

On one side of his body was placed a pile of white pebbles, which mostly represented his youth, when he was happy and carefree. On the other side was placed a pile of black pebbles, representing the darkness of his spirit, the torment and strife over his burden of solving the challenges facing his realm.

But amongst the black ones, a few white ones stood out, and they surrounded another golden rhyton he had ordered

Truxos to make, with the head of the same maiden.

They represented the few happy days he had spent with Evmondia.

- SEVENTY-FOUR -
2016

IT WAS EARLY IN THE MORNING. THE BEACH WAS DE-serted and quiet. The only sounds to be heard were the chirping of the birds, wind rustling through the pines, and the waves of the Pacific rushing to the shore.

Zenon stood gazing at the sun as it rose from behind the ocean. Basking in its rays, he stood at the spot where, three months prior, he had been tempted to follow the song of the sirens—to be lured deep into the sea, to be drowned. To be lost forever. At the spot where he had followed instead the song of the Thracian muse, which had led him to dry ground.

He now knew that by taking the journey of writing and reviewing *The Mask*, the fascinating world of ancient Thrace had become his healing ground, the story itself resembling a prophetic dream. And, unbeknownst to him, by taking him on a path down into the darkness, it had helped him to emerge back into the light.

Evmondia...

He hadn't seen her since that day at Mr. Clifton's apartment. And yet, she'd had an incredible, life-changing impact on him. She'd had a rare, natural beauty, and the fact that she had seemed so unaware of it had made her even more attractive to him. She had shined with the distinctive aura of her faraway land, the depth of her country's ancient history, and the enchanting spell of its many myths and legends.

He wanted to tell her about *The Mask*. How it was meant to pay homage to the mysterious culture that history had overlooked, how it had helped him dig deep into his being, and how it had forced him to find answers to the most terrifying questions. More than anything, he wished she could know that the manuscript was a mirror to his soul.

Maybe one day he would be able to tell her. To show her the unmasked him.

It had all been a lie. A deceit. An illusion.

The mask had been his imprisonment. A false tale of appearance, and a false reflection of his aspirations and dreams. The mask had never suited him. But it had been powerful, always finding excuses to hang on, refusing to let go—confusing him and fueling his inner inferno.

The mask had been cold and unfeeling. Under its influence, he had pulled a grand scam—not just on Accruement Finance, but on himself as well. And the embers had seared him.

Zenon stood for some time at the beach, feeling the placid waters of the ocean gently caress his feet. He then followed the pine trees fringing the beach and veered in the direction of the old water tower of Ouro.

- SEVENTY-FIVE -

CLIMBING TO THE TOP OF THE TOWER, ZENON STOOD perched on the edge and breathed in deeply, enjoying the fresh morning air. No one was around. It was still too early for the tourist bus. A perfect setting for reflection.

After completing his radiation treatments in Nouméa and returning to the Isle of Pines, he was determined to rethink the direction of his own life. He couldn't take it for granted any more. As much as he used to criticize and bemoan it, coming so close to having it taken away had made him realize how precious it truly was, and how fearful he was of actually losing it.

He recalled the words he had written, placing them in the mouth of the Bessian priestess.

Can you accept defeat as a gift from the gods?

He had come close to death. And indeed, it seemed that something in him had died.

Yet something new in him had been born.

He resolved to use his experiences as an opportunity for a new beginning. To find a new purpose in life. As the phoenix rises from the ashes, so would he rise with a new motivation.

Would his new life be better? He didn't know. But he was

determined to at least try to make it so.

He then recalled the words of his oncologist. "Don't focus on why it happened. You'll never know for sure. There is no person or thing worth blaming for it. What's important is that the lymphoma is in an early stage and treatable. You are young and have many years ahead of you."

Indeed, the spark of life within him had never been extinguished. There must have been some purpose for his existence; for his coming into this world. And he needed time to discover it.

It was no wonder, in *The Mask*, he had protected the young historian, and in the end had kept him away from the greatest danger.

Zenon understood that he had to learn to forgive. He no longer wanted the world to treat him differently just because of what he'd experienced. Instead, it was important for him to treat himself differently. And treat others differently, too.

One thing was for sure. The world he had known—of fighting, controlling, and resisting—could be no more. That had been the world of Ketriporis as well. But Ketriporis's world had ended. His didn't have to.

He thought of the way he had portrayed the Odrysian ruler in his novel. A deep sense of compassion toward the young king—who had fought and loved, been victorious and been defeated—enveloped him.

Then he thought of the other characters in *The Mask*. Major and minor. Protagonists and antagonists. Despite living in a completely different era of humanity, he had felt connected to their aspirations and plights.

The water tower he was standing on had been built by prisoners, stone by stone. Step by step, he was going to rebuild his life by the open sea, the wind, the sand, the sun. Just as the prisoners—his inner voice—had once told him.

It was time for him to stand on firm ground. To be rooted

again. Not spinning endlessly in a whirlpool of deception. Not hiding in places where he ultimately didn't belong.

It was time to open up to the possibility that the world was not such a bad place after all. One could live a good, honest life and be happy. Many people did it. Why couldn't he?

In the end, Ricardo had been right. Success was not a number. A successful person didn't need glamour, and glamour was not a prerequisite for success.

Millions upon millions of people around the world were living their own success stories every day. Some were big, some small, but they were success stories nevertheless. What was wrong with their stories? Nothing but the yardstick by which he had measured their success.

He recalled the dream he'd had in the Bronx; it felt like eons ago, now. He wanted to reinterpret it. Perhaps all those people at the poker table on the cruise ship were not afraid to gamble with life. Perhaps they weren't afraid of losing—they didn't see it as a defeat. They were willing to take the chance.

There were many stories Zenon could write. So far, there had been no one to share them with. Maybe he could take the chance to have them published. Maybe one day, *The Mask* could be his new beginning.

He had been living his life with a closed point of view and a closed heart. But he had tricked the sentries of his mind and snatched the key. By doing so, he had rediscovered the love that still dwelled deep within his heart. And it was that love he would trust to lead him to where he needed to go, and what he needed to do.

Zenon swiftly descended from the top of the tower, realizing there was something else he wanted to do. Another change he wanted to make. It was time to bring harmony and balance to his life.

He wanted to change the story, to change the outcome.

He rushed back to his hut and turned on his laptop. He

was ready to begin typing the new ending to King Ketriporis's story. But before he did that, he glanced at the title of his manuscript.

The Mask was a fitting name for the story he had written. The story he had needed to write. But it was no longer appropriate. There were three words he needed to add—so he did.

It now read *The Cracking of the Mask*.

THE CRACKING OF THE MASK

BY ZENON MCCLOW

THRACE, AUTUMN, 356 BCE

It was early in the morning. The young king's residence had not yet awakened when Ketriporis and twenty of his most elite bodyguards set out quietly and swiftly for the land of the Elethi.

They galloped through meadows covered in early autumn dew, shimmering silver under the rays of the rising sun. Upon reaching the Nestos, they took the same path the king had already traversed twice before.

The closer they got to the Elethian land, the more careful, discreet, and inconspicuous they became. The king led his men around and over steep hills, along sharp cliff faces, and across wide chasms in order to reach the goldsmith's dwelling from behind. They traveled quickly and silently, as nimble as foxes.

This time, I will not return empty-handed. I promise you, Father.

By the time they arrived, the goldsmith's household was awake. Hidden by the tall pine trees, the young king could see Kerza tending to the goats in the stockade. The goldsmith was sitting outside, basking in the sun and partaking of his morning meal.

As expected, Evmondia was nowhere in sight. He had carefully planned to arrive when she would be down in the village.

Seeing the masked men approaching, the goldsmith exclaimed, "Friend Rebulus, welcome back! The mask you are wearing—the one for the king—does not suit you well here."

"I am not Rebulus, old man, but King Ketriporis of the Odrysae himself! I am pleased with the mask you made for me. It suits me well."

"I know of you, son of Berisades. But why have you journeyed to my humble dwelling? Is there something else you want made for you?"

"You keep the secret of where your people's gold is hidden. You must know why I have come."

"Ah, so it is gold you seek. You have come to the right place, then."

"So lead me to it! If you do not want blood to be shed, that is."

"The gold you seek is not located in one place."

"How many places, then, are there?"

"Gold can be everywhere, young king. You seek it, and yet you cannot even see it."

"What nonsense do you speak, old man?"

"Rebulus—or should I now address you as King Ketriporis?—I knew that you would return one day with such an intent. And as one of the elders of the Elethi, it is fitting for me to be the one to tell you, but I fear you will be disappointed in what you shall hear."

"That is for me to decide."

"Very well, then. From the beginning of its creation, the gods have gifted our land with an abundance of gold. But for this gift, the gods wanted something in return from the elders of the Elethian people: to use the gold for good. Not as a means for inflicting harm or hardships upon others. The gods warned the elders that hoarding the gold would bring destruction to the people. That depleting the land of gold would impoverish not only those currently dwelling on it, but their children, and then the children of their children thereafter. They told the elders that they had given the Elethians enough gold to make the lives of their people better. But they also warned them not to abuse the gold, as they would not replenish it."

Pausing to take a deep breath of the fresh morning air and a sip of goats' milk, the goldsmith continued. "Thus, guided by the gods themselves, since the very beginning, the Elethian people have been using the gold in our land in moderation, striving to live in harmony with it and not to use it in a way that would result in harm or suffering, nor as a means to rule over one another. That is why there is no rich treasury hidden in our land, young king. Nor is there gold that wears a mask of death. As we do not fight over it, we mine and pan only what is needed to honor our gods, to bring beauty to us and to others, and to better the lives of our people."

"I knew you were wise, old man. And that is a fine tale. But I am not foolish enough to believe your people do not have a treasury!"

"We do, but it is insignificant. You already possess far more gold yourself, I am certain. You would be more successful if you simply took the gold that is in my workshop."

"You are lying, old man. Why do such tales and sayings surround you, then?"

"Look around you, young king. Do you think that if I were truly the keeper of such a secret, there would be no one here to guard and protect me? People tell tales—you are a king, what do they say of you? Besides, those tales have protected me from intruders into my old age—being a goldsmith, living up here in the mountain. But here I was born, here I belong, and here is where I will die."

"It is a fine talk, but I need gold, master goldsmith! If I do not replenish my treasury, my realm shall be conquered by the Macedonian king, and death will befall my people!"

"The more gold you have, the more enemies you shall

have. And the closer you will come to death. How could your death help your realm and your people? You are trapped in that thinking. You were wondering why we made a mask of death for you. Do you understand now? Let it fall, King Ketriporis... I have known all along who you were."

"I thought I played my character well."

"You tried. Do not vex yourself about it, young king. But it was the zeal, the ambition, and the determination I saw in your eyes—they all gave you away. You must use that zeal and determination to bring good to your realm, instead of destruction."

"How would I be able to accomplish that without wealth?"

"There are ways. You are wise, King Ketriporis. You will find them."

Ketriporis felt that the words of the goldsmith were true and sincere. There was no gold that he could raid. No secret, after all—at least not one that he wanted to hear. And there was no need for the mask. He reached for it and took it off.

"That is better!" the goldsmith exclaimed. "You have a handsome face with strong features. Do not hide it behind a mask."

"You have proven your wisdom, master goldsmith," said Ketriporis. "I feel differently, and even if I have not fully comprehended it, I suspect I have learned something by coming here."

"I am glad to hear it."

"But before I take my leave, there is a secret I want you to keep."

"You do not want Evmondia to know. Is that it?"

"Yes. If she is to know, I should be the one to tell her."

"I will keep your secret. I give you my word."

"I know I can trust you. Farewell, master."

"Farewell, King Ketriporis. May the gods show you the way and keep you safe."

With his confused bodyguards behind him, the king walked away hastily and disappeared among the tall pines.

I feel strange. Disappointed, yet relieved. Like I have failed, but like I have just had a major victory. Father, have I failed my promise to you? I am indeed returning empty-handed. But perhaps I have gained wisdom. Maybe I have fulfilled my promise to you after all.

Somehow, he knew where she would be. Having ordered his bodyguards to await his return, he hurried in the direction of the meadow. And there she was, picking berries, light as a butterfly and as beautiful as a spring flower.

He spotted the mother bear relaxing by the waterfall. She paid no heed to him and he made no attempt to harm her.

His heart fluttered as he approached the maiden he had been yearning to see again. The one whose image and memory brought the most guilt every time his thoughts turned to the raid he had planned.

"Rebulus!" she greeted him.

"Evmondia! It is good to see you."

She smiled at him, her face open and pure. "What brings you back to these lands?"

"I came to seek gold. And gold I found."

"You came to seek something else for your king? You must have visited the master."

"Indeed. Those are exquisite necklaces, bracelets, and ornamentations you have made, Evmondia."

"Oh, you know it is me! Master has been teaching me. He thinks I am good at this trade."

"He is right, Evmondia. Creating beauty suits you best."

"Is Brother Pitros well?"

"I left him in good spirits, Evmondia," replied the king.

"I am glad to hear it!"

Then Ketriporis said softly, "Evmondia, I would like to hear you sing."

"You look troubled, Rebulus. If it shall help you, I will!"

"I have indeed been troubled," he admitted. "Your singing is healing, Evmondia." Her song was relaxing him, beguiling him, carrying him back to the days when he was carefree and full of life and enthusiasm.

She looked straight into his eyes as she sang. Her gaze led him deep into the tranquil green forest where he belonged, healing and calming him.

After she finished her song, she smiled at him again with that open smile. It was then that Ketriporis felt the other mask he was wearing—the invisible one that had been suffocating him—begin to loosen. The false face that had been his companion all along was slipping, allowing him to breathe easier again.

"Evmondia, I will return to this land. Will you wait for me?" he heard himself ask.

The maiden blushed and lowered her eyes. "I will," she replied.

Then, picking up her basket that brimmed with berries, she ran away, quickly and gracefully.

LXXVII

I am bringing no good tidings. No new fortune. No new ways for the realm to restore its glory. Maybe there is another way. The people have been suffering from the increased tribute, fearing the wrath of the gods for cutting down the sacred forest. I should ease their worries. That is all I can do for now; at the least, I should not let them suffer through the cold winter.

"Ketriporis, my king. I am glad you have returned!" Mononius had rushed out to greet him at the fortress gate.

"What is it?" Ketriporis asked, seeing that his brother was deeply troubled.

"There is bad news, brother. The Macedonians attacked while you were away!"

"What about our fort on the Strymon?"

"The fort has fallen. General Akinestes could not defend it! The Macedonians are marching toward us with a large force. It is an invasion."

"How could this be?"

Clenching his fists, Mononius said, "Philip is acting quickly, brother. Much quicker than we could have anticipated. He surely knows about the weak state of our army. I believe he has learned about the secret alliance and wants to prevent us from joining forces with the other kings and the Athenian fleet. All the negotiating we did will be of no use now."

"I had always known he would be a threat to us, but I could not foresee that it would be so soon."

"Fear not, brother! In your absence, Skostos and I have been gathering the army. We cannot allow the Macedonians to conquer our land."

"How large is the Macedonian force?"

"About twenty thousand, the scouts estimate. We will fight to the death if we must. What is your command?" Mononius asked.

But the king just stared down, recalling the remarks of the Bessian priestess, not uttering a word.

"Brother, what is the matter?"

"There will be no fight, Mononius," Ketriporis replied firmly.

"Brother, did I hear you right?" Mononius asked, surprised.

"Yes, you did. Our army is not strong enough to fend off the Macedonians. We needed more time. More funds. More men. I had been working on a special weapon—a special sword to counter their force. Although the blacksmith has been working fast, only a few swords have been forged. Not enough to equip even my elite unit."

"What should we do then? We cannot allow defeat!"

"Even if we are defeated and conquered, Mononius, we shall not lose. The people shall not lose their lives. They shall not lose their land. Their homes shall not be burnt or destroyed by the Macedonians. Why do our warriors need to spill their blood? Why should their carcasses become food for the crows? We shall send an embassy to Philip, and we will meet his demands. Whatever it takes to ensure peace so that no hardship befalls our people. That way, our land, our homes will have a chance to survive."

I am speaking like the priestess now. I finally understand her words.

"Brother, you want to allow Philip to be victorious?"

"He may win this campaign, but he shall not be victorious over us," Ketriporis replied. "One day, we will rise again and rebuild this great realm, if the gods will it."

"But what about what the gods told you on Donuca's peak?"

"We cannot always understand the will of the gods, Mononius."

"Can you accept becoming a vassal king under the Macedonian, just like Lyppeios the Paeonian?"

"If I must."

"I shall respect your decision, brother," Mononius declared, striking his chest with his fist.

"I trust you, Mononius. And hear my words—if you are the one to succeed me, I will be honored."

"Do not speak like that, brother. There is no one better than you to rule over this land."

"I am grateful for your words, Mononius. But it is Philip who shall decide. Let us prepare now to greet the Macedonian king and show him the hospitality of Western Odrysia."

Ketriporis walked back to his chamber, his head held high. There, the sight of the golden mask, prominently displayed over his armor, took him by surprise.

"How could that be? It was made of solid gold!" he exclaimed, looking at the large crack that ran almost its full length.

Maybe it is for the better. I shall not wear it in battle after all.

KINGDOM OF MACEDONIA, 20 YEARS LATER

"Berisades, you have become the best archer in the kingdom."

King Ketriporis was watching his son's archery practice in the field with pride. Suddenly, the sight of his old advisor running toward him drew his attention.

"Sura, what is it? Catch your breath!"

"My king... Philip has been assassinated."

"Assassinated? By whom?"

"Some say Pausanias, but others say it was Olympias and Alexander who were behind it."

"It could have been anyone behind Pausanias, Sura. Philip had many enemies who would have wanted him dead."

So, in the end, I outlived him.

"Sura, prepare a feast and games," Ketriporis continued. "We shall give Philip the honor and respect he deserves. I cannot approve of everything he did, but it is undeniable that he was a great king."

Then, he saw her coming. Even after all their years together, his heart still skipped a beat at the sight of Evmondia. She was holding their daughter by the hand.

"Evmondia, did you hear the news?"

"Yes, Ketriporis. I knew you would be troubled," she replied gently, taking him by the hand.

"Indeed. Whatever Philip did, he was a king to be remembered."

"Shall we go home?" Evmondia asked.

Ketriporis nodded, and together with their daughter and son, hand in hand, they walked in the direction of the sun, breathing the crisp and fragrant air beneath a blue sky without a cloud in sight, and with the snowy peaks of Mount Orbelus glistening in the distance.

It was a beautiful day in Apollonia Pontica. Zenon was relaxing in the warmth of the sun, an activity of which he was becoming more and more fond.

That day, a letter had arrived from an old student of his, one he had not seen in many moons: Trysimachus of Athens.

Zenon was an old man now and relied on his students for many things. He gestured for one to read it to him.

"Esteemed Teacher," the student began. "Can you imagine that the young Athenian you once taught now has gray hair? I have been living here in Thrace that long.

"Now that King Alexander has ascended, much is occurring in the Macedonian dominion. The Thracians who dwell by Mount Haemus and the Istros are trying to overthrow his rule. The instigator of the uprising is the chief of the Brenae, Lord Bryzos. The old boar, they call him. Furthermore, King Kersebleptes remains discontented as a vassal under Alexander, and word has it that he is plotting a rebellion.

"In the west, by safeguarding his people and ensuring they remain on the sacred lands, King Ketriporis has found peace for them and for himself. Having come to accept his current fate and the fate of his once independent domain, he is governing the province in harmony with the help of his brothers.

And as his spirit has remained unconquered, he often says he firmly believes that the time will come when Odrysia will be restored to its former glory.

"Teacher, you surely remember Pitros the Bessian. He has been fighting together with his tribesmen, and they have so far fended off Alexander's army from their remote mountainous lands.

"As for myself, your words of so long ago were very wise, Teacher. Through the journey and the quest you sent me on, I indeed found myself. I now know myself much better than I did when I first became your student.

"During that journey, I was tested many times. I faced numerous dilemmas and challenges. I suffered through cold and heat, was injured, and feel certain I nearly lost my life more than once. But I came to know myself as a true historian, able to record what I see and hear and nothing more. I learned to accept the good and the bad, the black and the white, without taking sides. And I believe my life has been better for it.

"Through that quest, I matured and strengthened both in body and spirit. I also became less fearful, although I can never be entirely like the Ctistae priests, as fear is still present in my life. Indeed, my life as a historian can never be sustained with only a few ingredients. As you taught me, I need to explore all of life's flavors, colors, experiences, and complexities, as it is the variety of its numerous ingredients which make history what it is. And as a true observer, I must partake in all its variants.

"That is why, with much sadness in my heart, I have decided to depart from Macedonia—from western Thrace, as I still prefer to call it—and from King Ketriporis.

"There are many here whom I hold dear. There is Pitros, the king, even Sura and Medosades. And Evmondia, who is King Ketriporis's queen now, and the ruler of his heart.

"I shall greatly miss them all. But I must leave them behind. I cannot limit myself to the history of Thrace and Macedonia. Other kingdoms and lands—new quests and journeys—await me. And if I am fortunate to come out of them alive, one day, I shall return here.

"I remain as always, your eager student, Trysimachus of Athens and Thrace."

- EIGHTY -
2016

THE AUTOMATIC DOORS OF NOUMÉA – LA TONTOUTA International Airport were busy opening and closing. But the man whose passport read 'Felix Svoboda' stood outside, his face raised to the sun.

Zenon just wanted to feel the warmth of the sun on his skin, and the wind ruffling his hair.

He had renamed his story *The Cracking of the Mask* because he felt that his own mask had become cracked.

Now it was time to take it off, to let it fall. So he could feel his face again, in all of its imperfections, all of its weaknesses, all of its vulnerabilities, all of its pain and sorrows.

It had been a long time since he had truly felt it. The hairs on his face prickled his fingers. They were rough. But they were his, and they were genuine.

A group of Korean tourists kept the doors open for a while. Zenon brushed a few locks of hair that had fallen over his eyes, and he followed them inside, heading to the counter of Qantas. His luggage consisted of a backpack, which he held onto, and a medium-sized suitcase, which the airline agent checked in all the way to New York.

He was ready to return. Ready to surrender. Ready to

make things right.

Ready to live up to the word *Svoboda*.

He felt free.

IN HONOR OF

Peter Georgiev Lilov
Poet and avid reader
(1929-2021)
Father of Maria Petrova Green
Maternal grandfather of Alexander Green

Thank you for inspiring us to collaborate
and write a novel together.
We are deeply saddened you are not with us
to see this book come out into the world.

and

Captain John "Bud" McCloskey
United States Air Force
Royal Canadian Air Force
(1914-1943)
Paternal grandfather of Alexander Green

Your courage and sacrifice have not been forgotten.

- APPENDIX 1 -

CHARACTERS BASED ON HISTORICAL FIGURES

THRACIAN

- Kotys, Odrysian king
- Kersebleptes, son and successor of Kotys; one of the three kings in the divided Odrysia
- Amadokus II, one of the three kings in the divided Odrysia
- Berisades, one of the three kings in the divided Odrysia
- Ketriporis, son and successor of Berisades
- Mononius, brother of Ketriporis and envoy to Athens
- Miltokythes, former treasurer of Kotys who rebelled against him

ATHENIAN

- Aristocrates, defendant of the proposed decree to make Charidemus inviolable
- Demosthenes, writer of the speech *Against Aristocrates*
- Euthycles, delivered *Against Aristocrates*
- Athenodorus, mercenary general who fought for Berisades in the civil war

- Bianor, mercenary general who fought for Amadokus in the civil war
- Peisianax, Athenian ambassador to King Ketriporis

OTHER

- Charidemus of Oreus, Euboean mercenary general and minister for Kersebleptes
- Philip II, Macedonian king
- Alexander, son of Philip (commonly known as 'Alexander the Great')
- Parmenion, Macedonian general
- Lyppeios, Paeonian king, vassal to Philip
- Grabos, Illyrian king
- Ateas, Scythian king

- APPENDIX 2 -

CHARACTERS INSPIRED BY HISTORICAL FIGURES

- Skostos (inspired by Skostodokos, a possible son of Berisades in western Thrace based on numismatic evidence)
- Meda (inspired by Meda of Odessos, daughter of the Getic king Kothelas and a later wife of Philip of Macedonia)
- Zenon of Apollonia (inspired by philosopher Diogenes of Apollonia and historian Heracleides of Odessos)
- Sadalas (inspired by Sadalas I, a Thracian ruler or paradynast in the Pontic coastal region)
- Vologesus (inspired by Vologesus, Bessian chief and high priest who led an unsuccessful revolt against Roman rule)
- Abruporis (inspired by Abrupolis/Abruporis, a Sapaean ally of the Romans against the Macedonians in the Third Macedonian War)

- APPENDIX 3 -

GLOSSARY

amphora (plural: amphorae)- a tall, narrow jar with two handles

barbarian- a non-Greek speaker, generally looked down upon as being uncivilized

basileus (plural: basileis)- Greek term for "king"

centaur- a mythological creature; half-man, half-horse

chasing- hammering a malleable metal, such as gold, on the front side

chiton- a long tunic

cuirass- a breastplate and backplate of armor fastened together

emporium- a settlement primarily functioning as a market or trading center

fibula (plural: fibulae)- brooch for fastening garments on the right shoulder

hippodrome- a stadium for chariot or horse racing

hoplite- a heavily-armed foot soldier in Greek armies

hydria (plural: hydriai)- a liquid-carrying vessel

kantharos- a cup used to hold wine in Dionysian rituals

kline- a reclining couch

lochos (plural: lochoi)- a unit or regiment in ancient Greek armies

machaira- a large knife or sword with a single cutting edge

maenad- a frenzied female follower of Dionysus in mythology

muse- an inspirational goddess of the arts

mythos- a background story rooted in mythology

nymph- a spirit of the forest embodying the form of a beautiful maiden

oracle- a message from the gods communicated to a priest or priestess, usually mysterious and ambiguous

paradynast- sub-kings under the Odrysian king—often related by blood—who rule outlying territories (similar role to that of governor or warlord)

pelta (plural: peltae)- a crescent-shaped wicker shield carried by peltasts

peltast- a Thracian infantryman armed with a javelin and light shield

phalanx- a block of heavy infantry standing shoulder-to-shoulder several ranks deep

phiale (plural: phialae)- a shallow bowl used for drinking or pouring wine

polis (plural: poleis)- a political state in ancient Greece consisting of a main city and its immediate hinterland

rhomphaia (plural: rhomphaiae)- a powerful Thracian sword dating back to the fourth century BCE and most likely originating in the Rhodope Mountains

rhyton- an elaborate drinking vessel shaped like a horn with a small hole at the bottom

sald- word for 'gold' in the Thracian language

sarissa- a long spear or pike between thirteen and twenty feet in length, first introduced in the Macedonian army under Philip II

satyr- a mythological creature resembling a man with a horse's ear and tail

siren- a half-bird, half-woman creature who dangerously lures men to destruction with a sweet song

sophist- a paid teacher of wisdom and rhetoric in ancient Greece, often employing deceptive and fallacious reasoning

stadion (plural: stadia)- a measure of length, approximately two hundred yards

thyrsus (plural: thyrseis)- a staff carried by the followers of Dionysus covered with ivy vines and tipped with a pine cone

zibythides- 'bright ones', the Thracian nobility

zymlidrenos- a Thracian mythological water dragon

- APPENDIX 4 -

MODERN LOCATION EQUIVALENTS

LOCALES

- Apollonia Pontica (Sozopol, Bulgaria)
- Kabyle (Kabile, Bulgaria)
- Miletus (Balat, Turkey)
- Olbia (Parutyne, Ukraine)
- Valley of Bendis (based on the Rose Valley, Kazanlak, Bulgaria—also known as 'Valley of the Thracian Kings')
- Onocarsis (based on Starosel, Bulgaria and Hisarya, Bulgaria)
- Eumolpias (Plovdiv, Bulgaria)
- Temple of Dionysus (based on Perperikon, Bulgaria)
- Amphipolis (Amphipolis, Greece)
- Euboea (Euboea island, Greece)
- Chersonese (Gallipoli Peninsula, Turkey)
- Thasos (Thasos island, Greece)
- Doriscus (Doriskos, Greece)
- Neapolis (Kavala, Greece)
- Galepsos (Kariani, Greece)
- Pierian Valley (Pangaio municipality, Greece)
- Krenides/Philippi (Krinides, Greece)

REGIONS (roughly corresponding to)

- Thrace (Bulgaria, European Turkey, southern Romania, and Eastern Macedonia & Thrace in Greece)
- Eastern Odrysian realm (most likely: Eastern Thrace in Turkey and the eastern parts of Northern Thrace in Bulgaria)
- Central Odrysian realm (most likely: Western Thrace in Greece and the western parts of Northern Thrace in Bulgaria)
- Western Odrysian realm (most likely: parts of Eastern Macedonia in Greece and parts of Blagoevgrad Province in Bulgaria)
- Land of the Bessi (mountainous regions in South-Central Bulgaria)
- Land of the Dii (located by Thucydides in the Rhodope Mountains, Bulgaria and Greece)
- Land of the Elethi (located by Pliny the Elder upstream on the Nestos River; probably northeastern Blagoevgrad Province in Bulgaria)
- Land of the Getae (northeastern Bulgaria and southeastern Romania)
- Macedonia (Macedonia region in Greece and parts of North Macedonia)
- Paeonia (central North Macedonia)
- Illyria (parts of Albania, Montenegro, Croatia, Bosnia and Herzegovina, Serbia, Kosovo, and North Macedonia)
- Scythia (parts of Ukraine, Russia, Kazakhstan, and Moldova)

Note: The realms of Grabos and Ateas did not encompass the entirety of the ancient regions of Illyria and Scythia.

MOUNTAINS

- Haemus (Balkan Mountains, Bulgaria and Serbia)
- Rhodope (Rhodope Mountains, Bulgaria and Greece)
- Orbelus (thought to refer to Pirin in Bulgaria, Slavyanka/ Orvilos on the Bulgarian-Greek border, and/or Belasitsa divided between Greece, Bulgaria, and North Macedonia)
- Donuca (possibly Rila in Bulgaria)
- Pangaion (Pangaion Hills, Greece)
- Symbolon (Symbolon Hills, Greece)
- Serrium (Cape Makri, Greece)

RIVERS

- Hebros (Maritsa; Bulgaria, Turkey, and Greece)
- Nestos (Mesta; Bulgaria and Greece)
- Strymon (Struma; Bulgaria and Greece)
- Angites (Angites; Greece)
- Istros (Danube; Romania and Bulgaria in its lower course)

ACKNOWLEDGMENTS

We are deeply grateful to Brian Green, a wonderful father and husband. Your great love for history, together with your open-mindedness and acceptance of other people and cultures, has inspired every page.

We are also immensely grateful to Peter Lilov, our number one cheerleader. Although you are no longer with us, your big and loving heart, as well as your poems, will live with us forever. This novel is the result of your encouragement and faith in us. Without your support, publishing a book may have remained only a dream. Your spirit continues to illuminate our way.

Alexander would like to send his warm thanks to:

Everyone who has supported my creative projects, including my podcasts and YouTube channels, since 2008. I would like to give a special shout-out to Ascension participants. Your time, effort, and most importantly, friendship, are greatly appreciated.

All the excellent teachers I had during my student years at Cash Elementary, Brunson Elementary, Hanes Middle, Early College of Forsyth/Forsyth Technical Community College, and UNC Greensboro. I would especially like to express my gratitude to the teachers, instructors, and professors I had the honor of studying under in the disciplines of English, History, Philosophy, Psychology, and Geography. Not only did I learn a lot, but your passion for these subjects definitely rubbed off on me.

Maria would like to acknowledge her Bulgarian family:

Although you are long departed, you have been inspirational in this writing journey:

My paternal grandparents, Maria and Georgi Hadzhililovi. Thank you for your generosity, wisdom, and loving care.

My mother, Teofana Lilova, for your work in cancer research.

My maternal grandmother, Olga Raleva, for your work as Director of the Library of the Bulgarian Academy of Sciences, and for your work with UNESCO in establishing libraries in Lebanon.

And together:

We are very grateful to the historians (ancient and contemporary!) who have written about the Thracians, as well as the archaeologists who have helped unearth the enthralling Thracian artifacts. Without your work, it would have been next to impossible to bring this rich ancient culture to life. A list of primary and secondary sources we used while writing the historical chapters is available on our website.

Last but not least, we would like to thank the forward-thinking team at Atmosphere Press, as well as the independent editors and beta readers we worked with on this project. Thanks to you, our rough draft is no longer a rough draft but a book!

ABOUT ATMOSPHERE PRESS

Atmosphere Press is an independent, full-service publisher for excellent books in all genres and for all audiences. Learn more about what we do at atmospherepress.com.

We encourage you to check out some of Atmosphere's latest releases, which are available at Amazon.com and via order from your local bookstore:

Dancing with David, a novel by Siegfried Johnson
The Friendship Quilts, a novel by June Calender
My Significant Nobody, a novel by Stevie D. Parker
Nine Days, a novel by Judy Lannon
Shadows of Robyst, a novel by K. E. Maroudas
Home Within a Landscape, a novel by Alexey L. Kovalev
Motherhood, a novel by Siamak Vakili
Death, The Pharmacist, a novel by D. Ike Horst
Mystery of the Lost Years, a novel by Bobby J. Bixler
Bone Deep Bonds, a novel by B. G. Arnold
Terriers in the Jungle, a novel by Georja Umano
Into the Emerald Dream, a novel by Autumn Allen
His Name Was Ellis, a novel by Joseph Libonati
The Cup, a novel by D. P. Hardwick
The Empathy Academy, a novel by Dustin Grinnell
Tholocco's Wake, a novel by W. W. VanOverbeke
Dying to Live, a novel by Barbara Macpherson Reyelts
Looking for Lawson, a novel by Mark Kirby
Yosef's Path: Lessons from my Father, a novel by Jane Leclere Doyle
Surrogate Colony, a novel by Boshra Rasti

ABOUT THE AUTHORS

When Maria and Alexander Green, a mother and son, teamed up to write a novel, *Cracking of the Mask* was born.

Alexander is passionate about honoring both his American and ethnic Bulgarian roots. A lover of learning, he remains incessantly curious about the world and its inhabitants. His interests include public speaking, organizing tours, bringing people of various backgrounds together, and studying the humanities and social sciences. Alexander graduated from the University of North Carolina at Greensboro with a B.A. in Economics, minoring in Philosophy.

Maria was born and raised in Sofia, Bulgaria, in a family of writers and book lovers. She came to the United States through marriage, having met her American husband in Sofia. She is continually drawn to the lesser-known and always looks forward to learning about new historical discoveries. Maria is passionate about using the art of creative writing as a tool for self-discovery and healing.

www.travelthroughtimebooks.com

Lightning Source UK Ltd.
Milton Keynes UK
UKHW012242081122
411848UK00001B/125